To: Mika

P Raslim

THE LOVE MATCH

PRIYANKA TASLIM

SALAAM
READS

New York   London   Toronto
Sydney   New Delhi

An imprint of Simon & Schuster Children's Publishing Division
1230 Avenue of the Americas, New York, New York 10020

For information about special discounts for bulk purchases, please contact Simon & Schuster
Special Sales at 1-866-506-1949 or business@simonandschuster.com.
The Simon & Schuster Speakers Bureau can bring authors to your live event.
For more information or to book an event, contact the Simon & Schuster Speakers Bureau
at 1-866-248-3049 or visit our website at www.simonspeakers.com.
Interior design by Tom Daly
The text for this book was set in Adobe Caslon Pro.
Manufactured in the United States of America
First Edition
2 4 6 8 10 9 7 5 3 1
Library of Congress Cataloging-in-Publication Data
Names: Taslim, Priyanka, author.
Title: The love match / Priyanka Taslim.
Description: First edition. | New York : Salaam Reads, [2022] | Audience: Ages 12 up |
Audience: Grades 7–9. | Summary: When her mother sets her up with handsome, aloof Harun,
eighteen-year-old Zahra pretends to date him while she pursues
her coworker, Nayim, but she quickly finds herself second-guessing her true feelings.
Identifiers: LCCN 2022032732 (print) | LCCN 2022032733 (ebook) | ISBN 9781665901109
(hardcover) | ISBN 9781665901123 (ebook)
Subjects: CYAC: Love—Fiction. | Dating—Fiction. | Bengali Americans—Fiction. | Family life—
Fiction. | BISAC: YOUNG ADULT FICTION / Romance / Romantic Comedy | YOUNG ADULT
FICTION / Social Themes / Emotions & Feelings | LCGFT: Novels.
Classification: LCC PZ7.1.T3836 Lo 2022 (print) | LCC PZ7.1.T3836 (ebook) | DDC [Fic]—dc23
LC record available at https://lccn.loc.gov/2022032732
LC ebook record available at https://lccn.loc.gov/2022032733

To any brown girl who has ever felt unwelcome in the pages of her favorite book. You deserve love, magic, and wonder.

And to my parents, for always supporting me—
even when I didn't want to be a doctor, lawyer, or engineer.

Dear Readers:

Although it's a work of fiction, this book *is* inspired by a few of the more interesting elements of my own (usually boring) life: my upbringing in the colorful Bangladeshi, Muslim diaspora community of Paterson, New Jersey; my parents' and various aunties' well-meaning but misguided attempts to matchmake me with Good Bangladeshi Boys™; how big of a part family lineage plays in these matches; modern day Deshi social politics that remind me a bit too much of Austenian romantic comedies of error; and my inability to write a single word or function as a human being without a properly brewed cup of saa.

See how I spelled it "saa" and not "chai" (and "Deshi" instead of "Desi")? Throughout the book, I'll often use the Sylheti Bengali (and Banglish) that I grew up hearing and speaking in lieu of spellings and pronunciations that might be more commonplace.

I hope that this book feels like the celebration of being Bangladeshi (particularly, a diaspora Bangladeshi) that I always wanted it to be. In addition to writing what I hope reads like a natok set in America (expect forbidden romances! Family drama! Singing and dancing! Lots of wordplay!), this book truly is a love letter from me to the city and culture I grew up in, and my deepest wish is that this love comes across.

May it be your cup of tea! Your love match! Your— (okay, I'll stop now . . .)

Hugs, kisses, and lots of saa,
Priyanka

THE WORLD ACCORDING TO BENGALI NATOKS

What is a natok, you might ask?

Technically, natoks started with the Bengali theater in the nineteenth century, during British rule of Bangladesh, before it was even called Bangladesh. But it wasn't until they were televised by Dhallywood—Bangladesh's film industry—that natoks really took off.

Even outside of Bangladesh and West Bengal, loads of Bengalis now tune in to view them, my family included. Sitting on Amma's and Nanu's laps while they watched these movies and TV series first taught me about storytelling. Like Shakespearean comedies, they frequently feature big, dramatic weddings—either at the beginning, the end, or *both*.

If a natok ends with a wedding, it's almost always a happily-ever-after. An estranged family reunited; lovers returning to one another's arms after fighting off the forces that strove to keep them apart; evil kings, monsters, and mobsters defeated.

If a natok *begins* with one, however . . .

Let's just say it's asking for nothing but trouble.

Chapter ❤ 1

Bangladeshi weddings can be brutal.

Sure, like most South Asian ceremonies, they *seem* magical. There's a reason why everyone from Selena Gomez to Coldplay has attempted to cop our glamour. The vibrant clothes, plentiful food, and impromptu dance numbers will take the most average wedding and turn it into something straight out of a Bollywood blockbuster.

Or, in this case, a natok.

But the ugly truth is, in or out of the movies, weddings are as treacherous as a jungle—the prime hunting ground of matchmaking aunties and uncles, who herd together in the buffet line, dressed in their peacock-bright sharis and fanjabis, munching on somosas and zilafis as they set their sights on any Bengal tiger cubs foolish enough to stray from their streaks.

Enter me: Zahra Khan. I may be a cub, but I'm hardly a fool.

Usually, I'm smart enough to avoid weddings *and* busybodies.

Now, don't get me wrong. I'm not immune to the occasional fairy-tale wedding fantasy. It's hard to be when all my favorite stories are romances. *Pride and Prejudice*, *Crazy Rich Asians*, *When Dimple Met Rishi*, *Yeh Jawaani Hai Deewani* . . . If it involves extended eye contact, an eventual kiss, and hand holding, sign me up.

But a love story of my own is a fantasy for a future-Zahra. One with time to date and dream. *Present*-Zahra is only eighteen, graduated from high school less than a week ago, and has plenty on her plate already, thank-you-very-much.

Too bad I can't get that through my mother's stubborn skull.

Since senior year began, she's been dropping less-than-subtle hints that a proper—read: *rich*—match for me would be the end of all our woes. You see, since my father's passing two years ago, Amma and I have had to work our butts off to keep food on the table for our family of five. A well-suited match, Jane Austen–style, would certainly help pay the bills.

So here we are at yet another ritzy banquet hall as Amma scopes out potential suitors, dragging me around like a show poodle on a leash. Her eyes flit toward a boy a couple of years older than me who sat in front of me in public speaking. He lifts a hand to wave. Before I can return the gesture, my best Good Bangladeshi Daughter smile glued in place, I'm yanked unceremoniously into the buffet line.

Jerking my wrist out of my mother's grasp, I exclaim, "Amma, that was so rude! I thought you wanted me to mingle."

"Rude?" She frowns between me and the table, laden with heaping platters of fragrant jasmine rice and vindaloo, before responding in exasperated Bengali, "Hireh, rude is the earful I'd get from your aunties if you married Mahmud Miah's bedisha son. Two years out of high school, and what is he doing with his life? Last I heard, he's waiting tables and planning to go to Hollywood to *act*."

Disdain drips off every word.

"*I'm* a waitress too," I bite back, swallowing a lump of rising hurt. "Besides, we went to school together. He was only saying hi, *not* declaring his undying love."

Not to mention, he's the only person I know here, if doing his share of our group project on, ironically, dream careers counts as "knowing." I catch glimpses of other people who live in our hometown, but it's *Amma* who knows everyone who's anyone in Paterson. I've always been too busy with work and school to socialize.

When I told her I was too tired to take a bus all the way to New York City for this dawath after my shift, she claimed we simply couldn't skip my *prio* cousin Anika's wedding, but I doubt I could pick Anika Afa out of a police lineup even with the romantic slideshow of her and her fiancé flickering across the mounted television screens around us.

Oblivious to my misgivings, Amma continues darkly, "I'd let a boy like that steal my daughter across the country over *my* dead body. Your fufus in Bangladesh would happily finish the job for me if they found out."

My lips press together, the reminder that I'm here as a favor to her, not to hunt for a boyfriend—much less a *husband*—trapped behind them. I don't like how often she makes light of dying, but I've never met a Bengali mother without a flair for the dramatic.

She ushers me forward with an impatient wave of her bangled arm. I decide to let it go, not wanting to pick a fight in public with so many onlookers. As she seeks out a table, I totter behind her in three-inch heels, the flared skirt of my glittery purple lehenga swishing around my ankles. She flings her purse onto an available chair, casting a challenging scowl at the unsuspecting woman who'd been about to take it like a tigress marking her territory. The poor lady scuttles away faster than a fleeing antelope, two empty seats in her wake.

Having attained her prize, my mother appraises the other faces staring back at us over a centerpiece strung with pearls that matches the ornamented decor of the banquet hall. "Assalamualaikum. Amar naam Zaynab Khan are oh oilo amar furi, Zahra."

I sigh, then greet the guests as well. "Assalamualaikum, Khala, Khalu."

Hardly giving them a chance to reply, "Walaikum salaam," Amma begins interrogating them about where they're from "back home." By "home," she means Bangladesh, of course, although our family settled in Paterson, New Jersey, on the outskirts of New York City, almost a decade ago. It's the question all Bengalis of her generation ask whenever they happen upon each other.

"Afnar bari koi?" my mother inquires.

Two of them are from the same family, sisters-in-law accompanied by their respective husbands, who chat with each other while sipping steaming cups of saa, keeping an eye on a trio of toddlers in pigtails and frilly dresses playing tag. The third is a woman wearing more makeup and jewelry than the mother of the bride, perhaps the bride herself, with henna-dyed hair in such a striking hue of red, it might be visible from space.

"And where are *you* from, Zaynab?" the bejeweled woman shoots back at Amma.

My mother takes a deep breath. "*Well*, Pushpita Afa—"

Here it comes. The *princess* story.

"Sadly, I haven't returned to my father's bari in decades, but perhaps you've heard of it? The Choudhury Zamindari of Sunamganj?" She pauses dramatically as the women around the table exchange eager glances, then drives her point home. "But my husband, Allah yarhemuhu, hailed from the Khan Rajbari of Moulvibazar."

The many-ringed lady emits a theatrical gasp audible over the *clink clink* of forks. Regardless of whether they've been to Sunamganj or Moulvibazar, Amma has name-dropped plenty. Zamindars, Khans, Rajas—all are titles associated with the people who ruled princely estates and kingdoms in Bangladesh, making us the descendants of *royalty*.

Or . . . well . . . close enough.

Never mind that my parents' families fell onto hard times after the Partition and the Liberation War. Never mind that we can barely pay our rent in New Jersey. Never mind that *I* have to take a year off before college to save while the rest of my friends move on. Amma reclines in her chair with an imperious smirk, a queen among her fawning subjects.

I resist the urge to roll my eyes, shoving another bite of beef and potato into my mouth. Debt collectors don't care about our family lineage, so why should we? But she has had so few pleasures since Baba's death that I can't take this from her. Better she tells these aunties about our vaunted bongsho than me or my brother and sister, at least.

The many-ringed lady parts her very red lips to answer when, suddenly, "Leelabali" fades from the speakers. Aside from hushed murmurs, the banquet hall falls into silence as everyone's wonder-struck eyes rise to the stage. There, under an archway lush with marigolds and roses, on a gilded bench that looks like a throne, the groom sits, attired in a scarlet sherwani with gold buttons down to the knees, feathers in the ornate pagri crowning his head.

He can't take his eyes off the bride, who enters from an adjoining hallway. Her mother, sisters, and other female relatives hold a fluttering scarlet urna above her head as she sashays slowly over to the stage, a vision of beauty in her matching shari and the floral mehndi that weaves like vines through her dozen bangles. When she reaches the stage, the groom springs off his bench to offer her a hand. Their fingers intertwine and linger.

My heart stutters in my ribs as I watch.

This—

"Must be a love marriage," Amma exclaims, in an awed whisper of her own.

The women at our table begin to chatter anew. Someone says, "Kids these days, so reckless and *romantic*." She spits the word like a curse. "Love marriages never last. Children should trust their elders to arrange suitable matches."

"The divorce rate is so high now," another laments. "Nearly *fifty* percent."

I swallow the urge to inform them that's only because women of older generations were blamed if they couldn't make marriages work, and were looked down on with pity, no matter how young they were, if they became widowed like Amma. As if their lives began and ended with their husbands'. The rebuke burns down my throat, hotter than the not-particularly-spicy vindaloo, but if I unleash it, it'd be about as unseemly as throwing up.

Despite my best efforts to tune them out, I sense someone contemplating me and turn to find the bejeweled woman. She introduced herself to Amma earlier as Pushpita Emon, but like most other aunties I meet through my mother, I simply call her Khala. Her lips quirk upon catching my gaze, her eyes as glittering and sharp as the knife near my plate.

"Your daughter is such a shundori, Zaynab," she declares

in Bengali. "How tall is she? Surely five-four, five-five? And what a sweet complexion! Even that dress is the most stylish thing I've seen this entire evening. You must beat the boys away with a broom."

My cheeks flush beneath the shade-too-pale foundation Amma caked on them earlier. It's not the first time an auntie has called me pretty. If you're paper-bag fair, thin, and taller than the Bangladeshi national average of four feet eleven, you're practically pageant queen Manushi Chhillar in their eyes. I try not to let their gross Eurocentric beauty standards give me a big head, but gift her a pleasant smile for my mother's sake.

"Goodness, no," Amma says, to my great relief, though she's preening at the compliments to both of her creations: me *and* the lehenga she designed for the occasion. While I love that she's taken an I'll-do-it-myself approach to our wardrobe situation after learning how expensive it could be for a single mother to dress three kids, I feel like a walking advertisement for her seamstress service tonight. Better than making me stand up and twirl, I suppose. "My Zahra worries about me and the little ones too much to think about a husband yet. But what mother doesn't dream of her child's wedding day?"

"Oh, I know a thing or two about weddings," Pushpita Khala replies. "Gitanjali is my restaurant, you see. We host many receptions here."

Amma chokes on a swig of mango lassi. "*Y-your* restaurant?"

"Technically, the restaurant is attached. This banquet hall is where we host events." Pushpita Khala grants us a self-effacing smile, then sighs. "We're set to open a second in Paterson by the end of the summer, but I worry. . . . With our son preparing to study engineering at Columbia, what will Mansif and I do with the Emon family business when it's time to retire?"

My gut clenches at the mention of college.

And why does it have to be Columbia of all places?

Amma's eyes, meanwhile, dart all around us, as if expecting a perfect specimen of a brown boy to materialize out of thin air. "Is he here? Your—"

"Harun," replies Pushpita Khala, reciting her son's name like a prayer. In her plump hand is an iPhone, and Harun's photo must be her wallpaper, because she slides it across the table for Amma's perusal, beaming at my mother's awed, "Mashallah."

I frown between the two women, but my mother has all but forgotten my existence, as if I'm no more than a spectator at a chess match. She leans forward, the brown eyes we share bright as polished mahogany, while Pushpita Khala sizes me up. I can't fathom which queen is about to checkmate the other's king, but I know one thing with 100 percent certainty.

Harun and I have just become their pawns.

Chapter 2

Life in the Khan house is far from glamorous.

When we lost Baba, we had no choice but to move into an apartment so tiny, my mother, brother, sister, grandmother, and I are packed inside it like a family of squabbling djinn in a particularly cramped lamp.

Amma sleeps next to my five-year-old sister, Resna, while Nanu and I share a room that used to be a walk-in closet. My fourteen-year-old brother, Arif, got the shortest end of the stick. He sleeps on a pullout couch in the living room, and his "bedroom" doubles as Amma's work space and our hangout spot.

Worlds away from the grand estates of the stories my mother told at the wedding a couple of days ago.

"Resu, please just get dressed! I'm going to be late for work!" I shout, leaping over a bolt of beaded velvet. A teetering stack of library books almost topples as I attempt to catch my sister's giggling, half-naked form. She ducks under the wooden coffee table that holds Amma's sewing machine, but I'm not so quick. "Ow! Shit!"

Amma's tired eyes narrow as she undoes a skewed stitch. "*Zahra.*"

My sister blows a raspberry from the other side of the table.

I throw my hands into the air. "She refuses to wear any pants, Amma."

Now our mother's stern gaze veers to Resna, who scurries to hide her pantsless form behind the torso of a mannequin. Whenever Amma's busy with a particularly involved job, Arif and I take turns making sure Resna looks presentable while Nanu cooks. My brother conveniently claimed kitchen duty before I even woke up this morning, giving me the sneaking suspicion he'd bribed her into bed with too much sugar last night.

"Besides," I add more urgently, "my shift at Chai Ho starts at nine. I *just* convinced Mr. Tahir to give me overtime. If I'm late again, he'll change his mind."

Maybe even fire me, I don't have to clarify.

Amma already knows, if her weary sigh is anything to go by. Rising creakily to her feet, she crooks a finger at Resna. Immediately, my sister hastens to stand at attention in front of her, chubby hands bunched in the hem of her baby blue Queen Elsa nightie. A pout darkens her pudgy face as our mother dresses her.

"Now, go eat," Amma orders us both.

Chai Ho isn't far, but we don't have a car anymore. When Baba died, I was only sixteen and Amma never got her license, so we used the thousand dollars from selling our beat-up old Toyota Camry as the security deposit for a cheaper apartment.

Paterson, New Jersey, rushes by as I sprint to the other end of Union Avenue, having left too late for the bus. Two- and three-family homes much like ours flank bodegas, bars, laundromats, and homey restaurants serving up a hundred different kinds of cultural cuisines. Beyond them, old brick-work factory buildings ascend to meet the smoke-kissed blue sky, some boarded up, others repurposed to host charter schools and apartment complexes.

Over the beeping of cars and the disgruntled complaints of the pedestrians I swerve around, the low burble of the Great Falls drifts toward my ears. It probably never comes up in the musical, but Alexander Hamilton himself saw the falls in the late 1700s and proposed building a city around them. It's a wonder they didn't call it Hamiltonville.

Amma, Nanu, and I applied for naturalization together when I turned eighteen a few months ago. Though I doubt the proctor will ask any questions about Paterson, we all memorized these facts by heart, because the city is special to us Bengalis. It contains one of the largest Bangladeshi diaspora populations in the entire United States.

Even someone who doesn't know its history can guess that the instant they enter Union Avenue. Five times a day, the call to prayer echoes from the local mosque, pulsing through the boulevard like a heartbeat. All along the block are Bengali restaurants, grocers, and garment stores.

Then there's Chai Ho, the only Pakistani establishment in Little Bangladesh.

A stenciled window displays the name of the shop—a pun on Jai Ho, roughly translated to mean *let tea* rather than *victory prevail*. It wisps out of a painted teapot like steam. Behind the image, I spot my two best friends, Dalia and Daniya Tahir. Dani spots me and drags a thumb across her neck, the universal gesture for *you're dead*, while her twin sister directs an uneasy glance at the clock over the counter.

9:07.

Shit, shit, shit.

I skulk into the shop, wincing at the bells that chime overhead like a death knell. Mr. Tahir stomps out from the kitchen on cue, stocky arms crossed over an apron too lacy to be as intimidating as it is on him. For a second, it looks like smoke billows out of his hairy ears, but I know it's just my imagination.

"I'm really, really, really sorry, Mr. Tahir. I was helping my mother get my sister dressed this morning, but she wouldn't cooperate and—"

"And nothing! You were late twice last week. Is this your grandfather's shop, for you to come and go as you please?"

His voice pitches louder with each word, as if he's a teapot growing hotter and hotter, the lid about to burst right off. I recoil, *please don't fire me* running through my head on a loop, but before he can progress to proper shouting, Dalia says, "Abbu, stop!"

"Zahra's only a couple of minutes late," Dani adds. "We haven't had a single customer yet. Do your blood pressure a favor and chill out."

As always, he deflates at his daughters' reprimand, but still wags a thick finger in my face. "Weren't you the one asking for more hours?" I mumble an affirmative without meeting his gaze. "You're lucky Daniya and Dalia are starting full-time classes in the fall. I need help, but I won't be so generous if you're late again. Understand?"

It's the millionth time he's mentioned that my best friends will soon be going to college *without me*. The reminder fills my mouth with such a bitter taste that I'm afraid I'll throw up on his shiny leather loafers if I try to answer.

I manage a nod.

He orders me behind the counter, where his daughters flock to cheer me up. Since the three of us moved to Paterson in the second grade, we've all been joined at the hip, bonded by our shared new-kid status. I was there when Dalia began veiling and when Dani admitted to liking girls. They helped me through my grief after Baba died.

Dalia wraps an arm around me. I drop my head onto her shoulder, the tassels of her pastel pink hijab tickling my cheek. Dani, meanwhile, hands me a cool glass of falooda.

"What'll I do without you two?" I ask with a watery smile.

They exchange an apprehensive glance.

Dani says, "Zar, we're going to Rutgers, not Rajpur."

Dalia pokes my stomach. "Besides, you can still enroll, Miss Ivy League."

I know they're trying to console me, but the sago pearls on my tongue are suddenly too thick to swallow. The thing is, even if a djinn popped out of one of the shop's decorative teapots and granted our family enough money for tuition, it's too late for me to attend this semester. I've already deferred all my acceptances, including to my dream school, Columbia University. Although many colleges promised scholarships, most were contingent on attending full-time, and we have bills to pay at home.

Trust me, I've crunched the numbers. Maybe if it were just Amma and me, we could figure out how to survive without my paycheck and pay off student loans, but we're not alone. What happens when it's Arif's turn? Or Resna's? I need to consider everything. Every*one*. There's no way to keep the lights on, even if I go to school part-time and work the rest, much less if I don't contribute at all.

I shake my head. "It's not in the stars this year, but if I keep saving half my paychecks, I might be able to enroll at PCCC by next semester."

The twins share another frown.

They don't think I should give up attending a prestigious school like Columbia for Passaic County Community College, especially after working myself to the bone to get in, but PCCC is cheap, close to home, and has a less rigorous course load that

I can work around if I need to keep my job. After two years there, perhaps I can transfer to a four-year university. By then, Arif should be old enough to chip in.

But for now, things are what they are.

The bells above the door jangle to announce the arrival of our first customer. We hurry to reprise our respective roles. Dalia joins her father in the kitchen, Dani brews the drinks, and I wait tables. It's easy to become Chai Ho Zahra.

The day ticks by in a busy but blissful monotony. I pour tea, clean up after a string of customers, and make small talk whenever possible with our regulars: elderly aunties and uncles who enjoy reminiscing about the good old days over a cup of masala chai and a plate of somosas.

The city is full of characters who frequent the shop.

I move on automatic, but my brain buzzes with activity as it runs through a brand-new round of the People-Watching Game. It's something I started playing with my friends when I first got hired at Chai Ho, where we made up increasingly hilarious backstories for customers.

Baba had just died, so Dani's girlfriend, Ximena Mondesir-Martínez, suggested the game to distract me, promising it would spark my creativity like it did hers. It hasn't helped me write a single word, but it *is* fun to let my imagination run wild.

Ximena drops by over lunch and seems to be having better luck with her art, her curly head bowed over a sketch pad, a smudge of charcoal on her brown cheek and one strap of her overalls.

Before I can pour her a drink, someone else enters the tea shop. Clearly not a local, the red-haired woman points at the screen of her phone to show me a photo of a cup of creamy pink tea sprinkled with chopped pistachios and almonds.

"I want this chai tea," she enunciates slowly, squinting at me over designer sunglasses.

Ximena catches Dani's eye over my shoulder and mouths the word, *Gringa*.

Without turning, I know Dani is smirking and whispering, "Gora," right back.

Paterson isn't exactly a gentrifier hotspot like Newark or New York City, but hipsters like Ginger Lady sometimes wander in to switch up their Starbucks orders, thanks to the scrumptious pictures Dalia posts online under the hashtag *ChaiHoes*.

Smothering a snort, I start to explain to the gringora in question that Kashmiri chai, although very Instagrammable, is deceptively bitter—in fact, in Bengali, we call it noon saa, which means "salty tea"—when the bells over the door tinkle for the umpteenth time. I turn to greet the new arrival and almost drop the teapot in my hands.

In the past two years that I've worked at Chai Ho, my mother has never once come to the shop, though she's never kept me from the twins or acted anything short of civil to them the entire time they've been my friends. When I told her and Nanu that Mr. Tahir gave me a job, even my usually mild-mannered grandmother ranted for weeks about the

Bangladeshi Liberation War, when Bangladesh was East Pakistan and Pakistan—then West Pakistan—placed us under martial law, forbidding us from speaking our language. Fifty years later, there's still bad blood.

"Why do you have to work at all? I can take care of us somehow," my mother pleaded, and when it became apparent both of us knew that wasn't true, "Couldn't it at least have been a Bangladeshi restaurant? It's a slap to the face that they don't use Bangla in our own neighborhood."

"All that matters is that their money is in USD," I replied.

She couldn't argue with that, not with a nagging landlord and mounting debt. But knowing that Chai Ho is such a big part of my life hasn't stopped her or Nanu from pretending it doesn't exist. Needing Mr. Tahir's money to survive was a step too far for their pride, my personal relationship with the twins aside.

"Wh-what are you doing here, Amma?" I whisper, after hurriedly handing the redhead her Kashmiri chai.

She scans the bustling shop before returning her focus to me, exaggerated innocence on her face. "I was in the area, picking up groceries. Can't you take a break now?"

"Assalamualaikum, Mrs. Khan." Dalia materializes beside me and flashes Amma a disarming grin before I can turn my mother down, holding a tray of confections, teacups, and a fresh pot of chai. "Can I offer you some of our best tea and desserts?"

"Oh, how kind!" Amma is already setting down her grocery bags so she can sit. "Zahra, join me."

Left without a choice, I lower myself into a chair. "Why are you really here?"

Amma takes a bite of spongy gulab jamun, pink at its heart and drizzled in rose syrup, but rather than complain that it's not as big as kalajam, the Bengali equivalent, she pulls out her phone from her purse. The WhatsApp icon opens as soon as she inputs her PIN. I groan.

WhatsApp can only mean one thing: the Auntie Network.

That's what I call my mother's group chats. Her hotline blings so often, even Drake would get jealous. A group for customers of her business, one for relatives in Bangladesh, another for acquaintances in Paterson, more for friends and family in New York, Michigan, Texas, and London—anywhere and everywhere a Bengali may have settled.

If there's juicy gossip to be shared, the Auntie Network will know it.

Already, a thrum of activity simmers in the tea shop as the aunties inside it take note of my mother's rare appearance and prick their ears in our direction.

"Do you remember the Emons?"

"Who?"

Amma frowns at my inability to name every single Bangladeshi person on the planet. She slides the phone over to me, and on the screen I see a grainy photo of a glum teenage boy with a serious case of Batman Jaw in a black graduation gown standing behind a podium. Between his glasses and cap, I can hardly make out any other distinguishing features.

I look from the image to her blankly. She gusts a vexed sigh. "That's *Harun*. We sat with his mother during the wedding Friday, mono nai? It's hardly been three days!"

I snap my fingers. "Oh, right! The lady with all the rings."

"Yes! Well, I've been doing some research"—when Amma leans in, I inch close enough that no one else can overhear—"and do you know what your Meera Khala told me?" She pauses expectantly. I offer a dutiful shake of my head. "They don't come from much status back in Bangladesh, but they *are* rich, Zahra! So rich, they own not only that grand restaurant, but *three* convenience stores in Paterson alone. And didn't you hear his mother say they plan to open a second restaurant here?"

"Okaaay."

Amma's frown deepens at my lackluster reaction. Her gaze follows mine as it strays to the glaring chai tea lady, who's clearly dissatisfied about something. Before I can bow out using Kashmiri Karen as an excuse, she clicks her tongue, her doe-brown eyes suddenly big and imploring. "You've been working so hard lately, shuna. We never even had a chance to celebrate your graduation. Come home early tonight, accha? I'll have a special dinner ready."

"Really?"

The abrupt subject change gives me whiplash.

She stands and kisses the top of my head. "Yes, really. Don't be late."

Round-eyed, I watch her shuffle out of Chai Ho into

the bright afternoon light. Not a minute later, the woman in sunglasses marches past me, barking a parting complaint loud enough for the entire shop to hear: "That tea was disgusting. Yelp *will* be hearing about this."

Although Mr. Tahir's palpable ire radiates from the kitchen, and I predict dreadful bathroom duty in my not-so-distant future, my eyes are riveted to Amma's retreating figure.

What in God's ninety-nine names is she up to?

Chapter ❤ 3

A cool breeze blows through the window cracked over my head, carrying a medley of smells through the city. Sea salt from the Passaic River, the cloying odor of beer tingeing the parking lots of the bars on either side of the road, the mouthwatering aroma of food from restaurants getting ready for the five o'clock dinner rush.

Riding the bus is one of the few times I can daydream about the book I haven't written since Baba called me to his bedside and asked me to look after everyone. He got diagnosed with stage four stomach cancer so suddenly that Amma completely came apart at the seams. His words still haunt me to this day.

I wish you could be a child, Zahra, but I need you to be strong if your mother can't.

Giving up writing is something I have to do for him. For Amma.

At least for now.

Even if I could afford starting college in September, writing doesn't fall into the trifecta of Asian-Parent-Approved careers every kid I know strives for: doctor, lawyer, or engineer. It's not even a second-tier "respectable enough" career like accountant, teacher, or nurse.

Once upon a time, I had Amma to thank for my love of storytelling, but now she's become the reason I guard my hopes so deep inside my chest, where a callous comment can't blow them away like a stolen wish on dandelion fluff.

If she dismisses them—dismisses me—I don't think I can piece together the broken shards of my heart this time. It's much easier to play the role she wants, of the obedient daughter who dreams in secret, rather than risking that the only parent I have left will think less of me, after everything I've done for her.

But maybe tonight, since I don't have to help with dinner, I can scribble a few ideas in my notebook.

The screech of tires calls me back to reality at my stop. I exit the bus and hurry to my rickety old building. Champa Khala, the landlady, doesn't pester me about our overdue rent for once, busy sweeping the porch, so I salaam her and climb the steps to our second-floor apartment.

On the welcome mat, I freeze. Excitable chatter and the thump of my sister's footsteps float through the door. No one sounds irate or upset, but when I sniff the air, I don't smell anything cooking. Trepidation fills my belly, replacing any hunger. My sneaking suspicion that Amma has been cooking up something other than the special dinner she promised is all but confirmed. If I don't tread carefully, I might end up on the menu myself.

Arif lets me in before I can use my key. Past the threshold waits . . . pandemonium. There's no better way to describe it. Our apartment looks like a Sabyasachi factory exploded inside. Decorative scarves in every shade of the rainbow, made from any material you can imagine, are draped all over the couch, the coffee table, even the ceiling fan. A single jhumka earring crunches beneath the sole of my sneaker, reminding me to remove my shoes.

"Api, you're back!"

Resna catapults herself at my legs, nearly knocking me over. Only then do I notice that she's dressed in a pink frock with poofy sleeves and a tulle skirt, and has ribbons in her pigtails. After I manage to detach her, I get a proper look at my shifty brother. Arif is tugging at the too-short cuffs of the white button-up shirt that poke out of the suit jacket Amma made for his eighth-grade graduation. He's been growing so fast for the past few years that he'll be too tall for the whole thing before long.

"Aru, what the hell is going on?" I whisper, covering Resna's ears.

He shrugs his bony shoulders. "Amma."

As if summoned, our mother flounces into the living room from her bedroom, bringing with her a whiff of talcum powder and perfume.

Like my siblings, she's dressed in her best shari, one with a silver brocade on opulent Banarasi silk that Baba had shipped from India for the last anniversary they shared. Plum-colored lipstick to match the shari adorns her smiling lips, a far cry from the more muted "widow" colors she normally wears.

She looks so beautiful, so happy, that I don't have the heart to spoil it, until I recall my star-crossed plans to write and fold my arms over my chest. "I thought Eid wasn't for almost a month. Why are you so dressed up tonight?"

"Hmm?" Amma bats her eyelashes. "What do you mean? I told you you'd get a delicious dinner tonight, but I never said *I* would make it."

My jaw drops. "You *never* take us out to eat." I affect her prim, perfect Bengali as best I can. "'Why would we pay for food at a restaurant when we have perfectly good food we already paid for at home?'"

I look to Arif and Resna to back me up, but my brother won't meet my gaze, while my traitorous sister snickers behind her hand. Amma, meanwhile, harrumphs as if I've insulted the last ten generations of our ancestors.

"So that's what you think of your poor mother, eh? Here I got a coupon from one of my customers and thought I'd treat us for once, but *you* think I'm cheap and—and—and *unfeeling*." She sniffles, using the hanging pallu of her shari to dry her weepy eyes. "Perhaps we should cancel and call it a night. Your grandmother already said she's too tired to do anything but watch her natoks. You're probably tired too. Why did I bother with such a terrible surprise?"

I raise my palms to quell her tears. "Wait! I—I want to go. Really."

Immediately, every crocodile tear vanishes, leaving not a trace of runny kajol behind, as she begins to shove me toward the bathroom. "Good! Now, hurry and shower! You have to look perfect tonight!"

"Haza-fara, haza-fara!" Resna singsongs, thrilled about playing dress-up.

I spot Arif mouthing an apology at me and get the distinct impression that I've been played, but before I can grill him, I'm thrust into the bathroom, then ensnared in the natural disaster that is Hurricane Amma, a whirlwind of outfits, makeup, and curling-iron burns that ends with me dressed in a yellow anarkali suit trimmed with sparkling sunflowers, a billowing urna pinned into my braided hair, my kajol-lined eyes stinging from the perfume she sprayed right into my face.

For no more than a second, Amma strokes my cheek with her thumb, her smile tender. "Just like a princess," she says in her accented English, but before I can respond, she's already prodding me toward the door. "Let's go! We don't want to be late!"

Although I currently resemble a brown Cinderella with a particularly sassy fairy god-amma, our ride to the restaurant is more pumpkin than carriage. I dodge the stares of the people on the 150 bus as Amma, Arif, Resna, and I squish into an available row of seats, turning everything that's happened over and over in my mind, to no avail.

What the hell could Amma be plotting? Is there some creep waiting for us at the restaurant? Did she dress up Arif and Resna to throw me off? Am I honestly expected to sit through my first-ever date with my entire family gawking? Or is this a ploy to get into my good graces when she *does* pull the blind-date card?

I could just ask, but it's more likely than not that she'll burst into tears again, wounded that I don't trust her—not that there's anything to trust at the moment—and I'd rather spare the rest of the passengers her histrionics.

We transfer from one bus to another until the sign for a restaurant surfaces: GITANJALI. It rings a bell, but Amma has been dragging me to so many wedding venues in the city that they've all started blurring into one ostentatious blob. Tonight, I expected a hole-in-the-wall, but the sheer *size* of this place is jaw-dropping. This is the sort of restaurant where a Kardashian might get proposed to if they wanted some exotic ambiance.

I elbow Amma mid-stride. "Are you sure this is the place?"

"I'm sure."

"Are you *sure* it's not too expensive?"

She scowls. "I'm *sure*. Now, hurry before the humidity ruins your hair and makeup."

I click my teeth shut and follow her into Gitanjali. Another bout of déjà vu fills me at the sight of the red velvet carpet and the antique, metal-worked lanterns that suffuse the whole restaurant with a dim golden glow, strummed sitar music echoing off the tapestried walls. The welcoming smile of a pretty white hostess in an elegant black gown sidetracks me.

"You must be the Khans!"

"We are," answers my mother, and then to me, as we trail behind the blond hostess, "I made a reservation for us tonight."

She sounds so proud of herself that I smile. Perhaps I misjudged her, after all. "You didn't have to do all this for me, Amma. It's too much."

The elation on her face ebbs. Before I can determine what emotion takes its place—guilt?—someone cries, "Zaynab, is that you?"

My stomach plummets.

Amma waves at a table hosting a familiar figure. I recognize her henna-red coif at once: Pushpita Emon, the woman we sat next to at Anika Afa's wedding.

This is her restaurant.

"Oh no, Amma, tell me you didn't . . ."

"Chup!" she hisses at me, even as a sweet simper greets our audience. "Assalamualaikum, Pushpita Afa!"

"What a *surprise* to see you here." Pushpita Khala's overemphasis on the word "surprise" reveals it wasn't much of one at all. "Why, you simply must sit with us. Nai ni, Mansif?" The well-dressed man next to her nods, inspecting us above thin, wire-rimmed bifocals.

"Ji na, I couldn't impose," Amma replies.

"Nonsense! It's no imposition at all," Pushpita Khala says. "Zoey"—this she directs at the hostess, who snaps to attention—"get Nadir to push our tables together, please."

"Yes, ma'am!"

All too soon, we're at a long, makeshift table with the Emons, all of us on one end, the two of them on the other. While my brother does his best to keep our hyperactive sister from crawling around under it seeking dropped quarters— a task that normally falls to me when we go anywhere, though tonight, Amma clearly has another mission in mind for me— I stare up at the ceiling.

Et tu, Allah?

As always, there's no response.

Amma's query fractures my reverie. "Are you dining alone?"

"No, our son, Harun, will be joining us soon."

I slump into my chair. *Of course* their son is joining us.

"There he is now!" Pushpita Khala says with a bright smile.

She and her husband rise from their seats to hustle over to a teenage boy waiting next to the hostess stand, whom I can only assume is the infamous Harun. With his parents in front of him, I can't get a good look at his face, but I can tell he's a good half foot taller than me, even while hunching over to speak to them.

After a brief but heated back-and-forth, Pushpita Khala snatches something off her son's face and manhandles him over to the table, giving me my first proper glimpse of Harun. Tousled black curls that look as if he's run his fingers through them one time too many do little to hide his dour expression or the firm set of his jawline. Renewed humiliation burns in my cheeks.

"Assalamualaikum," he mutters.

Did you get ambushed into this too? I wonder, but my tongue sticks to the roof of my mouth, and I suddenly feel dizzy under the intensity of the lantern lights.

Not that my silence matters.

As if God is punishing me for my ungrateful whining, Resna barges out from under the table like a possessed Whack-a-Mole and asks, "Are you gonna marry my sister?"

"Resu!" I squeak, face red as a tomato.

Arif scrambles out of his seat to catch her, but she's too slippery, chanting, "Zahra and Harun sittin' in a tree, K-I-S-S-I-N-G—" while zipping between everyone's legs.

By the time he gets ahold of her, the damage is already done. Harun ducks his head, refusing to make eye contact with me or anyone else. The adults, meanwhile, are guffawing at Resna's antics. The conversation soon shifts to other topics without me. Without *us*. My unhappy date barely speaks unless spoken to, but no one else pays his reticence any mind, especially when platters overflowing with the menu's specialties arrive.

They talk about—*boast* about—all manner of things while stuffing their faces. Amma recounts the princess story for Harun's father, who explains how he went from waiting at an Indian restaurant after first immigrating to the US to opening up Gitanjali with his brother.

"This is that very restaurant." He smacks the table, a gold watch peeking out of his sleeve. "Now we're planning to open another in Paterson itself."

"Mashallah!" Amma gushes. "This is the most delicious meal I've had in ages."

I almost choke on a bland bite of chicken marinated in a watery tomato-butter gravy. It's not the worst tikka masala I've ever eaten, but it's under-seasoned, probably to appeal to the palates of the white customers sitting around us.

Oblivious, my mother continues, almost wistfully, "You've done well for yourself, Mansif Bhai."

Pushpita Khala pinches Harun's cheek, ignoring the way his bronze complexion tints faintly crimson. "All for our darling son. Did I tell you he's going to Columbia in the fall?"

What, like it's hard? snarks my inner Elle Woods.

After all, I got in too. I may not be going, but it's not because I don't belong. I wonder what the Emons would think if they knew. Would it make them excited that Harun and I have Columbia in common, or would they prefer a pretty girl with no other aspirations in life than being a perfect wife and daughter-in-law?

"He graduated at the top of his class from the Hillam Academy in the city and received a perfect score for math on the SAT *and* ACT," Mansif Khalu adds, puffed up with pride. "Most of the Ivies accepted him, but he wanted to stay close to home. Isn't that right, betta?"

Harun's face darkens further as he mutters, "I guess."

Amma sneaks a glimpse at me, and I know she's debating whether she should mention that I also got into Columbia. I can hear the cogs turning in her head. She looks sorely tempted.

But if she does, she'll have to confess that we couldn't afford for me to attend, and that would be a crack in my princess armor.

"Ah, Zahra loves math too!" she ultimately blurts.

This time, I actually choke. There are a dozen different things my mother could have bragged about. Although I wasn't valedictorian, I graduated in the top three of my year and won several essay competitions while in high school. The local paper even did a piece on my acceptance to Columbia.

Math, though? It might defy every Asian stereotype, but I *loathe* math. Of course, that's all she can come up with. A lie, because the truth isn't enough for her.

I'm not enough for her.

Harun's eyes flick toward me for the first time, pinning me in place until I stop hacking my lungs into my fist. They're a brown so deep and dark, fringed by such an enviably thick fan of lashes, they look almost black. Even with smudges of dark circles beneath them, they're the kind of eyes a weak-willed girl could get lost in—if he weren't *glaring* with them.

Before I can snap, *I don't want to be here either, asshole,* Pushpita Khala chimes in with an exuberant, "Harun wants to be a biomedical engineer someday and make prosthetics for amputees! It's like being a doctor and an engineer all at once, isn't it, betta?"

The doctor-engineer in question grunts.

I blink, begrudgingly impressed. "That's cool. You must be supersmart."

His inscrutable gaze returns to me, but he only says,

"Thanks," once his mother elbows him. I almost give up right then and there, until Amma kicks me under the table, forcing me to disguise my grimace with a smile.

"Are you excited to start studying engineering?"

Because *of course*, this paragon of a brown boy would choose one of the Holy Trinity of Bengali careers, as if to personally spite me with his perfection. Wait, scratch that, *two of the three*, if his mother's bragging is anything to go by.

"I guess," he replies again, pinching the bridge of his nose.

What the hell? Am I giving him a *headache*?

Gnashing my teeth at his audacity, I wring the napkin on my lap into twists, pretending it's his neck. Neither of us wants to be here, but at least I'm not acting like a brat about it.

This is what parents like ours *do*. Although it's nosy and intrusive and often exhausting, it comes from a place of love. I remind myself of that all the time.

But Harun Emon thinks he's too good for all this? Too good for me?

Even Amma must realize by now that this is a match made in hell.

Chapter 4

When our table gets cleared at the end of dinner, I attempt to flee from the circle of hell that awful blind dates belong in, but Amma's sturdy grip on my knee keeps me in my chair. A wily smile spreads across her lips as she surveys Harun, whose Adam's apple bobs at the sheer intensity of her scrutiny.

"I would *love* to take a photo," she says. "You know, to commemorate the occasion."

"What occasion?" I grumble, then yelp when she pinches me.

Harun's eyes grow huge. Before he can answer, Pushpita Khala claps her hands. "Oh, what a marvelous idea! Zoey"— she snaps her ring-laden fingers until the hostess emerges and accepts her iPhone—"take a picture of us with the Khans, won't you?"

Between our two mothers, the rest of us are soon herded in front of an intricate tapestry that hangs from an entire wall of the restaurant, portraying colorful deities out of Hindu epics that make zero sense in an establishment owned by Muslims—likely window dressing for any customers who ordered a side of orientalism with their dinners. Harun attempts to slink behind the drapery, but Pushpita Khala stays him with a hand.

"Why don't you stand next to Zahra?" she asks innocently.

It takes every ounce of my willpower not to scream as our mothers maneuver us close together. Harun stands rigid next to me, while Amma, Arif, and Resna hover at my other side—the latter rubbing her eyes with a chubby knuckle—and his parents pose on his side.

Then Zoey chirps, "Say chhena!"

Harun doesn't bother to smile, and he beats a hasty retreat the second we're done. Well, fine. I'm hardly about to fall swooning into his arms either.

Glaring daggers at his back, I tug at the veil of my mother's shari, summoning her away from where she's squealing over the photos with Pushpita Khala. "Amma, it's getting late." I incline my chin at Arif, who has lifted a drowsy Resna into his arms. "If we're going to catch a bus home, we have to leave now."

"Bus?" Pushpita Khala lifts a hand to her chest.

Between her scandalized expression and the warning glance my mother levels at me, I get the sense I've made some bhodro society blunder, but Amma just flaps her hand. "I told you about my late husband, didn't I? He was the one who drove . . . before."

"Oh, you poor things," Pushpita Khala tuts.

Amma's smile stiffens. "It's fine. Please don't fret, Afa."

"Don't be silly," says Pushpita Khala. "Mansif, we can't let these children take the *bus* home so late." She wrinkles her pierced nose like the very notion stinks. Amma opens her mouth to protest but stops in her tracks when Pushpita Khala adds, "Perhaps Harun can drop them off?"

Her husband *hmm*s in concession.

My jaw hits the carpeted floor. I wait with bated breath for Harun to decline, but he simply frowns at my sleepy siblings and consents with a shrug.

Amma beams. "Are you sure it won't be a bother?"

"Of course not," his mother says. "We're also returning to Paterson, and Harun drove here in his own car. Go on, Zaynab dear. I'll WhatsApp you the pictures soon."

"Thank you, Pushpita Afa," Amma replies. "For everything."

They share a hug and kiss each other on both cheeks. Harun observes them with practiced boredom, hands in his pockets. After a quick sidebar with his mother, she gives him something from her purse—a pair of thick-framed black glasses, which he immediately puts on.

Wait, is that why he's been glaring at me all night?

Narrowing my eyes in suspicion at his back in return, I start to follow him toward the parking lot, then notice Arif's struggle to see around Resna's sleep-mussed pigtails. As I stick out my arms to take her, I grumble, "You knew about this, didn't you?"

"Um. I plead the Fifth?"

I glower. "We *will* be talking about this."

When we don't have a gloomy, looming tagalong, anyway.

The valet drives Harun's car, a sleek silver BMW, up to the curb and tosses him the keys. Harun holds the door open for us, eliciting another charmed giggle from Amma. "Such a gentleman. Isn't he, Zahra?"

"A regular Sir Lancelot," I mutter too quietly for her to hear, but Harun's forehead creases like he has. Entering the backseat with Resna proves to be much less of a Herculean labor with his help, however, so I reward him with a reluctant, "Thanks, dude."

As he observes me, his big, dark eyes seem to swallow the twinkling fairy lights strung all around us. My own eyes dart away, unwilling to be complicit to the abrupt racing of my pulse.

Harun's voice prompts a reluctant glance back, so soft, like a secret between us, that I have to strain to pick it up over the whistle of the wind. "You're welcome."

Half an hour later, he pulls up to the sidewalk in front of our run-down multifamily house. I unlock the door and scoot out of the BMW as fast as humanly possible with Resna still hanging on to me like an octopus, not giving him the chance to repeat his earlier display of gallantry.

Not giving him a chance at all, perhaps, but I push that thought out of my mind.

"Good night," I call over my shoulder.

Without waiting to gauge his reaction or to see if Amma follows, I hoist Resna into the building and scale the creaking steps, my brother at my heels. Inside our apartment, my legs almost buckle, but I prop myself against the doorjamb, clinging to my sister.

"Never grow up," I breathe into her hair.

Maybe then, she can just keep *being* without having to worry about making herself smaller, prettier, quieter, for everyone else's sake but her own.

"I'm sorry, Afa," Arif mumbles as he takes her from me. "Amma told us this would make you happy, but I should've given you a heads-up."

Happy.

I flip the word over and over in my mind. How could she possibly think that? She doesn't understand me at all. I know that it's my fault because I don't tell her much, but it's because I'm afraid my dreams won't be enough for her. That *I* won't be enough for her.

But she *does* know I'd like to go to college someday. That I've been busting my ass at work and school for years for the chance to be something other than some guy's future wife. That I'm only eighteen, for God's sake.

That and you didn't want your first-ever date to end up like this, a pitiful voice in some dusty corner of my mind bemoans. How long had I fantasized of the day it would happen, only for my first date to be with a boy who can't stand my guts?

But none of that is my brother's fault. Forcing my fingers to unclench from the material of my skirt, I scuffle his scruffy hair. "It's okay. Go tuck Resu in."

Aiming one last troubled glance at me, he disappears into Amma's bedroom and doesn't return, wanting to give the two of us time to hash everything out. I round on our mother the minute she locks the door.

"Amma, what the hell?!"

"Don't curse," she says with a frown, as if *that's* the problem here.

"How could you lure me into a blind date like that?" When she opens her mouth to retort, I hold up a hand to stop her. "And please don't insult my intelligence by claiming it was all some random meet-cute."

If anything, it was a meet-*ugly*.

Her mouth snaps shut. "Accha, accha. It wasn't random. But your Pushpita Khala truly did extend the invite today. I didn't want you to say no without giving it a chance."

It's far from an apology. Brown parents don't have the capacity for those wired into their DNA. Normally, *any* admittance of wrongdoing on her part would satisfy me knowing that, but I narrow my eyes, cross my arms, and tap my foot. *Her* signature disappointed look.

She cringes, then changes course. "Wasn't it a lovely evening, though?"

"What?" I suck in a sharp, disbelieving breath at her chipper expression. "*Lovely?* Amma, that was a train wreck."

Now it's her turn to gasp. "How can you say that? You and Harun hit it off so well. Why, he couldn't take his eyes off you!"

"No," I counter, throwing my hands into the air. "You were acting like such a drama queen that he couldn't take his eyes off *you*. No one could." Amma sputters as if I've slapped her. Taking advantage of her rare bout of speechlessness, I add, "I can't believe you would do this to me. Even village girls in Bangladesh are graduating college before marrying these days. Kids don't *do* this anymore."

"Oh, Zahra . . ." She reaches for my cheek, and I resist the urge to recoil. "I know you think I'm some kind of evil mastermind, but I didn't plan this. I wanted to show you off at the wedding, so people in the community would know you'll be marriageable in a few years." As if I need preview trailers. "Sitting next to Pushpita Emon was a complete coincidence. I had my doubts when she first proposed introducing you two. Their family isn't what I would have envisioned for you before . . . But though you're both young, Harun is polite, good-looking, and clearly going places. Proper Bangladeshi boys like that don't come along often. Would getting to know him be so bad? You're so quick to be pessimistic, shuna. I only wanted you to give him a chance."

Some of the anger dims in me, leaving weary defeat.

She's not wrong: pessimism *is* my default, but she's had a hand in that herself. Over the years, all my hopes have become hobbies to her, my dream to be an author someday equally as

silly as when I was eight and begged her for a pet chicken like
the ones we had in Bangladesh. Even if I make it to college,
will I ever get to study writing? I'm afraid she won't be proud
of me, the way Harun's parents are of him, and then I won't be
brave enough to keep trying.

"Well," I say, "I sat through dinner and so did he, despite
wanting to be anywhere but there. We gave it a fair shot, okay?
Time to move on."

Amma fidgets with her urna. A sinking feeling anchors in
my gut. "What is it?"

"The Emons have invited us to another dinner this Friday,"
she replies, looking anywhere but at me. "I already accepted."

"What?!" I shout. "Without asking me? *Again?* I'm not
going."

"Don't be that way," she pleads, mouth set in a moue. "If
we don't go, I'll never be able to show my face in Paterson. I
don't know if they'd be willing to give us another chance."

I press my fingertips into my throbbing temples, stamping
down the ridiculous urge to protect her from the monster of her
own making. Are the Emons so much better than us because
they're rich? Is their irritatingly perfect, future doctor-engineer
son better than me?

"You should have thought about that earlier," I say.

We stare one another down for the longest time.

Amma's expression has transformed from cajoling to
unreadable, the dark eyes we share like flat shards of glass,
her plum-colored lips pressed so tightly together, all the blood

drains from her face. She's not used to me talking back to her. I'm not used to it either. But I lift my chin, a mulish set to my own jaw. She won't make me back down.

Not this time, because I *know* I'm right.

She knows I'm right.

But then the ice in her eyes cracks, leaking big, fat droplets of tears. Lifting her trembling hands to suppress her sobs, she pivots away from me and dashes toward her bedroom. The door slams so loudly, the lightbulbs above my head quiver in their fixtures.

Frankly, she could give Aishwarya Rai a lesson in crying on cue.

I take a few breaths to temper my frustration, then stoop to pick up the scarves and other accessories that got tossed all over the couches and carpet earlier that night. When I glance up at a rustle, I discover my grandmother watching me and shake off the disappointment that it isn't Amma coming to grovel.

"Did we wake you up, Nanu? Sorry."

Nanu evaluates me for another few seconds, a somber cast to her weathered face. You can tell she's Amma's mother because we all share the same doe-brown eyes, long upturned noses, and Cupid's bow lips, but that's where all resemblances end. While Amma has all the scorching passion of the sun, Nanu is like the moon, cool and soft and dark.

Usually, I appreciate that about her, that she's the stolid lighthouse at the heart of all our churning waves, the voice of reason I can turn to when Amma's theatrics make me want to tear clumps of hair out of my scalp, but right now, I can't tell what she's thinking.

She beckons me forward. "Obaidi ao."

Knot in my ribs, I plod after her into the kitchen. She raps on the nicked wooden table with her knuckles. When I sit down, a wisping cup of tea appears in front of me, and I blink, wondering if she's been puttering around in here the whole time Amma and I were at each other's throats. "Isn't it kinda late for caffeine, Nanu?"

A tiny smile graces her face. "I have a feeling none of us will be sleeping well tonight."

She's got me there.

"You heard everything, huh?"

Silence reigns as we sip from our cups. It's not milk tea, but rong saa—strong and black, with a pinch of grated ginger and salt, sweetened by honey—that immediately thaws me like a comforting blanket.

"You know, there's something to be said for the old ways," she says at last.

I groan. "Not you, too, Nanu. I thought you'd take *my* side."

She trains a meaningful look on me. "Kun deen tumar 'side' nee see na?"

"You're right. . . ." I force my hackles down. "You *do* usually take my side."

Nanu has always been my confidante. She's a good listener,

and though I know her vision of my future isn't that far off from Amma's, she's never turned her nose up at my hopes for college or writing. When I told her I couldn't go to Columbia, she was more devastated than Amma and me combined.

"I met your nana at seventeen. . . ."

My eyes spring to her face, but though she never talks about my grandfather, it's as placid as ever as she takes another sip of tea, lips red from the faan and gua she always chews.

"He was already twenty," she continues. "It's what was done when I was growing up. Much of my father's ancestral gram had been burned by Razakar soldiers during the Liberation War. I was one of five daughters. Baba thought we'd be happier married."

"Were you?" I whisper.

She peals a melodic laugh. "For a long time, no. I spent years of our marriage sleeping in his mother's bed, missing my own, not yet ready to be a wife, but . . ." Her eyes go misty from the memories. "He let me. During that time, he traveled to Saudi Arabia to work, wrote me letters, sent home money and gifts. Perhaps there's something to be said for *that*, too."

The affection in her voice is gossamer-fine, but so clearly present.

"So you came to love him?"

"Love?" she muses. "I know he worked hard every single day to keep a roof over our heads and food in our bellies. I know we laughed together when his business saw profits and mourned together when we lost our children before your mother to miscarriages." She considers the sifting surface of her tea. "He never told me 'ami tumare bhalo bashi,' like actors do in natoks. But when he died . . . I didn't know how to be without him. Your mother was only a girl then, not even twelve. Had I not had her to live for, I don't know that I could have gone on. Is that love?"

All I can do is nod, a lump in my throat and tears prickling in my eyes. I can't tell if what I'm feeling is sadness, just that I'm bursting with it.

Deeper crinkles form around her eyes. "The Emon boy . . . do you find him handsome?"

Snapshots of Harun's face return to me. The strong set of his jawline, the sharp angles of his cheekbones, those infinitely dark eyes and that thick head of curls.

"I—I guess he's not a complete raikhosh."

Too bad I can't say the same about his trollish *personality*.

A hint of mischief gleams in Nanu's eyes. "My, my. Young *and* good-looking. Shunar kofal faiso go, moyna." She pokes me right between the eyebrows, eternally fond of her Bengali expressions about foreheads predicting one's fortune. "I wasn't so lucky. Your nana had quite the beard back in the day, and it itched terribly whenever he kissed me."

"Nanu!" I yelp, scandalized.

I can't begrudge her belly-deep laughter, though.

Her wrinkled hand moves to trace a thumb over my cheek, as Amma's did earlier. "Just because something has always been done a certain way doesn't mean it's right. Every day, I thank Allah for giving you more prospects than your mother and I had. That's all most parents want for their children. Give the boy another chance, moyna. For me. He may surprise you."

She smiles, and I meet her gaze, sighing.

"Okay, but *only* for you."

Chapter ❤ 5

Fridays are holy days to Muslims, like Sundays for Christians and the Jewish Sabbath on Saturdays, but I can't shake the feeling that *mine* are cursed.

Last Friday, I attended the wedding where I had the great misfortune of sharing a table with Pushpita Emon. Tonight after work, I have to play the reluctant heroine in *Disaster Date: The Sequel* at her house.

My prayers to skip straight into Saturday have gone unanswered, so I shove the clothes and makeup Amma set out for me into my backpack and leave the house early enough that I can actually catch a bus to Chai Ho. I'm on time for once.

My best friends cock their heads in tandem as I step through the door.

"Dal, do my eyes deceive me or has our erstwhile third musketeer appeared?" Dani asks in a more-aghast-than-necessary tone, giving the table in front of her a wipe to punctuate each word.

I roll my eyes, accepting a rag from her sister to join them in cleaning. "Haha. I haven't been late *that* often, have I?"

"Only a handful of times since you started working full-time," Dalia supplies helpfully.

I heave a sigh. "Mr. Tahir keeping track?"

"Maybe he'll go easier on you now that he's hired a new employee," Dani muses.

My eyes bulge mid-wipe. "He did *what*?"

Mr. Tahir has been threatening to replace me since day one, but I dropped so many desserts and spilled so much tea in those early days without getting the boot—docked paychecks and withheld tips notwithstanding—that I figured it was our schtick. Sure, I'm occasionally a few minutes late, but I've always hoped he considered me a good employee, or at least that he pities my family too much to axe me.

Being poor has done no favors for my pride.

The twins must notice my dawning distress, because Dani says, "Breathe, Zar. He's not firing you. With us working only part-time starting September, he wants more hands on deck. If anything, he needs you now more than ever."

"You're *sure*?"

Dalia wiggles her smallest finger. "Pinky promise."

I sigh, relieved, and move to heft my bag onto the counter, table forgotten. "Good, because I need you to help me hide this somewhere he can't find."

"What's in there?" Dani asks. "Drugs?"

"Yep, a whole kilo," I deadpan. "Actually, it's an outfit for a dawath I have to attend after work. We're going straight from here and I can't let my shalwar kameez get bunched up or Amma will have my head. I told her Dalia would help me with my makeup too." I bat my eyes and smile at them in a way that says both *thank you* and *my bad*.

"A dawath, huh?" Dani wrinkles her nose. "Not another wedding, right?"

I shake my head. "No. It's an invitation to my mother's friend's house."

The twins share one of those twinny glances where they have a whole psychic conversation with each other, while I fidget. They used to look even more identical when we were younger, before Dani cut and bleached her hair—currently purple—and her sister began veiling. Dalia's also fat, with a face as bright and round and lovely as the moon. But though they've changed so much, it's no less eerie now. I've never kept secrets from them and am hoping the Harun situation resolves itself before there's ever anything to tell.

Dalia cracks first. "I'm always happy to help, Zar."

"Me too," Dani adds.

I brandish my most grateful smile as they smuggle the contents of my backpack, *Ocean's 8* style, into the supply closet the three of us pray in, hanging my flamingo-pink shalwar kameez on the dustpan hook next to the spare janamaz.

Jumu'ah services make Friday one of the most profitable days for Chai Ho. Some customers stop in for breakfast before them. More show up for the lunch rush. Today, we're even busier than the typical Friday. A choir of whispers and pointed glances toward the kitchen door accompany every visit to a table, signaling that the Auntie Network must have already heard about the new hire through the grapevine and are dying to find out their life story. It's so hectic that I don't have a second to breathe, let alone dwell on Harun.

"Have you met the new employee yet, Zahra?" my visiting landlady asks eagerly as I refill her cup. When I shake my head, she clucks her tongue. "I heard the poor thing is all alone here."

"I heard he's an orphan," adds her friend, sipping her own tea.

A bearded man in a fanjabi with a matching white tufi on his head chimes in from another table with, "Well, *I* heard the imam—"

I'm so distracted trying to parse their gossip while bringing desserts and tea to and from the hungry mosque-goers that when I carry a wobbling stack of plates to the kitchen door, I fail to notice someone opening it from within.

"Zar—" Dani warns from behind the counter.

It's too late. The door slams into my face and stars burst in my vision. The mountain of dishes topples right out of my arms, shattering as it makes impact. The momentum tips me too far in the other direction to do much more than grope for the plates and the lean, tall silhouette that appeared in the doorway, a cry escaping me.

Something wraps around my wrist and jerks me forward.

Air whooshes as the cacophony of breaking ceramic continues. I flinch, eyes screwed shut, bracing myself to tumble onto the floor like the dropped china. Very little pain follows my landing, though my "cushion" feels more like bone than padding. Only a blur of noise, heat, heavy breathing—my own and someone else's—and a heartbeat pounding in time with mine.

"Are you hurt?" the someone else asks from under me.

Under me!

My eyelids fly apart.

I find myself staring into a pair of unfamiliar, honey-brown irises, shimmering with worry. "Y-you're not Mr. Tahir."

Not-Mr.-Tahir smiles. "As far as I know, that's true."

The man himself manifests soon after, holding his balding head in shock. "Astaghfirullah, what's the meaning of this? So many ruined dishes!"

Only when his flinty gaze roves to me do I realize the compromising position I'm in, clutched in the arms of an unknown teenage boy on the floor of the tea shop, my forearms pressed to his chest, my hands gripping his shoulders for dear life. Jagged pieces of broken porcelain glitter at our feet, a reminder of how close I came to hurting myself.

"Oh God," I rasp, scrambling up off the boy, who must be the new employee. "Mr. Tahir, I am so sorry—"

"It's not her fault," says the boy, dusting himself off and rising to his feet. When he does, he towers over everyone else inside the shop, but Mr. Tahir still looks tempted to take off his loafer and lob it at him. "I thought I'd come out to get more dishes since I finished cleaning the last stack, and . . . well . . ."

Our boss evaluates us over crossed arms, then sighs when Dani and Dalia arrive. "It's fine. We can take it out of your paycheck later. Can you keep working, Miss Khan?" I poke my forehead, remembering my injury all at once. So much for what Nanu said about being lucky. It throbs, but at least there's no blood. I don't want to end my shift early, so I nod, even though the new boy and my friends seem skeptical. "Good. Nayim, clean this up, then go back to the kitchen, where I can keep an eye on you."

The kitchen door slams shut.

I grimace but assure Dalia and Dani that I'm not in imminent danger of collapse. "Go back to work before your dad blows another gasket, okay?"

Reluctantly, they do as asked, leaving me alone with our new coworker.

Nayim, Mr. Tahir called him.

I can't meet his gaze after my mortifying fall, especially after feeling him up in front of half the city, so I stoop beside the shattered dishes, carefully picking out larger shards until gentle hands land on top of mine, forcing them to still.

"Let me get a broom, Zahra," Nayim says, in a musical accent that's comfortingly familiar now that I'm paying attention. "You'll cut yourself if you aren't careful."

My eyes widen, then narrow. "How do you know my name?"

He taps the plastic name tag pinned to a ruffled blue apron that matches my own. It reads *Nayim A.* Blood rushes to my cheeks once more, but before I can muster up a clever quip, he disappears into the kitchen, carrying with him the handful of plates that survived my gracelessness. I can only gape.

He looks to be about my age, with thick, shoulder-length black locks that sweep into his catlike eyes, dressed in a T-shirt under an open flannel button-up that must be a hand-me-down from a much broader man, his jeans-clad legs taking confident strides till the door shuts between us. Once he's out of sight, I become aware of the renewed chatter within the shop. Eagle-eyed aunties and uncles stare after Nayim.

Like that, the conversation drifts away from my blunder. I should be happy, but my mood darkens as I try to make sense of the rumor mill. From the chatter, I can pick out words like "orphan" and "charity case." Did they talk about me like that when Mr. Tahir hired me after Baba's death?

"You sure you're not dizzy, Zar?"

It's Dani who asks from behind the counter. She's too preoccupied with a winding line of customers to come over and help me up, so I grab the empty chair nearest to me and do it myself. The door to the kitchen opens again at that exact moment and Nayim returns, clutching the broom and a dustpan. Which means that he went to the broom closet.

Oh God, did he see my dress? Did Mr. Tahir?

I gulp. "How mad was he?"

"Pretty upset," he concedes, before quirking a lopsided grin at me that almost wins one from me in return. *Almost.* "Don't worry, though. He's only miffed at me."

I frown, still confused by his decision to take all the blame. "Why did you do that?"

Mr. Tahir already vowed to charge him for the mess, and from the snippets of gossip I've grasped, it doesn't sound like he can afford that any more than me. He shrugs. "I already dropped a few plates in the sink when he was showing me the ropes earlier. What's a couple more if it means I've come to your rescue?"

"My rescue?" I scoff, but this time the grin is too difficult to resist any longer. "That line work on other girls?"

His dark brows pinch together. "On girls? Never. I was simply coming to the aid of a fellow coworker, whatever their gender."

I snort-laugh and his severe mask cracks. His own laugh is so infectious that I almost forget everyone else watching us, including a baby strapped into a polka-dotted stroller with a matching bottle between her pudgy fists.

My blush returns with a vengeance as I toe at the broken dishes and clear my throat. "Right. Well. Fridays are our busiest days, so we'd better get back to it before we really piss Mr. Tahir off, newbie. I think that table's flagging me down."

Nayim's smile falters, but he doesn't try to stop me, too engrossed with cleaning up my mess. He holds the broom and dustpan in each hand as if they might bite him, and a fresh tide of guilt crests over me for having inconvenienced him.

Trying not to think about *any* cute, confusing boys, I lose myself in the tedium again and mostly succeed until I flit behind Dani to grab an order from the pass-through window and catch myself face-to-face with my new coworker. He directs another dentist-approved grin at me.

My heart definitely does *not* skip any beats, no siree.

"Mr. Tahir banished me here," he says by way of greeting.

"That's nice?"

"We didn't have a chance to talk much earlier," he continues, clearly unaware of my self-consciousness. "The *A* stands for Aktar. In case you were wondering."

"Huh?"

He chuckles. "Do I have to tap the name tag again?"

"Oh! Your name! Duh!" I grab the golden laddu he holds out just to have somewhere else to look besides his teasing expression. "My name is Zahra. Zahra Khan."

"A pretty name," he says. "It suits you."

And what's *that* supposed to mean? Is he flirting?! With *me*?!

Memories of how solid and warm his body felt beneath mine don't take much of an imagination to summon up, despite me silently repeating *astaghfirullah* like a mantra to dispel the thought. The fact that he's the first boy I've been that close to physically doesn't escape me.

"Thank you?" I manage to squeak.

As fast as my feet will take me, I zip away to get the order of yet another customer, but as if the universe has decided to keep spurning my wishes, Nayim and I end up meeting at the pass-through window to exchange dishes over and over again throughout the rest of our shift.

Each time, he asks me exactly one question. Do I enjoy this job? (Yep, it's helping pay for college.) Am I from Paterson originally? (No, but I've lived here most of my life.) Am I friends with the Tahir girls? (Best and forever.)

By our fourth less-than-clandestine meeting, my curiosity gets the best of me, and I fire off my own query before he can speak. "I hope you don't mind me asking, but you're not from here, right?"

"What gave it away?" he wonders ruefully. "Do I look that clueless? I thought I was doing a decent job blending in."

Clueless isn't how I'd put it, but there's something different about him. Maybe it's that he's so *new* in this place where everyone knows each other.

I wave a plate-free hand. "Oh, no, it's not like that at all. It's just, you have a . . . British inflection? It's kind of like my mom." Except, well. *More* British. More crisp, lilting vowels that are at once soothing and like nothing else I've ever heard.

"Huh." Nayim picks up a plate to frown at his own reflection. "First I reminded you of Mr. Tahir and now your mother? I didn't realize I passed for middle-aged."

I drag a hand over my face. "Ugh, sorry. I'm totally stepping in it, aren't I?"

"It's fine," he replies, cupping his cheeks in both palms so his amused expression fills the entire window. "I rather like it."

Fighting another infuriating blush, I say, "What I meant was, your English is perfect, but it sounds more British than American."

"The colonization will do that to you," he answers with a chuckle. "But your instincts are spot-on. I immigrated here from Bangladesh."

"Oh, hey, I'm Bangladeshi too!"

"If you two could reserve the formal introductions until after your shift," Mr. Tahir intones in his matter-of-fact rumble from the kitchen, where Dalia is doing her best not to give in to a fit of giggles, "I would greatly appreciate it. I already have to replace those dishes you destroyed earlier without you lollygagging on top of everything."

We split apart from each other immediately, but not before I catch Dani wiggling her eyebrows at me from the latte machine. I scuttle away from the counter to welcome a new arrival.

Like this, the rest of the day passes by.

Whenever Nayim and I catch glimpses of each other, he flashes me another of his—friendly? flirty?—smiles, honeyed eyes twinkling with an emotion I can't translate. Between him and a rowdy group of customers, time flies. Before I know it, we've closed for the night.

It's time for my date.

After carefully tucking my paycheck and the day's tips into a unicorn fanny pack I borrowed from Resna, I trudge tiredly into the kitchen, making a mental note to add half the money to the ever-so-slowly-growing college savings under my bed.

Nayim is humming while he sweeps inside.

He's tall—more so, even, than a certain someone my mother has all but swooned over—and I can't help the way my eyes are drawn once more to his lanky frame, remembering how it felt when he held me. He smiles brightly and straightens the second he spots me, so I have to look up at him, like a sunflower leaning toward the sun.

Before he can say anything, Dani retrieves my bag from the broom closet, Dalia traipsing behind her with my dress. Both of them push me into the employee bathroom, while Nayim and Mr. Tahir stare in bemusement.

I shrug as the door shuts. *What can you do?*

"He's cute, isn't he?" Dalia asks as soon as it's closed. She pulls out her primer and begins dabbing it onto my face, then applies concealer to the bruise on my forehead I'd forgotten about.

"Eh," replies Dani, busy braiding my hair into a crown. "If you're into guys, I guess. *Somebody* sure seemed to be."

They both smirk at me.

"Oh, cut it out," I sputter. "I was just being polite to a fellow Bangladeshi."

"Polite?" Dani quips. "Is *that* what the kids are calling it these days?"

I'd shove her if it didn't mean looking like Miss Havisham tonight, but if I'm being honest, I can't help the hint of intrigue that bubbles in my belly. "What's his deal, anyway? I didn't think your dad was in the business of taking in any more Bangladeshi strays."

"You're so adorable, I guess he couldn't help it," Dalia says with a boop on my nose.

Having finished with my hair, Dani leans against the tiled wall, rubbing her chin. "He's actually more stray than you, Zar. Apparently, he's an orphan or something. He got here from Bangladesh all alone a week ago. When Ammu heard about it, she convinced Abbu to give Nayim a gig here, and the imam's wife let him stay with them. The Auntie Network works fast."

Never would I have guessed from Nayim's sunny disposition that he could be an orphan. Losing my father is a blow I might never fully recover from. I don't know if I could abandon my whole world on top of that. Lose *everyone* and *everything*.

My heart breaks for him.

I also feel a rare rush of gratitude for Mr. Tahir and the other aunties and uncles of our community, who swooped in to help Nayim without expecting anything in return . . . aside from hot gossip and manual labor. Every once in a blue moon, their prying comes in handy.

"Annnnnd all done," Dalia declares, taking in her handiwork. "You're a knockout, babe."

Although the reason I needed her help is bothersome, I grin at the Zahra in the mirror. Dalia curates body-positive content for hijabis online and has a delicate touch with makeup that doesn't make me look like a vampire-pale Fair & Lovely spokesmodel.

Just . . . me.

I can't help but wonder what Harun will think. Frankly, he doesn't deserve this much effort, but my pulse starts to race nevertheless.

Dani narrows her eyes at me. "Why are you so flushed, hmm?"

"'Cause of Nayim again?" Dalia adds.

"No," I choke out. "It's called blush, am I right?" They don't seem convinced, so I change the subject. "Anyway, I owe you two a box of Munchkins for rescuing me today. Amma wanted me to take the day off, but I can't afford to miss shifts."

"Anytime, Zar."

They both give me careful hugs that won't wrinkle my outfit, and then we pile out of the bathroom. My newest coworker is still sweeping, but alone. Mr. Tahir must already be sequestered in his office, counting today's profits. Nayim glances up at my arrival.

He freezes. "You look—"

"Yes?" My voice cracks, though I'd been aiming for blasé.

He seems too taken aback by my appearance to notice. "Different."

"Hey!" The twins grow indignant on my behalf, but I only cock my head at the horrified expression that steals over his face as he apologizes.

"Sorry. I guess I'm the one stepping in it now."

"Big-time." I grin.

He rubs the back of his neck. "I didn't mean it like that. You look . . . great."

A nervous giggle escapes me. I try my best to play it cool. "Thanks. You're not so bad yourself, newbie."

The sight of my smile invites one of his own. "Where're you off to?"

For some reason I don't want to unpack, I'd rather not tell him my mother has set me up with a boy who despises me. I'm rescued from having to explain by a series of knocks on the window of the tea shop. As expected, Arif is waiting outside in his second-best suit, an idling car behind him. He gestures for me to hurry.

"Gotta go," I say. "Duty calls."

But as I leave the shop, I can't resist glancing back and find Nayim watching me, too.

Butterflies flutter in my belly. I slam the Uber door shut hard enough to dislodge them, turning my attention to my family and what's to come instead.

Now is not the time for more boy-shaped distractions.

Not when I have plenty of boy-shaped problems ahead.

THE AUNTIE NETWORK

Sharmila:
Has anyone else met Mr. Tahir's latest hire? Is Chai Ho an etheem khana now?

Meera:
Sharmila, how could you say that? Fareh na ilan mathe! Did you see how he saved Zahra? It was like something out of a natok. What a dashing young man! √√

Champa:
Oh? Are you saying you'd introduce a dishwasher to your daughter? Just because she's fatherless doesn't mean Zahra can't do better. She is a Khan, after all.

Meera:
Chup koro! Of course not! Such a shame he doesn't come from a better family . . . but that won't be a problem for Zahra. I heard Pushpita Emon has been sniffing around her. √√

Sharmila:
Hassa ni? Khans and Emons? Some people will do anything for money. . . .

Chapter ❤6

"Are we theeeere yet?" Resna whines.

"Almost . . ."

I keep my hand on her knee to stop her from kicking Arif's seat as we peer out the window of the Uber our mother splurged on to bring us to Harun's. The houses grow more and more grand the farther we wind up the hill, nothing like our derelict multifamily home. Only a twelve-minute drive but entire worlds apart.

Amma goggles between the scenery and the glowing screen of her phone. "This article says the mayor lives in this neighborhood!"

The reverence in her voice prompts me to wipe my sweaty palms on the skirt of my shalwar kameez. The fancy embroidery leaves my skin itchy, and my scalp prickles under the heavy urna draped over my hair. I keep waiting for the car to stop somewhere—I keep praying for our destination to be some semblance of normal—but it continues to inch up the hill, until finally, it passes a sign that reads HILLCREST in gold.

The houses beyond it are like something out of *The Great Gatsby*. The Uber driver slows in front of one that could pass for a miniature castle, stone tiles plastered over pale pink and white stucco under a trio of pointed dome roofs. It sits on an emerald-green expanse of lawn, attached to a three-car garage and a long driveway with a basketball hoop at the end.

"This it?" asks the driver.

Even he seems skeptical that we would be invited to a place like this.

Amma practically hauls me out of the car but gives me a blessed few minutes to compose myself before she rings the doorbell outside the iron gate. Although an obstinate voice in my head insists I don't care what Harun or his family think of me, my heart feels too big for my rib cage—or maybe my push-up bra—as it does its damnedest to hurtle out of it.

I know I'm good enough, and also that *he* might not be, but the thought of being a disappointment to my family is a specter I can't ever exorcise.

Pushpita Khala's familiar accent cuts through the static and my nerves. "Ji?"

"Assalamualaikum, Afa," Amma greets her.

"Oh, Zaynab, waalaikumsalam! Come in, come in!"

She buzzes us through. Amma leads Arif and Resna by hand in front of me, letting me tread up the cobblestone path to the front porch alone. The door swings open before we reach it, revealing a dimpling Pushpita Emon, who launches herself at Amma as if she hasn't seen her in years rather than for a mere few days.

Amma is equally enthusiastic, kissing both of her cheeks. "Ah, your home is so elegant!"

Pushpita Khala smiles. Her dark eyes, the same spilled-ink black as Harun's, settle on me as I trek into the house after the rest of my family. She utters a dreamy sigh. "Oh, mashallah, you look so beautiful, my dear! Is this another of your mother's dazzling creations?"

"Thank you, Khala. It is." I blush, eyes on the Persian rug below my feet.

I doubt she hears me over her own shout. "Mansif, Harun, our guests have arrived!"

Harun's father steps into the long foyer from an adjoining room, and more niceties are exchanged. They're so animated, I don't realize that my date has slipped in to join us until he murmurs, "Hey," right next to me.

His sudden, looming *thereness* startles me in the middle of removing my strappy sandals. My arms pinwheel as I struggle to regain my balance, still wearing one wobbling heel, the other dangling from my fingertips.

Before I can crash backward into the doorway, Harun catches me by the wrist and yanks me upright. I trip head over heels—damsel-like—into his chest. It feels so firm under my palms that my face blazes feverishly hot. Astaghfirullah, between this and what happened at the tea shop with Nayim, I've become a ditzy rom-com heroine, haven't I?

Harun all but picks me up by the biceps and places me a foot away from his person as if I'm a boogery child, refusing to look at me any longer. "You good?"

I squeak something that passes for a *yes* while silently begging the earth to open wide and swallow me whole. Surely rich-people houses come with that feature equipped?

Our parents chortle at the scene. With a crafty gleam in her eyes, Pushpita Khala says, "Doesn't Zahra look like a princess tonight, betta?"

Harun's voice grows garbled with frustration. "Ma, c'mon."

I take the opportunity to scan him from head to toe while we're conducted into the mammoth living room, replete with a mounted TV, enough couches to seat five times as many guests, and an actual tea cart out of *Downton Abbey*. All that's missing is a butler.

Unlike his father, Harun has ditched his jacket for a pinstripe button-up that clings to his broad shoulders and narrow waist. His sleeves are rolled up to expose his forearms, covered in dark hair. He keeps his hands in the pockets of his black chinos, feet clad in navy-blue socks that match the shirt. Thick black frames complete the outfit, but they only make him look like the male models they always cast to play haughty—and *hot*—geniuses on CW shows.

Ugh! Why couldn't he be a dweeby Deshi guy?

Sadly, his fashion sense doesn't translate to his conversation skills. Just like our first date, he doesn't issue a single word of his own accord as his mother passes glasses of freshly squeezed lemon sharbat to my siblings and tea to the rest of us.

He sips from his cup, scrolling through his phone and pretending I'm invisible, while the adults make small talk about some mogul on the Bangladeshi news who hails from one of the only surviving princely estates in Bangladesh—"You know, *his* children must appreciate traditional values"—and Arif does his best to entertain a squirmy Resna.

At last, it's Harun's father who helps us along by suggesting, "Harun, while your mother prepares dinner, why don't you give Zahra a tour of the house?"

He nods and stands up, raising an expectant eyebrow at me when I don't immediately move to do the same. I gulp. Something about Harun's piercing gaze makes me feel very small when I'm with him, and I'm not sure I like it.

"Come on. Let's get this over with."

As he guides me from room to room, I try to keep my jaw from toppling to the polished wooden floor, mostly because I don't want to give him the satisfaction. A mahogany table long enough to feed a dozen people sits under a crystal chandelier, gleaming china arranged behind glass in a complementary showcase my mother would sell her soul to own.

"This is the dining room," he says, as if I'm too poor to have ever seen one.

"It's nice."

"Thanks."

The conversation drags on like this, rinse and repeat. He takes me through a gigantic kitchen with a marble island and countertops, several pristine bathrooms, his father's study, a guest bedroom, and a game room packed with an Xbox, a PlayStation, and a Nintendo. There's even a pool table, poker cards and chips scattered across the green surface.

"You must always have friends over," I say.

"Sometimes."

And that's that.

Although I'm certain Arif would combust from the pure excitement of being around so many gaming consoles, it's when I enter the library that I freeze mid-step, a wonder-struck gasp spilling from my lips. Towering wooden shelves cover every inch of the room, filled with more books than I've seen in my life. The *fancy* kind, with gold foil titles across leather spines. The kind you'd expect to flip open and find "First Edition" on the copyright page.

Harun turns to observe me, but while my pride shrivels at the idea of him sensing my envy, I can't help gazing longingly at the shelves.

I've always considered libraries my haven; they're not only where I learned to read, but where I learned to *love* reading—where little Zahra, at the tender age of ten, decided her lifelong dream was to see her own name on the cover of a book, in a place just like this.

My date regards me for an instant, while I squirm like Belle beneath the Beast's mercurial contemplation. When he speaks, his voice is soft, even sheepish. "These are my father's books. No one comes in here. The decorator ordered them when we moved in."

I read between the lines: the library is no more than a status symbol.

"That's so sad," I whisper, before I can stop myself. "No offense! I just meant . . . I love to read. But of course that doesn't mean *you* need to or anything."

He shrugs and motions for me to follow him upstairs, but I catch the slightest frown on his face. It vanishes by the time we reach the top of the steps.

"My parents' room," he explains, waving at a shut door. Next, he points at another door farther down the hall, this one half-cracked. "And that's mine."

"Can I see it?"

His forehead wrinkles at my eagerness, for once completely unfeigned. "I guess."

Before he turns away, I notice that his ears are scarlet beneath the black locks that curl around them. With his hands shoved inside his pockets, he skulks toward his room, then stops to hold the door open for me.

His bedroom is huge—as expected—but that's where all my predictions end. Unlike the game room, there isn't much to hint at hobbies or leisure. It's spartan and neat: a desk along one white wall holds a lamp, a closed laptop, a small calendar, and graphing paper.

There are trophies, model planes, trains, and colorful anime robots next to framed photographs set on top of a bookcase, lined with STEM textbooks and the occasional comic book or manga in shiny plastic. I wander closer to the photos, stooping to examine every picture.

Family vacations at tropical destinations. Harun presented with trophies, medals, or certificates. His parents and teachers on either side of him, proud expressions on their faces, his own indifferent despite being one of the few students of color present. Always indifferent, even when standing next to kids in the same school uniform who have their arms slung around his shoulders, presented in sharp contrast beside a grinning boy who looks a lot like him.

Maybe he's actually a cyborg who wasn't programmed to smile?

One frame lies facedown, shoved haphazardly behind the others. Before I can flip it over, another photo sucker punches the air from my lungs. Harun poses with a gold medal in nothing but a pair of black swimming briefs, his long legs, flat abdomen, and bulging biceps toned, water glistening in his curls, sliding down the sculpted copper planes of his six-pack and angular hips.

Whoa.

"Y-you swim?"

He cocks his head. "My mom didn't put that on my biodata?"

"Oh, um, yeah, she did. I—forgot. That's cool." My voice pitches high enough to crack glass as I pivot away from the frame, bolstering my back against the bookcase and chanting my mental mantra of *astaghfirullah* again, even though it's his fault for leaving it out like that.

A biodata is essentially a marriage résumé used to arrange matches. His mother sent one for me to peruse after the dinner at Gitanjali. It listed everything from his age, height, and blood type to all the clubs he's participated in over the years. In addition to robotics, he was apparently on the swim team. But seeing him, *er*, in action is another thing entirely.

"Are you okay?" Harun asks, more suspicious than concerned.

Trying not to let on how much his stoicism aggravates me, I reply, "Yep. All good. I just . . . Is there a bathroom I can use? Out in the hall?"

He inclines his chin at another door I'd assumed was a closet. "Through there."

I nod and click the lock behind me.

With the knob pressed into my spine, I survey the tile-covered room. It's nothing like the one in our apartment. There's not even a plastic bodna to clean up with next to the toilet, but the silver hose of a bidet instead. I notice four toothbrushes on the sink, each in its own glass cup. Who the hell needs so many toothbrushes? The glass-enclosed shower, meanwhile, is bigger than the one my entire family bickers over every morning.

Not that I want to think about him in the shower.

"I can't do this," I grouse to the Zahra in the mirror, releasing the breath I didn't know I was holding.

Without even meaning to, I recall the new boy and how he actually appeared interested in getting to know me—how pleasant and funny he was despite being all alone in New Jersey, of all places. Compared to Nayim, Harun is so privileged, but seems utterly miserable.

Could I ever be with a guy who acts like talking to me is as painful as getting his nails torn out? Who looks at me as if I'm a homework assignment he's forced to complete?

Sorry, Nanu. I tried my best.

After turning the spout on and off to sell my act, I dry my hands and throw open the door. Part of me wants to hunker down in his bathroom until the end of days, but the faster I get out, the faster dinner will be over, the faster we'll leave, and the faster I can confess to my mother that I foresee no universe in which Harun and I are happy with each other.

I stumble forward, and to his credit, genuine concern furrows his brow. "Are you sure you're all right? You wanna lie down or something?"

It's the most he's said to me in, well, *ever*. It would be sweet if I didn't suspect he has a potentially fatal case of gingivitis.

"Are *you* okay?"

He blinks at my rapid change of subject. "What?"

Cheeks aglow, with the pungent taste of foot in my mouth, I say, "Uh, it's just, I noticed you have *a lot* of toothbrushes. Like, a lot, a lot."

He shrugs. "One's mine, one's a spare, one's to clean my models, and one's for Rab."

"Rab?" My gaze flits unwittingly toward a terrarium in the corner. Taped on the glass is a laminated label that reads *Rabeardranath Tagore*. You've got to be kidding me. "Your lizard?"

A frown purses his full lips at my indignation. "He's a bearded dragon, actually."

My eyes rise heavenward. The longest conversation I've had with the guy my mother hopes I'll marry is about the semantics of reptilian nomenclature. A guy who doesn't read but has the audacity to name said reptile after one of the greatest Bengali poets of all time.

What sins did I commit to deserve this?

"He's actually not so bad," Harun says.

My head snaps in his direction. "Who?"

"Rab," he replies. "Sometimes people are scared of him. My last—" He cuts himself off, but I can almost hear him swallow the word "girlfriend." Oh, is Mr. Perfect Son maybe not-so-perfect, after all? "Uh, my mother still steers clear of his tank like she thinks he might jump out and go all *Jurassic World* on her. But once you get to know him, he's cute."

I can't keep the dubiousness off my face. To my surprise, Harun chuckles. It's a deep, husky sound that sends a tingle up my spine and makes my whole body heat up.

"Seriously," he says. "Come here."

My feet are rooted in place, my eyes huge. He hesitates at

my recalcitrance but holds a hand out to me. I glance between it and his uncomfortable expression, then set my hand inside it. It's much bigger than mine and warmer than I would have imagined. His fingers close around my wrist. My pulse thumps in the clammy flat of my palm, but he doesn't let on if he notices.

Instead he carefully lowers my hand into the terrarium. It quivers in his grasp, but I don't snatch it away, even when the lizard—scratch that, the *bearded dragon*—darts a tongue out at us. My eyelids do, however, screw shut. Before I know it, my fingertips graze across Rab's spikes. They're not sharp at all, but rubbery, the scales beneath smooth.

Harun pauses our joined fingers above the rigid plastic of Rab's tail. He remains close enough to me that I can sense the temperature radiating off his body and smell the minty toothpaste on his breath as he whispers, "I 3D-printed that for him after he got tail rot."

Definitely no gingivitis.

I open my eyes at last, if only to sneak a peek at him through my peripheral vision. He's smiling, but not at me. At the not-lizard, *of course*. But when he smiles, he gets a single, pokeable dimple in his right cheek. Not that I'm thinking about touching it.

"I guess it's not so bad. . . ."

Before I can decide whether I mean him or his not-lizard, Pushpita Khala calls up to us from downstairs, "Hurry up, you lovebirds, or dinner will get cold."

As if her voice has broken some spell, Harun yanks himself away from me and rakes a frazzled hand through his hair. We circle each other warily.

"Look, Zahra, before we go down . . . You seem like a nice girl, but you know this is never going to happen, right?" He gestures between us. "We're eighteen. Aren't we supposed to be focused on normal stuff like, you know, college?" His voice dips lower. "Besides, even if I get married someday, I wouldn't want to be arranged with someone interested in me for my family's money. I don't care that you're a princess or whatever."

I try to control the expression on my face so that the stinging rejection doesn't show.

Obviously, I don't want him, either, and I get where he's coming from. Obviously, I *agree* with every single point he's making and would have let him down gently by the end of the night myself. Obviously, while marriages of convenience are swoony in romance novels, I've never wanted to marry a guy I barely know—or become Zahra Emon of the House Khan, First of Her Name, Stepmother of Bearded Dragons—just because he's rich.

But I also wasn't expecting him to be so . . . blunt.

"Oh, trust me, dude," I scoff. "It's *allll goood.*"

A relieved smile dawns across his face, as if he couldn't imagine anything more repulsive than having me for a wife, and for the second time, that maddening solitary dimple winks at me. "I knew you were too cool to go for this. We on the same page, then?"

He extends his hand again. I frown at it, then give it a brisk shake.

"Same page. After tonight, I hope I never see you again."

For the first time, Harun laughs. A *real* laugh. "I hope I never see you again either."

Determined to present a united front, we return to the living room. Arif and Resna are gone, most likely banished to Harun's game room, but our parents sit together, chuckling and chatting like one big happy family. They turn to us simultaneously upon realizing we've come back, and I stiffen at their matching self-congratulatory expressions, suddenly feeling like we're a pair of defenseless deer that have wandered into a tiger ambush. While tigers aren't known to hunt in groups, when they *do*, you're pretty much screwed. Deader than dead.

With innuendo in her voice, Harun's mother says, "You two were certainly gone a while, eh?"

"It's wonderful to see you getting along," Amma adds.

Before we can convince them otherwise, Harun's father pounces. "We've discussed this long and hard and . . . we believe you two are a perfect match. Inshallah, we'll be moving forward with this courtship with the hope that it someday leads to marriage."

The pit in my stomach fractures into a yawning black hole. I can feel Harun's gaze at the nape of my neck and venture to meet it. Just yesterday, I would have called it blank, even bored, like I did during our first date. But now I see the tic in his jaw, the taut press of his lips, the trench between his thick, dark brows. I read the unspoken message in his obsidian eyes as clearly as the lines of my favorite Tagore poem.

Tell them!

I open my mouth to comply, but the rosy-cheeked joy on my mother's face chokes the words in my throat. I haven't seen her so happy in . . . well, more than two years. When I turn my pleading stare back to Harun, he meets it just as helplessly. Although my impression the night we met was that he didn't care as much as I do about parental expectations, it's clear he doesn't want to dash his family's hopes either.

My eyes narrow. *You tell them. Unless you're a chicken?*

Me? his scream back. *You're the chicken!*

The silence stretches on until Amma chimes in, "We couldn't be more delighted," beaming from ear to ear and rising to hug me. I hug back, watching Harun over her shoulder.

Being a Good Bengali Kid really bites sometimes.

Chapter 7

Throughout dinner, our parents end up devising a master plan: every Friday for the foreseeable future, Harun and I will have dinner together, either with our families or accompanied by another chaperone, until the two of us concede that we're head over heels for each other like they've predicted.

"This is like *Gilmore Girls*, but way more Austenian and miserable," I lament in a whisper to Harun from the passenger seat of his car. I didn't complain when he volunteered to drive us home again or when he asked me and Amma if he could talk to me for a minute after everyone else stepped out of the car, so I could reserve all my protests till we had more privacy. "Except Rory got to have like three epic romances and free tuition. If that isn't white privilege, I don't know what is."

Harun side-eyes me like I've grown two heads, the absolute heathen. It reinforces for the umpteenth time that the two of us aren't meant to be, but Amma arches both of her brows at me from the sidewalk, amusement in her brown eyes. She doesn't lurk to eavesdrop, prodding my siblings into the house. I squint up at the first-floor window but don't catch sight of the landlady, either.

We're totally alone.

"You know, my mother's going to become president of the Team Zahrun Fan Club if we give her reasons to think we're madly in love," I complain.

"Team Zahrun?" His brows pinch together in deliberation. "Sounds too much like the Bengali word for 'broom.'"

"Well, we're trying not to be romantic," I remind him. "What's less romantic than cleaning supplies?"

Harun ignores me to drop his head onto the steering wheel, one hand reaching up to roll the blue glass beads of the tasbih hung around the rearview through his fingers. I can't see his face, so I don't know if he's repeating zikirs under his breath like I sometimes do to help myself calm down, but he looks utterly defeated. Even his *curls* are droopy and dejected. I have to ball my fists in my lap to avoid patting his back.

"Are you okay?" I ask instead.

He sighs. "This is messed up. I know I should go back home and tell them no. They'd never actually *force* me."

Neither would my mother, but I can almost hear the *but* that's about to follow, and decide to voice what he hasn't. "But you don't want to upset them."

Harun removes his hand from the tasbih and shakes his head without lifting it from the steering wheel. "I'm about to go to college and I want to do it on good terms, not have the shadow of this over our heads for the next couple of months, or worse, when I bring home a girl I actually like."

Once again, it's as if we're reading each other's minds. Our lives couldn't be more different, but I completely get that feeling of not wanting to upset your parents. I can't shake the image of Amma smiling so happily for the first time in such a long time.

"It might be best to tear the bandage off fast . . . but I don't like the idea of letting my mom down either," I say. "I've worked so hard to avoid exactly that since my dad died, and Amma . . . she's been killing herself trying to give my siblings and me everything she thinks losing him took from us."

Tonight's matchmaking is yet another misguided attempt at that.

Harun lifts his head up at last. "Shit, sorry, Khan, I didn't mean—" I wave my hand to dispel his unease, but he keeps giving me that kicked-puppy look I've seen on too many faces since Baba passed.

"I can't ever understand everything you're going through," he murmurs instead, "but I know how you feel about your mom. My parents are the reason I have everything I do. I know it wasn't easy for them, starting over in a new country." His eyes catch and hold mine. "I respect them," he says simply, "and you respect her."

I nod.

It's astounding how much this boy gets me. We could go home and outright tell our parents no, but perhaps there's a way for Harun and me to navigate this that will end with the fewest broken hearts and future matchmaking attempts. Perhaps by pretending to go along with what she wants, I can even leverage my efforts to guilt-trip Amma and minimize any future disappointment on her part when she learns I'm planning to study writing next year, after all.

Perhaps . . .

"Give me your phone!"

"What?" Harun's forehead scrunches in bemusement. "Why?"

"Don't worry," I reply. "It's *just* so we can figure out how to get out of this on the down low. Your heart is safe with me, robot boy."

I try to keep my tone light and teasing, but nerves gnaw at my stomach. With so many people and feelings involved, we might screw things up worse if we're not careful.

He shoves a hand into his pocket and produces a smartphone despite his bewilderment. "Jeez, you're so pushy. Has the princess thing gone to your head?"

Glowering, I snatch the phone out of his hand and inspect the device. It's one of the newer models, so big I have to grasp it in both palms, with a shiny screen nearly as broad as a tablet's and a plain black silicone case around it. Even his lock screen is one of the default northern lights live wallpapers that come with the phone.

He's like a stock photo brought to life, I swear.

"There." My fingers move rapidly as I input my info into his contacts and send a text to my own refurbished phone. "You're in, robot boy. Or do you prefer lizard boy? Frog prince?"

"Haha," he deadpans. "You're a regular Mindy Kaling."

But a hint of a dimple flashes at me, and when I notice him changing my name to *Princess* in his contacts, I find that I don't mind. If we're going to be dealing with this together, I guess it's only fair that we have code names.

The wheels start turning in my head as we say good night.

After taking a shower, I notice that Harun has texted me.

I shoot a glance at Nanu, who is already snoring into her pillow inside the bottom bunk of our bed, then scale the ladder to the top bunk and scan his message:

Robot boy: You up?

Why do you text like a frat bro? I reply.

This is no laughing matter, Khan! My mother is already asking whether you'd like my nani's or dadi's engagement ring better . . . HELP?

A snuffling laugh escapes me at his blatant alarm, but I bury my face in the plush material of the khul balish I can't sleep without to muffle it, not wanting to alert my own grandmother. I'd rather Nanu not know that Harun and I are chatting outside of the Friday Date Nights our parents have arranged, but not for the typical you-must-not-talk-to-boys reasons. Neither Harun nor I need our families to get any more invested than they already are in our happily-ever-after together.

I'd have to see them first, I quip. That's a pretty big decision. Pics?

I hate you, is his immediate response.

Although we're still virtually strangers, something changed between us tonight, because we've discovered that we're strangers with a common enemy—and a common solution. Maybe not friends, but temporary allies. Enough so, in fact, that I know he doesn't mean it.

Curling a drying strand of hair around my pointer finger, I use my other thumb to text back, Okay, okay, I'm kidding. Wanna hear my plan?

You've got a plan? Oh, thank God.

A devilish grin takes possession of my face. Our parents want to play games? Fine. We're just going to have to win.

That's... not ominous at all, he replies. How do we win?

We wage guerrilla warfare. We'll "date," but sneak attack and sabotage them, until our folks are convinced we'd be a nightmare together and insist we break up themselves. In the meantime, because we're "together," they won't try to throw us at anyone else, either.

When we break up, I can probably bring up college and writing with my mother, and she'll be so grateful—so guilty— that she'll trust me to make my own choices at last.

Damn, Khan, maybe I should call you General instead of Princess. Harun's response elicits another laugh I have to muffle. How long can we keep something like that up, though?

How many Fridays are left this summer? We can both tell our

parents that we'll give this a chance until then, since you'll get busy with college in the fall and I—My fingers hover for a second. What *will* I be doing? The same thing as ever, I suppose, but Harun doesn't need to hear my sob story—have stuff to do, too.

Robot boy does his mathematical magic. Eight Fridays.

Eight dates, then. It's poetic, the way it almost rhymes. It'd make a cute Hallmark movie if so much didn't ride on it going well.

The Eight Dates of Summer, I type back.

Chapter ❤ 8

The next day at work, I'm determined to tell my friends about the arrangement—and the arrangement *within* the arrangement.

It was hard enough keeping things from them when I thought the Harun problem would fix itself yesterday, but now that I know it'll drag on for two more months, I'm bursting with the urge to reveal everything, if only to have other people to opine to.

Unfortunately, with Mr. Tahir, Nayim, and a shop full of customers to contend with, I don't get the chance until Chai Ho closes up for the night. On the weekends, we lock up even later than the rest of the week, to accommodate for increased business. Normally, the three extra hours of wages, which count as overtime, are a blessing. But the darker the sky grows outside, the more my mood dims as well. At least Ximena dropped by and stayed to hang out with Dani, so I can catch her up as well.

"Ay shallah," my boss curses under his breath, tugging at

the loose tie around his stiff collar in an effort to make it sit right. "If I'm any later to dinner at your mamu's, your ammu will use my skull for a bowl."

"Uhhh, then why don't you let us close up for you?"

His eyes narrow at my suggestion.

I bat my lashes, summoning my most innocent expression. The twins meet each other's gazes from where Dani is polishing the counter with Ximena and Dalia is standing on her tiptoes on a tabletop, dusting off the decorative umbrellas open over the light fixtures. Even Nayim watches through the open kitchen door, clasping a sudsy plate and a dish towel over the sink.

Okay, so I'm not about to win best actress anytime soon.

Thank God for my friends, though, because they pick up on my tactless cue and nod along. Dalia hops off the table to do up her father's tie, while Dani bulldozes him toward the door, catching the car keys Ximena tosses at her from a hook behind the counter and pushing them into his hands.

"Zahra's right. We've got this, Abbu!" says Dalia.

"Don't want Ammu to make ya sleep on the couch, do we?" Dani chimes.

The twins shove him out the door. Before he knows it, Mr. Tahir is blinking at us from the sidewalk. To his credit, he broaches the subject one last time with an incredulous, "Why so eager to close up all of a sudden? Usually, I can't pay you enough to do it, especially on weekends."

That's not strictly true. I'd take any extra shifts he offered.

Without missing a beat, the twins say in unison, "For old

times' sake, before we go off to college," and that's that.

He huffs and stomps toward his minivan, grumbling a final reminder for them to be careful on the way home. Although he comes off as very gruff, Mr. Tahir actually has a gooey marshmallow center—halal, of course—when it comes to his daughters and wife.

"You three are lifesavers," I declare once he's out of sight.

"How exactly did we save you this time?" Dani asks, hitting me with an unimpressed double-eyebrow arch nigh identical to her father's, arms crossed over a Ms. Marvel T-shirt.

"You've been acting kind of twitchy, Zar," Ximena adds.

Ah, so they *have* noticed my caginess.

Dalia tackles the topic with more decorum. "Is something going on at home?"

Yes. No. *Yes.*

I risk a peek over my shoulder at the open kitchen door, but now that Mr. Tahir is gone, a humming Nayim appears otherwise occupied with stacking dishes inside the wooden cupboards all around the kitchen without breaking any new ones.

Having clocked my unease, however, Dani strides casually behind the counter and kicks the door shut in one smooth motion while giving the surface one last exaggerated swipe. She then turns her no-nonsense gaze back to me and steeples her fingers, rag forgotten.

"Spill. The. Chai."

I all but blurt out everything that's happened in the past

week, starting with the wedding and ending with what was decided at Harun's house yesterday.

"But neither of us are into it," I hurry to assure them, out of breath after my long-winded explanation. "We're going to do whatever we can to make it seem like we'd be a disaster couple, so our parents put the whole matchmaking ruse out of their heads by September."

I don't admit that Harun is sort of cool.

And hot . . . if you're into the repressed Mr. Darcy type, which I'm totally not.

That's not as important right now as them not getting the wrong impression of me. They've always known that I didn't so much as look at boys in high school because I was too busy helping my mom with the bills, but I don't want them to think I'm the sort of person who'd hook up with one just because of the size of his wallet, like Harun apparently does.

Would it help us out? I guess so. Rich people who say, "Money can't buy you happiness," are bald-faced liars, 'cause being poor sure doesn't do it for me.

But trading my heart for wealth? That's *not who I am.*

I peer at the three of them helplessly, trying to convey all this. The twins exchange a look I can't quite decrypt. Another of their silent psychic conversations, even more formidable than the ones Harun and I shared last night.

At last, Dalia says, "I'm sorry you have to deal with this, Zar. Of course, we're happy to help however we can with staging the breakup."

"Yeah, girl," Dani adds. "Just say the word and I'll happily tell your mom you can't marry this guy because you and I are running off to Paris together."

I snort. "Yeah, because then my mother, your parents, *and* Mena would team up to hunt me down. Thanks, but no thanks."

Ximena fake-glares between us. "Mm-hmm, you'd better not leave me behind, Dan. I want to see the Eiffel Tower too."

The kitchen door creaks open.

"Did someone mention Paris?" Nayim asks, moving to join us.

His honey-brown eyes land on me as he hops on top of the counter, apron now discarded. Like the first time we met, he wears a shirt a size too big underneath it, splashed with so many hues that I can't help staring. The sort of vibrant that they warn about on the nature documentaries Nanu likes to watch, although his languid smile is welcoming. No one has any business looking that attractive in such a gaudy Hawaiian-print shirt.

My tongue feels too thick to maneuver into a response, but Ximena comes to my rescue. "Oh, we were just talking about college. I think I'd like to study abroad someday."

Dani blinks. "You would?"

"You should do it," Nayim replies. "Nothing beats gazing up at the Eiffel Tower from the Champ de Mars, lit up with the rest of the city."

My jaw drops. "You've been to Paris?"

He nods. "Didn't realize it got so cold there, though. Sleeping on benches is much easier in Bangladesh or India than it is in Europe during wintertime."

I gape at him, unsure what detail to pick up first. He's been to so many places? He's been *homeless*? I must not be alone in my curiosity, because the four of us crowd around him, a dozen questions simmering inside us.

Surprisingly, it's Ximena who has the most to say, asking him when he went, who he went with, what he did there, how he could afford to go, while a worried Dalia wonders whether he encountered any Islamophobia in France like she's read about.

Nayim's eyes grow owlish at all the attention as he waves his hands in front of us. "Er, no, I went alone. I—I guess it was lovely, and might be a nice place to return with someone"—he pauses, pupils darting briefly toward me and then away—"but I had other things on my mind, trying to save up for a ticket to the States."

Before I can figure out if I imagined his glance, or inquire why he wanted to come here so badly, Ximena emits a wistful sigh. "I want to see more of the world. Last summer, my folks took me to Hispaniola to visit my grandparents. I have family on both sides of the island, and it opened my eyes to how big the world can be."

Dani grins. "I guess if you enjoyed yourself, my Mena withdrawal last year wasn't in vain."

Ximena gazes back at her, expression in somber contrast to Dani's cheer. "There are so many beautiful places out there,

Dan. I wonder sometimes if I'm wasting my life getting into debt and spending four years studying art at RISD when I could broaden my horizons more by traveling."

"Whoa, babe." Dani's smile falters. "I didn't know you felt that way." When Ximena shrugs, her downcast face lost amid a sea of curls, Dani elbows her teasingly and jokes, "I'm invited if you run off, right? Or are you ditching me 'cause I said I'd elope with Zahra?"

Nayim's eyes flick to me.

Flushing, I reply, "She's kidding. These two have been dating since middle school. No one else is a match for how disgustingly cute they are."

There's a breath as we await his reaction. If he's a douche about the girls, Mr. Tahir will—and should—give him the boot, but he nods.

Dani, meanwhile, objects to my words. "Hey! I'm serious. I'd love to travel. I've only been to Pakistan twice my entire life and want to see stuff outside Jersey too."

Ximena brightens, but a wrinkle forms between Dalia's brows. "What? You whined constantly when we went to see Dada and Dadi. You claimed the mosquitoes were homophobic for biting you more than me."

"That was years ago," Dani insists, hands on her hips. "I'm a different person now."

Her sister sighs. "Well, that's a problem for the future. This summer, we've got to arrange our schedules and dorm rooms for fall."

"Yeah, yeah, Ammu," Dani mutters, but perks up when Ximena pecks her cheek.

Nayim turns to me. "What about you, Zahra? What are your summer plans?"

"Oh, well, I . . ." I tuck a loose strand of hair behind my ear, smiling at the floor more for their sakes than my own. "Nothing much. Traveling, college . . . All of that sounds magical, but like Dalia said, it's a problem for the future. I can't really afford much of anything right now."

Regardless of my best efforts, the inkling of melancholy in my voice saps the jovial mood from Chai Ho, and we awkwardly return to what we set out to do in the first place: shut down shop for the night. It goes a lot faster with Nayim's help—and his height, since he can dust in high places without needing to stand on anything. Soon the door is locked behind us.

Ximena gives her girlfriend one last kiss before dashing to her car, art supplies clutched to her chest. Dani jerks a thumb at the lime-green Mini Cooper that Mr. Tahir recently bought her and Dalia so they could travel between their dorm and home. "Need a ride, Zar?"

"Nope, I'm good. I've kept you long enough."

Dalia sets her hands on her hips, but before she can go full Mom Friend on me about all the potential dangers lurking in our neighborhood—flashers, drug dealers, gangbangers—Nayim says, "I can walk Zahra home."

I latch onto his offer, bobbing my head. "Yep. So you two

go on before your parents send out a search party, okay? I've got Nayim and my handy-dandy pepper spray."

Dalia's phone going off in her Vera Bradley tote—no doubt her mother checking up on them—seals the deal. With hurried goodbyes, they vanish into the Mini Cooper, not bothering to bicker over who gets to drive this time.

I wait until their car disappears around a curb, then start marching in the direction of my house. When Nayim's sandals crunch across an errant lollipop wrapper behind me, I stop so abruptly that he almost bumps into my back.

"Nuh-uh," I tell him. "I only said you could walk me home so Dalia would get off my case. The last thing I need is more Auntie Network gossip"—especially when he's as eye-catching as a neon sign—"so thanks for your chivalry, newbie, but you can go off on your merry way now."

Nayim's eyebrows squish together. "The what now?"

"The Auntie Network," I explain. "My mom's group chat. They know everything. About everyone. Always."

When I start walking again, however, I hear his footsteps continuing to pad along, and I whip around, reaching for my bag and the aforementioned pepper spray. "Are you stalking me?"

"Um, no," he responds, pointing in the direction of my house. "It's just . . . I live that way too. Or should I wait to go home?"

Mortification courses through me. "O-oh yeah, with the imam, right?"

Dam—er, darn it. I'd forgotten that Nayim would be living *right next door*.

He nods. "But I can wait. I'm aware I've become the subject of some imaginative rumors around here, and I wouldn't want to make things tougher for you. I didn't mean to eavesdrop, but it sounds like you're dealing with quite a lot right now."

I grimace. So he heard about Harun, huh?

"No, I'm fine. That's no big deal, just my mother meddling in my love life." We fidget on the sidewalk, looking all the more conspicuous for it, before I continue, "I guess you can keep doing what you're doing." Even though it's late June, the suggestion of rain clings to the air. I pull my sweater tighter around my torso. "Just . . . walk behind me. Like, six feet behind, so no one assumes we're together."

"I'll be a perfect stranger," he promises.

We commence trekking home for the third time, but though he does his best to keep up his end of the bargain, I can sense his eyes on my back. A flush creeps up the nape of my neck. Am I imagining his interest in me? But why would my masochistic brain dream that up, when I already have enough boy problems?

I break the silence first. "About earlier . . . Have you really been to Paris?"

A beat follows, before he answers, "I've been to many places."

"But . . . how?" I wonder, peeking over my shoulder. "Isn't it hard, when you're all alone? How do you pay for everything?"

He tilts his face toward the night sky. The full moon

chooses that exact moment to duck out from behind some clouds and cast its silver halo over him. It glimmers across his raven-wing hair and gold-coin eyes in a way that makes my mouth go dry.

"I suppose it isn't easy," he murmurs at last, "but to me, it's worth it, because it brought me one step closer to my dream."

"Your dream?" I whisper.

He eyes me, as if he's unsure whether he can trust me. I don't know why, but I want him to, enough that I slow down, the six feet between us becoming five, four, three, until we're side by side, my gaze affixed to his moonlit face. The intensity of it makes him stop in his tracks.

"When I was a kid, someone gave me a guitar," he says. "I hung on her every word when she told me how she'd found it in New York. She went away again, like she always did, but I kept the guitar, and I've taken care of it ever since."

"Do you still have it?" I ask. "Can you play it?"

His smile becomes a lovelorn thing, his eyes at once distant and dreamy. It makes my stomach do an unexpected flip. "I do. And I can. Never that well. I always had other obligations that prevented me from dedicating the time to playing it the way I wanted."

"I know what that's like," I whisper, almost to myself.

Nayim's pupils flick to my face. "But there's nothing in the world that makes me happier than holding that guitar, teaching others how to play, watching them fall in love with it too. So it became my dream to go to New York City someday and open my own guitar shop there." Without meaning to, I breathe a small gasp, and his mouth twitches self-consciously. "It sounds silly, huh?"

I shake my head. "No. Why would it if you're serious about it?"

He catches his lip between his teeth, as if to stop himself from explaining, and I wonder if whoever he left behind at home made him believe his dreams were unattainable, like Amma often does with me.

At my encouraging nod, he continues, "I was able to get enough money to go to Europe. It's closer to Bangladesh and the ticket was cheaper. But then I had to save up to get to the States. Take odd jobs, sleep on benches, busk for change. People weren't always kind, like they are here, but since it meant I could make my own way to my dream, I did my best. I may not be able to afford it yet, but I'm going to prove that it's not impossible. That I can do it all on my own."

I stare at Nayim, heart pounding wild fists against my chest as if it wants me to unlock the cage of my ribs so it can fly to him. Because he . . . he gets it. Nayim gets me in an intrinsic way that someone like Harun, who's always had everything handed to him on a gold platter, never could.

It isn't easy to come to America from Bangladesh. My father's older brother applied for our family to come before I was even born, and it took almost a decade for the US government to approve us getting green cards. I have no idea how Nayim did that on his own, but I'm positive it was harder than it ever was for me, and I admire his perseverance.

"You *will*," I insist, though the words are thick with emotion. "That's . . . That's how I feel about writing."

His head whips up. "You write?"

I cringe.

Ugh, why did I say *that* when I've barely written in the past two years? And why to him, an absolute stranger, of all people? One who traveled halfway around the world for his dream, while I let my own be deferred like Langston Hughes's raisin in the sun. . . .

"Not much, lately," I say. "It's romance and other silly stuff. Not literature."

"You told me my dreams aren't silly. I don't think yours are either." Nayim slants a glance at me. "Besides, isn't *every* story about love, one way or another? What makes that less important?"

Of course, he's right.

But I guess I'm so used to fearing other people will find my interests shallow that I sometimes talk them down before anyone else can.

Why do I care what Nayim thinks, though?

"It's nothing. Helping my family eats up most of my time and keeps me from writing. What about you?" I hedge, trying to steer the topic away from my deepest insecurities. "I got the impression you also shouldered your fair share of responsibilities in Bangladesh. Do you help take care of your family too? Send money back?"

Does anyone take care of you? I don't add, though I'm dying to know.

Surely, someone misses him there. Are they worried? Do they still talk? What happened to the woman who gave him the guitar?

He sighs. "What family? There's no one left in the world who needs me. But enough about me." A hint of teasing steals into his voice. "Tell me more about *you* and your romances."

Although I squawk at the flirtatious deflection, deep down inside, I foresaw it coming. Haven't I employed this sort of diversion tactic hundreds of times myself when the twins or Ximena or teachers touched on our financial situation?

It's my own fault for asking him such a probing, personal question when we don't know one another, but it serves to confirm what I already suspected: he's an orphan from a poor, fragmented family. Possibly even worse off than my own, if he's been homeless before.

Just then, a man shambles past: the owner of a bodega across the street called Bangla Villa. As his curious gaze traverses the two of us, I clam up, perspiration beginning to pool under my armpits. Nayim, for his part, drops to the sidewalk right away, where a stray black cat nibbles on a loaf of bread next to a tipped-over trash can.

He starts crooning nonsense at it, and I make my escape as the man stops to observe his antics, ignoring the nervous flutter of butterfly wings in my belly.

The feeling dissipates the instant I get home, when

Amma inquires, "Has Harun contacted you today?"

What would she think if she knew I'd walked home with another boy? A *poor* boy from a family of no reputation?

"Uh, no, Amma, he hasn't," I mutter, then add, "I'm tired tonight. Gonna turn in if you don't need anything," before she can browbeat me about skipping dinner.

Her perturbed retort dwindles as I flee into the bathroom to take a shower.

Later, blessedly alone in my bedroom, I drag myself over to the window, trying to find stars amid the smoggy sky, and catch Nayim doing the same, sitting in the window seat of his basement apartment with a notepad in his lap, chewing on the cap of a pen.

He must sense me watching, because his eyes lift to my window and crinkle at the corners. Before I know it, he scribbles a message onto the notepad and holds it up against the glass for me to see. *Sweet dreams, neighbor.*

The butterflies return with a vengeance.

Pressing a hand to my stomach to quiet them, I whisper a "Sweet dreams" he can't hear, then shut the blinds before Amma or Nanu can catch me in the act.

As I crawl into bed, I can no longer ignore what my galloping heartbeat betrays. I like Nayim. He is brave and funny and silver-tongued.

How messed up is it that he wouldn't be considered as eligible as Harun just because of the coincidence of his birth?

Life's not fair sometimes.

If it were, Nayim would have all the riches in the world.

Chapter ❤ 9

A week blinks by.

When I text Harun about kicking Operation Zahrun into motion, he replies, I think I can handle this one, princess, and doesn't bother to elaborate.

Fine, but you owe me if this backfires, robot boy, I concede, though I hate not being in charge.

The twins snoop on his social media with me, and we discover from Snapchat that he's part of some prestigious summer robotics program. I can't begrudge it when it means our parents have no way to throw us together any day other than Friday.

Nayim walks me home every night—always at a distance.

He even starts carrying treats for the stray cat—who he names Thara, because of how its yellow eyes gleam like stars in its inky face—so it will trot after us and give him an Auntie Approved™ excuse to ramble the entire time.

I guard my heart at first, simply listening, but by the third night, I can't help spilling my guts in return. I complain about the hoops Harun and I have to jump through, how frustrating it's been that I can't help my family enough on my own so we wouldn't need to degrade ourselves with these dates, how my dreams of writing and college feel at once so close and so very far.

He listens to every word like nothing else matters.

Friday arrives once more, and with it, Date Number One.

Just like the last two dinners with the Emons, Amma fusses with my clothes, hair, and makeup until we leave for their house, but this time, Nanu comes along for moral support, asserting that she should get to know the Emons before things go any further. Tonight, our hosts are waiting for us at the doorstep, a bearded man standing at Harun's side.

I scowl at my mother. "What now? Did you hire an imam to marry us off?"

"I don't know," she replies, and then, at my disbelieving squint, "Allahr duai! Your khala mentioned something extra special tonight, but I didn't think to ask her what."

"Uh-huh."

I narrow my eyes, recalling the last time Amma and her new bestie planned something "special." But she doesn't appear to be lying. Arif and Nanu are equally boggled by this turn of events, while Resna's tiny head bobs back and forth between us all.

I return my wary gaze to the Emons, making my way carefully up the stone pathway to join them. Upon closer inspection, the bearded man next to Harun is just another boy.

He must be no more than a year or two older than us, though the beard makes him look more mature.

He sizes up our family over a long nose, through steely eyes as dark as Harun's, before greeting us extra formally. "Assalamualaikum wa rahmatullahi wa barakatuh."

I glower at my date. *What the hell?*

Harun shrugs as his mother takes the initiative to explain. "Surprise! We thought it might be time for you two to get to know each other a little more privately, but of course we can't do that without a proper chaperone, can we?"

Amma has the decency to look gobsmacked. "Privately?"

"Don't you fuss, Zaynab," Pushpita Khala continues. "Hanif is my bhagna, Harun's cousin by my sister. He may only be nineteen, but he's already a hafiz who can recite the Quran cover to cover and would be the perfect chaperone to ensure that the children get to know each other without anything untoward happening. Harun asked Hanif to accompany you, in fact, Zahra."

My eyes jump to Harun, who has the nerve to smirk.

Oh! So his cousin Hanif must be in on Operation Zahrun somehow. I turn back to scan the older boy. He wears a severe frown that does little to imply he'll go along with our plan to deceive his aunt and uncle. If anything, he gives off the vibe that we're inconveniencing him by daring to exist. Then again, Harun has a resting bitch face too. Maybe it's just genetics?

"I suppose it's a good idea to give the kids some privacy," Amma acquiesces.

"It will give us more time to get to know each other as well," Pushpita Khala says, hooking one arm with Amma's and the other with Nanu's. "After all, it's important to seek khesha-kheshi with in-laws you'll get along with, isn't that right?"

Mansif Khalu claps Harun on the shoulder. "Ah, I remember some of my first dates with your mother. Back then, you only met once or twice before you made a lifelong commitment. Be a gentleman, betta, and don't do anything your old man wouldn't."

"Got it, Abba," Harun mutters, flushing as he avoids eye contact with his father, before catching my gaze.

We trade a long-suffering look, until I kneel beside my sister and whisper, "Resu . . ."

"I know, I know, 'Be good,'" she huffs.

I tap her button nose. "Nope. I was going to say, be yourself."

She cocks her head at the insinuation, while Arif frowns at us, but neither stops me from climbing into the backseat of Hanif's Prius.

When Harun attempts to do the same, his cousin exclaims, "You sit up front. No funny business on my watch."

Harun does as asked, but my phone vibrates in my purse a few seconds later, once Hanif has pulled away from the Emon house.

Sorry. He's a pain.

It's okay, I type back. If you think Hanif is the right call for OZ, then I'm in.

The... programming language? he asks.

I roll my eyes, which Hanif zeroes in on in the rearview. Operation Zahrun.

Harun sends me a series of confused emojis, followed by, Didn't we agree that name was kind of misleading?

You're the one who said it sounds like broom, so let's sweep this ridiculous idea right out of our parents' heads, I retort. If you can keep up with the plot, that is, Mr. Valedictorian.

Stop writing in codes I don't know then, Harun answers, ignoring his cousin. From my vantage point in the back middle seat, I can see how much they look alike from their profiles, but also how different they are. Hanif is glaring murder up at the road like he's just daring some foolhardy truck driver to try to cut his little Prius off. Meanwhile, the smile that twitches at one corner of Harun's lips contradicts his complaint as he continues, I'm more familiar with Java, C++, and Python tbh.

God, you're a nerd, I reply, smothering a laugh.

Takes one to know one, and thanks to this nerd, we've got a breakup expert on the crew.

Your cousin? Seriously?

Hanif is notoriously hard to please. He's already sent three "good Muslim girls" running for the hills since my khala pulled this matchmaking crap on him and tried to set him up with the daughters of her friends from masjid. Think you've got what it takes to make him hate you, Khan? 'Cause he will report your every flaw back to my parents without a second thought.

Harun turns in his seat to size me up.

Trying not to give away how much his doubt flatters me, I arch a lofty brow back. Puh-lease. I'm a professional disappointment at this point.

All my life, I've managed to let Amma down without making an effort, so turning off my date's snooty cousin should be a piece of chomchom.

Harun's smile dissipates, and I wince at the prospect of revealing too much, but when Hanif glares daggers between the rearview and his cousin, then growls, "Harun, you should respect your date by lowering your gaze," both of us get distracted.

Although the words are directed to his cousin, they're intended for us both. Good Muslim boys and girls are disciplined enough not to gawk at potential matches. But I'm not trying to impress our passive-aggressive chaperone, so I give Harun a good, hard stare, long enough to hear an audible gulp, even though he's turned back around in his seat. Hanif scowls lividly up at the road.

Only when both cousins are suitably unnerved do I swing my attention back to my phone to ask, So where are we going anyway?

I figure having Hanif along is punishment enough, so I picked a movie. Harun hesitates mid-type, before finishing his thought. AMC is doing a Bollywood night, and you seem like you'd be into that.

My cheeks grow warm at the way he's put real thought into our fake date. What tipped him off? Did he cyber-stalk me in return and seen the vintage posters of SRK alongside selfies with my friends, books, pics at the tea shop, and gorgeous BTS boys?

Aww, how cute! 😍

Harun sends me an eye-roll emoji. I resist the temptation to yield to a fresh fit of giggles. As much as we want the date to go badly, Hanif tossing us out of a speeding car would be the very last resort, if only because I don't want to damage the sundress Amma made me.

Luckily, we reach the parking lot of the AMC theater before our driver explodes. Hanif manages to find a spot close to the amphitheater-shaped building. As I ascend the winding stairs with the boys, gripping the metal handrail in one hand and my skirt in the other, notes of famous Bollywood songs carry over to us.

The ticket boy, a white teenager with a wispy mustache, appears as unenthused as Hanif about the whole affair while Harun buys three tickets from his booth. When he heads for the concession stand to get us popcorn and some drinks, I say, "Hold on a minute. I can buy my own snacks, you know."

The thought of wasting my pitiful savings on these fake dates makes me want to wither up like a salted slug and die, but my pride won't let him pay for me. Harun gives me a pointed look when I start digging through my purse for my beat-up wallet, jerking his head subtly at his observing cousin. My rummaging hands stop.

Shit. The plan.

I glue a simpering smile onto my face. "—is what I'd say if this weren't a date. But since it is and your family is filthy rich, you should pay. I like my popcorn extra buttery."

Hanif examines us for a moment more. Sweat begins to dot my forehead as I internally curse his unreadable face. *Think I'm a gold digger, think I'm a gold digger—*

At last, he says, "It's true. Gentlemen pay for dates, Harun."

Harun stares me dead in the eye before he extracts a twenty from his own wallet, knowing we've won. "You're so right, Hanif Bhaia. What was I thinking?"

I bat my eyes at Harun, getting ready to say something heinous and bratty, but Hanif plucks the bill out of his hand without letting our charade escalate. "The prices at these places are outrageous. One jumbo popcorn should be quite enough for three people, thanks."

I hesitate, watching Hanif march over to the concession stand himself. My own thriftiness has a reason, but aren't the Emons—and, by extension, Hanif—loaded enough to get pizza, popcorn, *and* nachos? Or is this vengeance for me acting too greedy?

Harun sighs and trails after his cousin, but doesn't put up a fight as we're handed small soda cups. Whatever the reason, I guess our ploy is working. On the way into the theater, Harun texts me, Nice save, general, and my cheeks hurt from smiling.

Soon we end up in center section seats. Hanif plops himself smack in the middle of us, the gigantic bucket of popcorn in his lap. Between him and the aunties—Bangladeshi,

Pakistani, and Indian—trickling in after us, Harun is right.

This date is effectively a nonstarter.

The dramatic instrumentals of *Kabhi Khushi Kabhie Gham* echo through the dimming room as the opening credits play across a black-and-white scene of a little boy and his mother. Hanif harrumphs and takes an angry bite of popcorn when a photo of Shah Rukh Khan fills the screen, muttering something about him being a Muslim sellout.

Harun and I grin at that, but it's when the tagline, a quote from director Karan Johar, materializes that I make faces at him: *It's all about loving your parents. . . .*

His blank expression divulges that he has no idea what the movie is about. I shake my head as he runs a chagrined hand through his hair, but I can't fault him. K3G is a Bollywood classic that was released years before either of us were born.

I watched it with Dalia, Dani, and Ximena when we were twelve, during a sleepover at the Tahirs', and while I still remember most of the best scenes—the four of us bounced on Mr. Tahir's bed to "It's Raining Men," pretending to be Pooja, until he got home from the tea shop and yelled at us to go to bed—I forgot *BE A GOOD KID* was the overarching theme.

My eyes roll skyward. *A bit on the nose, no?*

But once the film starts, even Hanif can't resist losing himself in the plot.

My whole heart aches when Anjali's father dies, leaving her and her younger sister destitute. When Rahul marries her and his rich family disowns him, a tiny sniffle escapes me, causing Harun to send me a stealthy, You okay?

I'm good, I reply just as surreptitiously, the darkened screen of my phone almost invisible inside my open purse. Hanif loudly blowing his nose into a crumpled tissue he found in his vest pocket draws all eyes to him before my "date" can express doubt at my emotional state.

The movie is long, and I'm grateful Hanif at least allowed us the one popcorn. Harun and I reach for the bucket at the same time. His searching fingertips brush against mine, slippery from the butter, and I almost recoil.

But then I get an idea.

Flinging a smirk past our chaperone, I entwine our hands together, marveling once more at how unexpectedly warm he feels. Although his fingers are stiff, his pulse thumps a beat quicker than mine in the flats of our touching palms.

A scandalized gasp erupts beside me, though I can't tell which cousin it belongs to. We're forced to jerk apart when Hanif gives the bucket between us a good shake, spilling kernels all over the floor and onto our laps.

I hear Harun slurping from his Coke cup like his life depends on it. He doesn't try to grab more popcorn for the rest of the movie, but whether he's simply doing his best impression of a Victorian gentleman appalled by a glimpse of ankle, or he's actually shy, the deed is done.

When the credits roll, we return to the world outside the theater in a daze.

Gruffly, as if he wasn't bawling his eyes out a mere minute

ago, Hanif says, "Dating requires a movie *and* dinner, correct? Where is there to eat around here?"

His dour gaze suggests we'll be disowned like SRK if we recommend anything other than a halal restaurant, which probably means it's a perfect time for me to insist we eat at a diner back in Paterson famous for "Texas" wieners made of questionable meat, but Harun replies, "That's okay, Bhaia. The movie was two hours too long and I'm wiped out. I'd rather not waste more time on this."

Although I might not have minded debating the ending with him, my head nods of its own volition. "If you're going to be a cheapskate, fine. I'm already full anyway. You know . . . from all that popcorn."

If Hanif picks up my jab at his popcorn hogging, he doesn't let on, but I notice Harun dimpling at me on our way back to the car. The ride to the Emons' is quiet, but not awkward.

When we arrive, the once-pristine living room is in shambles, Resna plunked amid the mess, playing with some of Harun's robot models exactly as I hoped.

With undue pride in his voice, Hanif announces to the gathered group of haggard adults, "You'll be pleased to hear that not a single inappropriate thing happened under my watch. They barely spoke at all. But Mansif Khalu, can I have a word?"

While he and Harun's father retire into another room to discuss my bad manners—with any luck—our mothers try not to reveal how disappointed they are. Harun and I share a sneaky eye roll and a snicker that quickly transform into identical, scornful stares the instant our audience's attention returns to us.

Later that night, on the car ride home, a new text pops up on my phone. **About that movie…**

I grin.

Date One was pretty successful, if you ask me.

Chapter 10

I come crashing back down to earth when we get home to a stack of bills in the mailbox, FINAL NOTICE stamped in big red letters across the one at the very top.

"Oh my God, is this the electricity bill?" I hiss.

It takes every ounce of my self-control not to wake Resna, who is being carried to bed by Arif and Nanu, exhausted from her Oscar-winning performance as a tantrum-throwing toddler.

Amma frowns at the envelope I'm waving. "Is it?"

I tear it open and discover that PSE&G warned us *three* previous times. The late fee alone makes my knees weak. "How did you let it get this high?"

A note of fluster creeps into Amma's voice as she takes the bill from me. She casts a nervous glance over her shoulder at the landlady's door. The hallway we stand in is so narrow, we have to talk in furtive whispers. "I—I've been so busy getting you ready for your dates with Harun that I—"

"And that's the problem," I say, cutting her off. "These last couple of weeks have felt like . . . well, the movie Harun and his cousin took me to. But this is real life, Amma. And in real life, you can't fix all your problems with a heartfelt musical number or a sudden inheritance. How are we supposed to afford this?"

It was well and good to wish for a handsome prince to swoop in and rescue us, but life doesn't play out like books or movies. We have to save ourselves. The fact that Amma still can't see that makes me hot with rage.

Amma must notice my anguish because she says, "Wait, please. Don't fret. I'll take care of this." She starts rooting through her purse until she brandishes a scrap of paper with a name and number. "Ah, here it is! Your Pushpita Khala gave me this earlier."

"What is it?"

"You know, the Emons are at the heart of our local wedding business," Amma says. "No matter what else you think of these dates, they've given your khala a firsthand look at my abilities as a seamstress. When she found out I made your dress tonight from scratch, she was so impressed, she gave me the contact information of a girl getting married at their banquet hall at the end of the summer. Apparently, she's something of a bride-zolad—"

"Bridezilla," I correct absently, though the sentiment remains the same.

"Right, yes, bridezilla," continues my mother, "and your

Pushpita Khala thought she might be more inclined to 'say yes to a dress' if it's one designed with her in mind."

I mull over her words, frowning at the threadbare entranceway carpet. "You've never made anything so elaborate."

"I haven't. But to keep our lights on, I'm willing to try."

Her eyes shine with grim determination, and despite my frustration at her reckless disregard of our finances—my frustration at *myself*, because *I've* been the one reminding her about bills since my father died—the knot in my gut loosens.

A touch of admiration replaces it.

When we lost Baba, Amma lost a part of herself, untethered now that she was no longer a housewife, now that she had to become the breadwinner. I saw the same determination in her then when she applied to work in the factory district, making paper and packaging and perfumes until she could take her seamstressing off the ground and come back to us.

She wasn't able to do it alone, but she *did* do it. I suck in a shuddering breath and Amma closes the distance between us, wrapping me in her arms so I can breathe in her soothing scent of sandalwood soap and spices. "Oh, amar shuna, amar jaan, everything will be fine."

I nod into her shoulder, willing it to be true.

The following day, the entire family waits with bated breath, surrounding Amma as she calls the number from the couch. A strained, mostly one-sided conversation follows.

Amma mentions Pushpita Khala, who gave her a glowing

recommendation. The bride-zolad retorts with something that drains the color from her face. A tense, "I'm not sure if I can do that, but I can try," follows before the call ends. My mother's eyes swivel toward us.

"Your Pushpita Khala was kind enough to send along photographs of my work. . . ."

The rest of us lean closer.

It's Resna who exclaims, "And?" from where she clings impatiently to the skirts of Nanu's white shari, though she understands the direness of the situation least of all.

"She loved every piece," Amma replies quietly. "She'd like to hire me not only to make her bridal, mehndi, and gaye holud sharis, but to outfit her entire bridal party."

"Yay!" Resna exclaims.

She takes Arif's and Nanu's hands in each of her own and starts skipping around the living room. Even as my grandmother reaches for mine, my eyes are drawn to my mother's crestfallen face and the listless way her fingertips trace over the keypad of the phone.

"What is it?"

The festivities fade at my query, the rest of the family taking notice of exactly what I had when Amma lifts her glistening gaze to mine. "It's a big order and would help us immensely, but she's only willing to pay a quarter in deposit until she sees the final pieces. It would cover the bills, if I didn't need it to purchase more materials. Bridal wear is so expensive."

Her words are like a bucket of ice water over my head.

"H-how can she ask that of us? That isn't *fair*. It's not—"

"Pushpita Afa warned me the bride would be a handful," Amma murmurs, and I remember how she called the customer in question a bride-zolad. Zolads in Bangladesh were exacting and cruel with the people in their service. Worse than the meanest *Say Yes to the Dress* bridezilla. "She said it'd be an investment. If we put a little in now, we'll get a larger return later when the bride pays, but I turned it down at first because we'd have to front the cost of the materials. . . ."

Though she trails off, I know the answer. It might be a *little* to the Emons, but it's our life savings. Everything we've worked to the bone for.

I suck in a deep breath and steel myself to ask, "How much?"

My mother's shiny eyes widen. "It's too much, shuna. We can't possibly—"

"How. Much?" I grit out.

Swallowing, she answers, "The silk for the garments, the gold and silver thread for the zari and embroidery, the various kinds of stone-work . . . I would have to call my suppliers, but perhaps two thousand?"

Two. Thousand.

Two.

Thousand.

In my two years of working at the tea shop, I've barely managed to scrape together that much, because I gave most to Amma to help with the bills, or to Arif so he wouldn't be left out when the rest of his classmates went on field trips, or to Nanu when insurance didn't cover her prescriptions.

My nest egg has always been a gooey, bleeding nest yolk, but the more I worked, the more shifts I took, the closer I got to affording a different life. Affording college.

I remember Nayim's words from the first night we walked home together: *to me, it's worth it, because it brought me one step closer to my dream.*

This is ten steps back, but if Amma can pull it off like she pulled off launching her seamstress business in the first place, maybe things will get better.

Maybe.

I don't know what storm of emotions sieges across my face, but my mother extending her hand to me and whispering, "Don't worry, Zahra, we can figure something else out," jolts me out of my stunned state enough that I can spin on my heel and walk slowly to my room.

Dropping to my knees next to the bunk bed, I grope under it until I find a book bound in cloth, an old edition of *Pride and Prejudice* that the library put on its free-to-take shelf because the pages were already yellowed and moth-eaten. Hands quivering, I crack it open and remove an envelope heavy with bills.

I know how much is in there without counting, because I've spent so many nights awake, calculating what I had to do with it, and what would remain after.

How much more it would take to pay for a semester. How

much my books might cost. Bus passes. Money for food. How much I would need to make it through two years. How many more hours, days, weeks, and months I had to work to afford it.

It's every single penny to my name.

Although I know it's the right move, my return to the living room is slower, more painful, than my departure. Amma's eyes grow huge in her pallid face when she catches sight of me, then fly to the fat envelope. Kneeling next to the coffee table, I take her hand and place the envelope into it, ignoring the way she shakes her head.

"Use this, Amma. Make dresses so beautiful even the bride-zolad won't have a complaint. Make everything okay again. Please."

My eyes burn, but my voice doesn't quiver and the teardrops don't fall. In an instant, her arms are wound around my neck, and they aren't alone. I feel Arif and Nanu join them, and even Resna's tiny limbs wrap around my waist.

"Thank you, Zahra," Amma breathes into my hair. "I will pay you back."

Chapter ♥ 11

Amma's new job is meant to save us but has created an assortment of brand-new problems. Because of the sheer amount of work involved in preparing outfits for a bridal party, she won't have time for many other jobs in the coming weeks.

When I volunteer to help her prepare, however, she waves me away. "I have three other perfectly good assistants. It's your first day off in ages. I insist you go enjoy it."

"Yeah, Afa," Arif chimes in, crossing his scrawny arms in a businesslike manner. It'd be cute if his face wasn't still puffy from our family cryfest yesterday. "Go act like a real teenager instead of an old lady for once."

Resna chimes a weak giggle. "Api is a bura betti."

"I'm not old," I protest, turning to Nanu for backup.

She only tuts as she brings Amma the old butterscotch candy tin containing her sewing supplies, but there's sad pride shimmering in her brown irises. "I'm sorry to say you don't have the coloring to pull off white like me yet, betti. You should listen to your mother."

"Fine, I can take a hint."

Drained like my savings, I lumber over to my room. For the briefest instant, my focus turns to the messy table-turned-desk that I used to write at, which Nanu has been using to pray on since her knees grew arthritic. The sight of the scattered Post-it notes stuck to the wall sends a surge of anxiety through me.

Not today.

It's been hard enough without having to contend with a blank document.

I could probably collapse in my bed and sleep until I've grown a Rip Van Winkle–esque beard, but what I sorely need is a distraction, so I text the twins and Ximena to ask if they've got plans. With Mr. Tahir taking the day to train Nayim in tasks other than dishwashing, this is the perfect opportunity for the rest of us to catch up. I want to tell my friends everything that happened with Harun and at home.

Dalia replies, We're about to head downtown.

My lips purse.

They never hang out without inviting me along. I can't always swing it, whether because I've taken on extra shifts or I can't afford wherever they're going and my dignity won't let them pay for me. Hell, if Mr. Tahir didn't force me to take the day off so he could turn the full force of his Mr. Tahir–ness on poor Nayim, I'd still be at the tea shop. But at least my friends usually *ask*.

What's up downtown?

Just some summer sales, responds Dani.

My thumb lingers over the keypad, typing and deleting *I love sales!* once I accept that it makes me sound like a desperate loser.

But Dalia, bless her Mom Friend heart, must detect the conflicted ellipses across the screen, because she says, I'm sorry, Zar. We were going to look at stuff for our dorm rooms and didn't want to hurt you. Do you want to come? We can swing by on the way?

Yeah, girl, come! Ximena adds.

I hesitate, until Dani sends an animated GIF of a white bear grabbing a brown bear's paw and looking up at it with puppy eyes, the words *Plz . . . I'm sorry* flickering across the top.

Fighting a smile, I reply, I'd love to, and return one of the Golden Girls hugging.

Five minutes later, Dani yells from the Coop, "Get in, loser, we're going shopping."

I smack her shoulder, laughing, then enter the backseat next to Ximena, who drops her curly head on my shoulder at once, burrowing into my side like a koala. Dalia regards us through the rearview, a guilty expression furrowing her brows, until I say, "I'm okay, Dal. Thanks for worrying about my feelings, but if you're all going to be busy with college starting fall, I want to spend as much time with you this summer as humanly possible."

Ximena hugs me tighter and Dani reaches behind her seat

to pat my leg. Dalia, meanwhile, wipes at her mascara-lined eyes and dredges up a watery smile. "Oh, don't make me cry or I won't be able to drive."

"I'll do it," her sister volunteers.

Dalia kitten-glowers at her. "Not a chance. It's my turn."

"Then *I* get to pick the music!"

I sit back and smile, hoping that's the end of all the icky-sticky *feelings* and we can go back to normal. I've had as many Lifetime moments as I can handle in one day.

The wind blowing through my loose hair feels so soothing that even though I want to give them a status update on the Harun situation, my eyelids droop and the city blurs around me. I have to blink several times to wake myself up.

We pass the Great Falls National Park along the way, packed to the brim with parents pushing strollers, families barbecuing, and couples sitting on the benches.

An ice cream truck parked in the gravel lot plays a merry jingle. Screaming kids holding drippy Popsicles dash toward the railing around the wide cliff's edge, so enamored by the sight of the waterfalls that they pay no mind to the foamy, yellow-tinted water, the trash littering the grass, or the construction crews working high above. The air smells of sea salt and smoke.

Traffic picks up downtown.

As the central hub of Paterson, it contains not only city hall, the police station, and other important clerical buildings, but Passaic County Community College and dozens of local businesses, including food carts, electronic stores, boutiques, and other restaurants.

The Mini Cooper whooshes by a billboard announcing PCCC's impending open house.

Dalia parks next to a meter in front of a store with a sign that reads MO'S DISCOUNT FURNITURE. I scope the street before entering, recalling many wonderful memories of back-to-school shopping in the area with my family or the girls, snacking on churros and snow cones from the carts or a greasy but delicious slice of pizza from the parlor on Broadway.

"Salaam, little sisters!" greets the owner, a burly Middle Eastern man with close-cropped gray hair and Arabic script tattooed on his arms, noticing Dalia's shimmery purple turban.

"Salaam," we say in unison, and let him point out the ongoing sales.

While the girls amble off to ooh and aah, I check the price tag on a floor lamp that resembles a palm tree, wince, and release it. Not as much as it would cost outside downtown, in a department store, but way out of *my* price range.

"Surprised your dad didn't tag along," I tell the twins, who are bouncing on two of the garishly decked mattresses that take up the whole center of the shop.

"Psh, we had to ban him after he kept moaning about the cost when we went to Target," Dani says. "The white people started side-eyeing us. They were either about to offer donations or call security, but we left before we could find out."

Dalia shakes her head, though it's clear she's suppressing a smile. "Can you blame him? It's going to be an expensive four years, even with us chipping in."

"Well, that's why we're bargain-hunting, isn't it?" Dani replies. "Besides, Zahra knows more than any of us about helicopter brown parents." She turns to me. "How's that going, by the way? You'd tell us if you were already engaged, wouldn't you? 'Cause I think your smoking-hot new dishwasher bae might be less than pleased if you were taken."

"Dani!" Dalia scolds.

I laugh uncomfortably. "No. I already told you Harun isn't into it either, right? He's not a bad guy. The funniest thing happened on our last date, actually—"

Before I can tell them about Hanif's hilarious antics, how Harun texted me to chat about the movie after, and everything that occurred with Amma's job following our night together, Dalia gasps and points toward the rear of the shop. "Look, Dan, those twinkle lights are exactly like the ones we saw at Target but, like, half the price!"

"Hold that thought, Zar," Dani says, hopping off the bed to join her sister.

Ximena observes my downcast expression for a moment, then takes the space her girlfriend vacated, patting the spot next to her for me to join. "You sure everything's okay, Zahra?"

Although I'm tempted to lie again, I can't do it anymore. Not after what happened with Amma. But I don't want to cry, either, which I will if we get into all that now, so I merely say, "I guess it's hard not to feel like a fourth wheel these days. I mean, Dani and Dalia are twins, you're Dani's girlfriend, and all of you are going to college, while I'm only . . ."

Replaceable.

"You're not *only* anything," Ximena replies, putting a hand on my knee. "They're just . . . in their own world sometimes." Although she's talking to me, her eyes are on Dani, at once fond and something more complicated. "That doesn't mean that you're not an important part of their lives. Of all of ours." She smirks. "*Or* that there aren't things in your own world you should try exploring more . . . like certain eye-candy dishwashers."

Heat rushes up my face, her ribbing doing its trick as I squeak, "Nayim is more than just a pretty face, Men. He's a hard worker with big dreams and—" Ximena's smirk grows wolfish and my teeth snap together. "Okay, okay, I get it. Maybe you're right."

"I'm always right," she replies, but her grin takes on an edge. "Honestly, Zar, I know things have been hard for you. Losing your dad? I can't even start to imagine it. But I worry you get so lost in the bad sometimes that you don't notice the good."

"*Good?*" I recoil.

Ximena winces. "That came out wrong. It's just, your future being undecided doesn't have to be so awful. It means you get to make choices for yourself, in a way none of the rest of us can."

I'm about to answer, when Dani yells across the shop, "Oi,

Mena, come look at all the art they have hung up! You think I should buy one for my dorm?"

"Uhhh, you're buying this imitation BS over my dead body, babe," her girlfriend calls back, giving my knee one last squeeze before moving to find the Tahir girls, leaving me before I can respond. And honestly, I wouldn't even know what to say. There's not a single bone in my body that can see the silver lining she believes in.

I'm all alone.

This is the most stuck I've felt since the acceptance letters rolled in and I had to defer mine. Maybe it *was* a mistake to come.

My friends have been swept away by the magic of colorful fairy lights. I wish the biggest question in my life was what kinds of decorations to buy. They presume I have some caricature of freedom they don't, when just last night, Amma and I were arguing over how to keep the lights on at our apartment. *Any* of them.

Dread cracks open inside me, gaping and raw. Things are changing between us, whether I want them to or not.

I only hope they won't leave me behind.

Because without them, I'm scared of who I'll become.

Chapter ♥ 12

A few days later, I'm left to fend for myself once more, this time at Chai Ho.

Or at least, that seems to be Mr. Tahir's fear.

"Are you certain you can handle this on your own, Miss Khan?" he asks me for what must be the third time in as many minutes.

"We'll be fiiiiine," I reply. "I'm not actually on my own."

He shoots a narrow-eyed glare at Nayim, who lounges behind the counter, flipping through the tea shop's menu while humming some old rock anthem. "And that's *exactly* the problem. Your mother has put her trust in me to guard your, well . . ."

Nauzubillah, *please* don't say something extra embarrassing like *virtue*.

". . . reputation," he continues, which is only marginally less *Bridgerton*. "So I hesitate to leave you alone with a boy now after so many years of diligence."

He looks at me way too earnestly.

I grimace, deliberating how to respond in a way that's less rude than, *Being virtuous and reputable won't help me save up for college again, so I'd prefer the time and a half you're promising for today, thank-you-very-much.*

Mercifully, I'm saved from having to answer by Dani swanning into the shop from the curb, where her mother and sister wait inside the family's minivan. All three are dressed in elaborate cerulean lehengas that match their father's tie, purchased from Amma by Mrs. Tahir, in preparation for attending one of their cousins' birthday parties in Woodbridge.

"Okay, number one," Dani says, lifting a finger, "that's pretty sexist, Abbu." Mr. Tahir opens his mouth to defend himself, but a second finger cuts him off. "Number two, Nayim is bunking with the imam. I doubt he'd bring the wrath of God—or Zahra's Hello Kitty pepper spray—raining down on himself by trying anything gross. Number three, Zahra's looked after the shop before with me or Dalia. Lastly, what could she and Nayim possibly get up to? Making out right in the middle of the floor?"

Just then, Dalia beeps the minivan's horn as her mom waves for Dani and Mr. Tahir to hurry. Dani takes her sputtering father by the arm and drags him toward the exit. Before they depart, however, he turns to me one last time and whispers, "Don't forget the cricket bat I keep under the counter . . . for *safety.*"

I puff out a relieved sigh when he's out of earshot. It's nine in the morning and I'm already exhausted thanks to him. But in his defense, he's made it as easy as possible for Nayim and me to look after Chai Ho today, having preprepared all the baked goods so we just have to wrap them up in fancy to-go boxes and brew tea. Takeout-only days are the best.

"He's a funny guy, isn't he?" Nayim says, gazing out the door after our boss with one cheek in his upraised palm.

My own cheeks grow pink as I wonder how much of the Tahirs' conversation he overheard. Clearing my throat, I say, "I guess so, but we should be grateful he trusts us enough to take care of the shop while he's gone."

"You're always so responsible," Nayim remarks.

I begin to bristle, then notice his affectionate smile and force my hackles down, shrugging. "I've sort of had to be, as the oldest kid, the oldest *daughter*. Especially now with my dad gone, my mom, grandma, and siblings rely on me. I can't let them down."

I ponder whether he thinks he's better off than me. He's lost people too, but he only has to take care of himself now. Or is that worse? Am I a monster for even comparing us? I can't imagine myself in a world without my family in it.

His smile dims as he reads the conflict in my expression. I busy myself with hanging the chairs upside down on the tables and flipping the CLOSED sign over to OPEN.

Only when I'm done does he say, "But who can *you* rely on?"

I stiffen in front of the glass door, the corner of the sign gripped in my white-knuckled fingers, then chime a breezy laugh in an attempt to turn it into a joke. "You, today, I hope.

Mr. Tahir was going to keep Chai Ho closed but left it open because I begged him. I'm sure I'm not the only one who could use the paycheck, right?"

He meets my gaze with those keen eyes and quirks a grin at me. "Right."

Our first customer arrives, followed by a steady stream of others, undeterred by the limited take-out menu for the day. As I watch Nayim man the register, I can almost see why Mr. Tahir was so scandalized on my behalf.

Gossip spreads like the flu in Paterson, so a gaggle of avid new faces have turned up to meet Nayim for the first time, not all of them Bengali. A freshman-aged girl bats her eyelashes as he writes her name on her plastic iced chai latte cup with a flourish, while a few middle schoolers peek out at him from behind each other, giggling every time one of them makes eye contact.

The older women are hardly better. They march up to the counter to inspect him as if the confections aren't the only thing on sale, then have to be dragged away by their husbands or children when he gifts them one of his sweet, knee-melting smiles.

I've noticed people gawking at him whenever we walk home. He has the kind of charisma that summons every eye in a room, but I guess it's a survival instinct as much as anything else. How else would he attract an audience as a street performer or convince random people to hire an immigrant boy for the jobs they need done?

I get it. I *do*.

My hands squeeze the mop in my grasp hard, viciously sopping up a falooda someone spilled, as I watch a beautiful girl I recognize, who'll be a high school senior come September, twirling a lock of dyed purple hair while chatting with him. As if he senses my death glare, his eyes catch mine and crinkle at the corners.

Harrumphing, I whip around and dunk the mop into the bucket more savagely than necessary, splashing murky water and soap suds across the tiled floor and my own Vans.

Ugh, I hate boys.

Insufferable, adorable, bigheaded boys.

Despite my displeasure and Mr. Tahir's suspicions, the rest of our shift passes by without too much extra hassle. Before I know it, the clock has struck four and only an hour remains until we shut down for the night.

Nayim strolls over to the door, where he switches the sign to CLOSED and clicks the lock to match, then turns to me expectantly.

I put my hands on my hips. "What are you doing? We still have an hour."

He glances down at me with a gleam in his eye. "I thought we could close a little early. Mr. Tahir won't mind."

"Ummm, I'm pretty sure he will. You don't know him like I do. He'll put you on bathroom duty for a week, and I strongly suspect that toilet is a portal to Jahannam."

Nayim chuckles. "You're such a writer, with those clever

metaphors. Wouldn't you like to sit outside on this lovely summer evening and just . . . do that?"

His eyes are intent on me. I gulp. "Do *what*, exactly?"

"Write, Zar."

He arches both brows, as if the answer should be obvious. Perhaps it should have been, but the slight flux of excitement that spiked through my veins fizzles at the clarification, replaced by a persistent anxiety.

It's not a matter of sitting down and doing it. I've *tried* for the last two years, to no avail. It's like when Baba died, my ability to tell a story died with him. It's hard to write happily-ever-afters when my own "after" has been up in the air for so long. When, rather than the words I'm seeking, visions of every possible disastrous outcome that leads to my family begging on the street plague me.

Sometimes, a good imagination is a very dangerous thing.

I shake my head. "I don't want to do anything Mr. Tahir would get mad about when he trusted us tonight. I didn't think you were that sort of person either."

To his credit, Nayim appears chastised at the thought of breaking my—and, by extension, Mr. Tahir's—trust. He murmurs an apologetic, "Sorry. I only meant . . . You've been running around handling all the orders and cleaning up after customers while I ran the register, so I figured you could use a break."

"That's—"

. . . Actually very sweet.

"I'm fine," I say instead, but his gaze is somber.

"Earlier, I think it bothered you that you have so many people relying on you and no one you can do the same with," he says gently. "I want you to know, you *can* trust me, Zahra. With your writing hopes and anything else you want to share with me."

"I don't know if I can do that," I whisper, frowning down at my stained sneakers.

It's not in me to break the rules like this. To slack off. It was one thing being alone with him when we were working, but this . . . this is something else entirely. And yet, when he extends his hand, my own twitches at my side.

He takes it and steers me over to one of the tables, pulling out a chair for me. "You don't have to know yet. At least for tonight, can't we look out at the stars together, rather than with an alleyway between us?"

"It's too early for stars," I want to grouse, but can't bring myself to do it when his eyes are glittering imploringly at me like stars themselves. I turn to the windows to see if anyone might be snooping or eavesdropping, but he's already drawn the curtains together to give us some semblance of privacy. The last weight of indecisiveness on my shoulders lifts as I give my consent.

"Okay . . ."

Sucking in a trembling breath, I observe Nayim through wide eyes as he dims the lights of the shop and brings me a bowl of creamy rossomalai and a cup of masala chai—extra sweet and milky, exactly as I like it. After I murmur a thank-you, he vanishes into the back room and returns with a wooden guitar. If possible, my eyes get rounder.

"Is that—"

"The guitar I told you about," he says, running reverential fingertips over the polished arches of the instrument. His attention turns to me, his honey eyes hooded. "If you want, we can write together? You, your book, while I try to finish a new song?"

"But what if I can't do it?" I mumble. "What if I try and nothing happens?"

"It's okay." His casual words make me scowl, until he continues, "I've learned that you sometimes find inspiration in unexpected places. Like in the Middle of Nowhere, New Jersey, for example."

Swallowing the thick lump in my throat, I nod. "Okay. But you have to play me a song."

"I can do that," Nayim agrees.

I notice the tension in his shoulders, however, as I sling my backpack over my own, an untouched notebook inside it, and carry the treats he prepared for me into the enclosed yard behind Chai Ho. Potted herbs and plants like mint, lemongrass, and lavender, which Mr. Tahir grows for his recipes, soon encircle us.

Nayim sits across from me on an upturned milk crate, the guitar in his lap. Although there are no stars, when he bows his head and his thick, shoulder-length hair curtains his face, the sun halos his figure like a crown, casting the shadows of his inky eyelashes across his high cheekbones.

God, he's beautiful. Polaris in his own right.

His long, graceful fingers strum a chord, but he soon pulls them back, laughing nervously. "Sorry, I'm a bit rusty."

I wave my empty notebook. "Hello. Girl who hasn't written a word in two years here. No judgment, Nayim. Seriously."

That makes him grin again, in that irresistible, lopsided way. "All right. I'll try to play if you try to write. Deal?"

"Deal," I reply, sounding more confident than I am.

He strums more and more chords, until they become a yearning melody I've never heard before. Something he's written? It sends a thrill through me like I've touched a live wire. This is the sort of "rusty" that treasure glints beneath.

I tear my gaze away only when his eyes rise and catch mine, my ears burning, but as I frown at the blank first page of my notebook, I realize it no longer feels like an insurmountable mountain to climb, because I'm not alone on my quest anymore. Bringing my sparkly pen to the paper, I start to write.

Nowhere near as bewitching as Nayim's song.

Nonsensical things, about raven hair and golden eyes, siren songs and sumptuous lips, but soon I'm stringing them together into sentences, into a story.

A love story.

He's right: having the right muse makes all the difference.

Chapter ♥ 13

Harun picks me up for the second of our eight dates, but he's not alone.

I do a double take at the drop-dead gorgeous woman in the passenger seat of his BMW. Curly hair cut in layers with ombre highlights shot through them frames her heart-shaped face, spilling in elegant waves down her shoulders.

Long-lashed brown eyes take me in from head to toe while I squirm on the sidewalk in front of our building, before her lips curve into a crimson smile. "Harun, you dog! I didn't know you snagged yourself such a cute new girlfriend."

Harun glares, but she's too busy stepping out of the BMW to notice. She takes my hand in both of hers and presses it against her sequined bosom, oblivious to my bashfulness. "Zahra, right? My name is Sharmin, but everyone calls me Sammi. I'm Haru-moni's oldest cousin, and I'll be your chaperone tonight."

I blink. *Haru-moni?*

Ice prince Harun has such a cutesy dakh-nahm?

For his part, Harun groans and thunks his forehead against the steering wheel. Sammi ignores the ensuing *beeeeeep* to help me into the passenger seat. "Don't worry, I know you two would rather be together. I can chaperone fiiiiine from the backseat."

"Um." I self-consciously buckle the seat belt over the tunic Amma beaded for me. "What happened to Hanif Bhai?"

"Oh, that stick-in-the-mud?" Sammi flaps a manicured hand. "He's probably at some symposium to discuss the reproductive habits of worms."

Harun frowns again. "Or something." To me, he explains, "Hanif Bhai went to a retreat planned by the Muslim Student Association of NYU."

"Close enough," Sammi mumbles.

Harun breezes right past her snarky comment. "Anyway, my parents thought it was for the best. They think we can 'get to know each other better' with Sammi Afa."

Sammi leans over the center console to wink. "I've gotcha, babes."

Harun grimaces like her proximity is giving him a headache. I wonder if Pushpita Khala and Mansif Khalu have somehow seen through my—*our*—ploy to avoid exactly this scenario. Days of texting new ways to make Hanif clutch his pearls, going so far as to draw up a *script* for us, have gone out the window.

Guess the students haven't quite surpassed the masters.

There's no time to freak out about it, though. Meeting his gaze with resolution in my own, I nod once, an unspoken message: *We just need to make it through tonight. Nothing has changed with Operation Zahrun.*

Sammi's squeal as she pops her torso between us again nearly causes Harun to swerve on the highway. "Oh my God, you two are precious! I can't take these lovestruck stares!"

"L-lovestruck?" I stammer.

Harun barks, "Can you please put on your seat belt?"

Pouting, Sammi does so, but her stream of intrusive questions doesn't subside even when we reach our destination. I work my jaw, wondering if she's truly related to Harun and Hanif, who are both so stoic, or a changeling left by the pari who stole the real Sharmin in her infancy. Then again, who but family are such experts in annoying the hell out of you?

Case in point: this date.

"So what do you think about our Haru-moni?" she sing-songs as we veer into the parking-lot area of Willowbrook Mall, not far from the theater where we had our last date.

Are we doing dinner and a movie again?

A bit unimaginative, but we can put our plans into action anywhere.

I arch an appraising brow at my date.

"He's passable, I guess, but I doubt I'll be calling him 'moni' anytime soon."

"Thanks for the rave review," Harun intones dryly, ducking

out of the car, a glare fixed in place as he steps perfectly into his own role.

Sammi droops at our incompatible act. "Oh . . ."

I bow my head to hide a victorious smirk, pleased that she's showing her hand more than Hanif did. Maybe Harun's parents sending her will be a blessing in disguise.

But then she snatches up Harun's arm so we're less than a foot apart and says, "You mustn't let his grumpy face fool you, Zahra. Harun is a sensitive soul when you get to know him. He even wore a special cologne to impress you." She wrinkles her nose. "A bit too much, possibly, but it's the thought that counts. I made him change that shirt, so you're welcome."

I snort at said sensitive soul. *Really?*

His shoulders hunch as he glances away, muttering something about how it was supposed to set off Hanif's allergy.

"He seems so much happier since you met," Sammi barrels on without paying him any mind. "After the way he got his heart broken, I'm glad he's—"

"Afa," Harun snaps, agitated for real now.

She slaps a hand against her lips in a clear *oops* while I swivel my head between them.

Heart broken? *Harun?* I'm learning so much about him today.

He *did* hint at a girlfriend, and when I snooped on his social media profiles, although most of his stories featured Rabeardranath, his family, and some guy friends, there were a few older Instagram posts of Harun with a dazzling blond girl.

They no longer follow each other.

He refuses to look up from the pavement, his jaw set tight, but I don't have a chance to check in because Sammi skips the last couple of paces to the setting of our date and flings an arm at it with a flourish. "Ta-da!"

It's TGI Fridays.

"Have you been?" she asks.

I nod. Ximena invited me and Dani here when she got a summer job as a waitress at the restaurant, but although I'm not as strict about eating halal as Dalia—I just don't order anything with pork or alcohol and say "bismillah," hoping for the best—the prices were way too high for me to willingly return, even after her friends and family discount.

Ignorant of my penny-pinching musings, Sammi struts into the dimly lit restaurant, pointing at a sign as we enter. "Would you look at that? They're having a karaoke night! I should come back with my darling hubby."

She's *married*?

The last thing I hear before loud music drowns out every other noise is Harun groaning. Not ten minutes later, a waiter carrying three laminated menus directs us to our table. Harun and I sit across from each other, Sammi cozying up next to me. There's indeed a gold band with a hunk of diamond on her ring finger.

She puckers her lips at her own reflection in her iPhone's camera. "Why did no one tell me my hair was a mess? Excuse me while I freshen up in the bathroom, Zahra."

I watch her sashay away, confused since I don't spot a single strand out of place, then shift my wary eyes back to Harun, who's carefully reading the menu in front of him. He no longer seems upset about Sammi's slipup. Though curiosity burns inside me at what she revealed, do I really have a right to know intimate details about his life and past? Would I be willing to spill about Nayim in return?

These past few weeks, it's almost started to feel like we could be friends . . . in the totally platonic, comrades-in-arms sort of way. But the fact of the matter is, we're faking everything.

"So . . . Sammi Afa sure is something," I venture.

He snorts. "You can say *that* again."

I worry my lip at the undercurrent of irritation in his voice. "Sorry you got stuck with her. And me. I'm sure you had better things to do on a Friday night."

I'd be working, babysitting, or sleeping if I weren't here, but he could have been going out on *actual* dates to mend his supposedly broken heart if we didn't have to carry on with this ruse. In spite of his hang-ups, plenty of girls would line up for a chance with his chiseled good looks.

Including stunning blondes, apparently.

But he shakes his head, dragging a hand over his face. "No. It's not your fault. We're *both* stuck doing this to make our parents happy." His voice dips lower as a smirk quirks his lips, his eyes meeting mine. "Besides, you're not as bad as I thought when we first met."

"Uh, thanks." My stomach does a nervous flip that I blame on hunger.

Harun must be feeling something too, because he goes back to focusing on the menu and adds hurriedly, "Neither is Sammi Afa."

"What?"

"Not that bad, I mean," he says. "She's always been there for me, like a big sis. And her brother Shaad is probably my best friend. Oh, and Afa can hand us all our asses at *Mario Kart*. She made Hanif Bhaia cry last Eid, though he blamed it on fasting all month."

I giggle. "That's cute. She must really love you guys if she's practicing *Mario Kart* in her spare time."

"Yeah, yeah." He rolls his eyes. "But honestly, I think she acts like this to blow off steam. She and her husband are both neurosurgeons at Mount Sinai."

My jaw hits the metaphorical table. "Neurosurgeons? She's like *Grey's Anatomy*–level gorgeous."

"Are you bragging about me again, cuz?" Sammi drawls, sliding into Harun's side of the booth to give his curly hair a good muss before releasing him.

Harun looks adorably disheveled and murderous.

Sammi then aims her inquisitive eyes at me. "It's true, though. Our parents introduced me to Bilal while I was in my last year of medical school and he was completing his residency. I was *sooo* not into the whole arranged marriage schtick, but then we met and it was love at first sight."

"Wow . . ."

That she can have a career *and* love *and* her parents' approval, while being so completely herself, fills me with both envy and awe. Even Harun looks at her in a way that betrays the childish hero worship beneath his standoffish veneer.

As if sensing she's gotten back into his good graces, she flags down the waitress who shows up to take our orders and says, "Can you please add us to the karaoke list?"

"Us?" demands Harun. "Speak for yourself."

Sammi juts out her bottom lip. "Come *on*, cuz. Don't you remember the Bengali folk dance class Pushpita Sasi enrolled you in as a kid? You were so cute. It'll be just like that!"

I whip my head toward him, delighted. *Folk dance?!*

"I've been trying to *forget*, thanks," he grits out.

"Don't be such a spoilsport," she says. "These places always have a long wait for your food. We may as well have a good time. Zahra will do it. Won't you, Zahra?"

My grin freezes into place. "I, that is—"

She slams me with the full force of her persuasive gaze, until I crumble and nod.

Maybe arguing onstage and embarrassing our families in front of a bunch of hangry people will be the final nail in the coffin of our relationship? But my date scowls like I've taken the butter knife off the table to stab him in the back.

I don't realize the ramifications of my actions until I find myself standing next to a petrified Harun onstage, ready to perform a duet before an apathetic audience—and Sammi Afa, who already looks prepared to give us a standing ovation.

"You just *had* to volunteer us, Bollywood," he hisses.

"Oh, shut up. I don't want to do this either!"

"Coulda had me fooled," he counters. "I thought you liked musical numbers."

"Yeah, *in movies.*"

Now that I'm in the spotlight, I remember how my friends have always teased me for having a singing voice that could shatter glass.

How whenever I sing in the shower, Arif pounds on the bathroom door to tell me I sound like a pair of cats fighting. How Mr. Tahir lasted only one slumber party after buying the twins a karaoke machine for their tenth birthday before he realized our heartfelt renderings of BLACKPINK songs wouldn't be winning any Grammys anytime soon.

Then I notice a movement from the corner of my eye and realize how pale Harun has become, knuckles blanched almost white around the microphone in his rigid, trembling grasp.

Oh, crap, he's legit scared.

Glancing between him and the dispassionate audience, I realize I have to take one for the team, since he's gone along with everything I've suggested so far, including this duet. His blown-out pupils flick toward me in surprise when I move to take his hands in mine, bringing the microphone between us.

A peppy collaboration between Ariana Grande and Justin Bieber blasts from the speakers. I start yowling along, purposely loud so all eyes—and formal noise complaints—fall to me instead of him, and then smile when thirty seconds in, his brisk voice choruses mine.

Our gazes lock, our lips part, and—

Well, we're as cringey as you'd imagine, though Harun, with his gravelly baritone, is marginally better than my awful, keening pitch. At least our enthusiasm can give the Biebs a run for his money.

We screech the chorus simultaneously, not even bothering to attempt a sound that resembles the correct pitch. Even Sammi pokes her fingers into her ears at the highest notes, but by then, we're fully committed, yelling into the mic and bopping our heads so hard, his glasses almost fall off.

In that instant, our faces are mere inches apart, his hand a comforting weight around mine. My feet move of their own accord. Harun's eyes widen behind their frames when I retreat two steps and offer him my free hand. He shakes his head but doesn't resist as I pull him into an awkward, bumbling dance.

It's nothing like the choreographed numbers in K3G. Nothing like Nayim, with his deft, poised fingers. But I don't mind because I'm breathless and dizzy beneath the beam of the spotlights, my heart drumming in my chest, veins, and temples as I spin, confident that dependable Harun won't let me fall.

Chapter 14

The hostess practically snatches the mic away the instant the song ends. "Wasn't that, er, energetic? Let's give a round of applause to these two very brave guests."

Scattered claps follow.

It doesn't matter, because Harun and I barely make it back to our table before dissolving into raucous guffaws that summon disapproving tuts from the other customers sitting around us. Harun is looking at me like he's seeing me in a new light and doesn't entirely hate it.

Fair. Dalia likes to say I'm *wonderfully weird*.

It takes several minutes before we catch our breath enough for him to whisper, "Thanks. I don't—I hate being the center of attention, especially with so many strangers."

I bask in the warmth of something other than the lingering heat and adrenaline. It seems like he's growing more comfortable opening up to me, too. "You're welcome, partner."

Only then do we notice Sammi isn't there, though our

orders have arrived. The white cheddar and broccoli soup I picked looks woefully tragic next to Harun's fish and chips and Sammi's braised salmon, but at least letting him pay for it while posing as a gold digger won't dent my pride as much. With the complimentary breadsticks, it might even keep me full.

Our chaperone returns from where she was speaking to the waiter, putting her hands together in an apologetic gesture. "Sorry, darlings. I have to go."

"Was our singing *that* bad?" quips Harun.

"No! You were great!" she lies. "But Bilal called. We have some surprise guests and they're waiting for me. Don't worry, though! You two enjoy dinner—on me. There's no reason your parents have to know."

With another wink, she's gone, leaving behind a fistful of twenties and the faintest whiff of expensive-smelling floral perfume.

Harun and I turn to each other, then burst into a fresh round of laughter. Sure, we haven't done a convincing job of proving to Sammi that we aren't meant for each other, but I have a feeling she made up her mind about our compatibility before ever meeting me, simply because her cousin's happiness was the most important thing to her. I can respect that.

"If she's paying, we may as well order another app," Harun says.

I fake-glare. "You rich people are terrible."

He chuckles, but I can't help stealing glimpses at him as

I nibble on the salmon he slides toward me without another word, some unnamed emotion bubbling up inside me.

It isn't true, no matter how much I once willed it to be. He *isn't* terrible. He could have easily rejected his parents and me when this whole matchmaking thing came up, saving us both the trouble, but he didn't, because he wants them to be proud of him.

Just like me with Amma.

"Are we friends?" I blurt.

Harun's incredulous expression makes my stomach plummet, until he huffs, "Are you kidding me, Khan? No shit."

"Oh, good." I sag into the booth, at once relieved and thrown by his surety. "It would have been pathetic if my platonic feelings were unrequited."

I expect him to retort with another snarky crack, but he becomes earnest. "I'm glad I'm stuck with *you*, Zahra. I don't think I could make it through this godforsaken summer with anyone else. Even when you use SAT words like unrequited and platonic in casual conversation, I don't hate hanging out with you."

"I don't hate hanging out with you, either," I whisper, thankful that the restaurant's mood lighting hides how rosy my cheeks are. "It's been nice, getting to act like a real teenager again. Things changed when my dad died. Before this, I could probably count on one hand how often I'd been to a movie or eaten at a restaurant or sung karaoke with friends in the last two years."

His expression softens. "I can't imagine. I'm sorry."

"Don't be," I murmur. "It's not your fault. If nothing else, at least this farce of ours has given me the chance to experience those things again. My world was beginning to feel so small." And it might go *back* to being small when he heads off to college, but I don't want to be a downer, so I crook a smile at him, extending my hand across the table. "Friends."

Harun dimples at me and we shake on it. He sneaks a few more peeks my way as we go back to our food, then says, "I think this has been good for me, too. I'd become a shut-in ever since"—he visibly considers his words, then settles on—"since graduation."

Was that when he got his heart broken? I watch him through the fringe of my lashes, my voice quiet so as not to spook him. "Is that when you had that breakup Afa mentioned?"

"Sammi Afa exaggerates," he rumbles, but doesn't otherwise deny it, chewing so intently for the next minute that I figure that's all I'll get out of him. It's *plenty* already, considering who he is, but then he adds, "We did date for a while, though. Years. So I may have taken it extra hard when she dumped me, but I'm getting to be okay again."

I meet his gaze properly, stunned not only that he had such a long-term relationship before—the same broody Harun who loves robots, reptiles, nerdy jokes, and his family—but that he's being forthcoming about it to *me*, of all people.

"That's understandable," I murmur. "To feel a little lost when someone is suddenly gone, when you're used to them being there. I know what that's like."

That fear has clung to me like Saran Wrap since Baba died. I'm scared to lose any more of the people I care about, even though I know letting them go is an inevitable part of life.

Harun searches my face, perceptive as ever. "Jeez, it's not even in the same ballpark as what you went through. I'm sorry if it's hard to think about."

"It's okay." I smile down at the grooved surface of the wooden table. "It's actually nice to talk about him sometimes. Amma doesn't do it much, so the rest of us avoid bringing him up too. But there are lots of great memories I wish we could reminisce about, you know?"

"Yeah?" Harun says, voice soft.

I smile sadly. "Amma and I always butted heads, but I could do no wrong in Baba's eyes. Even when Amma would complain about bills, he used to wink and sneak me some money to buy snacks after school or get a book I wanted to read. . . ." I chuckle, remembering the time I hid under the sheets reading my stash from the book fair, afraid Amma would find me out and be upset with Baba. But then I recall why we were talking about him in the first place, and clap my hands together, breaking the spell. "So your ex. Tell me about her."

"Lily . . ." Harun sighs heavily. He's frowning very determinedly at the french fry in his hand, as if there's some golden ketchup-to-fry ratio he can't afford to mess up. "It's a totally different story. By the end, we brought out the worst in each other."

"But you still miss her, right?" I ask, reading it in the subdued set of his shoulders.

He shrugs. "I . . . don't know. I don't think I know how to be without her yet?" His fingers tap across the tabletop, and I resist the urge to set mine on top of them, letting him find the words he's seeking. "My cousin Shaad and I . . . We had targets on our backs at school from day one. New money, Muslim brown kids from one of the poorest cities in New Jersey at an academy like that, with the kids of politicians, celebrities, and CEOs."

Here I'd assumed his private-school life must have been glossy and cosmopolitan, like something out of *Gossip Girl*. I level a sympathetic wince at him. "I never thought about what it must have been like for you."

"It was miserable," he admits. "I got the worst of it because Shaad was outgoing and funny and would turn things around so everyone was laughing with him, not at him. People couldn't help liking him. But me? I hid away in the science building, feeding the reptiles and making Lego bots. Hell, I was probably asking for the bullying at that point." I open my mouth to argue, but an imploring glance stops me. "Then, in high school, Lily Whitlock, hands-down the prettiest girl in our year, suddenly wanted to breathe the same air as me."

"That's not surprising," I reply casually. "You're, like, really good-looking, Harun."

His lips twitch. "I guess. Looking back, that's around when I had a growth spurt and joined the swim team. But it blew my mind. She decided I'd be her boyfriend, and everyone else started falling over themselves to welcome me into their social circles. That's the way things were for the next few years. I was . . . happy, I guess."

"You don't sound so sure. . . ."

He considers his words as he chews another bite. "Despite her best efforts, despite my best efforts, I didn't fit into her world. I didn't like her friends, who pretended they hadn't treated me like dirt only a year ago. Her folks weren't exactly rolling out the red carpet for me either. Did you know, in all that time, her dad never learned I wasn't Indian?"

"Ugh." I grimace as I try to picture Harun, who is painfully shy, struggling to figure out a way to correct someone without it seeming impolite. I come up short.

"Yeah," he agrees, divesting himself of his half-eaten fry at last so he can comb a hand through his unruly hair. "But even though it was hard, I convinced myself I was lucky she gave me a chance. I thought I loved her. Maybe I did? It was enough that we agreed we should both go to Stanford together."

An invisible fist squeezes my heart. If he's here, obviously that didn't work out. "What happened?"

Harun smiles, but it's sad, and there's a faraway glaze to his eyes. "I never introduced her to my parents. I—I don't know why. Maybe I was scared that if they hated each other, everything would have to change. I kept putting it off and she kept pushing me. She always felt like I didn't put her first, like I was under my parents' thumb."

"I'm sorry," I whisper.

He sighs, pinching the bridge of his nose. "No. Don't be. She was right. I was a bad boyfriend. I didn't even know how bad until college acceptances rolled out."

"My mom's always been a diabetic," he continues, "and that spring, she had a bad hypoglycemic episode. Dad's been busy with the restaurant for basically ever, especially after he got it in his head to open a second one in Paterson. I got home late from a date with Lily and found my mom just in time. It . . . scared me."

"Oh, Harun . . ." I finally reach for his hand.

"I realized then that I didn't want to go so far that I couldn't drive back if they needed me," he confesses, meeting my gaze like he's desperately willing me to understand. "Shaad, Sammi, and Hanif all have siblings, but my parents only have me. When I tried to explain that to Lily, explain why I was choosing Columbia, even though I promised we could fly out to visit each other, she said she was tired of me being such a codependent loser and dumped me."

Righteous anger flares in my chest. "What the hell? She could have broken up with you without being so—so—so rude." Choicer words dance on the tip of my tongue, but I bite it and glance up to find Harun grinning at me. "What?"

He shakes his head. "Yeah, she was pretty harsh, but I guess I deserved it. If Stanford was some sort of test to choose her over my parents, I flunked it, big-time."

"At . . . least you did well on the SAT?" I reply, in an effort to make him laugh.

Harun snorts. "Truth be told, it was the best thing for us both. I *had* grown codependent, but with her. I thought I should be grateful she even chose me, but I never stopped to consider why that was. When she dumped me, all I did was brood around the house like some kind of ghost." His eyes dart to mine, crinkling at the corners. "And then there was you."

"Me?" I squeak.

I wonder if he realizes how rom-com he sounds right now. Probably not, but that doesn't stop my heartbeat from pulsing in my veins.

"Yeah, you, Khan." He half dimples. "My folks probably figured they'd get me out of my funk by setting us up, but I didn't realize until we met how badly I needed a friend who didn't know Lily." He sighs and then smiles apologetically. "Thanks for listening."

"No need to thank me," I whisper, suddenly feeling shy and looking down at my bowl.

Perhaps Harun also senses the shift in the air between us, because he coughs into his fist. "Anyway. That's over. So you don't have to worry about Lily coming after you or anything."

The truth of his words sinks in, anchored to guilt.

Swallowing a mouthful of soup, I say, "I'm not dating anyone either, but . . . there's this boy. Amma doesn't know. She wouldn't approve."

Harun's brows knit together, his expression unreadable. I can't bear to look at him too closely, in case I find familiar judgment in his gaze. He isn't the only one with far too few friends, and now that I have him, the prospect of losing him sooner because he thinks poorly of me makes me want to puke.

Technically, I've never *dated* like him, but though Islam has the same rules in place about romance regardless of gender, people have double standards for what brown boys and girls do. Perhaps he hid it from his parents too, but even if he didn't, him dating is *boys being boys, he'll settle down eventually.* If I do it without the parental stamp of approval, a long list of rules, and chaperones, will it ruin my reputation? Will *he* think less of me for it, like Amma and the aunties and uncles of our city?

Gossip is a sin, too, but somehow, retribution always blows back on girls.

Only girls.

Harun's basket of french fries slides into my line of sight, prompting me to blink at him. His smile is kind. "If it makes you happy, you should go for it, Zar."

"Zar, huh?" The sound of the nickname my best friends use, and his immediate acceptance of my feelings for Nayim, sends delight bubbling through me, but I paste a teasing expression onto my face. "Does that mean I can call you 'Haru-moni'?"

"Shut up," he laughs.

Although I don't know if he's right about Nayim, his conviction comforts me.

I accept a fry. A *friendship* fry.

Chapter 15

That Saturday morning, I learn Chai Ho will be closing early because the Tahir family has another engagement—quite literally. It's an engagement party.

Mr. Tahir scowls when I ask why Nayim and I can't mind the shop again, and I fear he somehow discovered that we locked up before we should have last time.

Fortunately, he says, "Believe you me, I'd rather keep it open. Time is money! But Nayim said he has some errands to run tonight. If you'd like, perhaps you can open up tomorrow for a little extra pay?"

Although disappointment eddies through me at the thought of Nayim being too busy to walk me home for the first time since we met, I rally up a smile, accepting the ring of keys Mr. Tahir holds out. "Thank you, sir. I won't let you down."

"Just don't be late," he scolds.

When I salute, he snorts and waves me away.

It ends up being a sleepy day at Chai Ho. After the

lunch rush, Dani FaceTimes a paint-splattered Ximena, who volunteered to help restore the old Ivanhoe Mill Wheelhouse so it could once again become a hub for local artists, musicians, and writers. The four of us chat, with me catching them all up on what's been going on with Harun.

"I know you don't *like him* like him," Dalia says, as we swipe through some Snaps Harun sent me of Rabeardranath riding around on a Roomba, captioned *Kaiju attack*, "but it's cute, isn't it? How close you've gotten? I think you text him more than us these days."

She gusts a dreamy sigh, while I huff, "No way. He's just trying to convince me to come feed his lizard flies or whatever. As if."

I pointedly ignore the memory of Harun correcting me: *bearded dragon.*

"Come on, Zar." Dani smirks like she can read my mind. "Is it possible not to catch feelings for a hot guy who's taking you out on romantic dates every week?"

"Romantic?" I squawk, casting a nervous glance at the closed kitchen door. "The two of us are friends. We shook on it and everything. Plus, you don't even like guys, Dan."

"Maybe not, but I wouldn't say no to free food," she replies, then spins away, laughing, to dodge the dish towel I snap in her direction, still clutching her phone.

Ximena observes our antics over steepled fingers through its screen, the rusted sign of the wheelhouse visible above her curly bun. "That's adorable. Baby's first boyfriend."

"I am *not* a baby and Harun isn't my boyfriend." Crossing my arms, I sulk exactly like a baby might. "This is just something we have to do. We're like Batman and Superman when they had to team up to defeat that axe-headed dude in that never-ending movie Dani made us watch."

"Did Bats and Supes make out?" Ximena asks. "I don't remember that part."

Dani snickers. "It probably would have been a lot more exciting if they did."

"But then *we* might have kissed less," Ximena points out.

"Very true," her girlfriend agrees sagely.

I pout until Dalia says, "Okay, let's not bully poor Zahra. Plenty of people are friends without ever falling in love. I know that better than most."

"Thank you," I tell her.

Her smile grows impish. "Plus, Zahra already *has* a Prince Charming, so she doesn't need to kiss any frogs."

"Ooooooh," Dani and Ximena say in sync.

Them being so stinking adorable and happy together rubs salt in the wounds of my own complicated love life . . . if I can even call fake-dating one boy while walking home with another a love life, since Harun and I are comrades in arms and Nayim hasn't said a word about wanting to be more than my nightly bodyguard.

"Argh! This is why I need new friends!"

The girls giggle but take mercy on me and let the matter go before Mr. Tahir or Nayim overhear. Or at least, I *hope* neither have overheard. Nayim and I met at the pass-through window of the shop a few times today, but he seemed distracted and unlike his normal affable self. I'd rather he not hear any jokes about my nonexistent feelings for Harun and misunderstand.

Or worse. If I discover he doesn't actually care what I do, I don't know that I could show my face at the tea shop ever again.

The rest of our shift ticks by without us getting much of a chance to talk. Afterward, once the Tahirs have left for their party, accompanied by Ximena, who has shown up in a gorgeous lehenga Mr. and Mrs. Tahir gifted her for her last birthday, I find Nayim kneeling next to Thara the stray outside the shop, offering her a bowl of milk, a gym bag next to him.

"You can't come with me today, love," he says.

For a second, I think he means me—and my cheeks burn—until the cat issues a tragic mew. I squint between her, the bag, and his guarded expression. "Is that for your errands? Mr. Tahir mentioned you had something to do, so don't worry if you can't take me home. Paterson gets a bad rap, but I used to walk by myself all the time before you came along."

His throat bobs and I follow the jerky motion of it, wondering why he seems so jittery. He looks good, in a plain white T-shirt and black skinny jeans, colorful rubber bands up and down one wrist, another tying his hair into a bun. He could easily be on the cover of *Rolling Stone* as the front man of a band . . . if poor kids from Bangladesh got shots like that.

"Actually," he says softly, "I was hoping you'd go with me."

"Where?" I cock my head. "The gym?"

He chuckles. "Maybe later. I was hoping we could go somewhere more special tonight."

I catch my lip between my teeth and don't miss the way his eyes dart to it. My ears flush as anticipation and anxiety war inside my belly. Of course I want to go with him, but what if someone sees us together and reports back to Amma? What if the Emons hear? It would end my need to fake a relationship but unearth a million other problems I'd rather not deal with.

Good Bengali Muslim girls shouldn't be alone with boys.

Harun's words return to me: *You should go for it. . . .*

I meet Nayim's gaze, resolved to tell him no, but when his imploring eyes land on mine, the rejection seizes in my throat, an insect confined in the amber of his irises. I swallow and try again. What comes out is a weak, "I guess since we finished work early, Amma doesn't expect me home. . . ."

"Perfect!" He beams. "We won't need long."

I follow him at a distance as he leads me to the special place in question. By the time we make it to Hinchliffe Stadium, the graffiti-stained baseball field between Public School No. Five and the Great Falls National Park, I have a hunch where we're going, but Nayim's long strides don't slow until we've tramped past the grass and the gravel-covered pavilion across from the small brickwork wheelhouse Ximena called from earlier.

At the winding path that leads down to the historic factory Alexander Hamilton once built, he turns and extends his hand.

I hesitate for only a second more, before taking it. Sunlight glints off the construction equipment of the Emons' partially erected cliffside second restaurant, but the crew, busy packing up for the day, is too far away to pay us mind.

The recent drizzle also deters most aunties and uncles from lurking, so I let Nayim usher me to the colossal stone stairway monument, which overlooks the old factory, the wooden bridge that connects one end of the park to the other, and one of the larger waterfalls.

"It's breathtaking here, isn't it?" Nayim's eyes bore into me rather than the view.

I nod, hyperaware that he hasn't released my hand. "It's easy to forget because I've lived here most of my life . . . but yeah, it is. My father used to bring us here. He'd read all the plaques on the statues in the area and take us to the Paterson Museum."

Ignoring my half-hearted protests, Baba would pick me up by the waist so I could join a then-much-younger Arif and Resna on one of the rusty locomotive displays that represented our city's industrial history. He'd snap photos until his camera roll filled up, a good third featuring his thumb. Later, I would grumble while deleting those.

What I wouldn't give to go back.

Nayim studies my suddenly stricken face. "He sounds like a great man."

"He was," I reply. "He was always so proud to have gotten us to the US. He wanted us to have more than he did."

The reminder makes me ache.

Even now, the falls are somewhere I like to come when I need to be alone. I can almost sense Baba's presence when I close my eyes here, but what would he think about my present company? Would he see some of his own drive for a better life in Nayim? What would he think of my choices? That he worked himself to death so I could study and be something *more*, only to end up doing exactly what he never wanted for me?

The fact that Nayim brought me here of all places makes my heart thump so hard in my chest, I worry that it will burst through a crack in my rib cage and fly to him. Or at the very least, that he can hear it, see the sheen of tears in my eyes, and must hate me for ruining whatever special thing he wanted to show me.

Instead he smiles at me with such tenderness that my knees turn to jelly. Before I can sit down, he blurts, "Wait!"

I gape as he retrieves a red-checked blanket and a picnic basket from the gym bag, as well as a fancy-looking bottle of apple cider with a shiny foil label and two tall glasses from Chai Ho. My jaw drops when he lays out all the food on the step just below us and pats the now-blanketed spot at his side.

"You—how—why—?"

"It just rained," he murmurs, as if that's the reason for my shock.

"You did this for me?" I whisper.

He nods, taking out paper plates, plastic utensils, and oyster-pail containers with the logo of the nearest halal Chinese restaurant stamped all over the boxes. I spot desserts from the tea shop inside the basket too. In my head, I do a mental calculation of it all.

A box of fried rice, another of lo mein, yet more of prettily crimped dumplings, and then there's the clearly expensive cider among all the desserts. The snobby customers who'll someday dine at the cliffside Gitanjali would never bat an eye at this humble fare, but even with our employee discount, I know the sheer number of things he's purchased had to have cost over a hundred dollars.

"Nayim . . . ," I breathe. "This is way too much. You can't afford to splurge like this. All you ever have for lunch are Maggi noodles and rice with dhal. How will you feed yourself? Pay this month's rent?"

Save up for his guitar shop?

A hand covers mine as he shakes his head, eyes never once leaving my face. "No, Zahra. It's not nearly enough."

Oh.

No one but my immediate family or best friends have ever done something like this for me. Even Harun has only paid for our dates because of his code of chivalry and our colluding. Or maybe pity for the poor girl with the dead dad.

"But why?" I whisper.

There's nothing special about me. Nothing that could make a boy sacrifice his livelihood and passion. Not when there are plenty of beautiful girls with approving parents and the means to support his dreams.

He squeezes my hand tighter, smile dwindling even as

sincerity shines in his gaze. "My whole life, people thought I was too lazy or not smart enough to achieve anything on my own. That I wasn't deserving of happiness . . . and I believed it."

He emits a weary breath, and my heart breaks at the thought of him doubting himself like that, though I don't know why I'm surprised. People always think less of poor brown kids. Think we're charity cases and diversity picks. Here to steal their jobs and opportunities.

"That isn't true," I say with such fervor that he jolts. "You're incredible, Nayim. Those people can say what they'd like, but they couldn't do half of what you are. You've been working so hard to achieve your dreams."

The smile returns, but it feels as brittle as it is bright, like a diamond. He raises his palm to cup my cheek, tracing a calloused thumb over the arch of my cheekbone to catch an errant teardrop. His confession is quiet and fragile in the air between us. "It's been harder being here than I thought it'd be. There are so many nights I've stayed up asking myself, what the hell am I doing? Would I be better off if I gave up and went back to Bangladesh?"

"Nayim . . ." My eyes go wide.

He's always so upbeat that I never would have guessed, but before I can tell him I'm glad he stayed, that I hope he keeps staying, he says, "There must have been a dozen times when I almost quit. But you . . . *you* believe in me, Zahra. Not only that, but you *inspire* me. Ever since we met, I keep wondering what a future together could look like. A guitar shop in New

York. The two of us writing together every night like we did at the tea shop."

There it is again—that unshakable surety in his voice. When he talks like this, I can picture everything he's imagining right alongside him. It appears we both have more faith in each other than we do in ourselves.

His gaze flicks to my lips. Not giving myself the chance to second-guess the rare hum of adrenaline that trills through my veins, I careen forward and brush them against his. His mouth is soft and sweet and I sigh against him.

Never have I let myself dream about a boy like Nayim.

Except, here Nayim is, real.

He smiles in return, more genuinely this time, pulling back just enough to whisper, "Are you sure this is okay? It won't cause any problems with the guy you're dating?"

"Harun?" The mention of my fake boyfriend sends me spiraling back to earth. I cringe and shake my head. "You don't have to worry about that. There's nothing between us."

Amma, on the other hand . . .

"Good." Nayim's reddened lips stretch wider. "Because I'd really like to kiss you again."

I bite my lower lip. We're not supposed to be doing this. Being alone. Holding hands. Kissing. Our religion forbids any physical intimacy before marriage.

Isn't he worried? Guilty?

But even if I wanted to wait for him, even if we did everything by the book, would Amma ever let us be together?

And yet . . . another look in Nayim's eyes, and I see an entire future waiting for me to take hold of it. It's so easy to believe it can be real.

Taking a deep breath, I say, "I want this."

When his lips brush against mine for the second time, all thoughts of my mother, spying aunties, my fake relationship, and eternal damnation fade away.

THE AUNTIE NETWORK 📞 🔗 ⋮

Sharmila:
Meera Afa, didn't you say Zaynab matched Zahra with the Emon boy?

Meera:
Heh. They had their second date not long ago. Khenno? √√

Sharmila:
Khatun, do you want to tell Afa what you saw or should I?

Khatun:
Ya Rasul, you're always putting me on the spot! I suppose it can't be helped. The other day during the rainstorm . . .

Meera:
Yes? √√

Khatun:
I saw Zahra and the dishwasher boy at the falls together . . . but it's probably nothing, right?

Meera:
That can't be right. Zahra is a good girl. She wouldn't break her mother's heart. √√

Sharmila:
Monor khobor khew tho zanee na, Afa . . . Children in the West don't have the same principles we did, growing up. Who knows what they're thinking?

Chapter 16

It's been only a day since the picnic, but I've felt like a new Zahra since.

A braver, bolder, reborn Zahra. A Zahra who isn't afraid to dream.

It's as if I'm Ariel from *The Little Mermaid*, and the dashing prince kissed the girl—actually, *I* kissed *him*—to return my stolen voice.

After walking home with Nayim tonight, I sit at my desk and type up more of my novel, ignoring Amma's warnings about staring at screens for too long or staying up too late. Several new chapters pour from my fingertips, quieting only when Nanu comes to bed, so the clacking keys don't bother her.

It's a book I've been working on since before Baba died. Struggling with for a long time. I'm shocked how quickly the story comes now. Before long, I somehow end up with forty thousand words of a manuscript.

A whole half!

Most of it is from *before* and probably not particularly good, but it feels so nice to be able to create anything after such a long time.

This progress, combined with my lack of sleep, persuades me to call out from work to visit Passaic County Community College during its open house on Monday. Mr. Tahir is so shocked, he doesn't even complain about being left shorthanded. Before my friends can panic, or Nayim can think I'm avoiding him, I text them an update.

All of their encouragement keeps me from chickening out on the bus ride downtown, but I can't help fidgeting once I reach Broadway, gripping the straps of my backpack, a pamphlet from the school crumpled in one fist, my dinosaur of a laptop inside the bag. A cheery welcome banner hangs over the glass door a few feet away, framed by bright red columns.

Nervousness makes my sneakered feet tap the sidewalk. More than once, I have to move over so another pedestrian can pass me.

I'm going in.

I *am*.

I just . . . need a minute.

Or maybe that minute is only giving me more time to doubt myself. My imposter syndrome sounds a lot like my mother. I grimace, recalling how she asked what kind of jobs an English degree would get for me when she read my acceptance letter from Columbia in the spring.

She didn't say no, exactly, but she didn't have to. The

exorbitant cost to attend, the scholarship I lost since I could only study part-time, and the four years of splitting myself between school and a job . . . only to get a degree in a language I already spoke.

She didn't think it was worth it. That I was worth it.

I didn't want to worry her just to prove her right.

I'm so lost in the whirlpool of my fears that I don't notice the tiny woman standing next to me until she says, "I suppose it is a nice building, but not so nice that I could look at it for four and a half straight minutes."

"Wh-what?"

She frowns at the smartwatch on her wrist. "You've been looking at it for, *ah*, five minutes now." Her dark eyes shoot up to my face. "Will you be coming inside or do you need more time to etch it into your memory? No judgment either way, dear."

"N-no, I am."

My eyes dart from the top of her head, which only reaches my ear, to the bottom of her feet. She's dressed in a gray blazer, a matching skirt, and heels that do little to rectify her height situation, with a leather briefcase gripped in one hand, but neither her minuscule size nor her drab outfit nor even her youthful demeanor do her justice. She *feels* larger than life, somehow.

My gaze freezes at the lanyard and ID badge hanging from her neck, and I realize why. CECILIA LIU, it reads under the college's logo, surrounded in the same bright red as the columns ahead. She's a professor here, and oh God, what a first impression I must be making.

Professor Liu smiles at me. It's friendly, but utilitarian. "Here for the open house?" I nod, unable to manage much else. Undeterred by my reticence, she continues, "Very well. I'm on my way there. You may as well come with me."

She sets off at a brisk pace into the building, not giving me a chance to respond. My legs move of their own volition to catch up with her surprisingly quick strides, but I slow as our surroundings attract my attention.

The reception desk gives way to red walls lined with framed artwork created by past and present students, circling a much grander mural that displays the school's name and its mascot. Inside some of the classrooms we pass along the way, there are plush beanbag chairs and circular tables strewn with art supplies.

"The child development center," Professor Liu explains.

Farther down the hall, we enter what must be the main academic center. It's teeming with potential students around my age and quite a few adults who must be going back to school after a long break. Waiting in the midst of them, between signs welcoming people to the open house, are peppy-looking students in their late teens or early twenties, with clip-on badges that read STUDENT GUIDES on their school apparel.

There's a genial girl with cupcakes on her lanyard who waves at us, but before the professor can pass me off to her, I ask, "What do you teach, ma'am?"

Professor Liu stops in her tracks so fast, I almost bump into her. "I'm the co-chair of the English department. In fact, I'm due to give a presentation on degree requirements in five minutes." She studies me. "Is that something you might be interested in?"

"Um, yes." I nod so vigorously, she smiles. "I'd love to study English."

"Then I'm the woman for the job," Professor Liu says. "Follow me."

We lope through linoleum halls past the rest of the campus tour to our destination. There's a sign outside the lecture hall and an assortment of prospective students waiting within. I enter and seat myself at one of the long tables in the very back.

Professor Liu offers a nod as she passes. Beneath the steady weight of her regard, my shoulders unhunch and I sit up straight. One corner of her lips twitches in approval.

As she discusses the requirements for an English certificate with me and other potential students, I become completely engrossed. Some appear skeptical, flipping through the pamphlet to seek other options. But hearing Professor Liu discuss different genres of literature and fields of writing buoys me, particularly when I discover she's going to be teaching the creative writing course in late summer and fall. My own pamphlet ends up littered with notes.

At the end of her session, I hover next to her desk while she packs. Without turning to me, Professor Liu says, "I hope that was enlightening."

"Oh, er, it was. Thanks, Professor."

She evaluates me, eyes shrewd. "You have something to say. Tell me."

I suck in a deep breath, reminding myself: *Be a braver Zahra. Be a bolder Zahra.*

"My name is Zahra Khan," I tell her. "I don't know if I can do it next semester or even in the spring, but I'd like to enroll in your creative writing course someday."

Now she smiles, pleased. "You're a writer. I should have known."

"C-can you tell?" I wonder, awed at the possibility.

She nods. "There's something in the way we writers look at the world. I could tell as I watched you staking out the campus. At once observant and lost in your own head."

We, she said.

My heart does a merry flip. Her words are a shot of daring in my veins. I bob my head. "That happens to me a lot. I, um, taught myself to write."

"Very impressive," she replies, eyes alight.

I'm not sure she'd feel the same way if she knew it was because a popular show pissed me off so much by fridging its only brown character that I ended up writing a hundred-thousand-word fanfic to rectify the loose ending and get my one true pairing together. That eventually led to more and more fanfics and a Wattpad account with original work.

"But I'd love to learn from you and other real teachers one day," I tell her. "There's so much I still want to know."

"A hunger for learning is important for writers," she agrees. "But what's stopping you from enrolling in September? We have rolling admissions here, and you can sign up anytime."

I lower my head, clenching my backpack straps tighter. "I don't think I can afford it yet. . . ." Not if Amma doesn't pay me back. "But that's okay. Hopefully by spring or the following fall, I'll have finished my novel and be able to enroll so I can learn how to revise it."

"You have a novel?" Her eyes go round, and now she sounds excited.

My cheeks flush. "It's a work in progress. An incomplete first draft. No biggie."

"My dear," she replies, "we are *all* works in progress. I'm sorry to hear you can't attend in the fall. It's been ages since I had such a driven young writer in my ranks."

"I'm sorry too," I murmur. "But I *will* be back. I know it."

For once, I genuinely believe it.

Once the summer goes by and Harun and I "break up," I can take on more hours, save up again, get a second job if I must. By the time I need to start working less to attend school, we'll have enough. We will.

Then I can take Professor Liu's class.

"I know you will," she says. "Until then, would you be willing to let me read any of your work? I'm off for a few weeks and have time to offer constructive feedback."

My head jerks up. "Really? You'd do that, even though I'm not your student?"

"You *will* be," she replies, "so of course I would."

Before I can talk myself out of it, I pull out my laptop and share a copy of my manuscript with her on Google Docs, rambling all the while. "I'm super sorry in advance if there are lots of typos and plot holes. My feelings won't be hurt if you end up not finishing. I once tried and failed to finish *The Hobbit* four times before deciding it just wasn't for me, *not* that you have to suffer through my writing four times or anything, once is more than enough, and I'm no—"

A hand closing my laptop interrupts my babbling. I glance up to find Professor Liu grinning from ear to ear. "You truly are a writer, Miss Khan. I'll be in touch."

The words are at once dismissal and reassurance.

I skip out of her classroom and down the hall with a renewed pep in my step, feeling for the first time in a very long time—perhaps even *ever*—that my dream to be a writer someday isn't out of the question.

Perhaps it's time for this work in progress to become a final draft.

Chapter 17

I toss and turn all of Monday night. By the next morning, I have the seeds of a plan.

Oh hoh, do I have a plan! And it happens to be named after a common Bengali expression following an epiphany or the realization that you've made a big mistake: OH HOH!

It's a classic foil for Operation Zahrun. If *that's* supposed to make Amma think Harun and I are incompatible, Operation Head over Heels—or OH HOH—will hopefully help her realize that *Nayim* is my perfect match.

If she simply meets him, perhaps she'll be swept off her feet by his irresistible charm like the rest of the aunties who visit the tea shop, and by Eid, we can all laugh together.

A girl can dream, right?

Because lately, all my dreams have started to feel possible.

On Wednesday, I roll out of bed before my alarm rings.

It's so early, I'm able to corner the Tahir twins at Chai Ho without their dad present and fill them in on the specifics of my intrepid plan for the evening. As they have another of their psychic conversations, I squirm from foot to foot, wringing my hands.

"Do you think I should just leave well enough alone with Nayim?"

"No!" they exclaim simultaneously, startling me with their assurance.

Dani heaves a sigh. "Look, Zar, you've gotta be selfish every once in a while, especially when it comes to something like falling in love."

Her voice goes whisper-soft, her eyes uncharacteristically serious, and God, I could just smack myself.

When Dani first came out to us, she was so scared we wouldn't accept her and Ximena. Then Dalia burst into tears and hugged them, and I joined in, and soon we were a desperate tangle of blubbering preteen limbs rolling around the floor of Ximena's bedroom until Mrs. Mondesir-Martínez found us all, wiped our snotty faces, and made us chocolate de maní to sip.

That was the easy part.

Coming out to her parents was so much harder. Eventually, they came to believe their love for their daughter overcame every other obstacle, but it was a long, rocky journey back to a happy family for the Tahirs.

Ximena's finally gotten to the point where she's invited to family events without either of Dani's parents complaining when they have innocent moments of PDA in public. Most of the community assumes they're just "gals being pals," because while Ximena is essentially out and proud, brandishing bi flag pins on most of her belongings, Dani's not *out-out* as a lesbian with extended family or many other people. It might never be safe for her to be.

Meanwhile, here I am complaining about my straight-girl problems.

As Dalia wraps an arm around her sister, I suck in a grounding breath. "You're right, Dan. I'm going to be *so* selfish. The *most* selfish. I promise."

Dani cracks a smile. "Yeah, you'd better, goody two-shoes."

"Better what?" asks Nayim, loping into Chai Ho with one hand gripping his guitar case. He staggers back a step when we turn to face him in one synchronized motion, like a pack of wolves closing in on their prey, but the instant I see him, I freeze up.

Nayim looks . . . perfect.

He picks at the button on the cuff of his white dress shirt, probably resisting the urge to drag his fingers through his hair, which appears to be a few inches shorter than when I brought up the possibility of him meeting my family during our walk home last night.

"The imam's wife gave me a makeover," he tells me ruefully. "I told her I was interviewing for another job, but clothes like this always feel so stuffy to me. Do I look too much like a waiter?"

I shake my head, but the words are stuck.

I don't know why I ever doubted him. Of course he could pull off playing the part of the perfect boyfriend. He's so good at being exactly what he needs to survive, like a chameleon changing colors. But he doesn't look like *my* Nayim anymore, and a wave of guilt crests over me at the thought of forcing him into something he isn't, even for one night.

Can it be only for tonight?

Or will he have to keep up this pretense forever, as long as we're together?

Aren't I doing to him exactly what Amma has done to me?

"Zar, you all right?" he asks, brows knitting together in concern. "Did I . . . step in it again? I can go home and change, if you want me to? I've never met a girlfriend's family before, and I have to admit, I'm out of my element here."

The twins exchange a glance at "girlfriend."

My stomach does a flip. I shake my head once more.

Luckily, my friends have the wherewithal to take over for me and flit to either side of Nayim. While her sister supervises, Dani untucks the hem of his shirt from his dress pants, removes his belt, and tugs up his sleeves to expose his forearms, oblivious to his, "H-hey."

"Much better," Dalia says, appraising their work.

"Less office worker on the verge of going postal, more *Vogue*," adds Dani.

"*Vogue?*" Nayim parrots.

"Yeah, you know," she explains. "When they have the

models looking all rumpled, but on purpose. It's hot, trust me."

"If you say so," he relents, but he's watching me.

The Tahir girls peer between us, then make up some excuse about smelling smoke in the kitchen to give us time alone, with a final warning from Dalia about being careful not to wrinkle or get stains on his shirt. Nayim frowns at his shoes, which look pinchy and uncomfortable, and that's the last straw.

Uncaring of whether anyone's spying, I barrel into his arms and ignore his resulting *"Oomph!"* to whisper into his chest, "Thank you. I swear never to make you do this again."

The comforting thump of his heart lulls me. I feel him smile into my hair as his arms settle at my waist. "Don't worry. I'm doing this because I want to."

And in that moment, there's no more denying it.

I think I'm falling in love with him.

My revelation about Nayim is yet another frayed thread on my nerves.

I'm a ball of contained panic throughout my shift, a bomb on the verge of exploding into bits of frilly apron, but somehow, I manage to contain the eruption until we close at five.

Dalia and Dani exile me and Nayim with a box of ribbon-wrapped treats to go, stressing that they're on the house, while their father watches on in consternation. On the walk home, I become a rambling wreck—reminding Nayim of all the best ways to get into my family's good graces.

"At least you're bringing her mishti," I finally finish, trying to find a bright spot in my chaotic chasm of angst. Bangladeshis don't visit anywhere without bringing some sort of gift, typically in the form of sweets like cookies—which everyone calls biscoot even in the US—or mishti or boxes of mangoes.

Nayim frowns. "If you're that worried, we don't have to do this tonight. We can do something more fun like—"

"No!" I exclaim. He shuffles back a step at my shout, but our eyes remain locked. "We're doing this tonight. I won't back out. Just—"

"Just?"

Stay with me.

"Do to my mom that thing you do to all the other old ladies of the world, okay?"

A jaunty smile draws my gaze to his mouth. "I promise, Zahra."

Chapter 18

It feels like an answer to the silent hope in my heart I haven't been able to give voice to yet. Although I know getting caught would ruin everything, Nayim's assuredness emboldens me to grab his swinging hand in mine. We run the rest of the short distance to my house, the world blurring in our periphery, then release each other a step away from it.

Amma greets me at the door already talking: "I made shorishar ilish and bhuna murug with moong dhal tharkari, so hurry before it gets cold—"

The instant her gaze lands on Nayim, who hovers behind me, her mouth snaps shut with an audible click of her teeth. Her pupils dart between us. With the flicker of the television light behind her, an eerie shadow is cast over her face.

Swallowing a shiver, I try to remember that she's sprung a few surprise dinner guests on *me* in recent memory. Turnabout is fair play, right?

Nayim breaks the silence. "Assalamualaikum, Fufu."

"Who's this?" Amma asks at last, directing the question to me.

I feign a nonchalant smile. "This is my coworker, Nayim Aktar. You've probably heard about him from Meera Khala? The boy staying with the imam's family?"

Amma nods.

"Well, he told me he was about to go home and have instant noodles for dinner for like the third time this week," I continue, imbuing outrage into my tone so her mother-compelled-to-feed-skinny-kids instinct will kick in. It is a truth universally acknowledged among Bangladeshis that a guest on one's doorstep must be in want of at least two helpings of curry. "Can you believe that?"

Amma eyes Nayim from head to toe, taking in the present he holds and his outfit. He does his best to appear waifish and pathetic in spite of his lanky, towering frame. I, meanwhile, hold my breath. After a minute of this standoff, it's Nanu who declares, "Let them in already, Zaynab."

Score: Zahra.

I may have to listen to Amma, but *she* has to listen to Nanu.

A tense, smiling mask shrouds my mother's face as she greets Nayim properly and opens the door wider for us to enter, accepting the mishti with a dispassionate, "Oh, you shouldn't have," that sounds more literal than ever before.

She bolts into the kitchen, leaving us standing awkwardly

in the living room, scattered with incomplete pieces for the bride-zolad, until Nanu pats the space next to her on the old plaid couch for Nayim to join her.

Shaken out of his trance, he salaams her the extra-formal way and frowns at the table while setting his guitar case down on it, careful not to disrupt any sewing equipment. "I'm sorry I didn't bring anything for you, Dadi. Should I go get some mishti?"

Nanu tugs him onto the cushion. "Don't do that, betta. You're a guest. Sit."

As he moves to comply, he takes in the movie playing on the TV and his eyes grow round. "Is that *Amar Jaaneh Tumake Dhake*?"

Nanu and I trade a bemused glance, before I ask, "You watch classic natoks?"

"Uh, not much," he replies, but there's a waver in his voice and his knuckles have gone bone-pale on his lap. "My . . . mother loved them."

Crap!

When will I learn to keep my big fat mouth shut?

Thank God for Nanu, who must have also heard some of the gossip about Nayim's tragic past, because she changes the subject back to the movie. "This is an old film, older than either of you, but it's one of the greatest natoks of Nasrin Aktar's career. Her very last." She taps her chin. "Most kids these days only watch Bollywood. Your mother must have been a true fan if you know Nasrin's work on sight alone."

Nayim's Adam's apple bobs. "The biggest."

Nanu turns back to the film, where an achingly beautiful woman in her twenties sings a heartrending melody about the loss of her lover in war as she dances nimbly through her village. There's something about her ballerina grace and large eyes that glitter like gold that draws me to her, but I suppose since she's my grandmother's favorite actress, we've watched Nasrin in other natoks before. Nanu has loads of DVDs and a DVD player to play them.

"What happened to her?" I ask. "Why did she stop acting so young?"

Nanu tuts. "She had a real-life fairy tale of her own. One day, on the set of this very film, she met the heir of the illustrious Shah family. The Shahs are as close as you can come to Bangladeshi royalty. Abdul Rahim Shah was spellbound by Nasrin's beauty and they were married within a year. She gave up her Dhallywood career to be a wife and run the Shah estate, but she must have children by now."

"Heavy is the head that wears the crown," Nayim mutters.

I frown at him, worry curdling in my gut. Normally, I might tease him for misquoting Shakespeare, but I feel bad for triggering memories of his parents—or lack thereof.

Before I can move to comfort him, Nanu sets her hand on top of his. Startled, Nayim faces her and seems to soften at the tender expression she wears as she says, "Loss of one's parents can be a difficult thing, but when you get to be my age, anger and sadness fade to nostalgia and become more bearable. Live a life filled with no regrets until then, won't you?"

Nayim nods, swallowing again. This time, his irises glitter like coins themselves. My own eyes prickle at the sight of two of my favorite people getting along, but Resna saves us all from drowning the night in our tears by bounding into the room and right into Nayim's lap.

"Why, hullo?" He tips his head to the side.

"You have a guitar," she says matter-of-factly.

Nayim reaches for his guitar case as if he'd forgotten its presence, then utters a sheepish chuckle. "You're quite right, I do. Would you like me to play something for you?"

Resna considers him with healthy skepticism. "Do you know any Cocomelon songs?"

"I've only heard a few while babysitting for the imam," he admits, "but I'm not in the habit of denying requests from such pretty girls, so I'll do my best."

My sister giggles.

Only then do I hear my brother whisper, "Psst, Afa."

Arif is peeking out from Amma's bedroom, scowling at me. Casting one last look back at Nayim, Resna, and Nanu, who are all singing along to some song about the importance of eating veggies, I sneak into the room beside him and shut the door behind me.

"Is that your boyfriend?" he demands.

The raging blush that claims my face is all the answer he needs, but before he can blow up at me, I say, "Please, Aru, this is going to be hard enough with Amma. I need the rest of you on my side if I'm going to have any shot at happiness."

"Happiness?" My brother sags. "It's that serious with this Nayim dude, then? Like, *marriage* serious? What about Harun?"

I pointedly *do not* think about Harun or marriage. "What are you, Baba?" I don't think about how much more Arif resembles our father the older he gets, either. "Nayim . . . makes me happy. I just want to see where that goes without feeling like I'm bringing shame on our entire family. Is that so wrong?"

He folds his arms across his chest and mulls this over, looking more profound than any fourteen-year-old has a right to, before he nods. "I want you to be happy, Afa." A well of love bubbles in my chest. I crush him against it and pepper his face with smooches. "Ew, let go." He shoves me away and fixes his hair. "I *also* figured if I take your side now, you'll have to back me up later when I ask Amma to let me try out for the high school basketball team."

I grin. "Whatever you say, tough guy."

Amma calls for us to come to dinner.

Arif pats my arm as he passes me, one last wordless vow to have my back. I give myself a few seconds to regain my composure, then trail after him into the living room. Amma's standing at the kitchen door, watching Nayim show Resna how to play a chord.

At my arrival, she clears her throat and says tersely, "I

think we've wasted enough time on silly instruments. Let's eat while the food is hot."

Dinner goes . . . well, perfectly.

Nayim thanks Amma for going out of her way to feed him and compliments every single bite he eats so profusely that her natural instinct to preen wins out. He answers every question she can think of without so much as a flicker of annoyance, and whenever uncomfortable silences descend, the rest of us tag in to prod the conversation along.

He even plays along patiently when Nanu pulls out our family album and starts gushing about pictures of toddler-age me and present-age Resna in tiny red bridal sharis made by Amma—a time-honored brown girl tradition—until a naked baby Arif with a black string tied around his waist and a big black dot on his temple to ward off the evil eye appears.

At this point, my furiously blushing brother says, "Ugh, that's enough show-and-tell," and slams the album shut.

It goes *so* well, in fact, that Amma lets me tell Nayim goodbye alone once we've enjoyed the desserts he brought from Chai Ho. Out on the porch, we gaze at each other, then say simultaneously, "I think that went okay."

Nayim laughs, and I can't help joining him, but when I catch my breath, I realize his eyes are dark with some unknown emotion, an enamored smile that makes my knees weak stretching across his lips.

"God," he murmurs. "I wish I could kiss you right now."

"You can't. My—"

"I know. Your mother will see. Or your siblings or your grandmother or your landlady, who I hear hanging about downstairs."

"Yeah," I mumble. "Sorry."

He reaches a hand toward my cheek but doesn't quite cup it, before letting it fall away. "It's fine for now, but I hate saying goodbye, so I'll say good night."

"Night, Nayim . . ."

"Good night, Zahra."

My heart still hasn't quieted when I get back inside.

Chapter ❤ 19

Contrary to my expectations, almost no one is attempting to eavesdrop in the living room. I bet I can thank Nanu for that. She must have roped Resna and Arif into helping her wash the dishes. But Amma is sitting on the couch.

The hopeful butterflies fluttering in my belly gain wings of wax when our eyes meet, hers ablaze with grim determination. I clutch my stomach as I force my legs to take me to the couch and sit. Her hand splays across my back, rubbing up and down my spine.

"Amma, please—"

"Don't make me do this, Zahra," she pleads. "Don't force me to be the evil mother who has to tell you no."

"Why do you have to, though?" I demand.

"You're so young. You don't understand the ways of the world yet."

"That didn't stop you from setting me up with Harun!" I yell, surging to my feet despite my original intention to keep it down so no one else could listen in. I can't help it, though. Her hypocrisy makes me fume. "Why am I old enough for *marriage* with Harun, but not getting to know Nayim? I like him and he believes in my dreams."

"It's because of your dreams that I want Harun for you," she replies quietly.

My eyelids fly apart. It's the first time in years that I've brought up writing with her, though she's seen me working on it recently and has only bothered to comment that I shouldn't stay up too long doing it, clearly prioritizing my job. What could she possibly mean about Harun making my dreams come true? "How does that make any sense? How would becoming his wife at eighteen help me with college or writing?"

"Harun can take care of you!" When I start at her harsh words, she grows soft again, reaching to take my hand in hers. I'm too shaken to stop her from pulling me back down next to her. "You don't think I've seen you writing by the light of your laptop so late at night? You think I haven't seen those pamphlets of universities you hide around your room? Of course I have, and I've always wished I could give you those things, Zahra, but I can't. Not by myself. I also know, if Harun loves you, *he* can. Let you go to college. Support the family while you write."

In a convoluted way, it makes sense.

Baba took care of her when he was alive. When she lost him, she lost more than just her husband. She lost her entire sense of self and had to find it again. *Remake* herself again.

She's a very different person now from the one she was two years ago. Overnight, she went from a housewife to a single working mother.

In her generation, it's not uncommon for many women to want nothing more than to be mothers and wives. Sometimes because they choose it, to which I say more power to them. But many times, because it's all they know. It's all *she* knows.

It's the only future she can imagine where I'll be safe and happy.

"But I don't *want* someone else to *let me* do things, Amma," I answer, glaring at the coffee table, which was cleared of everything but her sewing machine when Nayim came. "I can support myself, the way Nayim does, if I have to. I've already been working—"

"I know," she interrupts. "How do you think I feel, seeing you throw your childhood away to help me keep a roof over our heads? I don't want to watch you struggle forever, shuna. I refuse to. What's more, I don't think *you* will feel the same way about Nayim when you're, what, following him from Paterson to his next destination, begging for change on the streets? You won't feel the same about writing, either. You'll be too tired for dreams."

My whole body goes cold. "How long have you known about Nayim?"

"Long enough," Amma replies wearily, pupils flitting toward her phone on the coffee table. I glare at it. Of course, the Auntie Network has always been a step ahead of me. "When I first heard about it, I hoped he was just a passing curiosity, but after the way you looked at him tonight . . ." She shakes her head. "You're more like me than either of us want to admit. I couldn't let go of your father, either."

"What?" I gasp. "Baba?"

My mother's smile is tired and sad. "We met when he came to my boro sasa's bari to meet my oldest cousin. Although his family couldn't offer much money, your father would go to America someday, like his brother. We all knew that. How could we not, with how often my Jui Afa boasted about how he'd bring her along once they married?"

A dozen responses claw up my throat, only to dissolve like acrid salt on my tongue. She's avoided talking about Baba since his death, but even before then, neither of them revealed much about how they met. Anytime I'd prompted them, their wedding album in my lap, my father would only chuckle and say he'd tell me when I was older, while Amma would claim their parents introduced them, as was good and proper. I would then lug the heavy thing back to my own bed and stare in wonder at their unlined faces.

As I grew older, it became clear that they hadn't had a luxurious ceremony. But despite the old Bengali adage that a bride should cry on her wedding day, in mourning for her previous life, beneath the veil of Amma's shari, her crimson lips had been curved in a subtle smile.

"What happened?" I finally ask, curiosity stamping out my anger enough that I unintentionally scoot closer to her on the couch. "How did you two meet?"

"We bumped into each other on the way to Jui Afa's," Amma whispers like a confession. "I knew it was wrong to like him, especially when I'd been tasked to make a dress for Jui that would take his breath away. But he was so handsome, and he looked at me, *listened* to me, in a way no one else ever had with my pretty cousin around. He saw me as more than the always-underfoot, fatherless burden I'd become to my family, so when he asked my boro sasa if *I* was of marriageable age, I begged him and your nanu to let us be together."

"So you and Baba were . . . a love match?"

My voice sounds distant to my own ears. The living room spins as I peer around it without truly seeing, my thoughts tumbling.

After everything she and the other aunties proclaimed at that wedding, after the way she's been intent on matchmaking me with Harun and orchestrating our future marriage, could it be true that she and Baba were a love match all along?

When I try to think back to how they acted with each other before his death, the memories surface bloated beyond recognition. I try to remember a sign of affection—of true love—between them and come up short.

"Yes," she replies. "We couldn't 'date' like you are with Harun. Within a week of knowing each other, arrangements had been made for us to marry. Jui Afa seethed, but her father had the final say, and he would no longer have to take care of his brother's widowed wife or daughter if I became someone else's responsibility." A humorless laugh escapes her. "It was because of my cousin's stories that I imagined America would be some fairy-tale land. That we would never want for anything in such a plentiful place." Her eyes lift and hold mine. "She never forgave me until your father died. I've often wondered if her bodwa tainted our future together from the start, because in America, we found only hardship."

Her words send a pang of hurt through my chest.

"Were things *that* bad?" I grit out.

Sure, it wasn't all sunshine and rainbows when Baba was alive. He worked six days a week at a local factory and we barely saw him, but while we still rented too-small apartments and I still couldn't splurge on the latest phones or clothes, we ate out whenever Amma didn't feel like cooking, went on trips together during vacations, never worried about the power getting cut off.

Back then, I used to ask if I could get a job for extra spending money, and he wouldn't let me, wanting me to focus on my studies, on being his little girl for a while longer.

The whole rest of your life will be full of struggles, he'd say, *so let me protect you from them for a little while longer. For as long as I can.*

My mother's revelation that our life was not simply imperfect, but *bad* for her, feels like a betrayal of my father and everything he did for us.

For her.

Amma reaches for me again, but I shrink against the opposite arm of the couch. Her hand freezes midair as she gusts a sigh. "I know you're a romantic, shuna. But love isn't the same in reality as it is in your books or Nanu's natoks. It can't fill your belly or give you a comfortable life like becoming an Emon could."

A thick lump rises in my throat. I shake my head to dislodge it, refusing to fall under her spell this time. "You can't decide what I want for me. I can't be happy as no more than some rich guy's prize, no matter how much he might dote on me."

Amma falls silent, and I hope that's that. That she will let me march off to bed and maybe tackle the issue again tomorrow, or let it go altogether, if I'm lucky.

Then she says, with all the velvet gentleness of a rose's petals, "As the oldest, you can't only think of your future, Zahra. Especially without your father to help us. As an Emon, you'll have status and someone to take care of you the way I can't, yes, but so will Arif and Resna. When it's time to find them suitable matches, people will remember their brother-in-law, the engineer, whose family owns several successful businesses."

"But—"

Her grip tightens on her knees and the thorns come out. "If, instead, you fool around with a boy like Nayim, lost in your happiness *now*, there will be a black mark on our family's reputation forever. We'll always be the Khans who lost their money in Bangladesh and their self-respect out West. Don't give up a perfect match for a summer fling."

"Amma . . ." My voice breaks. It takes several minutes to

piece it back together into some semblance of comprehensibility. "I think I could love him."

"But I *know* you love our family," she answers. "I know this is for the best. Love comes with a price like everything else. I don't want you to end up like your grandmother and me, paying it for the rest of your life."

She moves to hold me, and I almost allow it, because my heart is splintering into a million jagged shards that I can't possibly pick up all by myself without cutting my fingers on them. But I'm too angry, and she's not the one I need right now.

"I'm tired," I tell her coldly, raising my palms to halt her in her tracks. "I'm going to bed, if you don't need me to give up anything else for you."

She flinches but doesn't stop me as I march off to the bathroom and lock the door. Only then do I let the tears fall, but I'm already calling Harun.

He picks up after three rings. "Khan? Are we call-each-other friends now? Because my parents might get the wrong idea if they catch—" All traces of teasing evaporate, however, when he hears my shuddery inhale. "What's wrong?"

"We have to crank Operation Zahrun into high gear," I say. "We have to break up *now*."

Because until he's out of the picture for good, Amma will *never* give Nayim a chance.

Chapter 20

Harun and I stay up plotting well into the night, switching back over from furtive whispers to texting when Nanu enters the room with leftover mishti to cheer me up.

By the time I fall asleep, phone clutched in my fingers and dried tear tracks on my cheeks, I'm less panicked, or maybe too tired to be.

Unfortunately, that only leaves me a few hours to rest before I'm woken up by Nanu for Fajr at sunrise. The familiar motions and words help clear my head. Rather than contemplate a nap, I decide to escape to work extra early when I hear Amma puttering around in the kitchen, not wanting another confrontation.

Perhaps Allah hears my prayers, because we end up closed for inventory at Chai Ho. We've been enlisted to cater dessert for the forthcoming Bangladeshi community picnic on Garret Mountain, known colloquially as "the hill," and Mr. Tahir wants to make sure we have enough stock to feed everyone attending.

I like doing inventory. Mr. Tahir leaves me and the girls to it while he goes on a supply run to the giant Patel Brothers in Edison, which means we spend the day getting paid to chat. Ximena usually pops by but didn't pick up when Dani called to invite her.

"She's always too busy for me lately," Dani whines, rummaging despondently through the shop's collection of tea bags. "If it wasn't bad enough that we're going to colleges in different states, she's spending all her time at the wheelhouse this summer. Do you think she's going to dump me for some hot home-wrecker artist?"

I flick the back of her currently teal head as I walk past. "Mena would *never* cheat."

"She's probably prepping for art school," Dalia adds, ignoring her sister's indignant squawk. "Not everyone's undeclared like you, Dan. She has to get a portfolio ready for her professors."

Rubbing her wound dramatically, Dani concedes that we're probably right, and the Ximena problem is set aside for the time being.

Nayim, however . . .

Nayim is here.

My gut clenches every time he smiles at me with that expectant gleam in his honey eyes. I resist his every attempt to get me alone, not yet ready to talk to him about what went down with Amma last night after he left or the plan I've concocted with Harun, in case he thinks it won't work or decides I'm not worth the effort, after all.

Soon the smile melts away, and he looks hurt and confused by my chilliness. *That* breaks my heart too. God, what I wouldn't give to spare him more pain.

The bells above the bolted front door jangle as someone tries the knob. Without looking away from the spices and clipboard I have spread out in front of me, I shout, "We're closed, sorry. Come back tomorrow."

"Uh, Zar," Dalia says.

"What?" I ask, jotting down amounts of turmeric.

"Isn't that—"

"—your fake boyfriend?" finishes Dani.

My head whips up so fast, I almost break my neck. Despite my hopes that the twins were pulling my leg, there Harun is, in all his curly-haired glory, lingering outside the shop with his arms crossed over a black T-shirt, a familiar surly expression on his face.

Vaulting out of my chair, I throw the door open and blurt, "It's Thursday."

He blinks. "I . . . know?"

Upon closer inspection, he's less incensed than intrigued. He shifts from foot to foot in white joggers and black sneakers with the Nike logo across the sides as he glances past my shoulder into the shop, dark eyes unobstructed by his glasses for once. The faint notes of a Fetty Wap rap drift from his AirPods.

I poke his chest and hiss, "Don't act like *I'm* the weird one here, robot boy. Our date's not till tomorrow. They're *always* on Fridays."

"I know that," he mutters. "It's just, I usually grab coffee on my morning runs, and I was worried about you after yesterday, so I thought I'd check on you. Two birds, one stone."

Some of my ire diminishes as I take in the way he shuffles his sneakers, clearly embarrassed by his own concern. Sometime during our plotting session last night, he pressed me about whether I'd be okay at work and I made an offhand comment about him trying our drinks, but I didn't think he'd show up so soon.

Didn't think he would be *worried* about me.

In spite of everything going on, I grin up at him impishly. He glowers as if he can read my mind, then adds with a smirk, "Besides, if you're going to be breaking my heart, shouldn't I at least get to meet the guy you're dumping me for? Gotta make sure your Prince Charming isn't a dragon in disguise, princess."

It's my turn to scowl, though I still find this protective big brother act oddly adorable. I cross my arms. "Too bad, 'cause we're closed today. You'll have to come back."

"Yeah, yeah. Guess I'll see you tomorrow."

Before he can carry on with his jog, the twins dash past me and grab him by a sleeve each, declaring, "Oh, come on, Zahraaaa, we can get Pretty Boy his coffee" (Dani) and "It's absolutely no trouble" (Dalia).

In a flash, Harun is seated on one of the barstools in front of the counter, glancing around like he has no idea how he got there. Although he's the one who claimed to be curious about my workplace and coworkers, his shoulders have tightened up as if he's only now grasping what he signed up for.

I can't blame him—the twins are a force of nature. You know how a tsunami sometimes follows an earthquake? Yeah, that.

Meanwhile, I do my best not to bang my forehead against the door. When I turn around, to make matters worse, Nayim slinks out of the kitchen, arms piled with cardboard boxes of flour and sugar. He cocks his head. "Thought we weren't taking customers."

Dalia and Dani shoot me a look.

Catching my bottom lip between my teeth, I offer a brisk nod to assure them he already knows about my matchmaking debacle. Or . . . most of it, minus this latest development. The twins introduce the boys to each other, taking great care not to refer to Harun as my fake boyfriend this time, lest Nayim feel threatened.

I tense up, awaiting my boyfriend's reaction, but he only snaps his fingers. "Oh, yeah. Zahra talks about you all the time, mate."

Harun scowls at the hand Nayim holds out for long enough that the latter's sunny expression clouds over, then deigns to accept it. In the frigid voice I haven't heard since the first date at his house, he says, "She's mentioned you, too. Once or twice."

Ouch.

"Um, yeah," I laugh awkwardly. "We haven't talked much about our personal lives. The friendship thing is pretty new."

Nayim's cordial smile returns, but Harun barely looks up from the counter at him, fingers drumming on the marble. I stand there, unable to understand why he's acting like such a jerk when *he* wanted to meet Nayim, before giving myself a mental smack.

Of course. He's uncomfortable around new people. I know that well enough from our first couple of meetings, from what Sammi Afa revealed about his allegedly sensitive nature, and straight from the source after our impromptu performance at TGI Fridays.

It can't help that no one else knows about the blowup with Amma except him, putting him in a tough spot. I place a hand on his shoulder, in the hopes of setting him at ease. "Even though that's the case, you've been a very good friend to me, robot boy. If it weren't for your encouragement, I don't know that I would have taken a chance with Nayim."

"Oh?" The boy in question's eyebrows arch into his hairline. "Then I owe you one, mate. Zahra is the best thing that's happened to me in a while."

"I know," Harun mutters, before his eyes widen a fraction, as if he hadn't meant to speak aloud. My face reddens as his closes off, his pupils lowering to regard the countertop like imitation marble is the most fascinating thing in the world. When he continues, his voice is light. "I'm happy to help. The sooner you get serious with someone else, the sooner we can end our fake relationship and go back to our normal lives, right?"

All I can manage is a nod. I have no idea what to make of him or all this right now. Dani comes to the rescue by slinging an arm around my neck. "Come on, that's not entirely true. Zahra called you her friend, didn't she? That doesn't have to change."

Harun stiffens, while Nayim reclines against the table holding the espresso machine, both clearly interested in my answer. I nod, and Harun's sullen expression softens into something more familiar, like it usually does when we're alone together.

"Cool," continues Dani. "I'll whip us up some drinks."

She releases me to push past Nayim to the machine, but Dalia fills the void left behind at once, giving me an encouraging smile as she steers me over to the barstool next to Harun. Wincing, I realize that I must not be hiding my trepidation very well if the twins are going out of their way to be so vigilant.

"Let me guess," Dani tells Harun, looking between the punny menu board she came up with and his sour expression. "Coffee, black, one cube of sugar? I call that our un-espresso-ive." His brows press together at her sixth sense, but he doesn't deny it. Dani directs her attention to her sister next. "Iced Kashmiri chai latte with extra whipped cream, right?"

"Yes, please," Dalia chirps.

"And for Zahra—"

"I'll take care of Zahra," Nayim interrupts.

Before any of us can respond, he sets out to complete the task of preparing my order, filling a kettle with Assam and Darjeeling tea leaves, milk, pinches of cardamom, cinnamon, and cloves. The mouthwatering smell saturates the entire shop in pleasant steam. When the kettle whistles, he pours the tea into a glass teacup, adds the exact amount of sugar, and decorates the mildly frothy, aromatic concoction with a single star anise.

He slides it over to me.

"Th-thanks," I stammer, hyperaware of Harun observing the exchange.

"Tell me if you like it," Nayim says. "I've been practicing."

Although there's a strange tension simmering in the shop outside his kettle of tea, the masala chai tastes perfect. I release a contented sigh without meaning to as I take a tiny sip.

Harun glares at the shifting black surface of his own coffee, then downs it so quickly that I flinch at the prospect of him burning himself. He slides the mug back to Dani and stands up. "I've gotta go. Busy."

Nayim cocks his head and both brows, then glances over at the box of ingredients he abandoned. "I suppose I'd better sort out my errands too, before Mr. Tahir comes back and chews me out for slacking off."

"Wouldn't that be tragic?" comes Harun's snarky reply.

"Are you okay?" I ask him. "You're being moodier and more monosyllabic than usual."

There's no way the roof of his mouth isn't peeling right now, but he turns to me with the subtlest approximation of a smile. "Peachy. We're still on for Operation Zahrun tomorrow at my folks' Eid party, right?"

Wordlessly, I nod, and his jaw tightens.

"What's that?" Nayim peers between us.

Before I can figure out if I imagined Harun's injured expression or decipher what it means, it's replaced by one that veers on smug. He claps Nayim on the bicep as he heads toward the exit. "Inside joke. Don't worry about it."

A bewildered Nayim glances at me next, but I only shrug, not yet ready to tell him everything that happened last night because I don't want to hurt his feelings. I know firsthand how much it stings when you're told you're not good enough.

"It's not a big deal," I say. "You should finish with the inventory."

For a few seconds, Nayim considers me with such serious intensity that I break out into a sweat. It's clear that even if he wasn't suspicious about my relationship with Harun earlier, my cold shoulder and Harun's caginess have changed that. I want to admit everything, but the explanation snags in my throat, chased by the hope that it will be easier after tomorrow.

At least, that's what I tell myself after both boys leave me to my thoughts and I get back to work and try to figure out what the hell just happened.

Chapter ❤ 21

When I was a kid, I would rise with the sun for Eid, sneak into my parents' bedroom, and crawl under their blanket while they slept, oblivious to the fact that they'd only just returned to bed after morning prayers.

I couldn't help it.

The whole house smelled different during Eid, of fresh dhonia fatha, dried thez fatha, and other herbs; the spiced beef minced or braised for somosas, biryani, and haleem; the eggs that were boiled alongside roasting chicken for kurmas and chickpeas for chotpoti.

In the days preceding it, Amma and Nanu would let us kids crimp the edges of naikol fitas once they filled the pastry with coconut or cut shapes into the turmeric-yellow dough for lobonor fitas. When they weren't looking, my brother and I would grab fistfuls of the salty dough to eat raw, until they chased us away, giggling, with wooden spoons.

It was like swallowing sunshine.

Although we were too excited to sleep the night before, the whole world would wake for Eid. Visitors and video calls would pervade our apartment with cheery cries of "Eid Mubarak." Baba and Amma's cousins in Bangladesh would WhatsApp them pictures of the cattle they'd purchased for Eid al-Adha.

We'd dress up and visit others, eat till our bellies burst, and go to the masjid for jamaat, returning home after midnight carried in our parents' arms, with treats and money that cooing adults had pressed into our fists after pinching our cheeks red.

These are some of my loveliest memories.

But as you get older, holidays lose their wonderment.

Amma's done her best to rally us in the years since Baba's death, for Resna's sake, and the Tahirs always welcome me with open arms to celebrate with them. But if it weren't for my sister's innocent anticipation and the increase in the chores expected of me around then, I'm not sure I'd remember Eid al-Adha anymore.

At least for the Ruzar Eid, Eid al-Fitr, breaking the monthlong fast feels noteworthy, but the Kurbanir Eid is yet another day in America, even in a place like Paterson.

That's why it feels so strange to be standing in front of Amma's bedroom mirror now, the ruffled skirt of my multicolored lehenga swishing over my ankles like the train of a peacock's feathers. Rather than spend the night cooking, my mother and grandmother pieced this outfit together for me by repurposing scraps of the bride-zolad's fabric so I could steal the show at the Emons', but enthusiasm and hunger don't flutter in my belly today, only drunken butterflies I attribute to the beaded bodice being too tight.

Amma comes up behind me and puts her chin on my shoulder, lighting up at my reflection. "Do you like it?"

I almost shake her off, but her sallow cheeks give me pause. Although I'm angry at what she's forcing me to do, it's become a weary sort of anger, a flame doused in a bottle, and it won't serve me well to unleash the smoke yet.

Remember the plan, I remind myself, nodding as I say aloud, "Everything you make is lovely, but Harun and I have been trying this dating thing for weeks now and . . ."

My already crimson bottom lip flushes darker when I trap it between my teeth. Her gaze travels to it at once, like I expected it to. Her sigh reverberates down my back. "And? I hoped you two were getting along. If this is because of that other boy—"

There it is.

"This has nothing to do with Nayim!" I pivot in her arms, eyes big and solemn. "I know you like that the Emons have money, and that they want a princess-in-law, but Harun hates me."

Amma scoffs, "How can that be so? You're a beautiful, resourceful, and kind girl from a respectable family. Ar bala khoi faitho?"

I suppress a groan. A more naive Zahra might be flattered that Amma doubts Harun could find anyone better, but I see through the ploy. Thankfully, I've already rehearsed these lines, so they tumble out without preamble: "American kids don't

care about stuff like that, Harun least of all. You remember
that he grew up around white people, right?"

"What does that have to do with anything?" she asks. "He
seems mindful of tradition. Wasn't he the one who requested a
chaperone in the first place?"

I throw my hands into the air. "Because he wanted to get
away from you. All of you. His cousin Sammi was too busy
powdering her nose to watch us properly and ended up ditching
us to hang out with her own friends."

For a second, the idea of insulting Sammi's good name
gives me pause. Bad-mouthing Harun is awful enough, though
both of us have agreed to do whatever's necessary to end this
matchmaking masquerade, but Sammi genuinely believed she
was doing a favor for her cousin, helping him heal his broken
heart.

Then the bangles on my mother's wrist clink when she
covers her mouth, and I know I'm too close to stop now. I drop
my voice a decibel, peering up at her through my kajol-caked
lashes pleadingly. "I've tried so hard to make this work for you,
Amma. Like I always do." She flinches at my words. They're
a low blow—a reminder of the money I lent her—but a short
guilt trip won't hurt her after the many she's taken me on.
"Can't I please stop?"

I watch her struggle to process everything I've confessed.
Her rouged lips pinch into a thin line as she peers blankly at a
small grape juice stain on the carpet.

She looks more exhausted than usual, despite her makeup

and the shari she's chosen for the occasion. Another blade of guilt lodges in my chest at the awareness that I'm the reason when I've always worked so hard to ease her burden.

Before she can respond, Arif and a skipping Resna pop up beside Nanu, attired in their own Eid outfits. They each clutch Tupperware containers of the dishes Amma prepared for the Emons—because we can't possibly go empty-handed no matter what else is on our plate.

Amma's bleary eyes lift to us and she sighs. "We can't cancel at the last minute when the Emons have been preparing for this. Let's get through the day and we'll figure out how to move forward later. Accha?"

I nod, having expected that.

Soon we're in the Uber to the Emons', but though I should be buoyed by this first victory in the coming war, I can't help stealing glances at Amma, noting the lines around her eyes and mouth, the sad stories that they tell.

The urge to confess right then and there rushes up my throat, but I bite the inside of my cheek until a familiar house materializes at the top of the hill.

Harun opens the door.

I trudge up the stone path to his porch last, and for an ephemeral eternity, the two of us simply stare at each other, his frame in the doorway shielding both of our faces from the audience of our curious families.

He sucks in a sharp breath as he takes me in but doesn't

speak while beckoning me inside. I flash a secret smile, then let it fall away.

He looks good, as always, but it's the first time I've seen him in traditional attire. His black fanjabi is simple, silver jacquard floral patterns threading the collar without any other adornment, tailored to be taut across his shoulders while loose and flowy over his legs.

Elegant and efficient, just like him.

Brown girl TikTok would have a field day at the sight. Hell, one day he's going to make some other girl *very lucky*, but today's not that day and I'm not that girl.

If only we can prove that to our parents.

Like clockwork, Pushpita Khala gives me the customary three consecutive Eid hugs, then spins toward her son. "Betta, isn't Zahra such a shundori? This dress—"

"—is way too colorful," he deadpans. "Did a rainbow throw up on you? It might give me a migraine if I stare at it for too long."

Her jaw drops. My family gapes too. Harun, for his part, pinches the bridge of his nose for full effect. I hide a grin behind the hands I bring to my mouth in an effort to play at affront, lowering them only to sputter, "W-well, yours is so dull! You couldn't add a colorful scarf or something so you didn't look like Edgar Allan Poe?"

The furrow of his brows clearly asks, *Edgar Allan Poe, Khan? Seriously?*

Aloud, he sneers, "I think you're wearing enough color for all of us."

We glare at each other.

Internally, I commend Harun for being such a great actor, musing whether he can give me any tips, until Mansif Khalu takes him by the elbow. "Now, now, you both look like you could use a nice meal. That always makes your mother feel better when she's in a mood, na keetha?"

"Dhuro go, you're embarrassing me!" chides his wife, but there's no heat in it.

Everyone is watching Harun and me, expressing varying levels of alarm, so the two of us cross our arms in synchronized outrage and declare, "Fine!"

"You will *love* how the Paterson restaurant is coming along, Zaynab," Pushpita Khala continues, trying valiantly to steer the subject to something less cantankerous. "You should come with us to the grand opening at the end of the summer. Inshallah, we may even have *other* reasons to celebrate by then."

"I would love that!" Amma replies, her earlier reassurances to me forgotten.

Of course.

Gnashing my teeth, I take my sweet time removing my heels to give myself a few extra seconds alone. That hot coal of anger has rekindled in my chest, pulsing like a fever through my veins, but if I stop to let it run its course, it will consume me—turn everything I've worked so hard for, everything *Harun and I* have done, into ash.

Instead I run through the plan again and again like a mantra, not even noticing that I'm huddled in a crouch next to my shoes, until Harun's light touch and quiet, "Hey," snap me out of my trance.

I look up at him.

His dark eyes are luminous in the golden light of the room, as steady on my face as his hand is on my shoulder. The solid presence of him anchors the tempest in my heart enough that I accept his help to stand, clinging to his hand for a moment too long.

"You still want this, don't you, Zar?" he asks, in that same gentle way.

I swallow the lump in my throat and jerk a nod. "More than anything."

Even if I didn't need this to work out so I could finally have a shot at being with Nayim, this has never been about me alone. I pressured Harun into my attempt to turn the tables on my mother, forced him time and again into situations where he wasn't comfortable, troubled him with my confidence. But rather than resent me for it, he's chosen to stay by my side.

Dalia was right. Somehow, without my ever realizing it, this boy has become one of my closest friends. I owe it to him as much as myself or Nayim to end things tonight. It's fitting that our third official date will be the last.

"Right," Harun whispers, a sound so soft, it's no more than an exhale. My eyes dart to his lips when he quirks a tiny, half-dimpled smile. "Then put your game face on, general. You can't get cold feet on me now."

A brilliant grin overtakes me as I give in to the temptation to poke the dimple at long last. His skin heats up at my touch. "Don't you chicken out either, robot boy."

He bats my finger away, huffing a laugh, but the expression smooths into his usual mask of disgruntled apathy the instant we enter the dining room to find everyone gawking in our direction, waiting for us. Harun stomps past me without so much as a second glance, taking one of the two empty seats between his mother's and mine.

Not for the first time, I marvel at how easy this facade is for him, and how different it is from the Harun I now see beneath it.

What might have been, if the two of us simply . . . met somewhere, before all this? If he decided to go to Chai Ho for his coffee before a morning run by pure coincidence, or if someday, we bumped into each other on the Columbia University campus?

Would we still become friends?

In all likelihood, Harun and I would be nothing but strangers exchanging brief pleasantries, two planets spinning in opposite orbits around the same sun, never converging long enough to realize how similar we were at our cores.

I scowl at his back and try to imitate his heavy footsteps. If the Emons want a princess-in-law so badly, I'll show them *exactly* what kind I am.

As I march past Arif, my brother whispers, "Oh, good, I worried you strangled each other."

"The night is still young," I snipe back, throwing myself

into my seat so dramatically that my skirt balloons around my legs and makes the table tremble.

"Zahra," Amma grits out through a smile, a warning for my ears only.

Ignoring her, I take stock of my surroundings. The Emons' dining room resembles something out of the home-and-garden magazines I sometimes flip through while standing in line at the supermarket. Bone china plates trimmed in painted gold flowers, cloth napkins in rings shinier than the ones I wear on my fingers, freshly prepared dishes covered by gilded lids on matching trays, a tiered tower of somosas and other fitas comprising the centerpiece. More settings than there are people.

Amma's Tupperware containers seem woefully tacky in comparison.

"Who else is coming tonight?" I demand.

My rudeness renders Pushpita Khala momentarily speechless, while the young man sitting across from Harun next to Mansif Khalu clears his throat. I turn, half-surprised, to find Hanif Bhai, looking as severe and reproachful as ever.

"Oh, hi," I continue, before tacking on, as if an afterthought, "Assalamualaikum."

"Walaikum as-salaam," he responds tersely, clearly so irked by my behavior that he can only muster up the will to be somewhat formal, not go all-out.

It's too bad. I like Harun's cousins and have felt no small amount of envy at how close they all are, since most of my extended family lives far away. In Bengali, there's not even a word for cousins. They're simply an extension of your siblings, and though I don't have many of my own nearby, it's been nice to feel included with Harun's recently.

Making them hate me is a casualty of this war that I can't avoid, though.

Pushpita Khala regains her composure enough to chirp, "I invited Hanif and Sharmin to thank them for their help these past few weeks. Her husband can't leave the hospital tonight, but Sharmin is bringing her brother, too. Shaad couldn't wait to meet you! Did Harun tell you the two of them have been inseparable since they were in Pampers? Why, his mother and I would coordinate their clothes—"

"Ma, stop," Harun cuts in, a note of genuine fluster creeping into his voice. "Zahra doesn't care about stuff like that."

In any other situation, I'd kill to hear every painstaking, blackmail-worthy detail about Harun twinning with his cousin, but I clear my throat and say, "I *am* getting hungry."

"Oh, of course." The way his mother deflates almost makes me tack on a compliment about how good everything smells out of guilt, but Pushpita Khala perks back up. "The others are on the way. I'd hoped we could all catch up on the patio before they arrived, but . . ."

But Harun and me acting like spoiled brats ruined all her plans.

Good.

At least that means *our* plans are going off without a hitch.

Chapter ❤ 22

Sensing the imminent defeat of Team Parents, Amma strikes the next blow, but the waver of her voice betrays her nervousness. "You've worked so hard, Afa. Khoshto theelam. Can I help serve?"

Pushpita Khala shakes her head. "Na, khoshto arbar keetha? I prepared appetizers to tide us over until dinner. It wouldn't be Eid without those, would it?"

She lifts the gold-plated lids off an array of painted ceramic tureens: cool, pink custard flecked with chunks of strawberries and bananas; mishti doi with a delicate crust of brown sugar and date molasses that must be cracked to reach the yogurt, steaming hot chotpoti with tamarind chutney, boiled egg halves, sliced onions, and whole chilis in smaller metal containers around the main bowl; shredded beef swimming in the golden broth of haleem.

So many appetizers, I could happily give up dinner for the rest of my life.

My stomach utters an unseemly grumble. Paying no mind to the heat that crawls up my neck, I grab one of the stacked, empty glass bowls next to the tureen containing custard and pour some of the dessert into it. A little sweetness will make this night a less bitter pill to swallow.

Pushpita Khala beams but hesitates before handing me a spoon. "Harun told me you don't eat away from home often, Zahra. If you're not comfortable using a dessert spoon, I can get you a ladle to sip out of? We wouldn't want you to spill on that beautiful dress your mother made."

Hanif's thick brows vanish into his hairline. Mansif Khalu chokes on his own bite of haleem, but manages to cover it up with a sputtered, "Whatever Zahra prefers is fine."

"What!" Amma exclaims, in time with Arif's mouthed, *Afa, what the heck?*

Harun flashes me a smirk. The glower I shoot back at him is less fake than the others, although we both agreed we'd accept any humiliation levied tonight to make our disdain for one another appear that much more authentic.

Before my mother can disabuse the Emons of the misunderstanding, I push aside the offered spoon and slide my bowl closer, a patented Good Bangladeshi Daughter smile plastered on my soon-to-be-smudged lips. "Thank you, Khala. I prefer eating with my hands."

"If Api is eating with her hands," Resna announces, slamming a tiny fist, "I want to too!"

Amma buries her face in her palms.

Nanu cocks her head at me, as flabbergasted as anyone else, then says, in her best impression of a referee, "Zaynab, don't fuss. Eating with our hands is the Bengali way."

In spite of this, I note she and the rest of my family *do* accept spoons.

I almost regret not doing the same when I realize how slippery each fruit has become in the gloopy custard. It takes every bit of my hand-eye coordination not to stain my dress, but I stubbornly refuse to stop shoveling it into my mouth with my fingers, going so far as to lift the bowl to my lips to slurp out the last dregs.

Then I slam the bowl back down onto the table. In the reflective glass of the showcase across from me, I spy a mean custard-stache on my upper lip, accompanied by a slowly dripping custard-beard and a blot of custard on my nose.

Turning to Harun sweetly, I say, "Can you pass me some tissues from that roll over there? My napkin is already messed up."

His face scrunches up in passable disgust at the grungy cloth I wave in front of it, but the faintest hint of a smothered laugh is at odds with his ire. "Why're you asking me? They're closer to you."

"Zahra, shuna, let Amma help you," my mother interrupts in a reed-thin voice I can tell is on the verge of snapping. She practically throws a wad of paper towels that she must have torn off the roll on the table while I was focused on Harun.

I bite my lip to keep from laughing.

It's working! Operation Zahrun is *finally* working!

We both know our parents enough to target their Achilles' heels.

The Emons want a mild-mannered daughter-in-law from a reputable family, so the rest of the community stops looking down on them for their own checkered family history. Amma desperately wants a rich son-in-law who'll take care of me.

We're showing them the polar opposite.

And it's time to hammer the final nail into the coffin.

Fuming, I shove my face an inch from Harun's and poke his chest. "No, I don't want it from anyone else. I want it from you, asshole. You couldn't do one nice thing for me?"

He jerks back, chair scraping and pupils blown wide. "N-not when you're getting this crap all over my face. What the hell is wrong with you? Princess thing getting to your head?"

"Me?" I seethe, jabbing him again. "*You're* the spoiled rich boy."

We both hold our breath as time freezes around us for an instant, waiting, waiting, waiting for the inevitable thud of the other shoe dropping. For our parents to acknowledge that this was a terrible mistake. For Amma to take me home and chew me out about humiliating her, but have no choice aside from letting me have my chance with Nayim, since a future with Harun will be out of the question.

It's not what I hoped for when we began this.

I wanted her to respect my efforts to please her and trust

me to make my own choices. If anything, my antics tonight might prove to her I'm not just the opposite of what Harun's parents want, but the opposite of someone who can make good decisions for herself, like what her future career should be.

I never anticipated falling for Nayim when all this happened, but once I fix things with him, I can figure out how to glue everything else back together again, like I always do.

I *can.*

The tension is broken by yet more custard.

Harun yelps as a gloop of it is pitched right into his open mouth by my sister, who is now standing on top of the table like a rampaging sugarplum fairy. Arif's grip on her knobby knees does little to tame her, the custard smearing her own face transformed into war-paint.

She points at my date and shouts, "Stop being mean to my api, you big jerk-face!"

Harun looks at a genuine loss for words. The one eye that I can see behind his smeared glasses is bigger than the dishware.

I haven't escaped the custard-splatter either, but the beginnings of a toothy grin are stretching across my face, because *this* must be it.

The point of no return.

There's no way any of our parents can salvage this wreckage.

"Perhaps," Amma says tightly, "I should take my children home."

Pushpita Khala tries to respond but manages no more than a nod, while her husband replies, "Ahem, that might be best."

If it didn't mean getting found out, I would fling my arms around Harun and do a victory dance. One corner of his lip twitches beneath all the custard in acknowledgment of the glee that must be glinting in my eyes.

But before the triumph can truly sink in, my mother continues, "I don't know what's gotten into Zahra tonight. I think she was upset with me and took it out on Harun, but that's no excuse. Afa, Bhai, amare maaf kori deo."

"There's nothing to forgive," Pushpita Khala answers, smiling tentatively back. "They're very young and have only been on a few dates. Harun was the one to ask to try this until the summer ended, but clearly, that was a rash decision."

"Why don't we see how things are coming along at the grand opening?" Mansif Khalu adds, prompting his wife to clap her bangled hands together, clearly pleased at their ingenuity.

Hanif slams his hands on the table and rises to his feet. "Khala, Khalu, hold on! Hasn't this gone on long enough? This girl—"

But the rest of his words grow tinny and distant as my stomach plunges to my feet. How can the Emons still want to keep going with this sham of a relationship after tonight? My eyes take in the blurry shapes of the figures around me.

Harun grimaces at this blow, but doesn't otherwise object.

Resna hides her face in Nanu's neck while Arif wags a finger at her.

And Amma . . .

Relief dawns across her face like a sunrise, brightening her rouged smile and flushed cheeks. After everything that's happened, she has the gall to be *happy* that the Emons will give us another chance. Despite every awful thing Harun and I said and did to each other.

Despite how I begged her to stop.

It's not that I can't stop it myself. That I'm some shrinking violet in an ATN Bangla tragedy where brown girls are forced to bend to others' wills. I could have ended this farce at any time. But I've been desperately waiting for her to finally look at me, see me, and *understand* me. To say, of her own accord, that she has faith in my choices and will support me no matter what.

It would be easy to tell Amma, once and for all, that I'm no longer playing this game with Harun and the Emons, and she would have to live with it.

Would forgive me eventually, and things would return to normal.

But I'm tired of always taking the high road. I want to know what exactly it will take for her to decide *I'm* worth more to her than the wealthy son-in-law of her dreams.

The fire I've been bottling in my chest since she first tricked me into going on that blind date with Harun erupts from my lips like molten lava as I whirl to face her, unable to contain my own words: "Enough is enough, Amma! I can't do this anymore. Tonight was miserable enough, but I refuse to spend the rest of my life with someone who's still in love with his secret ex-girlfriend!"

My tirade silences everyone else at once.

Somehow, during the course of it, I'd screwed my eyelids shut without noticing, but open one now to find myself face-to-face with my ashen mother, who whispers, "That can't be . . ."

"Harun, is that true?" a still-seated Hanif asks quietly.

"What?" Mansif Khalu booms, while Pushpita Khala shakes her head and says, "Na, na, na, na, my betta would never do that. He wouldn't keep anything like that from us, nai ni, Harun?"

I bite my lip, pupils flicking to Harun as the realization of what I've done sinks in. His lips part in shock, then press together so tightly, it's obvious they're trembling. The hurt he wears is blatant, and so is the fact that I've majorly messed up.

"Harun, I didn't mean—"

He ignores me, his sole focus on his livid parents. "Ma, Abba, we're not—we didn't—we broke up already. I'm not—"

"So there was a girl?" his father challenges.

His mother's dark eyes film over with tears. "You hid her from us, betta? For how long?"

"Harun," I attempt again, reaching for his arm. "I'm—I'm sorry—"

"No." He cuts me off with a shake of his head, voice growing frigid even as his fists quiver at his sides. "No, go on. Tell them. It means getting what you want, doesn't it? So do it."

I peer between him and Amma, who is clearly waiting for an explanation. Harun's parents and cousin are tense with anticipation too, while the rest of my own family gawks.

Although we never discussed using this particular leverage, we did agree to do whatever was necessary. I guess that makes this okay, but guilt curdles in my belly as I explain, "He had a girlfriend he'd been seeing for years. A girl he knows from school."

"An American girl?" his father asks, pivoting toward his son again. "Is that what the tuition money I worked seven days a week to afford went toward? For you to fool around with bideshis? To mortify me now?"

Pushpita Khala speaks more gently, but the pain in her words makes Harun flinch. "Is she the reason why you've been so withdrawn from us? This whole time, I thought it was something we did, but you . . . This girl . . ."

"Lily." Her name is a weapon on Harun's tongue. He directs the blow at me, curling his upper lip in disgust. "At least *she's* studying to be a doctor. You think I'm supposed to beg to support some freeloading starving artist for the rest of my life?"

I flinch away from him and hiss, "Low blow, Emon."

"Well, that's all you know how to take," he retorts.

Okay, ouch.

Before the situation can escalate further, Mansif Khalu steps in with a brisk, "That's enough."

"I think it's time for our guests to go," adds Pushpita Khala, coming to stand between me and Harun. "We have some things we need to discuss as a family. Clearly."

This time, there's no underlying warmth or understanding in either of their responses, but Amma wriggles her way toward us with her palms up in surrender, nonetheless. "Ji, of course that would be best. We can discuss this more once everyone's cooled off?"

That infuriating note of hope remains in the query.

Pushpita Khala's smile grows stiff. "Dekha zaibo."

It's not a no, but certainly not a yes. A polite dismissal.

Harun refuses to so much as look at me as we plod past him to the door, but Hanif glares daggers that I almost expect to slice me.

This is what I wanted.

What we wanted.

An irrefutable win.

But if I've won, why don't I feel like celebrating?

Chapter 23

We hover awkwardly in front of the Emons' gate for our Uber, avoiding the stares of their dog-walking and barbecuing neighbors.

Although I'm sweating buckets in my long-sleeved dress outside the house's central air, the summer heat is preferable to staying in there.

It was worse than anything I imagined leading up to tonight.

That should be a *good* thing, but I already find myself missing how things were before. Pushpita Khala sending us home with leftovers to replace the original contents of our Tupperware. Harun's offers to drive us back. Meeting his gaze in the rearview and sharing a secret glance, a smile no one else was privy to.

We both got what we wanted . . . right?

It takes every ounce of my willpower not to sneak a peek at his bedroom window.

In all fairness to my mother, she's the picture of calm that entire time—unnervingly so, in fact, while the rest of us squirm on the sidewalk, cicada song suffusing the silence.

The instant we enter the minivan, our Decidedly Not Harun driver closes the partition separating us, bopping his head along to Egyptian house music. Nanu shoos Arif and Resna into the very back seats alongside her, affording Amma and me a modicum of privacy in the middle passenger seats.

Amma pounces on me. "How could you do that?"

"Do what?" I ask, crossing my arms.

A blotchy flush flares across the bridge of her nose even as her lips whiten from being squeezed together so tightly. "Amare keetha faiso? Do you take me for a fool, Zahra?"

I heave a breath.

Despite acting so flighty, and often doubting her own ability to take care of our family without Baba, Amma is one of the smartest and most resilient people I know. Which is why it bothers me all the more that I'm the one puzzle she either can't figure out or doesn't want to.

"No," I murmur at last. "I know I was acting weird—"

"Your behavior was completely unacceptable," she interrupts. "Since when could you not *use a spoon*? You made our family seem so backward in front of them. How can I ever show my face in town again? I did not raise you to behave like such a—a—"

Behaya, beshorom, be-other qualities I'm lacking because I'm such a flagrantly disrespectful daughter and person.

"I *know*, okay?" I proclaim before she can choose one, so loud that the startled driver meets my eyes in the rearview disapprovingly. *Get in line,* I glare back at him. Harun's words cut me deep enough for tonight, fake or not, and I don't have any room left for Amma to rub salt into that wound. "I just . . . it was all I could think to do. No matter what Harun or I said or did in there, you and the Emons seemed dead set on us being together. I couldn't take it anymore."

She's quiet for a moment, playing with the lids of the half-full plastic containers in her lap that Pushpita Khala returned earlier. I wince when she says, in that *I'm not mad, just disappointed* hollow voice that's somehow worse than getting yelled at, "If your behavior wasn't appalling enough, what you did to that boy was wrong, Zahra."

"What?" I gape at her, unable to believe what she's saying. "I tell you *he's been with some white girl* and you still find a way to blame this on me?" I whip toward the window. "I should have known all that mattered to you was his money and not how I feel—or how he feels, for that matter. What kind of sexist garbage is this? He can do no wrong and I'm just supposed to accept—"

"Oh, stop," she says, frowning. "This isn't about any of that."

"It is, though," I reply, scowling at her again. "You're fine with him dating whoever he wants, because he's a boy, but when I told you I liked a boy, you—"

A sharp shake of her head interrupts me once more. "No,

Zahra. No matter what you might think, this isn't about Nayim. It's about Harun. I'm not sure how you learned about his girlfriend, but you shouldn't have flaunted his secret that way, in front of his parents and cousin. You did more than embarrass our family. You humiliated and hurt him."

"That was pretty messed up," I hear Arif whisper from the backseat.

"Messed up," Resna's squeaky voice agrees, though whether she comprehends the situation remains to be seen.

Although Nanu doesn't intervene, her silence is revealing enough.

Tears sting in my eyes and nostrils, but I refuse to let them fall, wrapping my arms around myself to quell my trembling. What hurts the most is that Amma's right. But that she can have so much sympathy for Harun and never me breaks my heart.

"No matter what, I was always going to be the disappointment if I didn't go along with your plans, wasn't I?" I ask in a hoarse whisper. "I try *so hard* to be what you want, but I can't do anything right in your eyes."

Her fists ball in her lap, but before she can retort, the driver tells us, "We're, ah, here."

Amma immediately storms out of the car. The rest hesitate, but follow her to the apartment. The driver watches me pityingly but says nothing. To reward him for not being a busybody, I give him five stars and a tip higher than I can afford.

That weekend is the Bangladeshi community picnic.

Folks from every part of Bangladesh gather to eat, socialize, and play games, competing for the honor of their districts—and prizes—*Hunger Games*-style.

When Mr. Tahir orders Nayim to come along and help carry boxes, I volunteer to accompany them, while Dalia and Dani supervise the shop.

Their father grunts but doesn't protest.

Nayim smiles and I make myself smile back, praying I'm doing a decent job of masking the residual sadness that roils in my gut. Between the financial blow I took and Harun's one-word responses every time I send him a text, I need to escape my life.

Even if only for a day.

The extra pay and fresh air won't hurt either.

In the nearly six hundred acres of land that encompass the reserves, surely I might get a minute to sneak away with my boyfriend? I'm not naive enough to believe true love's—or true "I really, really like you's"—kiss can solve my problems the way it does in fairy tales, but I worked so hard to get to be with Nayim that I may as well enjoy it, right?

A couple of rented yellow buses pick us up at the Great Falls. Some girls I know from school call me over to sit by them, while Mr. Tahir instructs Nayim to join him and a chatty group of uncles in the back, who hold covered trays, boxes of Dunkin' Donuts, and other assorted snacks on their laps. He nods at me as he passes, and I notice his guitar case strapped to his back. Maybe he has similar plans to be alone?

We reach the park in record time.

Garret Mountain overlooks Paterson, Woodland Park, and Clifton. Although I visited the park many times before Baba's death, we haven't had a chance to return since he passed, and not just because tickets to the picnic are a hundred dollars a family.

I can't help following Nayim to the railing above the city. The buildings below look like points of a broken crown, studded with jewels of glass and feathery smoke, framed against a bright blue tapestry of sky embroidered with clouds and sunshine.

"It's beautiful," Nayim says, watching me.

Before I can agree, a familiar voice bellows, "Api!" and then Resna's pudgy arms wind around my legs, her cherubic face squished against my knees.

"Resu, what are you doing here?"

The answer to my question appears from the direction of the parking lot: Amma and Arif, surrounded by a gaggle of aunties and their children. My mother's eyes widen when she notices where Resna has gotten off to, then narrow at the realization of our present company.

No doubt sensing the daggers she flings his way, Nayim says, "I'd better go help set up or Boss Man will throw me off a cliff."

Amma watches him go, then returns her attention to me.

I almost expect her to walk away without a word, since we've been giving each other the cold shoulder since the Eid party yesterday, but she says, "I didn't know you were coming to the picnic with Mr. Tahir."

"I didn't know *you'd* be here."

Amma's best friend, the Lady Whistledown of Paterson's gossip mill herself, Meera Hussain, answers in her stead with a teasing, "Your mother has been so busy with that new job of hers, I had to force her to take a break today, Zahra."

"You shouldn't have paid for us," Amma chides.

"Nonsense," says Meera Khala. "My own children are too old to be seen with me anymore. Rumon is out with his friends, and Raisa had a work function she couldn't skip. As you can see, your bhai is too busy for me too." She juts her chin at her husband, a short, portly bald man holding a clipboard who oversees many of our local events. "So let me live through you and your precious kids, Zaynab." Before Amma can raise another objection, she adds, "We can talk about the upcoming Bangla Mela, too. It would be wonderful for business, wouldn't it?"

My mother relents. "Ji oi, Afa. You're right, of course."

She shoos Arif and Resna off to sign up for the games. I try to beat a subtle retreat as well, since Mr. Tahir is scowling at me from the picnic area where he's setting up, but get swept into a tidal wave of eager aunties. They grip my arms and begin to carry me over to a secluded copse of dogwood trees, under which they spread out blankets away from the busier picnic area where the food is being prepared.

Sensing a lost cause when he sees one, Mr. Tahir marches over, carrying boxes of the tea shop's sweets. To Amma and the other women, he says, "Assalamualaikum, ladies. Please enjoy these desserts from Chai Ho and find me right over there if you'd like a cup of tea." He then lowers his head to whisper in my ear, "You can stay with your mother for the time being, so long as you're selling her friends on how delicious our treats are, Miss Khan." Gritting a smile at us all, he finishes his spiel with one last ingratiating advertisement, "If you like what you taste, find our booth at the Bangla Mela next weekend or visit the shop any day on Union Avenue."

Pink petals dust my ponytail as I sit with the box of treats, holding them out to the aunties like their personal waitress. Flakes of shonpapri fly from their mouths as they volley questions at me about work and school, and then at last, calculatedly, one maneuvers the topic to Harun. "I heard Zahra has been seeing the Emon boy. Is it serious?"

The others titter, heads bobbing between Amma and me.

"Well," my mother says demurely, wrists folded in her lap, "there isn't much to say anymore. Zahra and Harun are very young, after all. They only saw each other for a handful of chaperoned dates before we decided they weren't ready for an engagement."

A harmonized string of *ohhhhs* rings out.

"That's a shame," another auntie muses. "I met Harun at a wedding once. The Emons don't have the same family stature as you Khans, but what a good-looking, well-mannered boy!"

Her friend snorts. "I say it's for the best. His *mother* is so obnoxious. You'd never be able to stand her if she were Zahra's shashuri."

The first auntie gives her a playful smack on the knee but doesn't refute this. "Could you imagine if she were here? Her son may be the strong, silent type, but she'd boast our ears off about what she made him for breakfast if she could."

"More like, what their *cook* made him," scoffs her friend.

Picking uncomfortably at a loose thread on her shalwar, Amma tries to come to Pushpita Khala's defense. "She can be quite sweet once you get to know her. . . ."

"To think she's from a Gulam family, though," tuts yet another woman, blowing right past my mother's comment. "Who knows? Perhaps her great-grandfather served yours, back in the day. But I suppose family bongsho is less important these days than the groom's potential." Her gua-stained lips curve in wicked amusement. "And that boy certainly has potential."

"Handsome, rich, *and* educated," Meera Khala agrees with a milder smile. "He would have been a perfect match for our lovely Zahra. It's too bad it didn't work out."

None of them spare a second to wonder how I might feel about them discussing my love life right in front of me, but I'm used to their "children are meant to be seen and bragged about, not heard unless we're interrogating them" mentality. I almost wish Mr. Tahir had dragged me off to work, especially when the topic shifts away from the Emons to laser-focus on me.

"Zahra has grown into a beauty," a grandmotherly woman in a gray-and-white shari says. "I still remember when her knees used to knock against each other whenever she ran the relays at the picnic. Never did want to participate, that one."

"She used to bring a book to bury her nose in," laughs her daughter, as my ears turn pink, recalling how they'd joke, *Boys don't want girls who are smarter than them, so why do you read so much?* "Those books were bigger than she was."

Yet another auntie scans me from head to toe. This one I recognize from work, though she's dolled up in a heavily embroidered shalwar kameez today that must be hell in the sweltering summer heat, even beneath the shade of the dogwood trees. "At least her beauty means the Emon boy is only the first of many." She lowers her voice into something sneering. "But I'd be careful if I were you, Zaynab Afa. Ulubone mukto chorano. If you aren't careful who you give precious, pretty things to, they'll be damaged and lose their value."

I stiffen.

It's a backhanded compliment, calling me a pearl to be taken and lost, like I have no say in the matter. It throws me back to what my mother told me after that fateful dinner with Nayim, except it's Harun they're insulting now.

In a clipped tone, Amma says, "You don't need to worry about that. Zahra's a smart girl. Even if she weren't, she has me looking out for her."

Just then, a rousing cheer erupts as Resna and the other

children in her age group bolt down the hill toward a finish line set up for the picnic's first relay race. My baby sister elbows aside the two boys closest to her and throws herself over the ribbon, shrieking a battle cry.

Arif, on the sandy pitch not far from the race, becomes a recognizable speck when he stops his soccer game to whoop, "Woo, yeah, that's my sister!"

I grin and clap, until I notice the auntie from earlier evaluating the exchange with her nose scrunched like she's been sucking on a lemon. "Charming. I saw your littlest one making the boys cry while playing kabaddi, too, Zaynab. Respectable in-laws will come in handy when it comes time to marry *that* one off."

"She's already darker than Zahra and burning worse in this sun," laments her friend.

The first auntie lifts her chin, vindicated. "I hope she never becomes as tomboyish as the one Tahir girl. I don't know how their parents will ever find matches for those sisters when one dresses like a boy and the other is so fat. My sons wouldn't spare them a second glance."

Annnnnnd that's about as much as I can take.

Ignoring my mother's warning look, I bare my teeth in a Good Bangladeshi Daughter smile so sweet, it would rot your gums. "It's *so* kind of you to worry about the rest of us, Khala, but isn't that your youngest son in the baseball jersey pulling worms out of the ground? You might want to stop him before he eats them. . . ."

The auntie gasps and leaps to her feet, shouting, "Shubie, not again!"

Meera Khala slaps her knee and guffaws. When Amma frowns between the two of us, she says, "What, can you blame the girl? Zoba had it coming, running her mouth like that. I find those who judge other people's children always end up weeping over their own one day."

Her words censure the rest of the group. Soon they focus on less scandalous subjects, like the Bangla Mela, and whether they want to see the equestrian center, Barbour Pond, or Lambert Castle today.

"I heard the castle is closed," one of the surviving aunties points out.

Only mildly thwarted, they decide to take a stroll around the pond first, giving me a window to escape at last. I should be happy to be free of their rumors and snooping, but though I managed to embarrass Zoba Khala with Shubie's help, I can't get her words out of my mind.

They sound like Amma's.

Chapter 24

I set off down a gravel trail, intent on finding Mr. Tahir and Nayim, but I'm so lost in my thoughts, I end up wandering farther than intended.

"Psst, Zahra," someone calls.

I glance around the forest on either side of me, unable to hear past the faint strains of conversations in Bengali and folk songs blasting from faraway speakers. Nayim waves at me from under the tree he's propped against.

"How'd you find me?" I ask.

"Once I helped him get ready, Mr. Tahir said I should go have fun," he replies. "It sounded more like a demand, actually. Then I noticed you all by yourself and figured I should follow so you don't end up getting eaten by a bear."

I scoff. "A bear? Are you serious?"

He points at a sign I somehow missed that reads BLACK BEAR CROSSING. "Deadly."

"My hero," I snark, then bite my tongue when the

conversation with the aunties rushes back. "Nayim, look, I—"

He closes the gap between us and takes my hand. "Whatever you have to say, it can wait. There's something I want to show you first."

"But—"

"We'll be all alone," he promises.

Reluctantly, I let the matter drop, since I'd rather not air my family's dirty laundry in front of a hundred gossipmongers who'll never let us live it down.

Running with his hand in mine is a familiar comfort. I try to write this moment into memory, despite Amma and the aunties warning me that I'm dooming everyone I love just by letting myself feel anything for him.

Nayim's breathless, "Ta-da!" stirs me from my waking nightmare.

He's shepherded us outside the barred-off entrance of Lambert Castle, the private-residence-turned-museum formerly owned by silk baron Catholina Lambert, who ran a prominent mill in historic Paterson.

"We shouldn't be here," I hiss. "It's closed."

"Only the museum," Nayim replies breezily.

He releases my hand and vaults himself over the wooden gate, then pitches a daring look my way—the same look that emboldened me to do things I never would have dreamed of until this summer. The look that always unleashes a dozen butterflies inside my belly.

Shaking off my nerves, I link my fingers with his and climb

into the granite and sandstone courtyard. Across from the stone lions that guard the arched doorway, facing a fountain, sits a wrought-iron bench. Rather than dropping ourselves onto it, Nayim lures me deeper into the castle until we reach the entrance to the observation tower.

Surprisingly, no one tries to stop us.

We're alone here.

Any remaining opposition dies in my throat when I stare out past the narrow stone columns of the tower toward the city. All around us, the world unfurls itself, providing a panoramic view of Paterson framed by the New York City skyline.

I've never been up here.

A breath catches in my throat as I stray to the lip of the tower, but it's the first note of Nayim's song that makes me hold it. I swivel to find him clasping his guitar and realize that's why he's brought me here, so he can play for me at last.

Before I can utter a single word, his enchanting voice permeates the gazebo. "Zahra, tumare sara zara zai tho nai."

The lyrics echo off the pillars surrounding us, cascading over me with such love and yearning that my eyelids fall shut of their own volition. Every other sound dies away, stripping the world empty of anything but Nayim and his assertation that he can't bear to be apart from me.

"My north star, to you my heart like a compass always guides."

His song is the most bewitching thing I've ever heard. On his perfect lips, my name is a prayer. Even in my wildest fantasies, I could never have imagined someone wanting me the way he claims to. It's an invocation in English and Bengali, at once only for me, and something he proclaims to the world.

"*Zahra,*

Zahra,

Zahra . . ."

My knees buckle me onto a convenient bench, but the cool stone does nothing to bring me back to my senses. Tears bead like dewdrops on my lashes, and in spite of my best efforts to blink them away, a few trickle down my cheeks to the hard floor.

Nayim's fingers fall still over his guitar strings when he notices. "Whoa, Zahra, you're crying! Do you . . . not like it?"

"No, I love it," I say on a shuddering breath, but I can't bear to look at him.

He sets his guitar on the ground and kneels in front of me, taking my hands in his own, his chin cradled atop our entwined fingers. His eyes shine like gold in the sunlight that streams between the pillars, though shadows dance across his cheekbones and frowning mouth.

"What is it?"

The sight of him only guts me more. "It's—you're so good, Nayim."

"That's no reason to cry, is it, love?" he asks, quirking a tiny smile.

I don't smile back. "It's not fair! It's not fair how no one will know but me, just because of who you are. Not fair how no one wants us together or how we can't pursue our dreams because we're poor. I always thought Amma and other adults were ridiculous for caring so much about something so vapid, but money decides everything, doesn't it? It isn't fair."

New teardrops leak from my eyes at every word.

Nayim murmurs soothing nonsense in an effort to comfort me, and when that doesn't work, says, "I've been writing this song for you for ages. I hoped this would be the most romantic place to sing it. Instead, you're sad."

"I'm sorry," I mumble, gazing over his head at the breathtaking view, which twists a knife in my heart. "It's beautiful here. Your song was beautiful." *You're beautiful.* "But being in this castle reminded me how easy Catholina Lambert must have had it. His lovely life, high above the clouds, watching people like us toil far below. It's been more than a century since this place was built, but nothing ever changes, does it?"

Nayim's brows draw together in concern. "You're scaring me, Zar. Are you okay?"

"No," I confess. "I'm not okay. I've always known it, but the fact that I'm far from a princess feels more real to me than ever."

"What's going on?" he asks. "Is it . . . your mother again?"

All at once, I blurt out everything that happened with Amma, as well as how the women at the picnic have only reinforced the idea that there's one path for me, the one where I let a nice wealthy guy like Harun take care of me forever, because otherwise I'm sentencing myself and my family to a lifetime of struggle.

By the time I finish, I'm sobbing openly, until Nayim's arms wrap around me. I dry my face on his soft shirt, which smells of sugar, the lullaby of his heartbeat against my moist cheek.

"Everything will be okay," he whispers into my hair.

I choke out a watery laugh. "It might not, actually, but if I have you, maybe at least some of it will. Thank you for being here."

His arms tighten around me, but he goes quiet. I worry I've offended him with my lack of faith, but then he pushes me back by the shoulders enough to peer into my face, the light in his golden eyes dimming.

"I mean it, Zahra," he says. "If you're unhappy here, you don't have to stay. Let's leave."

"L-leave?" I stare at him, uncomprehending. "What do you mean? Where would we go?"

"Anywhere you want," he replies. "Everywhere, if need be."

I laugh again and start to say, "That's sweet," but the stubborn set of his jaw doesn't falter, stopping me in my tracks. "Wait, are you serious? We can't run away. My whole life is here. What about your guitar shop? Didn't you always imagine it in New York City?"

"I did," he answers. "But Paterson, New York, Bangladesh . . . They're just places, and if I've learned anything since leaving home, it's that places are temporary. You, Zahra. *You* matter to me. As long as I'm with you, I can figure out somewhere else to open my shop. Texas, California—hell, maybe Paris, like we talked about that one night."

My head begins to shake of its own accord. This can't be the Nayim I know, who's sacrificed *everything* in pursuit of his dream. The Nayim who inspires me. It can't be so easy for *that* Nayim to up and leave the future he had his heart set on.

"Everything I know is here," I say. "My family is here. Even if we could somehow afford jetting around the world like that, I couldn't possibly abandon them."

Nayim's grip tightens on my shoulders. "Zar, please. I know something about families like yours, who try to make you into their puppet, pulling your strings till they snap and you're left broken. I don't want that to happen with you. We can leave before it does, and we'll be okay. I know . . . because I've done it before."

"You've done it before?" I parrot. "I don't understand. . . ."

I gape at him. How does this fit into the pieces of the Nayim puzzle I've collected so far? Now that I think about it, there are so few, because we've known each other for such a short time. Because he shares so little.

If he wants me to run away, perhaps he doesn't know me very well either. Losing my father changed my world for the worse. Robbed my sky of the sun, reaped the life from my earth. Nayim should know that. Nayim should know how much the people I have left mean to me. How scared I've been of them slipping through my fingers too.

How can he ask me to go?

"Zahra . . ." He licks his lips and considers his words very carefully. "The truth is . . . my family is still alive in Bangladesh."

Shock jolts me out of his grasp.

"Wh-what . . . ?" I stammer. My feet back away of their own volition, and I can't stop shaking my head in disbelief. "What do you mean, they're alive? How could you even joke about something like that, knowing what happened to me? Knowing . . ."

And yet, I desperately want it to be a joke, because if it isn't, it means he lied to me. That he's *been* lying to me since the moment we met.

"I didn't lie," he says, like he's reading my mind, smiling at me as if I'm some stray to mollify with crusts of kindness. "All those rumors about me started the second I arrived in Paterson, so I just . . . let everyone believe what they already wanted. It was harmless."

"But you let *me* believe it too," I snap, angry tears flowing freely now. When he tries to reach for me again, I slap his hand away. "I get that you didn't owe me anything at first, but after you found out about my dad . . . how could you not tell me?"

Nayim watches me for a long time, before he whispers, "I liked you not knowing who I was before. I spent my whole life trying to live up to what my father wanted me to be. Playing a role for everyone around me. But you, Zahra . . . You're the first person to like me as I am. Like me for me. I wanted to hold on to that for a little bit longer."

"Except this *isn't* you," I snarl, willing myself not to care about the hurt that makes him flinch. "You're still playing a role, Nayim, but what's a game to you is my *life*. I'm not just playing at the poor orphaned immigrant like you."

His lips tremble, then squeeze together. "I'm sorry I hurt you," he says, amber eyes piercing and voice suddenly forceful. "But what if that didn't have to be your life? No matter what you might believe, my feelings for you have always been true. We can run away. We can go to a place that has stars, see the *whole world*. Be each other's family."

Fresh tears well in my eyes as I shake my head. "No. You say your feelings for me are real, but if you actually loved me, you'd know I *have* to be here for my mother, grandmother, and siblings. I can't leave them. I'm sorry."

As I make to climb out of the observation tower, he calls after me, "I thought you were adventurous. I thought you were brave. A dreamer. The Zahra I was falling for would never be a puppet for her family."

His words are a slap to the face.

I spin around. "My family is all I have left in the world."

"Some families only hold you back and keep you small," Nayim says, fury rising in his voice. "If they cared about you half as much as you do about them, they'd want you to come with me. Don't you see that your amma is making you miserable?"

A flare of indignation sparks in my chest. My mother may be far from perfect, but how dare he judge her after two meetings without knowing all she's been through? All she's sacrificed?

"I don't *want* to go!"

At this, Nayim goes quiet for a moment before his jaw tightens. He picks up his guitar and straightens. "So what will you do now? Stay here and be with Harun like an obedient little girl, just because it's what she wants?"

The sparks billow into an outright flame.

How can he stand here talking about Harun when I ruined our friendship to keep him? To make him happy?

"Well, at least Harun isn't a selfish ass," I spit, fists balled at my sides. "Unlike you, Harun cares about the people he loves. Harun is reliable."

Nayim considers me, heartbreak written all over his face. "You're not who I thought you were. I thought you loved me."

I stare at him in total disbelief. Love? How could he presume to know what love is truly about after this? It's not just a feeling. It's about trust. And showing up, about commitment, about putting the needs of those precious to you before your own.

Like I did for him.

I set aside my dreams all over again, gave up Harun, for a chance for Nayim and me to be happy together, here, only for him to ask this of me. Ask me to choose between him and my family . . . that's not love. I'm starting to wonder if we knew each other at all.

"It's not enough," I whisper heatedly. I barely know myself

anymore, much less the boy who stands before me. "Goodbye, Nayim. It's—it's over."

He doesn't chase after me. I'm not sure if I wanted him to, but I wait until the tower is a speck in the distance to drop to my knees under a silver bell tree and cry.

Chapter 25

Nayim absconds from the picnic without telling Mr. Tahir,
which I don't hear the end of for the whole bus ride back. But
when he doesn't show up to work the next day or the following
or the one after that, even our gruff boss starts worrying.

"His phone is disconnected," Mr. Tahir tells us after making a tenth attempt at contact. "The imam says he suddenly
decided he had to go back home."

He ran away without me. The fact that he could disappear
from my life after insisting we were meant to be together
sends me reeling through a cycle of emotions—from despair
to anger to disdain and back again. Still, I can't help missing
him whenever I go to the pass-through window at Chai Ho
and don't find him there.

And I can't help wondering if he's okay.

After three days of my moping around and shooting constant,
fretful glances at my phone, hoping to hear that he's not dead in
a ditch somewhere, my friends reach their breaking point.

On Tuesday night, as I steel myself to walk home alone at half past five, Ximena pops up with her arms crossed like a bouncer's at the entrance to Chai Ho.

Her presence startles me, since Dani has been lamenting how hard it's been to pin her down for most of the summer. When I risk a peek over my shoulder, I find the Tahir girls hovering behind me, Dalia with a duffel bag over her arm, Dani with both of hers outstretched like a zombie who's found premium brains on sale.

I gulp at the three of them. "What's going on?"

"We're kidnapping you," Dalia says cheerily.

"We thought it was time for another epic sleepover at la casa de Tahirs," Dani adds, then pauses, deliberating over her words. "Or is it *de los Tahirs?*"

Ximena glares. "You promised you'd practice your articles, babe."

"I will, I will!" Dani grins. "I'll knock the socks off your abuelita one day with my Spanish, I swear. Can't say the same about Creole yet, though."

I groan. While I've always loved visiting the Tahirs since I was a kid, because they grew up in an actual *house* that their parents *owned*, and I'm relieved Dani and Ximena seem to have made up, the last thing I want right now is to watch them bicker like an old married couple when my own love story is a joke.

Nayim has vanished off the face of the planet. Although Harun hasn't ghosted me outright, he's been standoffish since the night of our fake-up. I tried to broach the topic of the dinner to apologize, but he dodges the subject every time I bring it up.

I'm not good at statistics, but I'm 98 percent sure I've betrayed him to the point of ruining our friendship for good. That, or he didn't mean what he said about being friends in the first place.

Either way, sorrow twinges in my chest every time I send him a math meme or ask how Rabeardranath Tagore and his cousins are doing, only to get a monosyllabic response. Should losing a friend I've had for a month hurt so much?

"There's too much going on right now," I tell the friends I still have.

"Which is *exactly* why you need a sleepover," Ximena argues.

I shake my head. "Look, I appreciate you going out of your way to put this together, but it's super last-minute. My mom will expect me home for dinner—"

"We already told her," Dalia singsongs, giving the bag a jostle. "She let me go over and pack your pj's, khul balish, and toothbrush during my break. I even snagged your copy of *To All the Boys*, in case you want to complain about the changes while we marathon the series."

"So stop doth protesting too much, lady," says Dani, utterly unashamed of her terrible ye olde English grammar. "You have zero excuses."

My eyes grow round, then abruptly brim with tears. All this time, I've been afraid of them abandoning me for college, yet here they are, considering every possible way to accommodate me so I have a good time.

"Oh, Zar," Dalia says.

"If you don't wanna go, you don't have to," a panicky Ximena adds.

"No, I want to," I blubber. "I just—I love you three so much."

"We love you, too," they chorus, moving to squish me into a group hug.

That's when Mr. Tahir lumbers out of his office, sees us, and sighs. "This is going to become a 'thing,' isn't it?" We nod in tandem. "Will you ladies be requiring a ride, then?"

Still gripping each other, we nod a second time.

I'm glad I relented to the slumber party, because it ends up being just what the doctor ordered, the perfect prescription for my bruised and battered heart.

Mrs. Tahir is on her way out the door to meet her husband after his car pulls into the driveway of their cookie-cutter house, but stops in her tracks upon noticing me and Ximena exiting with her daughters. Her round face lights up as I salaam her.

"Waalaikumsalam!" she exclaims. "Oh, I haven't seen you in ages, Zahra jaan. How have you been? Did you forget about your Hajar Auntie?"

A mix of shame and amusement prompts me to smile at her sheepishly. "No, Auntie. I've been busy since graduation."

All six of us are congregating on the front porch, no doubt

looking strange to the neighbors, but the probability of being watched doesn't stop Mrs. Tahir from extending a hand to pat my head the way she used to when I was a kid.

I've always liked her. The polar opposite of her stern husband, she would let her daughters, Ximena, and me do whatever we wanted during our childhood sleepovers, providing a steady supply of Pakistani snacks to fuel us. Not a regular auntie, but a *cool* auntie.

Her attention turns to Ximena next and she tuts, "What about you? Daniya has been moping endlessly for weeks because you bhooted her."

"Ghosted, Ammu," Dalia corrects, while Dani goes as red as her currently crimson-dyed hair and yelps, "Ammu! Don't tell her that!"

"My bad, Mrs. Tahir," Ximena replies, rubbing her neck.

Ignoring her daughter's indignation, Mrs. Tahir muses, "Perhaps I should stay and make my famous nihari. You loved it last time you came over."

Her husband groans. "Meri jaan, I see them every day. Too much, in fact!"

"Well, I don't!" she retorts.

"You were the one who asked for these date nights," he fumes. "Why don't you come see them at the shop, where I don't have to make a reservation?"

Before they can begin full-on arguing, I interrupt, "Thank you, Auntie, but I promise I'll come back another night. Mena too, right?" Ximena bobs her head. "You should go."

Mrs. Tahir frowns, but reluctantly succumbs when Dani says, "Ammu, we already ordered a bunch of pizza. The Domino's guy will be here in like thirty minutes."

Dalia tugs on the strap of my duffel bag. "And since Zahra and Mena are staying the night, you can make nihari for them tomorrow for breakfast."

"Now that that's settled, can we please leave?" Mr. Tahir asks.

"Ji, ji, calm down." Mrs. Tahir yanks me into one last bone-crushing hug, then does the same for the rest of the girls. "Khuda hafiz! We'll be back soon."

Mr. Tahir mouths, *Good job*, but even his undying appreciation is no match for his strict brown dad schtick. Before he returns to the car with Mrs. Tahir, he tells Dalia, "Make sure there's no funny business." He looks directly at Dani and her girlfriend at the last two words.

A beat of silence passes, before the Tahir girls whine, "They're so embarrassing!" while Ximena and I exchange an awkward shrug.

We pile into the house behind the twins. It's not Emon-huge by any means, a cozy two-story that always smells of spices and herbs, currently decorated with leftover moon-and-star-shaped lights, lanterns, and glittery hanging signs that read EID MUBARAK.

The twins have their own small bedrooms upstairs, which become relatively large when you open the door connecting them, but Dalia drops my bag on the carpet in front of the TV and says, "Cool if we camp out here? There's more space."

"Sure." I glance around for the closest closet, where I know their parents store extra blankets and pillows. "What can I do to help?"

She grins and pushes me onto the couch. "You can sit back, relax"—the remote magically materializes in my hand—"and enjoy five straight hours of *To All the Boys.*"

I hurry into the bathroom and change. When I return to the living room, everyone else is dressed in their pj's too, and Dalia has her hair tumbling in loose waves down her back, sitting on the couch. Her sister and Ximena, meanwhile, are snuggled up on the love seat, whispering to each other as an atmospheric Taylor Swift song plays from Ximena's phone.

Dalia pats her lap. "Let me braid your hair."

It's a demand, but such a sweetly phrased one that I can't help plopping onto the carpet in front of her. Within the next few minutes, Lana Condor's face fills the screen, and my copy of the book with all its dog-eared pages and Post-it notes is lying by my side.

Soon, the pizza arrives, and I'm stuffed full of food and contentment, but the more the trilogy continues, and the rifts between Lara Jean and Peter grow harder and harder to surpass, the more difficult it becomes to ignore the throb in my chest.

It's as the series comes to an end that the first tear drops.

Despite my attempts to muffle errant sniffles into my upraised knees, eagle-eyed Dalia notices the tremor in my shoulders and says, "Zar, what's wrong?"

That summons Ximena and Dani over to us at once, while Dalia kneels too.

I shake my head as I dig my palms into my eyes, scooting away to put some space between us. "No, please, don't let me spoil tonight. I feel like I'm always crying lately, and I don't know why. It's so cringey."

The Tahir girls trade a helpless glance from either side of me on the carpet, while Ximena digs her fingers into the cotton of her shorts, still standing over us. She's the one who breaks the silence first, with a heated, "No offense, but that's bullshit, Zar."

"Mena, what?" Dani gasps, her sister equally stunned.

Ximena's brown eyes blaze at us. "We've got to stop pretending everything's all right all the time. It isn't, and it's okay that it isn't."

"Mena . . . ," I whisper.

Her harsh tone takes me aback. I recall how she implied at the furniture store that I was being shortsighted, mourning something I couldn't have rather than appreciating what I do.

When I tense, she softens and sets a hand on my knee. Her skin is smudged with paint and charcoal in a few stubborn spots, a comforting and familiar sight. "We're your best friends, Zahra. If you can't be real with us, who can you talk to? If the reason you're sad now is because of what you told me downtown, then Dani and Dalia deserve to know too."

The twins gaze at me pleadingly.

I know they won't push me if I refuse to explain, but in that moment, I realize how right Ximena is. They want to know, they want to help, and it isn't fair that I've been building this wall between us without giving them a chance to find a ladder.

"Ever since we started getting our college acceptances, I've been scared," I tell them. "Maybe even before that."

Maybe since Baba died.

"Scared of what, Zar?" Dalia broaches gently.

I take a deep breath, then divulge every insecurity that's been eating away at me since spring. "Of . . . losing you. All of you. You have all these adventures waiting for you in college, while I'll keep living the same sorry life. I'm terrified you'll make better friends when you're there. I'm terrified to be without you."

Quiet follows. I take a quick breath in and hold it.

I can't look at them, because I'm afraid to see how selfish they think I am reflected in their expressions. While they're planning slumber parties to cheer me up, I'm resentful of the opportunities they have.

Except that isn't so.

I *am* happy for them. I'm just tired of being sad for myself all the damn time, and so desperately scared of letting anyone else slip away.

Dalia hugs me first, bowling me over onto the floor like a kingpin. "Zar, you could never lose us. Maybe we can't be around all the time, but you're stuck with us for life, no matter where any of us might go, so please, please, please stop torturing yourself with something that won't happen."

"Yeah, what she said," Dani adds, squirming into my other side, her fiery hair splayed around us on the cushy carpet. "It's true that I can't wait to go to college. I've daydreamed about Dalia and me having our own dorm room for years. But those dreams have always included you, Zahra, college or otherwise." She levels a dead-serious look at me. "Hell, you could decide to sell hyperrealistic unicorn figurines instead of going to college, and I'd support the crap out of you."

"Um, I might have a question or two first," Dalia says, "but me too."

A hysteric giggle bubbles up my chest, at odds with the rivulets of teardrops that continue to glimmer down my cheeks. My friends are somewhat teary-eyed as well.

Tugging them both closer, I murmur, "Thank you. Love you." Only then do I notice Ximena loitering above us, rubbing one of her biceps while frowning at our pile of gangly limbs. I flash her a smile. "You too, Men. Come here."

She wriggles between Dani and me right away, burying her nose in my neck. Her breath tickles when she says, "I love you all, too, but . . ."

Dani props herself up on one elbow. "But?"

Ximena turns to lie on her back, staring up at the ceiling. "But I don't think I want all that anymore. College. I meant what I told you at the furniture store, Zahra. There are other options out there, and . . . I think I want to explore them."

"What does that mean?" Dani asks, curling to face her.

Ximena swallows and licks her lips. "I'm not sure yet."

Another long stretch of silence follows, where none of us are quite sure how to react, until Dalia says, softly, "I know it's scary, but things are changing. That's why we're having this sleepover in the first place, isn't it? One last hurrah before they do?" One by one, the rest of us nod. "Then maybe . . . it's okay not to know everything, and just have a good time with each other, like we first planned? Even if only for tonight?"

Netflix choosing that moment to loudly blare the opening of the next show on the twins' queue makes our decision for us.

We finish the rest of the now-cold pizza and cheesy bread, squeal over brown girls in ball gowns on the Kate Sharma season of *Bridgerton*, and stream an episode of some Marvel show Dani's been dying to watch, before the other girls succumb to exhaustion sometime close to two a.m.

Dalia dozes off with her head pillowed on her arms on a couch cushion. Ximena and Dani aren't far behind, snoring on the love seat, the unanswered questions between them temporarily forgotten. Ximena's head rests on Dani's shoulder, while Dani's cheek flattens Ximena's curls. Poor Mena had been too drowsy to even remember her silk cap.

They'll all have cricks in their necks tomorrow, but I don't have the heart to wake them. Smiling tenderly, I tiptoe over to the hall closet and grab three spare quilts, draping one over Dani and Ximena and another over Dalia, who snuggles into it at once. The last one I wrap around myself like a cape.

I'm not sleepy yet, though. In fact, I've been struggling to sleep since Eid, which means Nanu hasn't had to tempt me out of bed with breakfast to do Fajr prayers for the first time in *ever*. Sadly, try as I might, none of my prayers have come true yet.

Cross-legged on the bottom step of the stairs so I don't disturb anyone else in the house, I rifle through Dalia's travel bag to see what else she's packed. My groping fingers tense when I feel the spirals of the notebook I wrote in that night with Nayim after work. I take it out and open it to a blank page.

Dalia must have swiped it from my desk before she left, figuring I might want something to write in, since she's also tossed in a few of my most glittery gel pens. But I haven't so much as looked at it since the night of the disastrous dinner with Nayim and my family. Our breakup and Professor Liu's radio silence haven't helped.

The pads of my fingertips brush over the page. It would be a shame to tarnish it when none of my thoughts make sense, when I don't even know if my so-called muse has left the country, if he's okay, if I'll ever see him again.

But it's not Nayim I miss like a lung as I trace the lines of the paper.

Harun . . .

Sweet, earnest, dorky Harun, who has been such a good friend to me ever since we met, even when I made it difficult for him.

Harun, who still replies, instead of deserting me entirely.

Ximena's wisdom returns to me, and I can't deny the truth

in it any longer: *We've got to stop pretending everything's all right all the time.*

I'm so sick and tired of pretending.

Before I can talk myself out of it, I retrieve my phone and press the FaceTime button, ensuring that the volume is too low to bother my slumbering friends.

It's only when he answers that I admit to myself how desperately I longed to see him, and how sad I was at the prospect that he wouldn't want to see me.

I drink in the sight of Harun.

His expression is guarded when he mutters, "What's up?" but I spy telltale signs of sleeplessness in the bruises beneath his eyes and his—admittedly adorable—rumpled curls.

"Are you okay?"

His pupils dart away from the screen. "Fine. Why?"

"Harun . . ." A lump rises in my throat. Before I can stop myself, I whisper, "I hate that you're looking at me like this again."

Harun scowls. "Like what? This is my face."

I shake my head. "Once upon a time, I would have bought that, but now I know you enough to know I hurt you." When he doesn't answer, jaw clenching, I continue, "I never should have used something you told me in confidence. I'm so sorry if it caused problems between you and your family."

"It didn't," Harun grits out, then droops when I flinch, dropping his forehead onto his knees. I can see Rab's empty terrarium behind him. "My parents were upset at first, but after we got a chance to talk, they were touched that Lily and I broke up because I chose a college close to them. It helped that I wasn't still seeing Lily." His voice is muffled, devoid of accusation, but remorse makes me swallow nevertheless. "It's just . . . I just thought you cared about me. I didn't think you'd throw me under the bus the first chance you got."

"Harun, no," I exclaim. "Of course, I care about you! I—"

His voice grows so quiet, I almost don't hear it. "I get why you did it. . . ." He lifts his head enough that his sorrowful eyes bore into me, glittering like polished ebony save for the blue glow of the screen. "If you're happy now, I'm glad for you, but it kind of sucks to always be the one tossed aside."

The weight of my betrayal hits me fully.

Harun has had a wall around his heart since we met, but through sheer chance, luck, and circumstance, I managed to worm myself through a crack. Made him laugh. Made him trust me with fears he couldn't share with anyone else. Made him privy to my own.

Only to double-cross him.

To use him like a pawn in my game against Amma, while berating her for doing the same to me. I'm such a hypocrite, but what's worse, a bad friend.

"I'm so sorry," I whisper again. "I'm so, so sorry. And I know you don't have to forgive me, but I miss you so much. I miss us."

There are tears beading in my lashes, but I blink them away, not wanting him to pretend things are okay simply because he wants me to feel better, regardless of his own pain.

Harun's eyes grow round. "Really?"

His blatant disbelief is a punch to the gut. I bob my head with a frantic nod. "I know neither of us wanted to be set up, but I didn't lie when I said our dates were some of the most fun I've had in years. I almost wish we could keep doing it."

Maybe it would be best if we said goodbye now, because Harun deserves better, but I don't want to let him go.

So, instead, I need to do better.

Be better, for him.

Harun is quiet as he processes this new information, pupils flicking in the direction of something out of my line of vision. I take the opportunity to observe every detail, my pulse thrumming for reasons beyond his answer.

His lower lip is plump and full as he chews on it, the glare of the phone screen in the dimness casting the fringe of his lashes in stark relief over his sculpted cheekbones. When his attention returns to me, it pierces right through me.

"I miss you, too, and I'm sorry," he admits, tentatively hopeful. "I never should have said what I did about you and your writing. Whatever happens with college, you're the smartest person I've ever known. Almost scarily smart, Zar."

Pure, sunshiny delight courses through me, and I can't keep the ear-to-ear grin off my face. "Then . . . maybe we can do something together soon?"

Harun hesitates. "We'd have to sneak around. I don't

want to come between you and your mother again. Not if everything's finally cool with you and Nayim."

I do my best to keep a straight face, but the truth is, I don't want to hear Nayim's name on Harun's lips so soon after I've been waxing poetic over the shape of them. Don't want the reminder of the boy who'd jilted me to taint my reconciliation with Harun.

If Nayim comes back tomorrow, I don't know how I'll feel. No one knows better than me how slow time can be to erase scars left by someone you'd gifted a piece of your heart to, but I meant what I told him in the castle. The Nayim I fell for isn't the Nayim I met then.

And now, part of me resents him for being the reason Harun and I fell out.

"This is pretty embarrassing, considering the lengths I went to at your folks' Eid party," I admit, eyes trained on the bottom of my screen to avoid Harun's, "but there is no me and Nayim anymore. He wasn't who I thought he was, and I . . . I hate that I let him come between us."

A beat goes by.

I forcibly meet his gaze, reminding myself that Harun has never judged me before. Even so, the bashful smile that alights like a sunrise across his face shoots a funny thrill through my chest. "Okay. That's . . . okay. That's good. Maybe we can do something Thursday?"

I beam. "I can't wait!"

"Me neither . . ."

We're content to sit in the dark, smiling goofily, until Harun suddenly yelps. "Ow, Rab!"

He must have dropped his phone because the world suddenly tilts on its axis. I hear the soft thump of the device hitting his sheets and find myself looking up at Harun rather than face-to-face with him.

When he raises his palm to cover his earlobe, I notice that his bearded dragon has scrambled its way up his shoulder to take a chomp out of it.

A laugh escapes me, so loud I have to slap a hand against my mouth. "Has he been crawling around this whole time?"

"He was helping me build a model plane," Harun grumbles, rubbing his red earlobe between the fingertips of one hand while holding the unrepentant culprit in the other. "Guess he got tired of waiting for bedtime."

I laugh again, soft and fond. "You're cute, Harun Emon."

"What?" comes his garbled reply. "Um. Well. Anyway . . . good night!"

He hangs up.

Warmth saturates my chest, and I don't bother attributing it to my phone or quilt for once. I crane my neck to grin up at the ceiling. That not-lizard has grown on me. He isn't the only one.

Even though I'm not ready to start writing tonight, for the first time since Nayim left, sleep drags at my eyelids. Wandering over to Dalia, I give in to its spell with a muffled yawn, wishing Harun an equally peaceful slumber.

Chapter 26

Wednesday finds me a nervous wreck.

I bite my nails to nubs until Amma thwaps them with a spoon and frets, "Boys won't like you if you don't have pretty hands. Meera's daughter gets manicures to make hers stylish and *French*."

Normally, I would: (A) tell her I don't care what boys think of me, (B) remind her we can't afford manicures, (C) attempt to explain how French tips work, and (D) ask why she's already plotting how to catch the eye of a new guy.

But I'm thrown by how much I'm looking forward to seeing Harun.

Leaving Amma, Nanu, and a coloring Resna in the kitchen, I drag myself over to the couch, where Arif is playing a Nintendo Switch his friend lent him, and plop next to him. Grunting, he budges over to give me more space. I grab a pillow and bury my face in it.

For the next minute, the only sounds in the room are the

pings from his game and my sighs, until Arif mutters, "Why don't you text him?"

I peek up at him over the pillow. "Who?"

"I can't keep track anymore," he counters dryly.

Glaring, I give him a good whack with the pillow but leave him to his game. He's not entirely wrong. Harun and I left off in a good place last night, and he even texted me a good morning selfie with a grumpy Rabeardranath, so it wouldn't be wrong if I checked in, would it?

After much internal debate, I settle on asking, What should I wear tomorrow? in a surreptitious effort to excavate clues about the location of our not-date.

Of course, his answer is as cryptic as ever: Something comfy.

Then I'll come in sweatpants and bunny slippers, I threaten.

I was imagining more along the line of sneakers, he replies, so you don't face-plant.

My mind spins with the possibilities of a destination where I'll need sturdy shoes to avoid falling. Before it can catch up to my fingertips, I type back, Psh, I'll be fine. You'd catch me, wouldn't you?

His ellipses disappear and my eyes grow huge.

Shit! Why'd I say that?

But then he responds, I would. Kinda comes with the territory of being with a princess.

My mouth goes dry. Is he flirting, poking fun, or being polite?

I can't think of a retort beyond, Much appreciated, my knight in robot armor.

Our current truce feels too fragile to survive my knowing what he meant, so the topic turns to how I might sneak out to meet him.

After we scheme, I toss my phone aside.

Comfy, huh?

Thursday night, an hour before sunset, I hurry home to freshen up and get dressed.

Dalia texts to let me know she's outside, since I told Amma I'd be hanging out with the twins after work.

Dalia drives me beyond Paterson's city limits to a leafy copse in aptly named Woodland Park. There's a playground next to the parking lot. Harun perches on the hood of his BMW at the far end of it, beneath the shade of a tall tree, frowning at his phone until the Mini Cooper stops beside him.

His cheeks half dimple as he grins. "You staged your escape."

It's hardly the first time he's smiled at me, but I swallow the sudden flutter in my stomach before I return it. Although I can sense Dalia smirking, I ignore her to clamber out of the car.

It's *not* a big deal, and less about Harun being attractive than it is about his resting broody face. If the sun were eclipsed every day, you'd want to see it when it shone too, wouldn't you?

"Perk of being a poor brown girl," I quip. "Your mom can't worry half as much as her friends when you spend most of the day out of the house working anyway."

"I'm just glad to see you." His eyes darken with some unreadable emotion as he appraises my outfit. "No sweatpants or slippers?"

"They're in the laundry," I deadpan.

"Too bad," he muses to himself. "You'd be cute in bunny slippers. . . ." His head shoots up the second the words sink in. Both of us flush in the awkward silence that follows, until Dalia coughs to remind us of her presence. We whip toward her like two guilty kids caught with our sticky fingers in the mishti batta. Harun sputters when she snaps a picture of him. "Wait, what are you doing with that?"

"Safety reasons," she chirps, then turns to me. "You trust him, and I trust you, but you've never been alone together, right?" Aside from that time when Sammi left early, and in the car, I suppose that's true. I nod. "Thought so. Share your location with me in case."

"Yes, Mom . . ."

Dalia scrunches up her nose, but the clever rejoinder never comes. Instead she leans in to give me a hug, whispering, "Have fun. But not too much fun."

"Yes, Mom," I say again, this time with more affection.

As she moves to enter her car, Harun blurts, "You can stay. Um, if you want. And Zahra wants." His voice softens when his gaze flicks to me. "I don't want you to be uncomfortable."

"That's sweet," Dalia says, "but I need to go home and pray before I let Paul Hollywood stare reproachfully into the depths of my soul while I'm trying to re-create this week's GBBO technical challenge."

I nod to let her know I'll be fine. "Nadiya's cooler."

"Fair," Dalia concedes.

Harun peers between us. "I have no idea what that is, but it sounds scary."

Dalia smiles beatifically. "So am I. Don't forget."

Blowing one last kiss at me and an *I know where you live* squint at Harun, she drives off. I watch her go, feeling insurmountably grateful. Dalia, my beautiful, protective friend, has often told me that she wants to focus on herself until she graduates from college, but when she does seek out love, she'll do it the traditional way, which a lot of modern Muslims call halal dating.

It's similar to what Harun and I were *supposed* to be doing, with chaperones and the chastest of contact until we agreed to a formal commitment. Now I'm sneaking around with a boy again, but Dalia doesn't judge me for doing things my own way.

It means a lot when so many others harbor nothing but judgment for me.

I move to the front passenger seat of Harun's BMW and click on the belt. After a beat, he says, "I mean it. I can take you home if you're not comfortable."

I *am*, though. I feel safe with him. I always have.

Not to mention, I'm dying to find out what he has planned. Rather than lay my heart bare, however, I shake my head.

"Nope. I was promised an adventure and an adventure I will get. Besides, Amma would hound me until I confessed all my sins if I came home early. She'll think my friends and I are fighting."

We start driving.

As we travel toward the highway, I ask Harun what he's been up to since we "broke up," and he hesitantly admits he'd been helping his father plan a surprise party for Pushpita Khala's birthday, then frowns at my wolfish grin. "What?"

"No, it's just, you're legitimately precious," I reply. "Mama's boy."

He scowls. "Stop calling me that. You're lucky it's over between us or *you'd* have been the one she force-fed sugar-free, gluten-free cake while my dad took a bunch of embarrassing photos to post on Facebook."

"Note to self," I say as I pretend to type into my phone, "make a Facebook just to add Pushpita Khala on it."

Regardless of his insistence that he didn't enjoy it, his veritable *pout* only confirms that he'd do almost anything to make the people he loves happy. I do my best not to laugh at his ruffled feathers, until he cracks a tiny smile.

The rest of the drive is like Harun himself: unexpected and quiet, but enjoyable. I watch New York City slowly come to life across the Hudson River. Once we reach the George Washington Bridge, Harun appears to come alive as well, spouting off facts about its history and construction.

Perhaps it's a trick of the lights strung on the arches of

the bridge, or those flickering in the many windows of the city's skyscrapers, but Harun practically glows beside me, dark brown irises sparkling like the night sky flecked with stars.

When he catches me staring, he cuts himself off. "Sorry. Was I talking too much? I get overenthusiastic about engineering sometimes."

It's the first time I've ever seen him excited about *anything* other than Rabeardranath Tagore. I shake my head. "Don't apologize. I like this side of you."

His eyes snap toward me, then back to the road. "You don't have to pretend."

Something about the *smallness* of his voice fires up my protective instincts. Have others made him feel like his interests were boring before? Or is it because our relationship has been built on so many lies and little hurts? "I'm not. I feel like you know so much about me because I'm always the one yammering on and on when we meet up."

"I like listening to you," he says. "And you're surprisingly good at saying a lot while sharing very little, general."

Ignoring the bubbly warmth his words cascade through me, I continue, "Did you always want to be an engineer, or was it something your parents pushed you into choosing?"

"If it were at all up to my mother, I'd be a doctor," he says. "I think that's why she keeps telling people I'm studying biomedical engineering, so she can brag that I'm *both*."

"That does sound like Pushpita Khala Logic."

His eyes flick toward me again. "I guess I do like

engineering a lot, for the same reason that I like Rab and swimming. It isn't . . . complicated."

I pull a face. "I beg to differ. I barely passed algebra, and I'd sink like a stone if we went to the beach."

Although I'm joking, Harun gnaws on his full bottom lip, fingers tightening on the steering wheel. "I was never . . . good with words, the way you are. In fact, I felt pretty damn *bad* with them when I first started private school. The other kids thought it was hilarious to fake Apu accents anytime the teacher called on me or my cousin. Shaad never let it bother him. I quickly learned it was better to keep my mouth shut."

"Harun . . ."

Not for the first time, the urge to hunt down and throw my shoe at some prissy private school kids assaults me.

He frowns at the road ahead, the glass-beaded tasbih around the rearview mirror casting shadows across his lenses. "It was awful for a while, and I couldn't even tell my parents. How could I when they worked so hard to get me in? But then I joined robotics. Everything else kind of fell into place. Math makes *sense*. There's only one answer. When I'm doing calculations, I don't think about anything else. It's the same way I feel when I'm underwater. There's no judgment for once. Is that weird?"

I think of all the voices I've been battling with in my own head.

Amma's and the aunties', with so many rules for being a good Bangladeshi, Muslim girl. I think about their group chats, worrying about what secrets they know. My characters', fighting with me over every word. Professor Liu's, utterly silent. My friends' and the fear of losing them. Nayim's, brimming with such disappointment.

An endless list of impossible choices.

My head shakes instinctively. "It isn't weird. Writing is like that for me. Thank you for trusting me."

Harun considers me through his periphery, as if he's gauging how honest I am. I sit up straight and peer back, hoping to convey that I mean every word. At last his shoulders sag, and his voice grows so soft, I almost don't hear it over the whir of traffic.

"Can I show you one more thing?"

The fact that he still thinks to ask sends affection rippling through me. Before I can talk myself out of it, I extend my arm until it brushes his next to the gear shift. "Please."

Swallowing audibly, he refocuses on the road, but his arm doesn't move away from mine. Moments later, we're parking the BMW in a ridiculously expensive garage. Harun shyly offering me a hand distracts me from the exorbitant prices, the stately city hall building at our rear, the roar of cars all around us, and the distant squeal of the subway below.

The Brooklyn Bridge arcs grandly above us.

My pulse thumps against his palm as he escorts me up a stairway to a cordoned-off pedestrian walk. Behind us, people mill out of the subway entrance, but though some sidestep us impatiently, Harun and I continue our stroll at a leisurely pace.

Cars zip by on either side of us on the busy highway roads, but it isn't until we reach the wooden planks that feed into the bridge that I realize how far up we are. The boards below our feet creak and wobble as tourists jostle and skateboards zoom past. I cling to Harun's arm, mindful of every step. No wonder he wanted me to wear sturdy shoes.

Then we stride onto Brooklyn Bridge proper and vertigo swoops through my belly. I'm suddenly hyperaware of the fact that only a thin wooden layer and a wide railing separate me from a violent death beneath a hundred oncoming wheels. It's narrower and less metallic than I would have pictured too. One well-placed push from a stranger is all it would take.

But when I turn to Harun, he's glowing again, the bulbs studding the cables of the bridge shimmering across his black hair and eyes through his glasses.

"This is my favorite place in the whole world," he says, guiding me over to a large patio where my legs grow steady once more, surrounded by walls and windows on every side.

I follow his gaze and gasp.

We can see *everything*.

Clusters of skyscrapers. The Empire State and Chrysler Buildings. The glass triangles that comprise One World Trade Center. Beneath our feet, the cars, and even farther below, boats sailing across the East River. The Statue of Liberty raising a torch to the blushing sky on Liberty Island.

Other bridges pierce the balmy mist that wisps around us. Harun points them all out to me: "The blue-gray that gets lost in the storm clouds when it rains is the Manhattan Bridge. You can see the train lines from there. And that almost pink one? That's the Williamsburg Bridge. But the Brooklyn Bridge is my favorite."

When he's like this, it makes no sense to me, what he said about not being good with words. Gently, I ask, "Why?"

He regales me with the history of the bridge. How it's one of the oldest suspension bridges in the United States. How its original architect died before its completion from an injury. How his son took over but was forced to watch the completion of the bridge from afar after contracting caisson disease, unprepared for the atmosphere. How his wife finished the project and was the first to walk the bridge.

I wince. "Sounds kinda Macbethian."

"That Shakespeare play?" His brows furrow. "How?"

"Well, it's called the cursed play, and this place sounds pretty damn cursed if it practically wiped out an entire family," I reply, casting an uneasy glance around us and recalling that I didn't have a chance to do Maghrib prayers before leaving with him.

Harun chuckles. "I mean, yeah, I guess you could see it that way. Me . . . I think it's a monument to the Roeblings' dedication to helping people cross the river. Once it was built, rumors started spreading that the bridge would collapse, but it's been standing over a century now. P. T. Barnum even sent a whole circus's worth of elephants across it a year after its completion to test the rumors, and it never once shook."

I sneak glimpses between him and the rosy sky. The setting sun glints off the steel and glass of the skyscrapers, refracting pink and red and iridescent light across the profile of his face. The arc of his cheekbone cuts a sharp line down to his jaw, but with his contented smile and the wind running invisible fingers through his hair, he feels approachable.

My fingers twitch on the railing. Our arms are touching again. All at once, his skin feels warm and electric against mine.

I glance back out the window.

It's quite possibly the most beautiful thing I've ever seen.

Although we're surrounded by other tourists snapping pictures and cycling across the bridge, I feel closer to Harun than ever before. There's definitely a metaphor in here somewhere.

"Thank you for bringing me to your favorite place," I tell him.

"It's even nicer in winter," he replies. "I like walking around the botanical garden nearby after visiting the bridge. I remember what you said about your world feeling small, but *this* is our world too. It's right at our doorstep if you're willing to go. Maybe we could come back?"

My head whips toward him. He's looking pointedly at the shifting river below, but the sky isn't the only thing that's gone red. What does it mean that he wants to come back with me, so long after our facade has ended? After he goes to college?

Does he mean as friends? Do friends hold hands so often?

Do they hang on every word the other speaks? Do they plan special outings like this? I don't think I can lie to myself anymore, even if I'm not yet ready to speak it aloud.

Harun has become one of my best friends, but he's something else, too. I feel things for him that I don't with Ximena or the Tahir girls.

Heart pounding at this revelation, I manage a faint, "Sure. I'd like that. Thanks."

"You're welcome." He dimples, and my stomach does another flip. "But I can tell I've talked about bridges for too long. I promise that's not all I had planned for tonight. Ready?"

I nod.

Fingers intertwined, we complete our trek across the bridge and find ourselves at the park on the other side, lush with trees and flowers. Bees and butterflies flutter in the air. We buy food from a Halal Guys cart and walk until we reach a stretch of lawn overlooking a pier, teeming with people sitting on picnic blankets, waiting for a large projector to play a movie.

SABRINA, reads the poster, portraying a black-and-white image of Audrey Hepburn, with one man gazing at her yearningly while another kisses her cheek.

"It's a romance," Harun says. "I thought you might like it."

A teeny-tiny part of me squirms at the love triangle depicted on the poster—haha, universe, I get it—but the consideration he's put into all this fragments my resolve.

"I'm sure I will."

Chapter 27

The Bangla Mela falls on Sunday just a few days later, giving me no time to angst over boys—well, a certain specific boy—since Amma and Chai Ho have stalls at the festival.

While my mother and grandmother push to complete as many individual pieces of clothing to sell as they can the day before the mela, I text Ximena to request her help in making an eye-catching banner. She comes over, and it's the first time we've hung out alone since school ended.

As we laugh watching Resna add colorful handprints around the borders of Ximena's creation, I find that I've really missed spending time with her, but I'm not sure what to do about it. She gives me a very long hug before she leaves, perhaps thinking along the same lines.

Later that night, Mr. Tahir calls to say, "Consider yourself on reserve during the festival, Miss Khan. I have the girls assisting me. Your mother needs you more."

I appreciate this, because the festival begins booming with

activity bright and early. The aromas of curries and kebabs, mishti and sanasur, float through the air, which pulses with the beating of drums. Police cruisers block off both ends of Union Avenue, from Totowa to Wayne. The everyday shops are shuttered and parked cars have been moved, replaced by hundreds of stalls selling everything from jewelry and henna designs to street food.

At the very heart, a tall stage has been set up with speakers arranged around it. A growing crowd gathers there, waiting for whatever shilpi has been flown in from Bangladesh to perform. Tiny children with bangles tinkling on their wrists and bells chiming on their ankles dance to the music the DJ plays, while their parents clap.

Other children, like my own sister, tear through the swarming bodies in vibrantly colored face paint and papier-mâché masks that make them look like packs of tigers, flocks of birds, and other wild beasts, out-of-breath chaperones—Arif, in Resna's case—at their heels. People from the neighborhood watch and whoop from their patios. Nanu, who can't walk for too long without her arthritis flaring, accompanies one of her fellow grandmas in doing exactly that.

Meanwhile, I'm stuck with Amma, who's still stubbornly giving me the silent treatment. I refuse to be the first to break, so it's through a series of grunts and meaningful glares that we communicate enough to get her garment stall set up—a foldout plastic table Meera Khala found in her shed, with Ximena's banner flapping above.

Before she busies herself with her sewing equipment, however, she raps me on the back with the length of her measuring tape, a wordless, *Stop hunching and model my dress properly*. Grumbling in the stuffy anarkali suit, I troubleshoot for customers as she haggles over prices and takes aunties' measurements.

A woman who must be all of four feet holds her bangled arms out for that purpose. When Amma kneels to wrap the tape around her waist, she says, "Ever since you got that wedding party job, you've been impossible to get ahold of, Zaynab Afa. How is that coming along?"

Pink-cheeked, my mother murmurs, "It hasn't been without its ups and downs."

Mostly downs, I grumble internally.

"I hope the bride likes the final pieces," Amma finishes, oblivious to my thoughts.

"Nonsense," drawls a new voice. "Don't be humble, Zaynab. Your work is impeccable."

To my absolute surprise, we turn to find Pushpita Emon. Harun skulks behind her, bags of his mother's purchases hanging off his arms. In spite of their weight, his fingers twitch in a covert greeting, before he clenches them into a fist and frowns.

My ears burn from the knowing stares of the crowd bustling around us, no doubt vibrating with curiosity over how we'll deal with seeing each other again. Ever since we fought, every reminder that he doesn't hate me has filled me with visceral relief, but since admitting my feelings for him to myself, just being together steals my breath.

I raise my hand, then pretend to tuck a loose strand behind my ear. Harun's eyes crinkle at the corners, like he sees right through my act but doesn't mind.

It's already gotten through town that Harun Emon and Zahra Khan famously do not get along. Somehow, the story of Resna throwing her mishti doi at him evolved into my siblings and I trashing the Emons' entire house. Some said uppity Pushpita Emon had it coming. Others tut as they observe us now. There really are no secrets in Paterson.

"You're too kind, Pushpita Afa," Amma says. "If it weren't for you, I wouldn't have gotten the commission in the first place. I can't thank you enough for that."

Pushpita Khala shakes her head. "I'm not the sort of woman who suffers fools, dear. I never would have recommended you if your work didn't merit it. Just because our, ah, little arrangement didn't work out doesn't mean I won't still support your business. So let your afa see what else you've been cooking up!"

Amma's incandescent smile makes my heart sing.

Harun must have smoothed things over with his parents. I think I see now why my own mother likes his so much, and why he's such a devoted son. There's compassion beneath her bluster. The same compassion in him.

Even knowing this doesn't stop my jaw from dropping when he strides past me toward Amma and clears his throat. "Khala . . . afnare help khortham farmu nee?"

Amma's jaw joins mine at his valiant effort at Bengali and the timid Good Bangladeshi Boy smile that accompanies it, but she manages a sputtered, "Oh, thank you, thank you! What a bhodro sele you are. Of course you can help. Will you be fine with Zahra?"

Pushpita Khala beams in approval.

Harun nods and slinks over to my side. "Need a hand?"

I squint. "You sure those delicate rich-boy hands can handle the manual labor?"

He rolls his eyes, but his cheek dimples. "My boss is pretty demanding, so I guess I'll have to learn on the job."

"You've got that right, Emon."

Despite my brazen assertion, a tingle courses up my fingertips as he accepts from me the money I'd been about to count, lingering for a second too long. His eyes widen and dart away from mine to the bills, but I can't help stealing peeks at his studious profile, admiring the sooty shadows cast by his lashes over his cheeks, the way he chews on his bottom lip when concentrating, and his frankly criminal cheekbone-to-jaw ratio.

Harun's mother glances up from our wares to consider us, and I sense another familiar stare boring into my back. Immediately, I snap my gaze away from Harun and fish out the customer-service smile I've perfected at Chai Ho, willing the heat to desert my face.

The other aunties exchange eager looks, then trail Pushpita Khala to our table, rifling through the sharis, shalwar kameezes, anarkali suits, and accompanying accessories Amma created. There are even a few hand-stitched khethas made by Nanu that will be perfect to decorate their beds with on cooler summer nights.

Soon I have fistfuls of twenties aimed at my head, and Amma is fielding query after query about whether she'll be taking future commissions.

In that way, although *they're* not the ones wearing animal costumes today, aunties are a lot like wolves: they take cues from the alpha, crowding around whatever carcass she's chosen. Whatever else they might say about her, Pushpita Emon is that alpha.

Like this, an hour trickles by.

Harun continues to collect the cash while I show off different materials to our customers. As we get more and more patrons, a sudden shrill squeal pierces through the crowd, louder than the bickering of the aunties fighting over the last beaded blouse.

The groping hands and griping voices around us fade when a colorful figure parts the bodies around her with a wave of her bell-sleeved arms. She's a young woman, probably around Sammi Afa's age or a little younger, and makes a statement in the heavily embroidered tunic she wears over jeans. An entourage of women varying in age follow her.

"Zaynab Khala, you didn't tell me you had a stand here today!" she squeals again. "And Pushpita Khala's here too?"

"Um." I glance between our loud new customer and my

mother, who has become a ghastly shade of pale. "Welcome?" It comes out as a question. "Please, take a look."

She already is, rummaging through our offerings and tossing whatever she doesn't like aside. Occasionally, one of her crew pipes up with input on the things she holds up, but more often than not, she brushes aside their commentary and the disapproving murmurs of the other customers she's cut ahead of at the booth.

I turn to Amma again, lifting a hand in a *WTF?* gesture.

She grimaces but mouths back, *Bride-zolad* . . .

Oh . . . Oh! Crap, talking to *her* never ends well. I haven't personally had the displeasure, but I *have* witnessed the fallout, with my mother and grandmother frantically trying to change the thread color in the hem stitches of every blouse, or whatever other bizarre request she's made.

Smile stiffening, I interrupt, "Is there something specific I can help you find today?"

"No," she snaps at once, before really taking notice of me. A slow smile spreads across her face as she eyes me from head to toe. "You must be Zaynab Khala's daughter! You're so lucky, having your mother around to make you such gorgeous clothes."

I start to nod, then blurt, "Hey!" when she reaches across the table to rub the material of my anarkali skirt between her fingertips, humming all the while.

Harun, for his part, jerks like he intends to put an arm between us, then resigns us both to our fates with a sigh. "Hey, Sonia Afa."

"Oh, hi, Harun," she says distractedly, without glancing away from my skirt. Her head whips up to beam at Amma behind my shoulder. "Khala, why haven't you ever shown me this darling tulle material?"

My mother's jaw works as her grip tightens on the measuring tape she holds. The auntie she's been tailoring gapes between her and the bride-zolad. Amma gulps, takes a breath, and in the meekest voice I've ever heard, says, "You told me which fabric to use from day one. Don't you remember the sketches and photos you sent me? There were *so many* photos."

"What do I know?" the bride-zolad scoffs. "You're clearly the expert. I mean, just look at this!" She tugs on my skirt again, ignoring the way I grab the edge of the table to keep from tipping forward, and Harun's steadying grasp on my elbow. "Layering lightly embroidered netting over the rest of the dress is inspired, I tell you!"

"Um, well, if you like it so much, you can have it!" I interject. "I'll take it off right now."

Harun's eyes go huge, but the bride-zolad waves her hand. "Aren't you funny? I meant for my wedding shari. None of my friends' sharis had such a unique feature."

"B-but," Amma says, "all the material has already been purchased. The pieces are close to being done. To make such a big change at this stage would be—"

"Money is no object," the bride-zolad counters breezily. "You know my fiancé works for a big hedge fund, don't you? He told me I could have whatever I want."

My eyes widen as the realization of what she's asking for hits me with the full force of a truck. After all the money and time and labor we've funneled into her wedding party outfits, she's suddenly had a drastic change of heart?

What's more, it's a costly one.

"Now, Sonia," Pushpita Khala steps in at last. "Don't you think you're being unreasonable? Your mother told me about the caterers and the florist and—"

A woman in an earth-toned shari behind the bride-zolad—presumably her mother—shakes her head for dear life.

Sonia's brown eyes turn icy and her upper lip curls. "Khala, I did you a favor by hiring your friend. Because you asked and I respect you so deeply. But I'm the customer, and the customer is always right. If she's not experienced enough to meet my needs, perhaps I should take my business elsewhere?"

"No!" Amma exclaims.

The sound of her outburst summons yet more murmurings from the surrounding aunties, this time of pity. Red splotches fill the apples of my mother's cheeks. She clears her throat. "That is, thank you, Pushpita Afa, but you don't need to fret. Sonia simply has superb taste, but I'm certain I can make exactly what she wants." She rubs her hands together, squeezing the measuring tape too tightly. "Perhaps after I close up my stand, we can discuss another advance on my payment? The cost of this—"

"My fiancé will handle all that at the end," Sonia says dismissively. I seethe. She's not the least bit grateful. "He's too busy right now."

Amma's eyes flick to me at once, glistening with an emotion she can't reveal in front of so many people, even if most can venture a guess at how she's feeling. Covering the cost of this new material without another advance will be impossible. If she bows to the bride-zolad, she can't pay me back as soon as we'd both like, but if she doesn't concede, the bride-zolad might not pay us at all, and then everything will be in vain.

Amma clears her throat once more. "Still. I'd like it if you could get him on the phone."

"We'll see," comes the breezy reply.

A white-hot blade of rage twists in my chest, the sting of it briefly overtaking the sadness that bleeds beneath. Before I can leap across the table to throw myself on the bride-zolad, who is already sashaying away now that the damage is done, Harun's fingers around my bicep stop me once more.

A few seconds later, she and her entourage vanish into the parade of people swarming us, leaving nothing but destruction in their wake. I stare after her blankly, so shocked by this sideswipe that I don't notice Harun speaking to me or the swell of other concerned voices rallying around my mother.

"You okay?" he whispers.

I shake my head, but thankfully, he doesn't push.

Amma puts on a brave face for her own audience, who tut at the rumors of the bride-zolad's treatment of her other employees.

"I heard that she just switched caterers," says one auntie.

"She fired the florist, too," adds another.

A third auntie peers off in the direction of the food stalls. "She's such a nightmare, even Mr. Tahir turned her down when she asked him to take over dessert catering, and you know he never says no to money. Made an excuse about being short-staffed now that the Aktar boy is gone."

Amma, who's been listening intently, jerks another glance at me upon hearing that, but I avoid her and Harun's gaze, not wanting to see the *I told you so* in the former or pity in the latter. Especially when aunties can smell secrets like sharks smell blood in the water.

"Ekh bar-eh zolad-nee," they all agree, denouncing her as a total mean girl.

Pushpita Khala shakes her head, wrapping an arm around Amma. "I can't help feeling responsible for this, Zaynab. She's demanding, but between her own family's money and that bush-managing fiancé of hers she's always going on about, I assumed she could at least be trusted to pay you properly."

"No, don't blame yourself," my mother replies. "I . . . she will pay. We'll be fine until then. Perhaps her fiancé will be more reasonable."

She forces a smile. Everyone is paying attention to her, so I let my own smiling mask crumble, fists shaking where they're balled up in my skirt.

That answer was her pride talking.

We're far from fine. My dreams for college might once again become as flimsy as the tulle that is currently ruining my life. It's hard to have my future ride on the gauzy whims of a person like the bride-zolad. There's only so much more I can take.

"Amma, can I go check on Chai Ho?" I ask, loud enough to cut through the chatter.

She hesitates, but then Harun jumps in. "I can stay and help khala clean up."

Amma looks surprised but smiles graciously at him and gives me a nod. "Go on then, Zahra, we've done as much as we can here."

Casting a grateful glance at Harun, I escape without another moment's notice.

It's not a lie that I want to go to Chai Ho, but when I get there, rather than the sympathetic ear I hoped for, I notice Dalia and Mr. Tahir working frantically to serve the customers lined up in front of their booth, no Dani in sight. Mrs. Tahir is there in her stead, an unusual sight.

Something's not right.

Dalia's round face is drawn, her brown eyes big and sad.

But I can hardly cut in front of all the customers like the bride-zolad did, so I reluctantly wade deeper into the mela, letting my feet take me anywhere they please.

Hours later, I make my way home.

I don't realize I must look like a tragic Bollywood heroine in my princess dress and runny makeup until I enter the apartment and startle a gasp out of Amma, who is stooped over the brocade of the wedding shari, carefully undoing the intricate golden pattern so she can replace it with the tulle the bride-zolad demanded.

"Ah, Zahra!" She does a double take at my appearance but doesn't comment on my tears, though her throat bobs. "Your brother and I looked for you earlier so I could show you some of the trinkets I picked up for you, but we couldn't find you or the Tahirs. You should have answered your phone." I bow my head at her reprimanding tone until her expression softens. "It doesn't matter. I'm glad you found some time to enjoy yourself with your friends."

I stand in the doorway, simply watching her. She keeps blinking her own bloodshot eyes and her hands are quivering. She shouldn't be working on the bride-zolad's commission after spending all day tailoring dresses for customers at the festival, but somehow, she even found the time to buy me a present.

I wonder where she got the money for it.

Where she'll get the money for the new fabric.

Nayim wasn't wrong. Sometimes I *do* feel suffocated by Amma's expectations for me. Sometimes I fear that her desires will suck all the life out of my own dreams. But as I observe her in the faint light of the lamp, I can't resist getting drawn in by something with no name other than love, and can't imagine going so far away that she wouldn't know where I am.

"Can I help, Amma?"

She taps her chin. "I suppose it may be time to try it on someone."

This time, I don't mind posing as her mannequin. Her brown eyes glaze over at the sight of me dressed like a bride.

I can tell she's imagining my wedding day, see the influx of emotions in the firm press of her quivering lips, the way a smile twitches at the corners, the way she uses an excuse to kneel so she can dab at her cheeks with the shari's hem. But she won't say so because she thinks I'll get mad, shattering the fragile cease-fire between us.

I'm grateful.

I desperately want to tell her everything.

Instead I return to my room to find a set of gold-plated suris on top of the library books on my desk. I rub my thumb over the floral embossment on each, more troubles in my head than there are jewels in the bangles.

It's not an apology, but it's close enough.

THE AUNTIE NETWORK

Champa Azad has added you and twelve others to the Bangla Mela Chat

Champa:
Can you believe that Sonia girl? Speaking to Zaynab Afa like that.

Lubna:
Such a rude young lady! Poor Zaynab. And what's going on with her daughter?

Champa:
Oh, yes, she and the Emon boy seemed awfully close, didn't they? I thought their parents had called off the arrangement?

Khatun:
Now that you mention it, they did seem rather friendly. Giggling together right in front of us all . . . Lojja nai ni itha bachainthor?

Champa:
Do you think that's that why the dishwasher left?

Meera:
Allahr duai, please tell me Zaynab isn't part of this group? √√

Chapter 28

Unable to get Dalia's ashen face out of my head, I end up at Chai Ho an hour before my shift Monday morning, hoping to strong-arm her into confessing whatever's the matter.

Even the Mom Friend needs a mom friend sometimes.

As soon as I cross the street over to the tea shop, I become aware that something is wrong. Faint yelling echoes through the glass door, though there's no one behind the counter. When I try the doorknob, I find that the door has been left unlocked, and I let myself in. Something crashes in the kitchen, jolting me into action.

Grabbing the first potential weapon within reach—a stainless-steel teapot—I charge through the kitchen door and shouting a war cry, only to find a puffy-eyed Dalia crouching on the floor, picking up shards of a broken teacup.

"Z-Zahra, what are you doing here?" she rasps.

But the source of the argument summons my attention: Dani and her father, shouting at each other in a combination

of Urdu and English. Urdu and Bengali have only some
terms and pronunciations in common, but because Dani has
always spoken it more crisply than her sister, it takes me no
more than a moment to decipher that they're arguing about
Ximena.

"Daniya, meri jaan—"

Dani cuts her father off with a screech. "No! Don't call
me that if your love for me is *conditional*, Abbu. If you and
Ammu only love me when I'm being a dutiful little girl who
does everything you say, I want no part of it."

Mr. Tahir throws his hands in the air. "That's not true. It's
because we love you that we don't want you to throw your life
away for some girl."

"Some girl?" Dani barks. "Mena and I have been together
since middle school. If you still can't accept her or who I
am—"

"You're eighteen! What do you know about who you are?"
her father fumes.

Dani's jaw snaps shut. Both panting, she and Mr. Tahir
stare each other down. At last, she says, "I know that legally, I
can do whatever I want."

I shrink at the ice in her voice, but when Mr. Tahir replies
with an equally cool, "Go ahead, break your mother's heart,
you ungrateful girl," the gravity of the situation sinks in.

The two of them march off in opposite directions, Dani
slamming the bathroom door in time with the thud of her
father's private office door. All the utensils around the kitchen

shake on their hooks, and another teacup falls and breaks. For a minute, Dalia and I are rooted in place.

Then she sniffles, and I drop to my knees next to her, putting my arms around her shoulders. "Oh, Dal. What happened? I thought your parents had come to terms with Dani and Mena's relationship years ago."

"Everything was going fine until the slumber party," she mumbles wetly into the crook of my neck. "It was already hard enough for Dani to accept that Mena wouldn't be coming to Rutgers with us, but now Mena wants to go back to the island."

Oh no . . .

Guilt sweeps through me.

I never checked in with any of them after that conversation at the sleepover. If I'm completely honest, I may even have been envious of how *sure* they've always been of each other. Remembering the tight hug Ximena gave me a couple of nights ago, I recognize it for what it was at last: a goodbye. An attempt to etch me into her memory. What kind of friend am I that I didn't stop her then to make her talk?

"What happened?" I whisper.

Dalia's voice is equally soft. "Yesterday during the fair, Mena asked Dani to come with her if she wants to stay together. Going to Haiti and her summer helping at the wheelhouse made her feel like there are more important things she's meant to do than go to college. Her uncle is opening a school in Pedernales and invited her to teach art there."

I sigh. "Dani took it hard, huh?"

Dalia nods against my neck. "We're supposed to move into our dorms in a couple of weeks. Tuition has already been paid. But she kept repeating how Mena said she still loves her. Dani thinks she can fix this if they just go together. She wants Abbu to give her back her half of our college savings for the trip."

Oh, that must not have gone over well *at all*.

Like most Asian parents, Mr. Tahir is dead serious about his daughters' studies. In fact, for as long as I've known them, I've known about the Tahir Twenty-Year Plan: the girls would go to college, get their MBAs, take over the shop together, franchise it, and make Chai Ho a nationwide name that would put Starbucks out of business, allowing Mr. and Mrs. Tahir to retire comfortably in Pakistan.

"Okay, we can fix this." I help Dalia up and dust off her skirt. "You go talk to your dad and I'll handle Dani. Once they cool off, things will be easier."

"Do you really think so, Zar?" she asks hopefully.

I give her one last squeeze. "I know so."

After releasing her, I advance into the den of the dragon— also known as the bathroom. Dani stands in front of the sink, splashing her tear-streaked face. She doesn't see my reflection in the mirror but must hear my footsteps, because she growls, "Go away, Dalia. I don't want to hear you make excuses for Abbu."

"It's not Dalia. . . ."

"Zahra!" She spins around and wilts, but despite her next stony remark, I'm not sure whether she's disappointed or relieved. "Oh, good. At least *you* understand how unreasonable he can be. How much of that did you hear?"

I shuffle next to her, close enough that she can lean against me if she wants. "Enough to know you need a friend. Wanna talk about it?"

Dani props herself against the rim of the sink, raking both hands through her bubblegum-pink hair in clear frustration. "Argh! He's *impossible*. When I told him and Ammu about visiting Mena, she said we could discuss it, but Abbu immediately forbade me. It pissed me off so much, I told him I'd use my college savings to go. And why shouldn't I? The world is *already* out there. What's stopping us from experiencing it now, instead of in four or six or however many years it takes to get a piece of paper that gives us permission?"

I cringe imagining how that conversation played out.

Although she sounds like she's reciting Ximena's speech from the slumber party back to me, neither of them is wrong. But Dani and her dad have a similar temperament, and when you fight fire with fire, you tend to get a bigger flame. No wonder Dalia looks like a husk of herself.

Scooting closer to Dani so our hips bump and make her lips twitch, I say, "So do you not want to go to college at all? I know you love Mena. I'll miss her if she goes too. But I thought you were excited about dorming with Dalia. You've been dreaming about being college roomies forever."

What happened to the fairy lights and furniture? The posters of her favorite anime series that she'd convinced her sister to let her put up on their dorm room's walls?

"I am! I *was*! I—" Dani drags a palm over her haggard face. "I'm not like you or Dal or even Mena. You've *always* known what you want to do." I shake my head, eyes wide, but before I can tell her none of my plans have ever worked out, she continues, "I was so amazed with the way you just . . . took charge after your dad died. Suddenly, you were a real adult with real adult problems, while the rest of us were still kids. But then college admissions happened and it became obvious *everyone* was growing up without me. Dalia has all these plans for herself and Chai Ho. Mena has her art. What will I have if she leaves me?"

That's when it hits me that I'm not the only one who's been terrified of what tomorrow will bring. No longer fighting the urge to hug her, I pull her into my arms and whisper, "Dan, you'd have us, no matter what. Even your parents will come around to it, whatever you decide. I've seen how much they love you. How much we all love you."

"But love isn't always enough," she chokes out. "I don't think Mena and I could survive a long-distance relationship. That's why she's giving me this ultimatum. Either we're together or we find other people."

I rub her back. "I know you don't want to hear it right now, but your dad's right about one thing."

She tenses. "What?"

"You *are* only eighteen," I reply. "You've got all the time in the world to figure out what *you* want to do. If you and Mena are meant to be, you will be. She'll find her way back to you. The same is true of your family. If they deserve to be in your life, they'll fight to stay in it. People who love you should want you to choose your own happiness."

Nayim's gorgeous face materializes in my mind.

Those honey-sweet eyes I could drown in. The spell of his voice, which dared me to be the boldest version of myself. His lips on mine.

Being with him was exciting, but excitement alone wouldn't have made us happy when we both misunderstood one another so deeply.

"What's going to make *you* happy, Dan?"

Dani and I rock together for a while, her head under my chin, until she emits a wobbly laugh. "Ugh. Here you are, having to comfort your friend choosing between college or travel, as if both aren't out of reach for you."

"You've always been there for me," I argue, shaking my head. "I want to return the favor because I love you. Besides—" A bitter chuckle escapes me, prompting her to gaze up. "I wish I had everything figured out, but I'm more confused than I've ever been."

Dani angles back enough to take me in. "What's wrong? Is it the guys? I thought Harun was pretty cool when he came by, but if you still like Nayim and you're telling me to be selfish, then you have to know it's okay for you, too."

"It *is* Nayim," I admit, "but not the way you think."

She and the others already know we broke up, but I didn't

think it was my place to expose his lies. Now that it's apparent he might be gone forever, I fill her in about our fallout at the picnic. Her brown eyes bulge at the revelation that he's not an orphan and ditched me when I refused to abandon my life in Paterson to run away with him.

"Holy crap," she says when I'm all done. "I thought it was bizarre how he just vanished off the face of the planet over a breakup, but I never guessed that—"

"Plot twist?" I finish for her wearily. "Yeah, me neither."

She studies me, a wrinkle between her brows. "Did you want to be with him? I—I know I keep telling you to be selfish, but the thought of you giving a second chance to some douche who left without saying goodbye seriously makes me want to throttle him." The frankness of this startles a snort out of me. She holds up her hands in defense. "But for real, Dalia, Mena, and I—and even your family—would learn to live with it if that's what you wanted."

I don't know if it's true that Amma would understand a choice like that.

Maybe if we were as rich as the Emons, our reputation would matter less if I all but eloped. But even they seem to be trapped by ideas of status, wealth, and lineage that our ancestors carried across three oceans and hundreds of years. Otherwise, why would they agree to the arrangement between me and Harun in the first place?

But that's not it, really.

Shaking my head, I murmur, "The boy I thought I had

feelings for isn't real. He lied to me and my family. To *everyone*. He looked me in the eye and let me think he knew what it was like to lose someone the way I did."

Disappointment swells again in my chest. Only now, I know that I deserve better.

Know, even, what better might look like.

The memory of Harun helping me during the mela rushes back. He didn't expect anything in return. He just stepped in where he was needed, silently promising me his presence.

Dani is quiet for a moment before saying, "I think I have to break up with Mena."

A fresh spring of tears wells in her eyes.

I hold her. Support her. And we cry.

Chapter 29

Tuesday morning, I wake up to the sound of Amma and Nanu in full triage mode.

Scrambling out of my top bunk, I trudge barefoot into the living room, then stumble back when a ball of thread rolls by. "Amma, what's—"

"Oh, Zahra, good morning," my mother says without looking up.

"You can heat up khisuri for breakfast," Nanu chimes in.

The tornado-swept living room has become a familiar sight by now. My mother and grandmother are stooped over a chaotic assemblage of fabric rolls, beads, zari-work, fake jewels, and mannequins with needles sticking out of them like voodoo dolls.

I still cock my head. "What's going on?"

"The bride-zolad and her fiancé are coming tomorrow to see what we've prepared so far," Amma replies. "Thanks to her unexpected material change, I'm far from ready."

Resisting the urge to give her awful client an earful, I say, "Can I help?"

The two of them blink up at me at last, wearing identical amused expressions, but it's Amma who says, "Nonsense. You can't possibly do much now that we're in the final stretch. It will only slow me down if I have to worry about you stabbing yourself while trying to thread a needle."

"Why don't you go check on your siblings?" Nanu adds. "Or your friends?"

That's a bit harsh. I'm great at pouring tea, which requires stellar hand-eye coordination if you don't want to spill it on the table or a customer's lap—ask me how I know.

They quickly return the topic to the bride-zolad's visit and what foods to serve her. I make my way to the kitchen. Arif and Resna are at the table, poring over stapled pages of coloring and alphabet worksheets, nubs of crayons scattered around them.

My brother taps a page. "Your uppercase *Q* is missing a line."

"Not a line," pouts my baby sister. "A *squiggle*."

Arif rolls his eyes. "If you know the squiggle is missing, add it."

Hiding my smile behind the rim of the cup of tea I pour myself from the kettle Nanu's left on the stove, I realize that I'd crave this if I ever left. Sure, my family can be messy, but they're *my* mess.

Back in my bedroom after finishing breakfast, I plop onto my creaky chair. It rolls for a second. I've been trying to write, so my laptop is open next to my notebook. When I pass my fingertips over the faded keys, the screen blinks on and my muscles go rigid.

Gmail displays one new message.

Unlike the spam I've been getting from colleges, financial aid scammers, and scholarship websites for the last six months, this one comes from a familiar sender—Professor Liu—with the subject *Manuscript Feedback*.

Oh my God!

Oh no, oh no, oh no, no, no, no, no starts running through my head on a loop, while I try to quell the tremor in my hands and lungs.

Aside from my friends, a handful of encouraging teachers, and fangirling internet strangers, very few people have read my writing. In most cases, it's been excerpts, essays, or fanfics, whereas this book is the most *me* thing I've ever written.

I was so excited to send it to Professor Liu, but I've been dreading that decision since, obsessively checking my email and feeling a blend of relief and disappointment every time she didn't write back. If she tells me my book is trash, I don't know if I can find the will to keep dreaming after getting so many signs to give it all up.

Somehow, I find my phone in my grasp, my fingers moving with a mind of their own. I shared some of my writing with a professor at the community college and she finally responded.

That's great, comes Harun's instant reply. Isn't it? What did she say?

I haven't opened it yet.... What if she hated it?

Then she'd be a shitty professor, he texts, matter-of-fact as ever.

I choke out a watery laugh. You're ridiculous.

I'm not. I just know you're a good writer.

Although I can't hear him, the conviction in his words rings clear. But did he actually track down some of my pieces? It wouldn't be particularly challenging. My school published some poetry, essays, and short stories in their online newsletter, while other snapshots of my work are available if you scroll for a while through my Instagram page.

But he actually *likes* them?

My silly heart flutters in my chest. I swallow the giddy feeling and defend Professor Liu. She probably won't tell me outright if it's godawful, anyway. She'll give constructive criticism.

It's kind of scary that I've bared my soul for someone else to measure its worth, but that's what's supposed to happen in creative writing classes. It can't be that much worse than the trolls on the internet who flamed me for writing about brown girls, could it?

Cool. Then you'll fix your book and impress her.

I glare half-heartedly at my phone. You are way too sure of my abilities.

You're not sure enough, he answers.

Ugh, this boy!

Perhaps I should be irritated by how easy he thinks this is, envious of how easy everything always seems to be for him, but

I've seen what lies beneath his unruffled demeanor by now and know he's far from perfect, with a far-from-perfect life. Just texting him has grounded me and eased some of my anxieties.

Okay, I'm going to check.

His response elicits an unbidden smile: Call me after?

Sucking in a deep breath and screwing my eyelids shut, I click Professor Liu's email. When nothing leaps off the screen to bite my head off, I open one eye and skim her message.

> *Miss Khan:*
> *Thank you for sharing your work with me. You are such a talented writer. You have a grasp of setting and character uncommon in writers your age, and I look forward to helping you further hone these skills. I've attached comments below, but I'd prefer to read the rest of the novel before giving you overarching feedback. Do you think you can send it to me before the semester starts and I get busy with my new students? Or at least an outline, so we can discuss weak links in your plot? Congratulations on an excellent start to your first draft. This book is going to be so special!*

My jaw drops.

Rather than opening the attached document to read her in-line comments, I blast my angry-girl playlist of Billie Eilish and Olivia Rodrigo from my laptop speakers to give us some privacy and immediately call Harun, who picks up on the first ring.

"Am I dreaming?"

"Um," comes his clever retort. "I guess it went well?"

"It was unreal!"

His smile practically radiates through the phone as I babble about Professor Liu's praise, and suddenly I wish I'd FaceTimed him instead, if only to see it.

I'm not sure what this means for me, especially after what happened with the bride-zolad, but I do know I'm finally ready to stop standing in my own way.

For the first time in the years since I started it, I know how my book ends.

It's impossible to write the number of words I need to finish the book in one sitting, so I split my time between outlining the rest of the plot in detail like Professor Liu suggested, and word-vomiting as much as I can of the new chapters into my Google Doc.

Day shifts to night outside.

When there are too many spots dancing in front of my vision to ignore any longer, I send the new outline and additional chapters to Professor Liu, shoot her an email, and trudge out of the kitchen, where I've been working to avoid disrupting Nanu's peaceful slumber.

Despite my best efforts, she cracks open an eye as I tiptoe

into our bedroom, deposit my laptop on my desk, and scale the ladder to my bunk. "Bala asso nee, moyna?"

Are you okay?

For once, the answer feels like yes.

I whisper for her to go back to sleep. My now-charging laptop sits on the desk across from us, but I still have my phone. The temptation to check my email gnaws at me, though I already know Professor Liu won't check it after midnight, so instead I text the *other* person I desperately want to hear from: Harun.

When can we see each other again?

He replies in just a few minutes, a boy after my own heart: Can you do tomorrow around 3-ish? There's somewhere I've been wanting to take you.

I'm scheduled for work tomorrow, so I should turn him down. The old Zahra certainly would have. Hell, she would have avoided *anything* that meant a smaller paycheck. But I've been that Zahra for such a long time, without getting anywhere for my efforts.

Harun wants to spend time with me. Take me somewhere lovely. I want that too, so I text the twins, asking them to cover for me at Chai Ho, before finally giving Harun my answer.

Yes!

If he says something after that, I'm not sure, because I nod off, smiling.

I wake up the next morning to a good-night text from Harun and an email from Professor Liu: *I had a chance to read your outline before my class. What an epic planned conclusion! Do you think you can stop by campus this morning so we can chat? My class finishes at ten.*

Yes, thank you, Professor!!! I respond, as ecstatic as I was last night.

Only then do I realize that I've double-booked my day. I don't have to meet up with Harun until later, but if I'm going to meet Professor Liu in time, I need to catch a bus downtown, which means I should get my butt dressed ASAP.

"Hi, Amma, bye Amma!" I shout as I snatch a couple of still-hot bhafa fita—round rice pastries with golden coconut flakes inside that I'd normally dip into my tea or drizzle all over in sticky honey—shove one into my mouth, toss the other between my hands to avoid scalding my fingers, and vault out the door.

She yells after me, but I don't hear what. It's worth it to reach the bus stop before my ride deserts me. I eat the second fita after dropping into an empty seat, and make it to the Passaic County Community College campus.

The girl at the front desk hands me a guest pass and points me toward the lecture hall, but I remember it from the last time I visited. When I enter this time, there are many more students, eyes affixed to Professor Liu's projected screen, though a few cast me irked glances.

She smiles and juts her chin at a chair toward the back, mouthing that it's almost over. The expression on her face is vaguely guilty, but I sit at the table she pointed out and peer around, adrenaline kicking through my veins. I'm in a real live college class!

No one treats me like I don't belong despite my earlier disruption. Soon I lose myself in the comforting inflection of Professor Liu's voice as she lectures on the concept of a three-act structure. When the class ends, I'm almost disappointed, although of course I'm dying to know what exactly she wants to discuss that required me to come all the way down here.

"Thank you so much for meeting me, Miss Khan," she says once we're alone. "There's someone I want to introduce you to."

I pick at a loose thread on my jeans. "Really? Who?"

"My co-chair," she replies. "Come along this way."

We stride down the long hallways toward what I presume is the faculty office area, where a harried-looking man wearing a yarmulke sits bent over a desk, a collection of papers fanned on top and a green pen in his hand.

He lifts his head upon hearing the clack of Professor Liu's heels, smiling warmly. "Ah, Cecilia! And this must be the illustrious Miss Khan?"

"Um, hi, sir."

Illustrious?!

Professor Liu nods. "Yes, the young novelist I've been telling you about." She turns to me. "And this is Professor Elijah Lewenberg, the co-chair of the English department. I've been apprising him of your ambitions since I finished what you sent me."

"Very impressive at your age," Professor Lewenberg says.

"Especially if you caught Cecilia's eye. Impressing her is a true feat."

A pleased blush warms my face. "Th-thank you."

"Why don't you take a seat, Miss Khan?" Professor Liu suggests, though she remains standing.

When I do as bidden, her co-chair says, kindly, "Cecilia also told me you won't be able to enroll next semester. Financial hardships, was it?"

Now my cheeks redden for a different reason. "Yes, sir. I don't think I can manage this semester, but maybe by the next one, or the following fall? I've been working hard to save up money, but I can't handle going full-time yet because I need to help my family."

"I see."

He has cornflower-blue eyes that harbor no judgment in them. They flick to meet Professor Liu's black ones, and the two of them nod.

"I don't want you to get your hopes up, but I asked Eli to meet you before the two of us talk to the office of the bursar," she says.

"Um, why?"

"I would very much like for you to be able to enroll in at least my creative writing class, Miss Khan," Professor Liu continues. "I hoped if Eli and I campaigned together, we could get the cost of the class reimbursed for you, so you could attend this fall."

My eyes grow huge. "Really? You'd do that for me? Why?"

Embarrassingly enough, my voice cracks on the last word.

Professor Liu sets her hands on my shoulders, while her co-chair's smile widens. It's he who says, "Because we see your vast potential, Miss Khan. Yours is a rare talent that will only grow if given the proper attention, and we'd like to do our part as educators in this community to see you harness it, without forcing you to choose between your passion and your next meal."

I'm so choked up, I can't reply right away, but finally direct another question at them. "How can I possibly repay you both?"

Professor Liu stoops closer to me to say, "You can put us in your acknowledgments when you become a famous novelist. And Miss Khan?"

"Yes, Professor?"

"Do finish up the rest of your manuscript so I can celebrate when my favorite heroine gets her happy ending, won't you?"

Laughing, I prance out of the campus more inspired than ever.

Maybe Harun was right: maybe the world is already here for me.

For us.

Chapter 30

Amma frowns when I return home before the typical end of my shift, and I curse myself for forgetting to tell her I called out.

Maybe it's for the best. I'm not sure I'm ready to talk to her about the class.

Thinking on my feet, I say, "Mr. Tahir let us out early. The twins and I were going to meet up with Mena at the wheelhouse." Amma's brows draw together, and I squirm in the kitchen doorway, wondering why she seems so troubled. "Is that okay? If you need me for something, I can cancel."

"No, I don't need you," she says, but she's slicing the eggplant she holds over the curved blade of her daa with more force than necessary. "Is it actually the twins you're seeing?"

Ice bleeds into my veins. Could she somehow have figured out my plans with Harun?

No way. Not after I objected to the match so heartily.

"Of course I am," I reply with as much affront as I can

muster. "Didn't you hear the aunties at the mela? You don't have to worry about Nayim anymore. We broke up."

Her grip tightens on the daa. "That's true, then? The imam's wife said he returned to Bangladesh. You haven't talked to him?"

"I don't know anything about him anymore." I shrug but can't quite keep the caustic edge from my voice at the revelation that she and her friends have been gossiping about Nayim. About us. Of course they have. "Your friends are probably right. They usually are. He's somewhere far, far away from me, in any case. Just like you wanted."

Such a long beat passes that I think she's done with me, until she stands up and claps her hands together. "The best way to cure a broken heart is to find something new to fill it! Perhaps we should find you something prettier to wear in case you bump into a nice Bengali boy?"

"Huh? S-something prettier? Another boy? What's wrong with this—"

Before I can protest her comment about fishing for a new suitor or finish listing the merits of the T-shirt and jeans I'd thrown on to meet Professor Liu, Amma has already manhandled me into her bedroom to cart out the luggage under her bed, where she stores the creations specially made for me, Arif, and Resna.

In no time at all, I end up waiting in Woodland Park, where Dalia has driven me again, dressed in a flowing pink, strawberry-print dress my mother modeled after a trend she saw on Pinterest a couple of years ago, dizzy from having gotten sucked into Hurricane Amma for the umpteenth time.

Her delight in getting rid of Nayim irks me, but I begrudgingly accept her wisdom when Harun swallows hard at the sight of me, eyes wide behind his glasses and cheeks ruddy.

"Y-you look pretty," he says, before remembering to greet Dalia.

She shoots me a smirk. "I can't believe you're already meeting the family, Zar."

By family, she means our not-chaperones for the night: Sammi and a martyr of a boy who can only be her younger brother, Harun's best friend and cousin, Shaad. He resembles Harun in every way but the most important, lacking the earnest sweetness Harun hides behind a frown. Shaad's loose curls are styled back using gel; there's a pout on his full lips; and red-soled Air Jordans don his feet, matching the tint of the Ray-Bans over his eyes.

The sulk and sunglasses vanish as he appraises Dalia, pulling the latter down his aristocratic nose. "Well, well, well. Maybe today won't suck, after all. Are you joining us too?"

He gives her a smolder that she breezes right past with a practiced smile. "Nope, sorry. Some of us have jobs, not inheritances."

If possible, the barb elicits a dopier grin. "Shame. Next time?"

Harun levels an apologetic glance my way. "Sorry about

that. Romeo over there wheedled today's plans out of me, and then Sammi Afa got it out of him. She said she'd only cover for us if we let them tag along."

Sammi slings her arms around her cousin's and brother's shoulders, forcing both to bend toward her almost comedically. "You can't imagine how delighted I was to hear about your escapades with Haru-moni, Zahra. Much as I love these two, I need you to rescue me from a testosterone overdose. We never did have enough girls in the family."

Dalia elbows me. "Who knows? If you play your cards right, that might change soon."

"Dal, please," I grit out, casting a long-suffering look at her.

She responds by pushing me toward the BMW like she can't wait to get rid of me. I stagger into Harun, who catches me. The two of us peer at each other for a second, hearts thumping in time with one another, until Shaad wolf-whistles and we jerk away.

Glaring at his cousin, Harun opens the front passenger door and I step in. Shaad and Sammi duck into the backseat. We all tell Dalia goodbye and drive off. Once we've gone a few blocks, I examine my three companions. "Where are we going?"

"The balloon festival," Harun says. "Have you been?"

"No . . . What do you do at a balloon festival?"

"If you don't know, don't Google it," he replies with an endearingly serious expression. "I want to see your face when we get there."

Oh, there's that blush again.

"O-okay." I flash him a timid smile, then glance over at Sammi and Shaad, who seem to be nitpicking each other's outfit choices. "So, they're actually coming?"

"Yes," Sammi answers in Harun's stead, prompting Shaad to groan as she presumably encroaches his personal space. "My darling baby brother is going away to school soon. Who knows when we'll get to spend time with each other again? So I forced him to come with me." I turn, bemused, in time to catch her wink. "But don't worry, Zahra. The festival is big enough that we won't be third-wheeling on your date with Haru-moni."

"Kill me now," Shaad grumbles, crossing his arms like a petulant child.

"Oh, hush," his sister replies. "If you're a good boy, I'll get you funnel cake."

His eyes narrow. "I can buy my *own* funnel cake!"

I giggle as they devolve into more bickering. They remind me of how I am with Arif, except he'd appreciate me more if he ever saw the way Sammi babies her brother.

The balloon festival is in suburban Readington Township, a part of New Jersey I've never been to before despite living only an hour away, but we spend so much of that time on the highway that we don't pass many impressive sights.

I'm still wondering what's so special about it when we drive into the township, with its uniform white houses on bright green lawns. Sure, they're cute, but I have a feeling very few people who look like us live here. Before I can make this crack to Harun, however, I see *them*. Bright, colorful specks dot the sky, the closer we get to the airport hosting the festival.

"Are those—"

"Hot-air balloons," Harun says.

Dozens of teardrop shapes in every color and pattern available float amid the clouds, above the rolling fields of green on which the Solberg Airport buildings are located. Most of the space is occupied by various stages and vendors, carnival rides, circus tents, and petting zoos. All remaining areas harbor grounded balloons and visiting families.

A giant banner proclaims the name of the festival, but there are other endorsements as well: a quote from the governor calling it one of New Jersey's best events, the American Bus Association dubbing it one of the greatest festivals in North America.

An old white ticket taker reads the tickets Harun hands her, squints between them and us, then finally says, "Two VIP tickets and two general? VIP flights are soon. Enjoy!"

Sammi snatches the two stubs with GENERAL stamped across them from her cousin, then drags her brother away, calling over her shoulder, "You two kids have fun! Don't do anything I wouldn't do!" then smacks Shaad's arm when he audibly adds, "That's not exactly much."

Harun pinches the bridge of his nose. "I'm sorry about them."

"It's okay," I say. "I'm just glad we could see each other again today. I didn't think you'd planned something so big, though. VIP tickets?"

"Sammi Afa foisted them on me, actually," he replies. "Repayment for extorting her way onto this trip. Hope this is okay? I know you were kinda jittery on the bridge, but you don't have a fear of heights, do you?"

I eye him. "I'm starting to think you taking me to all these lofty places is an excuse to get me to cling to you."

"My master plan is working?" he asks with a grin.

I pretend to consider this, then shrug. "Maybe."

"Good." His fingertips extend to brush mine. "Because I'd love to hear what happened with that professor."

Feeling bold, I take his swinging hand and hold it the entire time we make our way through the maze of stalls and rides.

"It was great!"

His brows arch as I explain exactly what went down at the community college. "Zar, that's amazing! *You* are amazing!"

"It's nothing," I mumble, though I'm secretly pleased by how impressed he is.

"It is *not* nothing. Trust me, I've spent enough money on writing tutors to know that, and that was just for essays," he chides. "You think you'll do it?"

I worry my lip. "I don't know how my mother will react. She's always seen writing as my hobby. While she might be pleased if I'm able to attend a free creative writing course, she'll probably think it's a waste of time. She already has all these other plans for me."

Now that she thinks Harun and I are a no-go, those

plans involve finding another suitable match. It would be the comfortable life that she's promised, I have no doubt, but it doesn't sit right with me, to rely on *any* husband so much.

Harun squeezes my hand, contemplation creasing his forehead. "Writing is your bridge." It takes me a minute to get it, but when I do, I snort, and he smiles. "Actually, that's not the same at all. My folks are all talk. They didn't actually mind when I told them I'm studying mechanical engineering. But Zar, you're so good at writing that you *have* to do it."

"Yeah?"

His eyes are dark and sincere as he nods. "Yeah."

I might have stood on my tiptoes to kiss him right then and there, if some guy with a bullhorn and mic didn't boom at that exact moment, "VIP tickets, please make your way over to the balloons listed at the bottoms of your stubs."

"Wait." My eyes bulge. "Are we getting *on* a hot-air balloon?"

"I did ask if you were afraid of heights," Harun reminds me.

"Well, yeah, but—"

"No buts," he replies. "You trust me, right?"

I hesitate for no more than a second, then nod. He's always taken such care with me during these fake dates, even though they were often more of an inconvenience to him, what with him providing the chaperone, ride, and dinner every single time we met up despite Operation Zahrun being *my* idea all along.

He gives our interlocked fingers one last squeeze, before leading me toward the balloon labeled on our ticket, one decorated with blooming flowers. The pilot opens the hatch for us, and Harun helps me climb aboard. The basket wobbles as I do. I turn to hold on to him, then go red when I realize what I've done, grateful that we're the only passengers.

Harun doesn't seem to mind. He hangs on to me in return as we make our way over to the rim of the basket, around the engine at the center. I keep my eyelids shut, my cheek pressed against his chest, feeling the thump of his heart beneath the soft cotton of his shirt.

My grip tightens when the whoosh of the flames blowing into the balloon joins the sound of his heartbeat, steadily lifting us off the ground to the cheers of people below. Sensing my nerves, Harun starts to explain to me in his deep, calm baritone the process by which hot-air balloons work, the safety procedures, and so on, until my panicked breathing and the basket grow level.

"Zahra," he murmurs next to my ear. "Open your eyes."

I peel my eyelids apart and gasp at the sight that awaits us.

Solberg Airport and Readington Township are far, far below. Hundreds of people crowd together like ants, waving their arms and glow sticks at the balloons and the musicians performing concerts onstage. Other balloons float, some higher, some lower, but so many, we can hardly see the twilight sky swirling between us.

I know I keep saying it, but I think *this* is the highest I've ever been, yet I've never felt more grounded than I do with Harun's arms around me. As I stare into his eyes, there's no more doubting any of what I've been feeling for him. How funny that I fought against this so long, only to fall for exactly the boy my mother wanted for me.

"I like you," I blurt.

"I like you, too," he says.

I shake my head. "No. I mean that I have feelings for you. The unplatonic kind."

Harun gapes at me.

I bury my face in his chest, muffling a frustrated whine against it.

Feelings. Like. They're both such inadequate descriptions of the swirl of emotions that squeeze my heart like an embrace, the emotions that have only steadily, inevitably been growing since I met this boy in the dimness of his family's restaurant.

"You've always been there for me, honest with me, understood me," I say. If I don't get this out, I'll regret it forever. "I get it if it's too soon, but I don't *just* like you. I'm pretty sure what I'm feeling is so much bigger. I've fallen in . . . love with you."

The last part I choke out in one flustered breath. His gasp reverberates through his chest into my skin, but despite being brave enough to confess my love for him, I don't have the courage to look up yet, in case he rejects me now.

"It's okay if you don't feel the same way, and—"

Gentle fingers ghosting under my chin coax me to lift it. Dark brown eyes sparkling, Harun smiles down at me, so wide my thumb twitches with the urge to rub circles around that infernal dimple. "For someone so smart, you can be awfully dense sometimes, Khan."

"Hey!"

Soft lips slotting against mine cut any complaints short, tasting of wintergreen mint and cocoa-butter ChapStick. My arms flail in the air in shock, before I regain enough sense to lean into him, lifting up my palms to cradle his cheeks, keeping his glasses from falling off.

His face is warm from the blush that spreads through us both like a sip of hot tea. I wonder if he likes the strawberry flavor of my own gloss.

His breath tickles my lips when he pulls away just enough to say, "I love you, too, Zahra."

"Y-you do?" I ask.

Now a chuckle ruffles the errant strands that escape my ponytail. "I think I've been falling for you for a long time. Maybe before karaoke?"

"You *have*?" I groan into the crook of his neck.

His eyes have darkened with emotion that sends a thrill through me when I gaze back up. This time, I stand on my tiptoes to meet him halfway the instant his lips begin to descend toward mine. We pull apart only when we're both breathless and giddy. His glasses are foggy and skewed, but he doesn't seem to mind as he leans his forehead against mine and asks, "What does this mean? Do we . . ."

He trails off, but I know exactly what he's wondering.

Does dating again mean a wedding for us on the horizon like it usually does for people? Like our parents expect of us? Does *he* want that? What do we tell them?

"I care about you more than I know what to do with," I say at last, "but we're so young."

Harun lets out a sigh of relief. "Yeah. What's the rush? We can go back to our parents and tell them we want to keep trying. I don't even mind having an annoying chaperone along for the rest of our lives, if it means I can be with you."

"Then you must really like me," I say with a smirk.

"We've already established that." His forehead scrunches against mine, and his frown is so cute, I have no choice but to peck it away. He lets me, then pulls away, ignoring my growled objection. "I think I'm going to tell our parents that I want to keep seeing you but will consider marriage only after we've graduated from college. *Both* of us."

He looks at me intently.

It takes me a moment to grasp his words, but when I do, my eyes overflow with tears and I throw myself back into his embrace. If *he* says that and Amma wants us to be happy together, she'll *have* to be okay with college.

"Thank you, Harun."

A gust of wind makes the basket sway from side to side. Recalling that we're thousands of feet in the air, I cling to Harun again, taking care not to budge another inch until we land. He holds me the whole time.

I feel at home, tucked safely in his arms.

And if we have to wait, if we have to endure an endless parade of chaperones and rules and rumors, if we have to fight for it, so be it.

If this is true love, it just might be worth it.

Chapter 31

Once upon a time, Amma could take one look and diagnose exactly what was the matter with me. She would know I was sick before I did, and tut, with the cool back of her wrist pressed to my forehead, "Na, na, na, na, shuna, you should stay in bed. I'll bring the Vicks, khisuri, and some rong saa to fix you right up."

Or she'd ask, "Zahra, shuna, keetha oise?" the instant I came from school, already knowing I'd fought with a friend or someone had been mean to me, which would prompt me to burst into tears and blubber into the material of her kameez while she rubbed my back.

But that was before Baba died, before we acquired so many troubles that it was no longer simple to keep track of them all. She still *tries*, but I've gotten better at hiding things for both our sakes. My siblings, who are younger, need more of her time anyway.

Tonight, however, she seems to sense a disturbance in

the force the instant I step into the apartment. She looks me up and down, like kissing Harun has changed something fundamental about me. "Furthi khorso nee?"

"Yes, I had fun. I'm happy!" I plunk down next to her on the couch, almost causing her to drop the needle she's threading when the cushion bounces. "I have a special surprise for you."

She sets her sewing equipment aside, like she doesn't want anything pointy and dangerous in her grasp when she hears this. "A . . . surprise?"

"A special one," I emphasize, mimicking what she told me at Chai Ho that first time I met Harun. "All you have to do is make sure everyone's dressed for a night out Saturday. I'll take care of everything else. Okay?"

"Saturday?" She tenses up. "I—I can't this weekend. I'm sorry."

"Oh."

Despite my best efforts, I can't keep my face from falling. Amma swallows at the sight of my disappointment, casting a glance toward the kitchen, where Nanu is teaching Arif how to roll out and make rutis by hand.

"It's because I have a surprise for you, too," she continues.

Before familiar apprehension can flood through me, she sets down her needlework to pick up her phone, scrolling through the Auntie Network WhatsApp group until she finds a picture of a poster bordered in flowers. She holds it up for me to read.

নাসরিন শাহ
কনসার্ট

I squint at the text, then remind her, "I can't read Bengali."

Her laugh is staccato and unusually nervous. "It's a free concert tomorrow night at the falls. With Nasrin Shah."

"Who?" I ask.

"Nanu's favorite natok actress," Amma explains. "Shah is her married name."

My eyebrows disappear into my hairline. "I thought she'd Meghan Markle'd her way out of that song and dance. Literally."

"Er, yes." Bemusement clouds Amma's features, but she doesn't let that stop her. "That's why this concert is so special. I promised your nanu I would take her and hoped we could make a family night out of it."

Hmm. While walking around the fair together after our balloon ride, Harun and I originally planned to *Parent Trap* our families at Gitanjali, but there's no reason it can't be at the falls. Although half the city will be there, there's a certain anonymity in a teeming crowd where everyone's attention is on a stage.

Besides, our folks will have to be on their best behavior in public, which will make it more likely that they accept the terms of Harun and me continuing to date.

"Okay," I say.

Her eyes widen. "Okay? You'll be there?"

"Wouldn't miss it for the world."

I flash her that Good Bangladeshi Daughter smile she loves so much. Amma drops a kiss on my temple, the last of her caginess draining out of her. I wait until my back is to her to grin.

Oh, how the tables have turned.

The second I've shut the door behind me in my blessedly empty bedroom, I shoot Harun a text. **Operation Zahrun Part Two is a go.**

This is the one where we don't break up, right? he responds.

I laugh. **We'd better not, robot boy, or I'll sic the twins on you.**

Not even those two could scare me away from you, he answers, and my breath hitches.

Leave it to Harun to turn our playful banter into heartfelt, romantic declarations. He's quick to agree when I inform him about the change in destination for our plans, having already heard about the concert from his own mother.

We can have dinner at the restaurant after, he suggests.

Perfect!

Once we say good night, I crawl into bed. Part of me feels bad for tricking Amma. I'm more than prepared for us to start being honest with each other . . . but all's fair in love and war, so honesty can wait till tomorrow night.

Besides, once she learns the truth, I suspect she'll be in a forgiving mood. For once, both our ideas of a happily-ever-after are aligned.

Either Nasrin Shah is the Bengali Beyoncé, rolling in dough, or *both*, because it's astonishing how quickly a Grammy-level comeback concert has been arranged for her.

Even from a block away, I can hear the gathering audience at the falls, their excited voices swelling louder than the ever-present *shhhhh* of the waterfalls and the Passaic River. The chaotic chorus is accompanied by the deep bass of drums and the sweet whistle of flutes.

Repurposed bedsheets dot every inch of green lawn in front of a newly built stage. A dedicated crew tinkers with the sound system and a spotlight, which offsets the golden glow of the string lights hung from the safety barriers and trees in the vicinity. Instrumentalists surround the stage and audience, dressed in elaborate costumes. A camera crew records the entire production from the fringes of the park.

Everyone is here.

Ushers clutching antique lanterns walk around, helping people find seats in the pandemonium. As one of them strides up to us, I whisper to Amma, "I thought this was a free concert. . . . Are there assigned seats? Tickets?"

She ignores me to introduce herself to the man. When he hears we're the Khans, he nods at another group of ushers conducting the growing crowd. Only when they nod back does he direct us toward the front of the stage. With him leading us, people part to make room, but I squint at his back, mystified.

Must be some Bengali concert etiquette I'm unfamiliar with or something.

Nanu stands on her tiptoes and cranes her neck every few steps to catch a glimpse of her favorite shilpi. Letting her set the pace, I allow Resna to drag me through the teeming bodies, Amma and Arif at our heels. There are vendors holding trays of snacks and drinks weaving past us, the Tahir girls and their father among them.

I even spot Ximena sitting on a boulder, clasping her iPad and a stylus. She's too far away to wave at, but I know the two of us will be okay. After my heart-to-heart with Dani on Monday, I called Ximena to let her know the two of us would still be friends no matter what. From now on, I'll even listen more.

No matter where the world takes us, we'll all be there for each other.

Giddiness wells inside my chest at the prospect of telling my friends about me and Harun, but it's only when Resna points and exclaims, "There's the mean boy!" that a true, ear-to-ear smile splits my lips.

"He is *not* mean," I correct her, redirecting her to the assorted picnic blankets a mere foot away from the stage where the extended Emon clan sits.

Nanu is still distracted, seeking out Nasrin, wizened hands gripping a tiny notepad and pen tightly in the hopes of getting an autograph, but I can sense the rest of my family watching me in confusion. Harun has noticed us by now, however, and I only have eyes for his brightening face.

But I can't seem too eager yet, so I wander close enough for him to point out to his mother, "Look, Ma, it's Zahra."

She glances away from the two women she's huddled beside. My own mother winces as if pained, though I can't fathom why, but manages a strangled, "Assalamualaikum, Afa."

"Walaikum salaam," Pushpita Khala says. "Do you need seats? Why don't you join us? We got here early and commandeered too much space."

"Pita tells us all the time about your dressmaking," adds a dark-eyed woman who must be her sister and Hanif's mother, if his scowl over her shoulder is any indication.

Another woman chimes in, "We'd love to see your work. Perhaps I could hire you to make something for my kids? A matching sherwani and shalwar kameez would look so lovely in new family portraits!"

"Jeez, you make it sound like we're toddlers," grumbles Shaad, eyes glued to his phone.

Sammi Afa, snuggled between him and a man who's presumably her husband, declares, "Um, yes, how adorable would that be?"

I turn to Amma.

The grimace hasn't left her face, but before she can retort, *I couldn't impose,* Nanu tells the others, "Onek dhanyabad. My old bones can't take any more walking." She plops down then and there, and when Amma reluctantly joins her, whispers, "They're the closest to the stage."

Fighting a smile, I let Sammi Afa corral me and my siblings onto the second blanket, where she and the other "kids" are. I don't protest my proximity to Harun. Arif frowns at the way our pinkies brush on top of the blanket but doesn't comment, instead ensuring Resna is affixed to his lap.

When Mansif Khalu returns with two other men, arms laden with Styrofoam dishes of mishti, chaat, and saa, Harun and I exchange a glance and a nod.

It's time to reveal the truth to everyone, once and for all.

Harun takes a deep breath. "There's something we have to tell you—"

The sound of drums, accompanied by a woman's lilting vocals, cuts him off. Spotlights flash across our picnic area, leading to the stage, where they shine above the thick velvet curtains. They part to expose the most beautiful woman I've ever seen, in an elaborate violet-and-gold shari, jewels crowning her long, thick black braid, threaded with silver strands. She's older than she was in the natok Nanu was watching when Nayim came over, but her more mature features do nothing to diminish her allure.

As soon as she appears, the music ceases to allow room for the deafening applause that fills the night. I doubt even Taylor Swift would get such a welcome. The entire crowd is now on their feet, whooping and cheering. Nanu might be the loudest of them all.

"Ekh asil ekh badsha," Nasrin croons before pausing to allow for another wave of applause. She's just uttered famous words that start many Bengali folktales—there once was a king. Her glittering eyes scan the assemblance, her lips upturned into a bright red smile. "I'm sure if you're here, you must know my story already?"

"Nasrin, Nasrin, Nasrin!" her faithful fans chant, led by Nanu.

Nasrin gives them a pageant wave, solid gold bangles tinkling on her wrists. "It fills my heart with such joy to know my fans continue to remember and celebrate my work almost twenty years after I retired from performing. But I never once stopped thinking of all of you. Now I'm a happy wife and mother. In fact, that's why I'm here tonight."

The crowd cheers again, tossing flowers up to the stage. They land at Nasrin's bare, nupur-adorned feet, bells chiming as she spins and holds her palms up toward the curtain. "It gives me great pleasure to perform tonight with my beloved son. I hope you, my fans, my family away from family, will welcome him with the same warmth you did me."

With that, she takes a breath and begins the song again: "Ekh asil ekh badsha—"

The drummers play in tandem with the melody, the heady beat pulsing like a heartbeat through the falls. With each echoing thump of their instruments, accentuated by the building tempo of the flutists, the curtains inch apart again. Several disembodied voices rise together in song, telling the story of two barren queens and their heirless king.

Even as they do, a giant pomegranate flower descends from the top of the stage, paper petals pressed together around a glowing pistil. The singers, women and girls in bright green and red shalwar kameezes with orange flowers in their hair, dance nimbly out of the curtains on either side of the stage and twirl beneath the bud, telling the tale of how the younger queen struck a bargain with a traveling magician for a child.

"Dalim Kumar, blessed by the stars," sings a pixie-like little girl Resna's age in English, joined by other costumed children. "Matchless near and far, Dalim Kumar!"

Nasrin's voice rises above the rest. "A prince like no other, treasure of me, his mother!"

She claps her hands—once, twice, thrice, each clap summoning the thunderous pounding of the drums. The pomegranate flower begins to tremble. By the third clap, the petals tear and scatter when a tall man in a golden mask bursts forth from it, waving a prop sword—presumably the famed Prince Dalim Kumar, played by Nasrin's son.

"Dalim Kumar, zeh naam amaar," he sings in a crisp, carrying tenor, introducing himself.

Although his face isn't visible, he certainly appears matchless, floating over the rest of the actors on a rising platform that escaped the pomegranate bud, wearing an opalescent pagri and a fanjabi beaded with pearls and gold thread.

"Nanu told me this kiccha," a round-eyed Resna stage-whispers from Arif's lap.

Nanu somehow hears her over the queen and prince's duet and nods. "It's a famous story from *Thakurmar Jhuli*. They took a few liberties, but I watched every week on NTV. Nasrin played the role of Dalim's princess then, but she looks so regal as the queen now."

"They're seriously going all out, huh?" Harun mumbles next to me.

Hanif narrows his eyes at the theatrics. "How do they have the production values for this? And how did they get a permit so fast?"

I shrug wordlessly, watching with bated breath as Nasrin's gaze passes over the gathering until stopping, almost eerily, on me. Conversationally, she asks, "Shouldn't a prince so handsome, so majestic, have a princess?"

The spectators scream their agreement.

Although his face is hidden, the smile in the prince's voice is apparent when he speaks. "What if I told you all . . . she's already here?"

Spotlights shine across the blankets where we sit.

A gasp rips out of me when I turn to find dancers flitting through the audience, stopping to gaze dramatically into the faces of girls in the throng, shaking their heads each time, until they finally convene in front of the stage and pirouette around to face—

Me.

I work my jaw as they open their bangled arms in my direction, not quite believing it even when they croon, "Zahra, tumare sara zara zai tho nai!"

Can't bear to . . . be without me?

I know that melody. But the last time I heard it was . . . my stomach drops.

I'm too stunned to stop the two dancers who reach for my arms and hoist me to my feet, though I feel someone attempting to grasp my skirt—perhaps Harun.

Twirling around me, they lead me up the steps to the stage. The crowd is practically feral, cheering so loudly that they drown out the singers' voices and the booming of the drums.

My feet move of their own accord toward the raised dais, where the masked prince lowers a hand to me. I can feel my pulse thrumming in every vein, my breath coming in short spurts, but the sooner I let this play out, the sooner I hope I can go back to Harun and my family. I steal a glance at the blanket where I was just seated and see my mother's beaming face. I look ahead once more and see the stage right before us. The prince reaches down toward me.

I take his hand.

The prince tugs me up so fast, I stumble into his chest, then glance up to meet his gaze at last. Familiar honey-gold eyes twinkle back at me.

A shaky breath wrenches out as I whisper, "How in the . . ."

Elegant fingers entwine around my own as the prince kneels in front of me. Gripping my hand in his, he uses his other hand to remove his mask and the pagri, baring his handsome face to the world.

A murmur begins to ripple through the audience as the onlookers in the front relay their discovery of the prince's identity to the others. I don't need to hear them to know what they're saying. *The dishwasher . . . orphan . . . Nasrin Shah's son? . . . That means . . .*

Louder than the rest, Mr. Tahir exclaims, "Nayim?!"

No longer singing, Nayim says, "Zahra, you were the first person to like me, to believe in me, for who I am, rather than because of my family's wealth or title. I missed you every breath we were apart. Without you, I was a total mess."

The mic taped to his cheek carries his speech throughout the entire park, to deafening gasps, cheers, and applause.

"Wh-what?" I manage to whisper, eyes darting between his radiant face and the congregation watching our every move. The lights are too bright for me to find my family or Harun. I sweat beneath them, my throat parched, hyperaware of the cameras broadcasting every second far beyond the city. "What are you doing back? You left! You—"

Lied to me.

Asked me to run away.

Left the scattered pieces of your life for me to clean up.

"Made a terrible mistake," he replies plaintively. "I needed that time away because I didn't know if I could be the man you needed me to be. I returned to Bangladesh to confront my parents. Told them about you and how you make me a better person. Told them everything."

"Of course," chimes Nasrin, sweeping over to stand beside us with a magnanimous smile, "I told my son, tumar dil eh dakher. Follow your heart. How could I deny my child a fairy-tale romance when I had one of my own?"

The audience crows in approval, but Nayim's hopeful smile is only for me. "When I kept getting signs that we should be together, I knew I had to return to Paterson, so I could ask you . . ."

"Ask me?" I repeat numbly.

The crowd clamors again, as if they know exactly what's coming.

"Zahra, I can't lose you again," he confesses. "Will you marry me?"

I stare down at his gorgeous face. Even with perspiration beading his brow and his hair mussed up from the pagri, Nayim looks every bit a prince straight out of a natok or a novel or one of Nanu's bedtime stories. Out of all the things I've always loved.

Because he is.

He's an honest-to-God, literal prince—the son of one of the wealthiest men in Bangladesh—and he's here to win me back.

In front of everyone.

My heart clenches. My lips part, but I can't speak.

The crowd is chanting, "Say yes!" "Hurry!" "Oi kho!" "Zolji!" in English and Bengali.

I want my mom. I want Harun. My friends. I want someone to talk this through with me, because I have no idea how to process what's going on, and I somehow feel more alone than ever, despite the dozens of musicians and dancers around me.

Does my head bob of its own volition? Because the next thing I know, he flings his arms around me and the audience is chanting our names, clapping, cheering.

I reach up, but suddenly I have no clue what to do with my own arms—whether to pull Nayim closer or push him away— so I just stand there, too stupefied to move, closing my eyes in an effort to escape the dizzying lights. The music swells in a jubilant chorus, and I can hear movement all around me.

When I open my eyes again, I see that dancers are twirling all around us once more and someone has spirited my family onto the stage. Arif is gaping at us. Resna, in his arms, glances around every which way, the apples of her cheeks flushed feverishly as the actors swarm around them both to invite them to dance.

Nanu is hugging her notepad to her chest, peering through dewy eyes at Nasrin, who puts an arm around her shoulder.

And Amma . . .

No surprise graces her face at this unpredictable turn of events. She stands with her hands linked together in front of her chest, beaming at me and Nayim, seemingly unaware of the growing crowd of well-wishers who flock to the stage to congratulate her on a job well done.

"Khubi bhalo kham khorso!"

A job.

As if an engagement is some sort of promotion or a business arrangement. The fact that the performance was only a ruse for Nayim's proposal doesn't bother her or anyone else.

Sometime during the flurry, Nayim slips a ring from his finger onto mine. Cameras flash as news crews and random people snap pictures and record. The whole time, I stand there unable to speak, unable to move, like some sort of doe-eyed doll. Not even the clamor of our entire city's congratulations can quell the deafening roar growing in my ears.

There's only one face in the crowd I seek, and yet it's nowhere in sight.

I feel numb. Shell-shocked.

Everyone in the town is here. Everyone approaches the stage and offers their congratulations.

"Thank you," I murmur, time and again, while Nayim shakes their hands wholeheartedly.

Is this really what he wants? To be his father's son? The heir to a princely estate? My *husband*?

I swallow the hard lump in my throat and my mouth goes dry.

But eventually, the crowd below the stage thins enough from people clambering on top of it that I can slip away with a muttered, "I need to go to the bathroom," while Nayim shakes his hundredth hand of the night, beaming so wide that his face must hurt.

I elbow through the crowd, ignoring any congratulations lobbed at me or jealous smiles that undoubtedly wonder how I, a poor girl from Paterson, managed to win a prince's affections.

My heart pounding, I make my way back to the picnic blanket. To Harun.

Pushpita Khala and Mansif Khalu are having such a heated discussion about something—me?—that they don't even notice me approaching. Sammi Afa has a phone up to her ear, looking worried. She sighs, presses a button, and lifts it back to her ear, trying again. Hanif glares at me, more disgusted than ever. Shaad immediately looks down and won't meet my gaze.

My eyes scan the blanket, but Harun is gone.

Not bothering to waste another second, I kick off my heels and run barefoot through the park, trying to find him.

Tears begins to blur my vision, but I keep running, wondering what the hell just happened.

And wondering how this fairy tale has gone so very wrong.

Chapter 32

Thankfully, he's not hard to find.

Even if I didn't already know about his fondness for bridges, I'm able to spot Harun's lonely figure on the usually crowded footbridge overlooking the waterfalls from a mile away.

He has his head buried in his arms on the rustic wooden railing of the footbridge, unable to hear my padded footsteps over the latent instrumentals of what has somehow turned into my engagement party, the voices of half the city, and the ceaseless flow of the water below.

Cautious of splinters, I tiptoe over to him and stand at his side, our arms an inch apart. Droplets of water spray across my skin, raising goose bumps across it, and I will him to close the distance so I can nestle into his warmth, but he doesn't.

I break the silence first, speaking around the lump in my throat. "Harun . . . I had no idea Nayim was planning all of this."

"You two haven't talked?" he asks without glancing up.

I shake my head, then feel foolish when I realize he can't see. My eyes are burning for some unfathomable reason, even though I know, *I know*, that if I can just convince him of this, convince him of the truth, everything will be fine again. "I haven't even seen him since the picnic, but I'm going to straighten all this out, okay?"

This time he says nothing, and despair creeps past all the logic I'd been assuring myself with earlier. I reach for his hand, but the weight of Nayim's ring on my finger sends another wave of shame through me and I drop my arm back to my side. Heat races to my cheeks. "Please . . . I love you, Harun. I, just . . . I don't know how this happened."

"I love you, too," he croaks back.

I can't help sucking in a relieved lungful of sea-salt air. "Good. That's—I'm glad. We can figure this out." I take several more deep, shuddering breaths. "We can figure this out," I say again, but I'm not sure if I'm saying it to him or to myself.

He peers up at me at last, eyes red-rimmed behind his glasses. "No, you should—you should accept his proposal, Zahra."

"What?" His words are a punch to the gut. I feel dizzy. Nauseous. I stare at him uncomprehendingly.

Desperately.

"You don't," I begin, and my breath hitches, "want me anymore?"

He turns toward me, jaw set. "It's *because* I love you that I have to let you go."

Understanding floods me. "No."

"Zahra—"

"No!" I interrupt, balling my hands into fists. "People who love each other try, Harun. They don't 'fall on their swords.'" I lift up my fingers in an attempt to do air quotes, but my hands are too clenched to do it properly. I can feel my body shutting down, shutting off, entirely, and move to cling to the railing to anchor myself.

He doesn't get to quit on us. Not after everything we've been through to get here.

His shoulders tense as he steels himself to answer. I feel my own grow rigid in response. "I can't promise you the kinds of things Nayim can. Can't promise you *forever* when I barely have a grip on now. Who knows if we'll be together in a month, much less for the rest of our lives?"

"Wow." Sarcasm drips from the word as my fingers tighten on the railing enough to cut into my palm. "So that's how much you love me, huh? You can't imagine lasting for more than a month?"

Harun shakes his head frantically. "No, it's—not that. I meant it when I said you were the best thing that's happened to me." He bites his lip, and when his eyes rise to mine, they're filled with fire. "But I'm only eighteen! The last time I thought I saw a future with someone, we broke up after *two years*. Who's to say the same won't happen with us in a year, a month, hell, maybe a few weeks from now?"

I clench my jaw, but don't answer.

More softly, he continues, "*Then what*, Zahra? I can't let you give up a sure thing for a maybe."

The defeat in his voice snaps me out of my trance.

Releasing the railing to encroach into his personal space, I glare up at him in spite of the tears that trail down my cheeks. "I'm so sick and tired of everyone trying to *let* me do anything. I don't need you or Nayim or my mother or *anyone* to save me. I've been doing a damn good job of that myself!"

"I know," he whispers, lifting a hand to cradle my face. It falls away and swings listless at his side when I recoil. "I— that's exactly what I love about you, Zahra. You care more than anyone else I've ever met. But I'm just . . . me. I'm not someone who can promise you all your wildest dreams. Not like Nayim. If you need to marry him for your family, I won't stop you, no matter how much it hurts me to let you go."

"I chose you," I reply, spitting the words. "I chose you, but you're not choosing me."

"I am, though," he says sadly. "I'm choosing the future where you'll be the happiest. God, you get to be a literal princess married to a guy who's head over heels for you. Who came scowl for you. He can give you everything you need."

I scowl down at the churning waves, hating how he manages to sound so sensible.

My silence makes him gnaw on his lower lip for a moment, before he murmurs, "A *good* guy, no matter how much I wish I could hate him. A future with him is best for everyone you care about." He offers me a tragic smile. "And you know it too. That's why you didn't tell Nayim no, right?"

I open my mouth to argue, but nothing comes out. "I . . . that's not—"

I want to dispute this. I want to list all the reasons why I didn't immediately reject Nayim. I was shocked speechless. I didn't want to humiliate him. I didn't want to embarrass *myself* or my family. Especially in front of the entire freaking city.

But . . . my family . . .

Could they have been the real reason why I held my tongue?

Have those ill omens the aunties gave me during the community picnic metamorphosed into a Greek choir in the back of my mind?

Harun looks away when I don't respond. "If you tell Nayim no, the whole community will be watching us. And they'll hate us if we don't end up getting engaged. Then you'll be the girl who snubbed a prince for the 'New-Money Emons' and couldn't make it work. I don't care about me, but if I'm the reason you can't find someone else, I won't be able to live with myself." He rakes his hand through his hair. "God, I don't know if I could live with that kind of pressure."

"I thought you didn't believe all that bullshit about my only value being as someone's wife," I say, my voice barely a whisper.

"I don't." He tries to smile, but his eyes shimmer behind his glasses. "If there's anyone in the world who deserves a happily-ever-after with the most eligible bachelor in Bangladesh, it's you, Zahra. I can't take that from you."

I look down at the water, training my eyes on the waves below. I thought Harun was different. I thought he understood me.

"You have so much to offer," he murmurs, turning away from me. "That's why I can't hold you back. I'm sorry if you don't believe me, but I really do love you, Zahra. Enough to live with a broken heart if it means you'll get everything you ever wanted. Everything you *need*."

I hate everything about this conversation. About this situation. About my life. I hate that I even *see* the merit in his twisted, backward logic. I hate that I don't feel like I have a choice. That he's making my choice for me.

Instead all that comes out is, "I hate you."

"I'm sorry." His voice breaks. "Goodbye, Zahra."

The second he's gone, I can admit that I was lying when I claimed to hate him. I love him so much, it feels as though my ribs can't contain it all. Like my heart might explode into star-stuff and fleck the night sky with its jagged shards. Watching him walk away hurts so much more than it did with Nayim, but there's anger stoking in the hollow that remains in my chest.

How could he tell me he loves me, then abandon me all the same? How could he tell me it was *for* me? If it's for my sake, then why does it feel like I'll never be okay again?

Why does everyone keep leaving?

I crumple to the wooden planks of the bridge with the railing at my back and cry, with only the roar of the waterfalls to keep me company.

Chapter 33

Some amount of time later, I tense up when someone slides down next to me.

My bitterness gives way to heartache, and I can't help wishing for it to be Harun. For him to have come back to say he's sorry, that he didn't mean it, that he loves me more than he's scared of the consequences.

But the comforting scent of sandalwood burrows into my senses, and I realize it's Amma. She tugs me into the warm cushion of her side. Immediately, I burst into shuddering sobs I thought I'd already cried out.

She rubs my back, unbothered by the way I get snot all over the pallu of her shari, or the dirt from the footbridge staining her pleats. Her words are soothing, quiet nonsense, "Oh, amar shuna, amar jaan." My tears eventually subside, and my breathing slows.

Only then does she tip my chin up and ask, "What's wrong, Zahra? I thought you *wanted* to see Nayim again? To be with him?"

There's a trace of something pleading in her voice, something in the way her other hand pets my hair. I study her anxious expression, then manage to ask the question hanging between us. "Did you . . . have something to do with him coming back?"

Try as I might, I can't figure out the how or the why.

She kept Nayim and me apart. She didn't think he was good enough for me. His disdain toward her was what prompted our breakup in the first place, sending him all the way back to Bangladesh.

But the way Amma drags a palm across her face does little to stifle her sigh or the truth. "For once, I thought I was doing what you wanted."

I stare at her. What could have changed her heart so thoroughly, that she and Nayim could go from blaming each other for my happiness, to conspiring to reunite us?

"Was it . . ." I try to swallow past the growing dread in my throat. "Was it because you found out his secret? That he's from a rich family?"

Not just *any* rich family, but the prominent Shahs, whose heir is part prince, part superstar. Even the Emons can't hope to compare to them.

Real live royalty.

Or . . . close enough.

I never would have guessed that Nayim is a prince.

And he wants me to be his princess.

But he also lied to me, even about something as simple as his name.

Nayim Aktar is Nayim Shah. Nayim Shah is not an orphan or poor or the child of a disreputable family. He was running away from his privilege and status and family expectations.

Can a real relationship be built on a foundation of so many lies?

"No." Amma pulls away enough for me to see the sincerity in her eyes. "I promise you, shuna, I never in my wildest dreams suspected that about him."

"Then . . . how?" I whisper.

How did my world tilt on its axis in so little time? How did we get here? I think of the expression on Harun's face before he left and my breath hitches again.

My mother frowns at an ant crawling down one of the wood planks, avoiding my eyes. "We haven't been talking to each other since he came to dinner, but I could see how sad it made you. I eventually realized it was because he was gone. I tried to tell myself I was doing the right thing and that you'd eventually thank me for everything, but the more I tried to make things better this summer, the worse they became."

She chuckles humorlessly.

Normally, I would chime in to comfort her, but I bite my tongue, unable to deny how much her wiles hurt me.

"Finally," she continues, "I had to admit to myself that I was the reason. That everything I thought I was doing to give you a better future was only making you unhappy in the present." Her lips tremble. "I wanted to make it up to you. Make up with you. So after the mela, I asked Meera and the others to start looking into Nayim's bari in Bangladesh to see if I could talk to him."

"Finding out his identity was just a twist of fate?" I mumble into my knees, more to myself than her, unable to wrap my head around a coincidence of such magnitude.

Amma nods. "It was. I was so . . . elated when Nayim reached out a few days ago to tell me he would try to win you back. That he had his mother's, Nasrin Shah's, blessing." She cups my cheek, thumb rubbing away the last dregs of teardrops. "Discovering the boy you loved could give you the world . . . I thought I'd done right by you at last."

I squeeze my eyes shut as she falls silent.

I know she did it for me. I know she's always done things for me, misguided or otherwise. I can't even be angry at her this time, because I hid Harun from her. For too long, our relationship has been tainted by secrets and scheming.

So I say, "There's something I have to tell you."

For the first time in a long time, Amma listens to my every word. Really and truly. Her eyes widen in shock when I reveal the truth of my fake dating plan with Harun. How we accidentally fell for each other along the way. What he told me on the bridge before her arrival.

"Everything I did, I did for you, too, Amma," I whisper. "For you and our family." I pause and reflect on my conversation with Harun. "I should accept Nayim's proposal, shouldn't I? Despite everything, his heart is in the right place. Maybe someday, I will want to be with him too, if I give him a chance, right?"

Like my grandmother before me, I could learn to love him and live with everything expected of me. She and my mother raised me to be strong enough for that.

"Oh, shuna . . ."

I hold my breath. I need to hear it. I need her assurance that this is the path of least resistance, the yellow brick road leading to our entire family's prosperity and happiness.

Instead her lips press into my hair, and she murmurs against my scalp, "I took a chance on your father. Although hardship followed, if I could go back and do it again, I would choose him every single time."

I gawk at her, chin quivering, lips parted but unable to form any words except a feeble, gossamer, "You would?"

"Very much so," she replies. "I've been thinking a lot about him recently. More than I've let myself since he died. He would be disappointed in me."

"Amma, no!" I shake my head. "He'd know how *hard* you worked to make sure we all—"

"Hush," she interrupts. "I put too much pressure on you, Zahra. As your mother, I never should have made you feel like it was up to you to save our family. You've worked too hard as it is. . . ."

"I always wanted to help," I insist. "You never forced me."

She strokes my cheek again. "I know that, shuna. But I need *you* to know that we will be fine if you choose your heart. No more matches or meddling."

"Hassa ni, Amma?" I ask. I look into her eyes, and

instead of my mother, I just see a woman. A person. A girl with her own hopes and dreams. "Do you mean it?"

"Hassa," she promises, eyes twinkling. "I've never meant anything more."

I collapse into her comforting arms. And as she holds me, I believe her.

"Mm," I say, burying my face in her neck. "How'd you find me, anyway?" She looks down sheepishly at her phone sitting at the top of her purse. For the first time all evening, I laugh. "Oh. The Auntie Network. Duh."

Her chuckles join mine, growing louder and louder. We feed off each other's laughter, and I realize I had all the love I needed right here all along.

THE AUNTIE NETWORK

Sharmila:
Meera Afa, tell me it isn't so!

Meera:
. . . Keetha? √√

Sharmila:
Don't play coy with me! Did Zahra truly reject the Shah heir?

Zoba:
Everyone knows by now . . . she did. I can't believe it! How could Zaynab let her daughter turn down that glorious estate in Bangladesh, that pampered life?

Meera:
Perhaps Zaynab knows her daughter's heart better than any of us can. √√

Sharmila:
Hmmm. I would never let my daughter act so imprudently.

Zoba:
I agree. If Zaynab had a better handle on her children, she'd be planning the wedding of the year right now.

Sharmila:
Anyway, you wouldn't happen to have Nasrin Shah's contact details, would you? My bhagni is even prettier than Zahra and about to graduate from Northwestern.

Meera:
There is no hope for you two, is there? √√

Zoba:
Afa, what on earth do you mean?

Meera Hussain has exited the chat

Chapter 34

Life returns to a quiet sort of normal after that.

The Tahir girls start college.

Dalia, Dani, Ximena, and I spend as much time as humanly possible together until the day comes that we drop Mena off at JFK for her flight to Haiti. She and Dani share one last tearful goodbye, with a vow to stay friends and keep in touch. Neither of them have an epic last-minute change of heart, but perhaps it's for the best that they'll get to learn who they are without each other. Who knows, maybe they'll even get back together one day, if it's meant to be?

Things are finally looking up for my family, too.

Irony of ironies, Amma's wedding dress business has really taken off. After the concert, she gave the bride-zolad a piece of her mind, threatened to back out too close to the wedding for her to find anything not—*shudder*—off-the-rack, and got a hefty bonus for her efforts.

I've never been prouder of her!

The bride-zolad ended up with a dress straight out of *Vogue India*. Pictures of her wedding outfits blew up the Auntie Network WhatsApp for weeks, giving Amma plenty of free advertising. While people might still be gossiping about us, in the end, getting the best outfits matters to them most. She's been up to her ears in commissions.

Resna starting kindergarten means Amma and Nanu have plenty of time for the business, especially since the imam's family picks her up with their own gaggle of elementary schoolers after school.

Arif has also gotten working papers from his guidance counselor, permitting him to pick up a few shifts at Chai Ho on the weekends without compromising his grades. Mr. Tahir has been having a field day taking my poor brother under his wing, but despite the frequent *please help me* eyes Arif shoots me, I don't think he genuinely minds our boss's antics. Mr. Tahir's not a father figure, exactly, but definitely a well-meaning, if cranky, uncle.

Then there's me.

I am killing it!

Amma finally paid me back (with interest!). Since I have financial aid this semester and don't need that money for classes right away, I've saved enough to buy a Frankenstein's monster of a Subaru to go to class and work and visit the people I care about, including the twins! Their dorm room is truly a pastel goth work of art.

So although I'm still working most days at the tea shop,

I'm getting to attend school twice a week. It's already helped a lot with my book.

Speaking of which . . . I finished the rough draft!

At first, I worried how Mr. Tahir would react to me working fewer hours due to school and writing, since with Nayim and the girls gone, he needs me more than ever. But he's been kind about it. Like, *really* kind. He even agreed right away when I asked if my brother could work with us . . . though maybe he had his own ulterior motives for that, being short-staffed and all.

"Thank you for convincing Daniya to stay. I can never repay you," he told me one night when the two of us were alone, manning the shop. "We're discussing allowing her to study abroad next semester. That way, she gets to travel for a *grade.*"

Peak Deshi dad, but at least the Tahirs are happy.

We're *all* happy.

I wouldn't have it any other way.

Chapter 35

There's a postcard sticking out of the mailbox when I leave the building.

It's an unassuming slip of a thing, so glossy that I drop it as I'm rifling through the rest of the envelopes, looking for bills. My heart still seizes in my throat as a reflex, but most of the mail ends up being junk or early notices, so I let the box fall shut.

A shiny red guitar embossed on card stock winks up at me from the top porch step. I bend to pick it up, rubbing my thumb across the curly script declaring the name and address of a shop.

It's close enough to my destination that I can swing by on the way, but I wonder if it was sent to me in particular, or if everyone in Paterson got one.

If it might be an accident.

Tucking it into the pocket of my hoodie, I hurry to the Subaru, leaves crunching under the soles of my sneakers. A chill kisses the air. Fall is well and truly here.

I almost change course a dozen times on the way to the address on the postcard, but by the time the half-hour drive into the city ends, I've made up my mind.

I want to go.

I can't help scowling at the amount flashing on the parking meter as I dip my credit card into the machine. I waste no time hurrying up West 48th Street.

A gaggle of college kids lurk outside the shop, giggling.

I don't want to stop to admire the sign while they're watching, so instead I clear my throat and ask the girl with hot-pink streaks in her hair closest to me, "Is there, um, a line?"

"Nah, Keelie's just scared to talk to the hot owner," says her friend, a silver ring glinting on his bottom lip as he smirks.

The girl called Keelie thumps him on the chest with one fist, hiding her face with her other hand, while the third member of their group whispers, "You've got this, Keel. Go ask him for a lesson like that other girl did."

In a garbled voice, the pink-haired girl tells me, "Please, go in before me."

I flash her a sympathetic look. Perhaps no one in the world knows better than me how it feels to be in her shoes.

Bells chime above my head as I enter. There's indeed already a customer with the owner. I observe them for a moment, noting the way he shoots her that irresistible lop-sided smile while showing her how to play basic chords.

"You're a natural already," he tells the red-headed girl.

Her face flushes to match the color of her hair. I won't

judge if she walks out of here with a guitar and six picks she never intends to touch again, but more power to her.

A familiar figure notices me first and slinks over to rub against my ankles, purring like a motor. I bend down to pick up Thara the cat, smiling at the music-note charm on her brand-new collar. "So that's where you got off to."

Nayim glances up at the sound of my voice, jaw dropping. "Z-Zahra, you came?"

Still holding Thara, I retrieve the postcard. "Was I not supposed to?"

"No, uh, you were!" he exclaims. "Of course you were! I asked the imam to put it in your mailbox. I just . . . wasn't sure he'd approve. Or that you'd be here so soon. Or ever."

Guitar girl takes the hint and wanders over to the other side of the counter, mumbling something about returning after her accounting class. Nayim offers her an energetic wave, though his eyes remain glued to me.

We take the opportunity to evaluate each other while she's exiting. Nayim looks as devastatingly handsome as ever. Maybe even more so, in his black leather jacket and beanie, like he stepped right off a *Rolling Stone* cover.

"I needed to come into the city anyway," I tell him when we're alone.

"Oh good!" he says, a bit too enthusiastically. He rubs the back of his neck. "I'm glad I didn't mess everything up for you when I came back. Sorry again for pulling that stunt on you without asking, by the way. Since you like romance novels so much, I figured a grand gesture would be the best way to win you back, and I let my mum go a bit overboard planning it out."

That night is still something of a haze in my mind.

Eventually, Amma was able to lure Nayim over to the bridge so I could give him back his ring and turn him down in relative privacy. Of course, news of our breakup managed to spread through the whole city despite my best efforts, anyway.

I didn't think he'd ever forgive me, or that I'd ever hear from him again . . . until today.

"Grand gestures are hit-or-miss in real life . . . but I'm over it," I tell him truthfully, smiling until he smiles back. "It honestly makes me happy to see you doing so well, Nayim. Just because we won't get married doesn't mean we can't stay friends."

He shakes his head with a chuckle. "True, even though getting rejected proper sucked, I don't regret it. I always thought both of my parents were hell-bent on shoving me into the Perfect Son box no matter how hard I screamed inside. But we understand each other better now because of you."

I frown down at Thara's fluffy head. "I swear I'm not hung up on it anymore, but all the stories you told me . . ."

Nayim senses the question in my voice at once, and answers ruefully, "Most of it was the truth, you know? Everything except my family."

I nod, but that's not quite the end of the story, so I gently venture, "Is everything going okay with them now?"

A grin alights on Nayim's face, chasing away all shadows.

"Bajan hasn't quite come around to the 'peddling guitars on the street' thing, as he calls it, but everything that's happened since has only convinced me that my mother, at least, will always have my back. She even got Bajan to invest in the shop. He's coming with her and my sister, Noreen, to visit it next time she's stateside. To make sure I'm not 'blowing through' his money. But hey, it's something."

It feels strange to hear him talk about his family so casually after all the secrets, but I'm glad we're finally being honest with each other. I cast a glance over my shoulder, where it appears Keelie has invited more friends to pine with her. Turning back to Nayim, I arch a brow. "I have a feeling finding business won't be a problem for you, Casanova. Especially when the other Paterson girls learn that Prince Dalim Kumar is still up for grabs."

"Maybe." He chuckles uneasily and shifts his weight from one foot to the other. "This isn't exactly how either of us imagined I'd accomplish my dream, though, is it? I have to admit, it's a bit gutting knowing I only got here with my family's money."

For a moment, I contemplate this, stroking Thara's soft black fur. Then I shake my head. "No. It's good you let them do that. I think they need to feel needed sometimes. To know you still want them around to take care of you."

It's a form of love, all on its own.

He smirks. "Speaking from experience?"

"Shut up." I glare even as begrudging amusement tugs at

the corners of my mouth. It's impossible to resist giving in to it. Nayim's joy always was infectious. "Besides, it's okay if your dream doesn't look exactly how you expected it to. Dreams are messy and difficult and important to hold on to because of that. I know that better than anyone."

"I guess you do," he replies, smile softening into something painfully tender.

I clear my throat and put Thara down. "Anyway, I'm jealous you have such a cute coworker, but glad you won't be lonely all by yourself out here."

"I'm just glad *someone* wanted to come with me," he jokes. "My ego couldn't have survived if Thara turned me down too."

I huff another laugh. "Thanks for inviting me here, Nayim."

"Thanks for coming," he responds. "Where are you off to now?"

"There's just one more thing I have to do."

We part as friends.

Chapter **36**

Visiting Columbia never ceases to be a wonder.

Although many things have changed since I first applied to the school last year, a tiny part of me will always delight in the way no one spares me a second glance while I stride through the Southfield section of the campus toward the freshman dorms.

It's only when I reach the John Jay Hall building that I stop in front of the three sets of black steel doors, admiring the matching trelliswork in the arches above them.

It doesn't take long for the center door to open.

"Hey, you," I say, already grinning.

Harun grins back, his whole face brightening in a manner that makes my heart dance inside my ribs. Like Columbia, he's still a bit of a wonder.

Or more than a bit.

"Hey." The word ghosts across my lips as he dips his head to kiss me, bringing up his palm to cup my cheek. I lift my own arms to wind around his neck and pout when he draws back, until he adds, "Man, I'll never get tired of that."

My brows arch. "Oh? Then aren't you glad I—"

"—hunted me down, shouted that I was being a 'chauvinistic douche-waffle' outside my window until my entire family practically threw me out to talk to you, and then convinced me it would be the biggest mistake of my life if I let my insecurities get in the way of our chance at a happy ending together?" he finishes, eyebrows arched. "Yeah, how could I forget? You ever gonna let me live that down, Khan?"

"Nope," I reply, beaming up at him angelically.

Some would say the night of the proposal wasn't my finest. After semipublicly dumping one boy, who just proposed to you in the most dramatic fashion humanly possible, it's not exactly the smartest move to go profess your love for another equally as publicly, but sometimes grand gestures work.

It's about fifty-fifty.

Although I'm pretty sure Harun's neighbors recorded me and I became a meme for the second time that night, I've forbidden Arif, Ximena, and the Tahir girls from sharing any of their internet sleuthing with me, ever, until I die.

I know the Zahra I used to be would be proud of the one last summer transformed me into: a Zahra with a boyfriend I adore, family and friends I love, a class I enjoy, and dreams worth fighting for. Who is loved and cherished in return.

Who says women can't have it all, am I right?

"Much as I hate to interrupt your gloating, because it's

actually adorable," Harun deadpans, "should we start making our way over to the library? We're kind of standing in front of the hall and getting a whole lot of dirty looks. I don't need the bio students leaving dead rats on my doorstep or something."

"Couldn't Rabeardranath eat them?" I reply innocently.

He shoots me an unamused frown. "Rab is a bearded dragon, not a snake."

"Okay, fine, we can go to the library," I relent, "but I have a surprise for you first."

"A surprise?" His dark brows vanish into the thick foliage of his curls, which have only gotten more unruly since he moved away from home and Pushpita Khala's coddling. They're exactly as fluffy as I always secretly hoped, though. "Uh . . . those haven't exactly gone well for us. Historically speaking."

Although he's joking, I take a step back from him, suddenly feeling nervous as I nudge my backpack off and start rifling through it. My fingers find the thick sheaf of papers that Dani and Dalia printed for me when I told them the news.

I hold it out to Harun with both hands. "I finally finished my book and . . . I wanted you to be the first one to read it." A flush blooms in my cheeks. "Except, of course, for Professor Liu. Because I had to give it to her. But you were the very next—"

His hand around my wrist stops my babbling. I glance up to find him smiling down at me, eyes sparkling in the midday sun. Without a word, he accepts the manuscript from me and runs reverential fingertips over the title, my name, the spiral binding.

Then he opens it up to the dedication page. I hold my breath as he takes in the words inscribed on it:

To Harun, my very own love match.

Harun gasps, soft and breathy. I might have wondered if I'd imagined it in another second, if not for the way his full lips press together like he's not sure if he wants to laugh or cry.

He does neither.

He sets his bag down and places my manuscript on top of it like something precious. I emit an "oomph" when he throws his arms around me again. He tucks his chin over my head and swallows hard. I can tell he's a little choked up when he says, "I love you an incalculable amount, Zahra Khan. Thank you."

I smile into his cozy Columbia Henley.

The stories I grew up with, the stories I'll always love, almost always conclude with a wedding. A wedding at the end of a natok means that the characters have overcome all other obstacles and can live happily ever after at last.

Harun and I won't end in a wedding. At least, not yet.

Perhaps not ever.

After all, our story is only getting started.

Yet as my arms rise to enfold his broad shoulders, bringing him ever closer, I feel like we can get through anything— quarreling families, meddling aunties, heck, even plotting princes—as long as we're together.

Harun frowns against my smiling lips. "You're scheming again, aren't you?"

"Always," I whisper back.

Because we're no longer pawns in this game of love. We're a matched set, and I'll be damned if I let anything else tear us apart again.

This time, I'm writing my own happily-ever-after.

Acknowledgments

Neither *The Love Match* nor I would be here without a loving and supportive team surrounding me, particularly since it was written in the midst of a global pandemic while I was teaching high school (yes, that was exactly as hard as it sounds), so I'm grateful for the opportunity to give a shout-out to my beloved habi-gushti.

First and foremost, thank you to my powerhouse agent, Quressa Robinson, for always standing in my corner, sharing your wisdom, and guiding me to this stage in my career. I appreciate you for letting me explore wherever my creative curiosity takes me. It's impossible to imagine a better champion for me or my work!

Next, I am so thankful to my incredible editors: Laura Barbiea, Dainese Santos, and Jennifer Ung. Laura, since day one, you have been so much fun to brainstorm ideas with to make *The Love Match* shine as much as it possibly could. Your eternal enthusiasm and respect for my creative choices mean a lot to me. We truly are a dream team! Jennifer, thank you for first taking a chance on Zahra and me. I have always admired your work as an editor and am glad we got to collaborate together, even for a short time. I know you'll continue acquiring wonderful books wherever you go. Dainese, although I was super nervous when Jen left, I don't think I could have moved on to a better editor, because you are so spectacular in innumerable ways. Your feedback is always spot-on, and when you, Laura, and I get together to plot, I always have such a blast! Sara Shandler and Josh Bank, I also have to thank you both for your visions of this book. So many of you have helped shape *The Love Match* into what it is.

To everyone else at Simon & Schuster, Salaam Reads, and Alloy Entertainment, I hope you know how valuable you have been to me even if we didn't work one on one. Thank you to Jenica Nasworthy, Jeannie Ng, Chava Wolin, and Sara Berko for taking *The Love Match* from a bunch of characters in a Word document and transforming it into a real book. Thank you to Sarah Creech and Fahmida Azim for making that book something beautiful. Thank you to Alex Kelleher, Maryam Ahmad, and everyone else in marketing and publicity for working hard to get the word out about the book. Thank you to Justin Chanda and Kendra Levin for welcoming me into the Simon & Schuster family. Thank you to everyone else who has worked on this book and will work on it in the future, such as the marvelous team at Simon & Schuster UK. I'm excited to continue collaborating on *The Love Match* and other projects with you!

Thank you in particular to Mehr Husain and Amanda Ramirez for helping me portray the characters in the book as authentically as possible. Mehr, you were one of the first people outside of my immediate team to read *The Love Match*, and your lovely words and nuanced perspective touched me deeply. I still think about them to this day.

Before I even had an agent or a publishing team, I had talented and hard-working people supporting me, those who I'm fortunate enough to call both critique partners and friends. To my Bengali Squad, Tammi and Adiba, thank you for the plotting assistance, helping me pin down the perfect Bengali word in any given situation, and our international Zoom catch-up sessions that easily last up to four hours simply because it's so lovely to talk to both of you! Adiba, you've already done wonders for Bangladeshi representation with your books and will only continue to do so. Tammi, I know your Bengali characters will also soon take the world by storm, and I am cheering for that day to arrive.

Similarly, I never could have survived so long in the industry without my Magic Sprinting Squad. Mara, thank you for always believing that *The Love Match* could go far and talking me off metaphorical cliffs whenever I panicked about publishing for the umpteenth time. Tana, thank you for giggling with me about auntie culture and helping me with songwriting when I was whining about lyrics. Thank you, Alisha, for having the patience of a saint and reading so many drafts of this book without complaint, providing me with such rich feedback each time. Cindy, thank you for threatening me with GIFs of a certain actor I do not get the appeal of every time I procrastinate. Cass, thank you for the steady supply of baby and cat photos, your eternal encouragement, and for also ensuring that I didn't let my anxiety swallow me whole before I could hold my book. Jen, Petula, Sabina, Lyla, Francesca, Laila, Aneeqah—thank you all too, for being part of my family away from family.

To others who have supported me over the years—like Ashley, Gayathri, Gayatri, Maria, Eunice, Morgan, and many others I'm probably forgetting right now but adore so much—thank you for your cheerleading, delicious treats and tea, and *Final Fantasy* memes. Many of you have been here since my spooky days and didn't blink once when I said I might try writing different genres. I would have missed out on so much fun if you deterred me!

Every single one of my CPs inspires me daily. I am always, always rooting for all of you, and will forever be grateful for the magic you've brought into my life. Like Zahra, everyone needs friends who not only support their choices, but constantly lift them up when imposter syndrome strikes them down, and I was blessed to have that long before there were any agents or book deals under my belt.

Moving on to my team at home: thank you to Amma and Abba for always believing in my dreams and doing whatever you could to help me make them come true. You have been my staunchest cheerleaders all my life, and I don't think I could have achieved this without your faith in me and prayers for me. Abba, you've always worked hard so I could focus on my education and future, never once doubting me because I wasn't a son. Every time I see stereotypical portrayals of sexist South Asian and/or Muslim dads, I think of you and how you only stopped pestering me about getting my PhD because this book deal was a suitable alternative. Amma, to this day, you bring me food when I'm too busy to eat, and are probably the only reason I didn't starve over the duration of my edits.

Thank you to my sister, Preeti, for being my sounding board anytime I need to bounce ideas with someone before I take them to my editors. Thank you to my brother, Ornob, for fueling my coffee cravings when my brain is about to give up (and needs something other than my usual, endless supply of tea). I appreciate both of my siblings for doing their best to explain to our parents how publishing works when they inevitably ask for the gazillionth time, "Why is it taking so long for Pinku's book to come out?" Supply chains bow to no woman, alas!

And, of course, thank you to my precious little fancy man, Loki, for being the balm to my mental health during the pandemic. I wrote a cat into *The Love Match* just for you.

To Sami, Meem, Noha, Zarin, and Mehreen, Harun's cool cousins were written in your honor, because you're more than just my cousins, you're like sisters to me, and in Zarin's case, my first friend, too. Nan, when you decided to go to Bangladesh during the start of the Muslim ban, I finally found the willpower to start taking writing seriously. There were so many unknowns at the ban's onset that writing became my escape from the fear that I might not get to see you again if Bangladesh got added to the list. I'm so glad you returned to us and that I can share *The Love Match* with you. Zahra's calm, cool Nanu is inspired by you. Shurji and Mami, you give aunties and uncles a good name.

To my extended family—every single Nana, Nanu, Dada, Dadi, Mama, Mami, Khala, Khalu, Sasa, Sasi, Fufa, Fufu, and the numerous cousins they've given me, whether by blood or otherwise—this book could never have existed without you. I hope I have done justice with my representation of the Bangladeshi diaspora in Paterson (Boro Mama, Lulu Mama, and too many others to name). I also have my relatives in Bangladesh and the UK, like Mezo Mama's, Jewel Fufu's, Hasna Khala's, and Jibu Sasa's families (which is why I'm so glad I get to publish simultaneously there) to thank for giving me a special appreciation of our heritage (plus all of you in NYC and other places throughout America, of course; Happy and Lippy Fufu, hi!). I'd apologize for the kissy parts, but let's be honest: forbidden love is a staple of all the natoks you love to watch, and this is something of an American natok itself.

Thank you to the colleagues who supported and mentored me for nearly a decade. I was very private about my writing at work for a long time, because I wasn't sure how others would react, but every single person I told about *The Love Match* has been absolutely wonderful. In my firm opinion, no one in the world does more important work than teachers, and my time with you has shaped me into the person I am today. In particular, thank you to Kara, Vivian, Nicole, Larry, Lorraine, Vanessa, Mary, Jessica, Nurdan . . . The list could go on and on. I wrote *The Love Match* with you and our students in mind, and I hope you will share it with any readers who you think will take joy from it.

I am also grateful to the alma maters I attended: to the school libraries and wonderful librarians at PS #2 and Tech I spent every moment outside of class with; to the English teachers who encouraged my love of reading and writing (Mr. Wacha, Ms. Spencer, Mr. Brower); to the professors of the creative writing minor at MSU. Professor Hodges, I have to thank you for being the one to ask why I wasn't submitting any stories about Bangladeshi characters, because you switched on a lightbulb over my head the moment you did. I never thought I would have a shot at taking my writing anywhere if I wasn't writing mostly white casts until then.

To my debut group(s), thank you for your constant wisdom. I'm an awkward introvert by nature, so it was daunting to introduce myself to a group as large as the #22debuts (shout-out especially to everyone in the 2k22 debuts and #YAsian22), then even more scary to learn my date had bumped so I'd be joining the 2023 releases instead. . . . But I've been fortunate to meet and learn from such welcoming people. I can't wait to keep supporting you all long after we've debuted!

Thank you to everyone who has taken time out of their day to read my book early, especially those who've provided it with blurbs. It's the greatest honor to receive your recommendations after being a fan of your work for so long. As an author of color, I know that I am standing on the shoulders of giants who have been working diligently for a very long time to pave the way for writers like me to tell stories like this. I'll never forget the authors who made this possible.

Thank you to bloggers who've been enthusiastic about *The Love Match* since I announced it would be published. I know there were a few bumps in the road with date delays, but your unshakeable excitement really motivated me when times were tough. I appreciate every list of most anticipated reads, every podcast, every interview, every guest post, every TikTok, every piece of art you've shared with me, and more. I hope that you enjoy the book now that it's finally, actually, really, truly out in the world!

To every single reader who picks up *The Love Match* and gives it a chance: may it bring you as much joy as it did to me in the years leading up to its release. Thank you for spending time in Paterson with Zahra and her loved ones.

Little Pri, who never, ever thought we could have this: we did it!

Last but not least, thank you to God. Your love and grace brought me here today.

In many ways, a book is like the perfect cup of masala chai. Of course, it needs the right hand to brew it, but it's only when everything comes together that it becomes what it's truly meant to be. My greatest hope is that this book has felt like taking a sip of a sweet, comforting saa.